UNTO THE TULIP GARDENS

Unto the Tulip Gardens: My Shadow

ANTHEM PRESS
An imprint of Wimbledon Publishing Company Limited (WPC)
First published in the United Kingdom in 2016 by
ANTHEM PRESS
75–76 Blackfriars Road
London SE1 8HA

www.anthempress.com

Original title: *Gölgemi Bıraktım Lale Bahçelerinde*
Copyright © Gül İrepoğlu 2014
Originally published by Doğan Kitap, Istanbul, Turkey
English translation copyright © Feyza Howell 2014

A CIP record for this book is available from the British Library.

ISBN 978–1–78308–455–5

This title is also available as an e-book.

UNTO THE TULIP GARDENS: MY SHADOW

A novel by

GÜL İREPOĞLU

Translated by Feyza Howell

ANTHEM PRESS

About the Author

Gül İrepoğlu

Architect, art historian, lecturer, broadcaster and novelist, Prof Dr Gül İrepoğlu was born in Istanbul. Her research on the life and works of Levnî resulted in the book entitled *Levnî: Painting, Poetry, Colour*. Her other books, some of which have already been published in other languages, are as follows:

> *The Concubine*, set in the latter half of the 18th century, is a love story woven around Sultan Abdülhamid I and a remarkable concubine in his harem.
> *An Istanbul Kaleidoscope with a Bow* is an autobiographical look at modern history through the medium of fashion.
> İrepoğlu is married, has two children and lives in Istanbul.

Feyza Howell

Born in Izmir, Howell is a graduate of Robert College in Istanbul with a UK Honours degree in Graphic Design. She holds an impressive backlist and is experienced in various aspects of international business from design, advertising, TV production, marketing and product management to business development. Throughout this period, she has always drawn, written and translated. Her interests include tennis, yoga and dance.

Howell is married, has a son and lives in Berkshire.

Letter to the Reader

What you hold in your hands was written as much more than a historical novel. True, the Ottoman court of the 18th century provides the backdrop, but it is people who matter, people who might not have behaved all that differently in a different time or place. This book might provide an insight into an Ottoman emperor as a man, into the invariable flaws and joys of human nature, or enable the reader to indulge in colourful speculation on the personality of a famous artist. And ultimately, yes, keeping the historical context foremost, scrutinise an era confined to predictable platitudes for far too long. Some incidents might be taken as symbolic and human relationships as factual, or vice versa. Yet, why shouldn't we transport ourselves to the opulence of the Tulip Era as we read? That was what drove me to include factual information; try as I might to extricate myself from the university lecturer's robes, this was the ideal environment in which to exercise my preferred method of teaching: wrapping intricate information in entertainment and surprise.

It wasn't a time for women; some women used their wits to advance their own causes or alter the course of events and some even succeeded in one or both. I examined this men's world from a woman's viewpoint and attempted to establish a link between details that remained fresh.

Reading into history is more rewarding than merely reading history: the spaces between the lines of social history, in particular – the dearth of published documentation notwithstanding – has so much capacity to inspire. The events in this novel may well suggest comparisons with other times.

The story is rich with trivia, largely taken for granted, but which once would have been crucial.

Speech patterns used in the novel refer to another time and place, but I did avoid writing entire conversations in Ottoman since that would have made the novel indecipherable.

I felt so close to these characters, as if I knew them personally. On occasion, I asked myself if I had lived then, in an earlier life. The more you delve into history, the more you begin to speculate on what else might have taken place. For someone who loves to write, the rest comes easy.

I was determined not to allow my love of writing hinder my existing commitments. Throughout the two and a half years it took to write this novel, I carried on with my academic research, and thus emerged my modus operandi – stolen time, the only time I had to write, time otherwise jealously safeguarded. At that strange time of night just before drifting off when the conscious mind wanders came inspiration, forcing me to leap out of bed, sneak up to my desk without disturbing the family and write a note or two in longhand on scraps of paper or fire up the computer for a longer session. I muted the start-up jingle to avoid waking my husband or daughters up at some ungodly hour. That was the sort of sneaking I loved!

What you hold in your hands is history brightened with imagination, or history with a topping of fiction.

Gül İrepoğlu

On the Art of Turkish Miniature Painting

Miniatures have illustrated manuscripts since the Middle Ages both in Western Europe and in Asia. The name is derived from the Latin *minium* – red lead – which was the most widely used pigment, and it does not refer to the size as is generally supposed. This art form is known as *nakış* in Turkish, the artist *nakkaş* and the workshop *nakkaşhane*.

The earliest examples of such illustrations in the Muslim world date back to 9th-century Egypt, and delicate works on pieces of silk prove portrait painting was popular amongst the pre-Islamic Turkic peoples in Central Asia.

Selçuk Turks painted miniatures despite religious restrictions on representative arts, and their successors, Ottoman illuminators, excelled from the 15th century onwards. Wherever there is censure, art invents its own method of circumventing it: deliberately avoiding any attempt at perspective, modelling or realism helped artists get away with painting portraits.

Brilliant colours and a graphic sensitivity to layout distinguish Turkish miniatures. The painter supported the chronicler to record both everyday events and special occasions. These miniatures would be bound into albums, either as part of a book or as an independent pictorial volume. Workshops frequently operated as reproduction studios whenever more than one patron commissioned a volume.

Miniatures deserve to be inspected at leisure, and both Topkapı Palace in Istanbul and the Chester Beatty Library in Dublin possess impressive collections. Further material on the art of miniature painting is found in Gül İrepoğlu's *Levnî: Painting, Poetry, Colour* and facsimile editions of Levnî's *Sûrname-i Vehbî*.

Gül İrepoğlu and Feyza Howell

Notes on Pronunciation

Ottoman names are spelt in modern Turkish throughout the book. Exceptions were made for the titles *pasha* and *agha*, words that had entered English long before Turkish alphabet reform.

Turkish is phonetic, with a single sound assigned to most letters. A circumflex accent [^] either elongates the vowel upon which it rests or 'thins' the k or l preceding it.

The consonants pronounced differently from English are as follows:

c = j in *jack*
ç = ch in *chat*
j = French j in *jour*
ş = sh in *ship*
ğ = 'soft g' is silent; it merely lengthens the vowel preceding it
r = r in *read*; at the end of syllables closest to the Welsh, as in *mawr*.
y = English y in *yellow*

The vowels are equally straightforward:

a = shorter than the English, as in *father*
e = e in *bed* (never as in *me*)
ı = schwa; the second syllable in *higher*
i = i in *bin*; never as in *eye*
ö and ü = like the corresponding German umlaut sounds

Given names are usually accented on the final syllable, so Ah-MED, Lev-NÎ or İb-ra-HİM. The title *sultan* precedes the name of an emperor and follows the names of royal women, so Sultan Ahmed, but Gülnuş Sultan.

Feyza Howell

Stefanaki
The amber-eyed child

It was the first day of April 1687, in the thirty-ninth year of the very long reign of the nineteenth Ottoman emperor, Padişah Sultan Mehmed the Fourth – known amongst common folk as Mehmed the Hunter – and this for him would be another ordinary day of customary concerns and pastimes.

In the western lands known as the Rumeli province of the vast empire, however, this cool April day was far from ordinary for some of his subjects, being the day of *devşirme* – of collecting the child tribute.

Stefanaki, one of the three sons of a farming family who lived in a village close to Salonika, was deemed fit to serve the Ottoman State. He was at the bottom end of the range, being then only eight years of age, and a healthy, fine-looking boy. Below his black eyebrows, honey-coloured eyes sparkled with intelligence belying the sadness of his gaze. He was well built for his age in contrast to his two thin, pale elder brothers.

He was holding his father's hand for the last time.

'Name?'

'Stefanaki.'

'Father's name?'

The details were recorded carefully, without haste. Conflicting expressions showed on the boy's father's face: submission to the inevitable and relief at the arrival of the dreaded event. His mother stood still at a distance, like a creature lost in a strange land, mutely witnessing something irreversible, with her swollen, red eyes indicating she had shed all the tears she had.

Stefanaki donned a thick red recruit outfit, much too big for him. His mother, father and brothers watched as he fumbled, tying the sash at his waist. They displayed neither enthusiasm nor sadness, a familiar scene in this part of the world. His family were farming folk, not poor by any means. Their monotonous lives would go on, just with one member fewer; that's all. And his place would be filled all too soon.

This was bittersweet for most of the families present. They were all seeing their sons for the last time, but their sons were embarking upon a future they would never have dreamt of had they stayed: a janissary commander, perhaps, or a minister in the great Ottoman State, or, if imagination ran wild, the grand vizier even ... at the very least, a soldier who would get his share of the spoils, or a distinguished official serving the emperor.

★   ★   ★

The emotional ceremony of selection and enrolment had come to an end. Children in red cloaks and white felt caps had joined the flock of recruited boys. The plain uniforms, often too big, created a sense of belonging – shared consolation for the boys on the way to accepting their new identities. Not to mention that it was much easier for the officials to keep an eye on the boys in their top-to-toe red outfits.

The colonel resembled a terrifying puppet, with a stern face, heavy eyebrows that extended to his temples shading his cruel eyes and an enormous, chestnut moustache. He seemed to have long forgotten how he himself had trodden the same path.

The boys lined up behind the colonel and set off for the barracks, the site of their first night away from their families. Some would not sleep at all this first night, others not even the second night. Some were teary-eyed, not caring who saw; others only focussed on following orders with a confused gaze, unable to make head or tail of this terrible change or to imagine anything beyond the immediate. Very few achieved a dignified walk, heads held high, challenging the blackness of that all-encompassing sadness, not once looking back, accompanied by the prayers of their families on this first step towards the new and the unknown.

The unique practice of *devşirme* formed the backbone of the Ottoman Empire for hundreds of years. The purpose was to select and train future janissaries – the foundation of the Ottoman military, servants of the emperor and state officials. Male children between eight and twenty years old were picked every three to five years from Christian families living in the empire. Recruiting officials of the relevant province would select healthy, strong boys, who would be converted and taken into public service. As members of the merchant class, Jewish boys were exempt. The number of boys each province had to supply would be determined beforehand. The appointment of recruiting official bestowed the mark of complete trust.

The recruiting officials picked one boy out of every forty homes with more than one son, choosing the strongest and best looking. Only families of high standing in the community qualified, so sons of cowherds or shepherds were not eligible. Physical disfigurements excluded the affected boys: baldness, hydrocephaly and congenital conditions such as beardlessness or hypospadias. Sons of the chief steward of the village were exempt in order to avoid compromising law and order in the area.

Boys who had already learnt a trade were similarly excused; a primary condition in the practice was that everything, including Islam, be taught after the boys entered service to the Ottoman State. Regardless of aptitude, the teachings of earlier life were not considered 'positive'. If a gem, then uncut; if a stone, then at least whole!

There was no room for chance in this system, which had been worked out down to the finest detail. The commander of the janissaries would personally examine the boys upon their arrival in Konstantiniyye. Circumcision and Muslim-Turkish names would follow. Those picked for court duty would be educated in one of the three palaces: Edirne, Galata or İbrahimpaşa. The imperial abode known as Darüssaade, Topkapı Palace or simply the seraglio awaited the best as the tallest joined the imperial guard and the rest became cavalry servants.

Grand Vizier Rüstem Pasha, Grand Vizier Sokollu Mehmed Pasha and Chief Architect Sinan were all *devşirmes*, all true Ottomans: loyalty and success were all that mattered for them.

Put emotion aside for a moment if you can and admire the internal consistency of the system. The Ottoman State implemented its own rules in adopting the children, raising them in a one-way boarding school. The state would be their only family. Who came from where might have mattered at first, but in time that terrific, centuries-old tradition would erase any trace of the past. The boys became true-born sons of the August Ottoman State: the inexorable power that was the janissaries, before whom all infidels trembled; the veteran statesmen who held the fine balance between the West and the East; the force that was the emperor's most trusted servants, who guarded his life and possessions; and the artists who elevated Islam and the Ottomans with their peerless masterpieces.

Master of the Hounds Colonel Mirza Mehmed Agha, who was entrusted with the collection around Salonika this year, enjoyed the satisfaction of having carried out his unusual orders. Yet he had to suppress his curiosity. It was the Commander-in-Chief of the Janissaries himself who had issued the top-secret order personally: pick one particular boy of one particular family in one particular village, whether the boy ticked the boxes or not. No explanation was vouchsafed: 'Our confidence in your person is complete, Mehmed Agha. Follow the orders as directed, and deliver the said lad to me safe and sound upon your return to the Abode of Felicity. Know that your promotion will be assured!'

That voice still rang in his ears. Enticed by the prospect, and curiosity piqued, the Master of the Hounds also knew to keep his silence.

Two identical logbooks were filled, as was the custom. Stefanaki was listed, as were all the other boys: name of the village, township, mother and father's names, the name of the farm, date of birth and eye and hair colour. One of the books accompanied the driver who would lead the boys to the centre.

Mirza Mehmed Agha guarded the other with his life. He had added, next to one of the entries: 'Amber eyes, angelic countenance, arched, heavy eyebrows, two moles on his neck'. Fate would deny the person described in these lines the chance to see these logbooks.

As day embraced the cold night, little Stefanaki did as countless others did before him for hundreds of years: he walked towards an unknown future, timid, disconsolate, angry, hopeless, curious and proud.

Gülnuş and Afife
'You look like Leyla when you don your black'

'The task has been discharged successfully. The boy you commanded has been recruited, My Lady; rest easy!'

Upon hearing these short sentences, militarily sparse and efficient, Rabia Gülnuş Emetullah Sultan, Chief Wife to Mehmed the Hunter, this most attractive, popular and intimidating of women, breathed a deep sigh of relief on the 14th of April 1687. Neither did she neglect rewarding their bearer.

Then she relived, as vividly as if it were happening again, that disquieting event of precisely eight years earlier, indelibly marked in the deepest reaches of her mind.

The harem of the Edirne Palace was all a-bustle eight years ago on that warm September morning she remembered oh so well, in the year 1679, a sweet commotion.

Afife, latest favourite to Sultan Mehmed IV, was about to endow her sovereign with a child. The baby's arrival was imminent; a boy – as predicted by fortune-tellers – would have meant one more heir to the Ottoman throne, alongside the fortunate two that she, that powerful, that magnificent Gülnuş Sultan had borne: the blond Mustafa, who took after his father, and the dark Ahmed, after her own colour.

Rabia Gülnuş Sultan was one of those rare women blessed with not only the desire but also the love of the ruler of the Ottomans. Therein lay the source of her power, just like Hürrem-Roxelana to Süleyman the Magnificent, Kösem to Ahmed II and Turhan to İbrahim the Mad.

True, her beloved Mehmed the Hunter had enjoyed others after her, but the plump, dark beauty with the sparkling black eyes had always managed to hold on to her privileged position despite her advancing years, never once – ostensibly – departing from the rules of the court. Hadn't even that legendary Hürrem Sultan learnt to share her Sultan Süleyman when the time came? But the indomitable Gülnuş, blessed with not inconsiderable intelligence, had ambition that knew no bounds; it was not for her to succumb quite so easily.

The Chief Wife had pretended to accept Sultan Mehmed's enjoyment of others as natural – that is, until she engineered the opportunity to somehow despatch her rivals. Even the most ruthless course of action was not beneath her. The first priority amongst the rules of the palace was total loyalty; the rest were no different from the merciless order of the world. To the victor the spoils!

Take for example the young concubine, Gülbeyaz by name and silken of skin, who had so beguiled the Emperor and who so unexpectedly found herself at the bottom of the Bosphorus, inside a sack flung off the Kandilli shore. Accompanied by his harem, Mehmed the Hunter had been summering in Kandilli Palace, cooled by the Bosphorus breeze; he had hunted in the hills behind the palace to dispel his grief.

He forgave Gülnuş, possibly mistaking her ambitions towards the throne for passionate jealousy.

Covert confrontations with the murky depths of the harem – dangerous women, armed only with their femininity, and emasculated males – must have seemed the more expedient course of action.

Yet Afife remained out of Gülnuş Sultan's reach. Never mind that the Gülbeyaz affair a few years earlier had been overlooked; the Chief Wife had been plagued by nightmares since then.

Afife was different; she was a poet. It wasn't only her beauty that had enchanted Sultan Mehmed; the couple conversed in poetry. This young woman knew how best to compliment the ruler's verses; her replies were femininely witty. She was clever enough never to outshine his talent. Moreover, she enveloped herself in a scent – whose composition she guarded jealously – whenever she was due to meet her sovereign. Word in the harem was that this blend of fruits and spices was bewitching. This heady, distinctive scent was a thinly veiled response to the unshakable harem-wide monopoly Gülnuş had over jasmine – Mehmed Han's favourite flower. She had expressly forbidden other harem women to wear jasmine.

But so besotted was the Emperor with his new fancy that he even neglected hunting. The romantic poem he wrote her whipped up jealousy to a fever pitch in the others.

> You look like a singular pearl when you don your white
> You look like Leyla when you don your black
> You look like a joyous parakeet when you don your green
> My fragrant Afife, you look like a fine rose.

Afife's response was an elegant echo, flattering a man in love in a much more refined style than the Emperor's. Hearing these lines – his hands in Afife's, eyes locked on Afife's, promising what sweet delights were to come ere long – made him truly believe he deserved every single simile and all his faults were erased:

> You look like the moon, My Emperor, when you don your white
> You look like Ka'aba Most Noble when you don your black
> You look like a gem buried deep when you don your scarlet
> My Formidable Sovereign, you look like the sea ...

Afife was wily enough not to show Gülnuş any disrespect. She was also quite probably genuinely kind, yes, a rare find in the harem.

Gülnuş would wait out the pregnancy and tolerate a baby girl. But... if the baby were to be a boy, the woman who had just given the Ottoman throne another prince would rise in rank.

And this would simply not do as far as Gülnuş was concerned.

No, it simply would not do.

* * *

Gülnuş Sultan was to recall much later the unfamiliar disquiet that had overcome her as she sat facing the fortune-teller. The dark-skinned woman had claimed to have travelled from distant western lands. This was the day before her rival's labour pains started.

A wave of excitement had swept through the Edirne Palace harem at the arrival of the fortune-teller. Gülnuş Sultan, as usual, was first in line. The sovereign was not fond of fortune-tellers or even astrologers. Loath to deny her, however, he tolerated the fortune-teller's occasional visits.

Fixing beady black eyes on the magnificent Chief Wife, the fortune-teller surveyed her from top to toe. Satisfied, she sighed, held Gülnuş by the thin wrist and scrutinised the open palm:

'Thy star, like a stellar pearly diamond, My Sultan; such dazzle, how it scintillates, denying its light from time to time, but never quite turning away. To thee I say: thy fate line looks tortuous. I also see that few members of the fair sex have dedicated themselves on this earth to their man as thou hast.'

She paused, held the palm up to the light and continued:

'I see two great crimes in thy long life, My August Sultan, but be they behind thee, or yet to come, I cannot say. Howsoever that may be, after the dark – and only a short time at that – thy fortunes brighten up, radiant, and like the sun in the heavens. Both thy male children will make thee proud, may Allah spare them to thee. I' faith, thy name will be remembered throughout the world, now and forever.'

She gazed deep into those kohl-lined black eyes once more before pronouncing her last:

'Hold fast, Gülnuş Sultan, when thy star dims! All things come to her who waits.'

The following day, on that warm September morning in the year 1679, Afife delivered a healthy boy in the Edirne Palace harem.

Mindful of this possibility, Gülnuş had taken precautions, assisted within and without the harem by dazzlingly generous – and surreptitious – gifts.

And so neither the august sovereign nor the young Afife would rejoice in the birth of a new crown prince. A plot – the like of which would have been hard to reproduce but for the audacity of the Chief Wife – had been hatched months earlier, a plan that could be flung aside and forgotten in case the baby was a girl.

But the baby's sex had determined his mother's and his own fate.

It all happened very quickly. The lady steward picked the baby up from the midwife's hands and walked off. The young mother, collapsed in the birthing chair and still sweaty and tearful, was informed of the sudden death of her baby at his first breath. A dead infant procured earlier was held up fleetingly before being removed on the pretext that a post-partum mother ought to be spared this sight.

Afife was left alone with her grief.

It was much easier to inform the father of the sad news; emperors were used to births and deaths in their families, so numerous were they.

Mehmed the Hunter would not look too long at that poor scrap of flesh enveloped in white muslin. He turned his head away, the better to avoid seeing the face of his dead prince, just as Gülnuş had guessed. Attributing the death to prematurity, the Emperor sought a stoically dignified manner, accepting the hand dealt by fate as befitted him: 'Allah Most High, His will not be defied, submission burdensome at times; yet perchance it were my own impatience that caused this boy to be born ere his time. Whatever the cause, may it not recur, this be all that I ask of Allah the Most High.'

In fact, he had almost felt certain his beloved Afife would have a boy and had already, in the depths of his heart, picked a formidable name meaning 'owner of the world': Cihangir. Had the fate of his poor son, who would not see daylight, been determined by this name, the name of Süleyman's ill-fated prince?

Loath to grieve in public, Mehmed Han remembered the dead fawn in the belly of his recent kill. Unusually slow of foot, the gazelle had been easy pickings. Right at the end of the hunt it was. The supremely graceful gazelle must have been generous in her mating season; the Emperor, in his hunting season. Mehmed Han took more pride in his huntsmanship than in his credentials as a warrior; yet this was a memory he wished he could bury, a memory that just wouldn't go away.

Chroniclers recorded a single sentence, one they had repeated countless times previously, without even mentioning the mother's name:

'A prince was born yesterday and he died. His body was washed by the imperial imam, laid out and interred, following the funeral prayer held in the palace square.'

* * *

Gülnuş checked her ruthlessness and spared the life of her beloved Emperor's child, thus alleviating her conscience a little. She too was a mother, however much she may have wielded the rules of supremacy in that ruinously competitive environment that was the harem.

'The Master at the Abode of Felicity has been presented with a baize-lined sable coat and a bejewelled dagger by Her Majesty, Most Virtuous Gülnuş Sultan.'

Yet another short note taken by the chroniclers, little they may have wondered over the detail. No one noted the sudden increase in the amount of gold saved by the eunuch. Gülnuş

Sultan was renowned for her generosity, and few would dare question the giving of presents.

Spiriting away the boy had not been difficult, the young son Mehmed the Hunter had never seen, brother to Mustafa and Ahmed. The mighty eunuch had his orders from Gülnuş Sultan:

'Find people who will not betray our confidence, who will appreciate that revealing this secret will result in eternal silence!'

His loyalty to the majestic Chief Wife, with whom he had shared so much for so many years, was deep enough to suppress the voice of his conscience. Neither was the veteran eunuch prepared to see the balance of power in the harem change.

Always equipped with a pretext for an excursion outside the palace, his groundwork was done months ago, and a suitable family had been picked ahead of time. So, the boy had been entrusted in the good care of a Christian family, until the day he would be recruited in *devşirme* to return to the palace on a day of Gülnuş Sultan's choosing; she would not exile her beloved master's issue from his rightful home for good.

The small farming family accepted a fortune they would otherwise never have seen and obeyed Gülnuş to the letter.

Eight years had passed, and the day of parting had come. They did their duty and handed that sweet little boy over to the grim officials of the state, the boy in whose fate they too had played a part. They were sorry to see him go; he had been a bright and joyful child in that silent home. The farmer knew that he had no choice but to keep his word.

★   ★   ★

Gülnuş believed the unique relationship she and Afife had, each acknowledging the supremacy of the other on some counts, would continue till eternity. But their worst fears came true at the accurs't end of the same year: in November 1687, seven months after the little boy had been recruited and brought to the palace, at a time when Gülnuş thought herself to be the mistress of destiny, their lives were uprooted.

Mehmed the Fourth, the poet emperor, whose birth had been celebrated with three days and nights of festivities in the Abode of Felicity, in Galata and in Üsküdar, for he would continue the Ottoman line, yea, whose birth had been joyfully greeted by the people, putting their problems aside, whose date of birth had been immortalised in the verses of poets, who, having ascended to the throne at the young age of six when carried by the Chief White Eunuch to the Gate of Felicity and placed on the saddle, who had taken his beloved Gülnuş along on hunts and even on the Hungarian campaign in a silver coach so as not to be parted from her and whose thirty-nine-year-long reign was marked more for his huntsmanship than his statesmanship, yes, this Mehmed the Fourth, son to İbrahim the Mad, was deposed.

The sultan-no-more asked terrified: 'Doth death await us?' Upon receiving the assurance, 'Heaven forbid, My Emperor, merely imprisonment orders!' he hung his head, relieved.

He was destined to fill the rest of his days in the Boxwood Quarters as was the custom.

And so Afife finally poured her grief into verse, addressing none other than Gülnuş in a feminine expression of this unique relationship:

Tell Gülnuş to don her black weeds
Each sigh piercing to the quick her lungs
Let Sultan Mehmed cry in the Boxwood Quarters
Woe is me, 'tis unfair, says Sultan Mehmed.

Abdülcelil and Süleyman
'No room for us at our old homes, anyway'

Little Abdülcelil was far from docile, ever wanting to know why before obeying. Yet he always moved with dignity – no unwarranted audacity for him. This little man appeared to exude an indefinable charm. Stefanaki no longer, his new name was Abdülcelil, 'servant of the mighty'.

The hazel-eyed boy from Salonika was clearly destined for the court after his basic training. He was too precious to squander in wars.

His Enderun – Inner Palace – school friend Süleyman bin Abdullah would join him after evening prayers when it quietened down, though this was infrequent. The two young boys would talk of their former lives. The veteran officer in charge of the recruits would not tolerate over-familiarity, both to prevent the formation of suspect groups and to save the boys from compromising themselves.

Süleyman was also a Balkan recruit; he still missed his mother's gentle words and the way she stroked his head.

Abdülcelil's eyes filled and the base of his nose ached at recalling the way his little sister rested her freckled nose on his cheek. Overt displays of affection were not common in families, but his former family had been the exception. Sometimes he wished it had not been so, for then he wouldn't have missed them quite so much! Some of his friends were almost pleased to have been recruited: this, after all, was a way out of the heavy toil of home or the beatings. Here was an altogether new life.

Children's lifespans in the villages were not easy to predict in this world of plagues and wars. Parents might have chosen not to get too attached to their offspring. Süleyman clearly was one of those who missed his home most and so sought refuge in Abdülcelil, in whom he perceived an intellectual superior.

Seated on the thin mattress in the dormitory, Süleyman said in an urgent whisper:

'One of the latest novices brought news of my folks. He wasn't gonna speak at first, but I made him. Mum's on her deathbed, calls out my name alla time. I made my mind up: I'll find a way and escape, Abdülcelil – I wanna hug mum one last time. If our master catches me he'll whip my soles for days, but I'll take the chance so long as I have hope.'

Abdülcelil didn't reply immediately; saving his friend from himself was crucial, he knew. This crazy venture was bound to end in tears. He picked his words carefully:

'Forget it, dear friend! No use in attempting to escape. Beware the temptations of simpletons! Everyone knows the outcome of such daring escapades.'

Abdülcelil read it in his friend's eyes: convincing him wasn't going to be easy. He didn't like this subject but had to stop Süleyman before he became the subject of an exemplary tale for future Enderun novices.

'Don't think I've not considered the same thing many a time ...' he said, ignoring Süleyman's rising hopes; the boy had sat up. Abdülcelil continued: '... and the conclusion is ever only one. This palace is what the order of the world saw fit to place us in. Rejecting the opportunities the palace college offers us would be ingratitude, and that is abhorrent to me. But in the future, when we have reached high positions, no one would stop us from taking good fortune to our birthplaces.'

His friend hung his head. 'Abdülcelil, my friend, you think like a grown man, bury your grief deep. You find solace in submission and turn hardship into something good. I know not what I would do if not for you.'

Süleyman, childish fervour calmed down, getting ready for sleep, missed the words Abdülcelil whispered to himself: 'No room for us at our old homes, anyway.'

Abdülcelil somehow knew that it wasn't just common sense that tied him here, to this palace, this fate; there was something else that had pulled him here. These unidentifiable emotions were not for sharing. Every once in a while he would join in the conversation when the topic was that old, common one that some wouldn't let go:

'Just a little information on how my former family are doing, and I would be happy. But they have disappeared off the face of the earth. I remember the name of my village, but none who hails from that region knows this name. Perchance some neighbourhood names were changed. 'Tis difficult to ascertain which district or province it belongs to. Even that single name is no longer distinct; sometimes I think I must have remembered it wrong.' Abdülcelil always finished with 'One day I shall solve this mystery in my life.'

★   ★   ★

One day, a distressed Süleyman bore disquieting news but to surprisingly little effect:

'Have you heard, Abdülcelil? Some logbooks burnt in the fire that broke out in the commander's quarters yesterday! From the year of our recruitment.'

Abdülcelil had somehow come to know about it. He replied in his usual mature manner, almost as if he were talking to himself:

'The cause of the fire is unknown. There is little need to ask; I am certain of the response I would receive. This may well be all for the best. My mother, father, homeland and village are etched in a corner of my heart, in any case.'

Abdülcelil and Illumination
'I think on my adulthood/I cry/ After my childhood'

It wasn't just his family he was leaving behind, that much he had sensed. The amber-eyed child knew he was bidding farewell to his childhood and innocence for good. He was quite mature for his age even at that early stage. That resistance would serve no purpose he had realised, but he wanted to write or draw to preserve those powerful emotions swelling up inside. Then he might be able to hold on to all that he never wanted to lose.

Drawing the pain of parting from those he loved on canvas was what he had wanted to do since he was very young, and the desire had grown. The pain that demanded acknowledgement could be felt when parting from not only a loved one but also from a place or a situation. He was going to pour pain, anger and anticipation into the endless curves of the flowers he had drawn and mostly into the petals that pierced one another like pointy swords. He remembered the poem-like words whispered by a fellow recruit walking alongside him, the first time he took a brush in hand: 'I think on my adulthood/I cry/After my childhood.'

Abdülcelil's sharp intellect, confidence and refined wit helped him shine in the college. Few could sense the sorrow deep within. It was this hidden sadness that guided him towards the arts, towards painting. Paint held the power to let pain, yes, but joy and excitement too, burst forth; each and every one an intense emotion. He was talented in so many fields: calligraphy, reciting poetry and decorating pages with flowers drawn in a fine brush.

* * *

'Her Majesty Gülnuş Sultan, mother to our benefactor, the Sultan, has heard of your skill in fine floral brush decorations. She wishes to see them. Go to her presence forthwith!'

Bewildered and excited, he followed the eunuch towards the Queen Mother's quarters, remembering the far-off sight years ago of the Sultan on his way to the hunt and of his legendary Chief Wife. It was just before his recruitment; he was bringing bread and cheese for his father and elder brothers working in the field when the royal hunting party passed by.

On that unforgettable day, Gülnuş Sultan was riding her steed alongside the man who was besotted with her, the man who ruled all the lands, and she flouted the wonderment of all. Surrounded she may have been by eunuchs, her body covered by a loose cloak and cape and her face behind a veil, but even the hunt masters, dog handlers and falconers nearby never hazarded a look in her direction. The peasants in the fields similarly pulled back, obeying the commands of the guards shooing them. Children were different, of course; they were truly curious and enjoying this scene.

Stefanaki had believed he had seen the phoenix of those fairy tales riding beside the Ottoman Sultan – in his eyes, the owner of the world – her green-gold cape fluttering like wings.

* * *

The stern gaze of the eunuch brought Abdülcelil back to the present. They had reached the heavy, gold-embroidered curtain hanging between the Queen Mother's quarters and the inquisitive eyes of the rest of the harem. He prepared himself for yet another unforgettable event in his short life.

It was not usual for the ruler of the harem, the majestic mother of the emperor, to take an interest in a student. But Gülnuş Sultan, now Queen Mother since the accession of her elder son Mustafa to the throne, was known for her unconventional ways.

The boy had only managed a brief glance at the Queen Mother, who was seated on a high sofa leaning on massive cushions. All he could see was a pair of bright black eyes – their vibrancy belying her advanced years – looking out at him over her veil, with her sparkling jewellery covering her almost completely. The phoenix was made flesh once more – and this time so close to him!

The eunuch indicated he should advance and kiss her hem; the boy did as he was bidden, trembling, before he retreated, hands clasped together deferentially.

After an interrogation on his skills, she had yet another surprise: she asked him to remove his turban and open his collar. She approached and checked the two moles on his neck. The boy obeyed, feeling bewildered and shy, overwhelmed by the powerful scent of jasmine that emanated from Gülnuş Sultan.

No one would dare question the great Queen Mother as to her reasons; he would have to content himself with remembering this perplexing event the rest of his life.

★ ★ ★

He was delighted to be apprenticed to the art studio in Edirne Palace, the very essence of a temple he relished belonging to: the ceiling and cornices bedecked with tiny plant motifs, the wide windows open to the sun, a sweet warmth radiating from the massive fireplace in the wall and a place of hushed voices. The colours were bright, shapes and voices soft, scents distinctive, hopes and light fresh. The first time he was allowed in here, he kissed the hand of the Chief Artist, listened to his advice and impatiently waited for instructions. Everything around him made him bubble up with joy. So this was what he had sought all along – painting.

He worked hard and learnt fast. He never tired of crushing the pigments, mixing and preparing the paints. Time stood still when he took the brush in hand. His work was favourably received; he was being treated well. The path to becoming a master had been very short for him. The young artist had very quickly learnt how to render his flowers, so lifelike on the page, and gracefully curving reeds; other painters flocked to fill in the leaves he had drawn.

His talent did arouse envy, as was to be expected. Take the older artist, for one: he whose work had previously found much favour – before, that is, the arrival in the studio of this young child whose inherent talent shone through.

The senior artist watched every single move, trying to find fault but failing.

Levnî Abdülcelil Çelebi
A new path, a new name

The elder artist approached; Abdülcelil had just finished the outlines of striking petals in bud and a leaf whose point curled violently, like it would pierce the heart of the viewer. At his elbow was a small paint pot of colour obtained from crushing the shell of a rare green insect. The older man's elbow accidentally brushed the pot, spilling the paint over the curling leaf. He proceeded to blame this simple accident on the inappropriately, unconventionally lifelike appearance of the accurs't flowers that one could almost smell, these modelled drawings that looked ready to leap out of the paper.

The entire studio held its collective breath for the young artist's reaction. Abdülcelil was well aware of the extraordinary talent his Creator had blessed him with. Abusing others would only make him lose it. Feigning belief this was an accident, he shamed the elder man by a further pretence not to have heard the muttered pronouncements on the inauspiciousness of modelled flowers.

'This little paint pot,' said the young artist, 'was upended to show me that I should paint much more lifelike flowers, instead of those I had painted. I am truly grateful to my master, who has caused me to see it. Had the paint not been upended, there would have been no room for the drawing I shall now start with renewed fervour.'

It was a time when modesty and sincerity could converge.

Through his knowledge, manners and, above all, maturity, he had come to a stage where he merited being called a gentleman. He was now artist Abdülcelil Çelebi.

His repute reached the ears of Sultan Mustafa, son to Gülnuş Sultan. Impressed with his skill, the Emperor rewarded the artist with an extra purse of silver. Yet none of this satisfied the young artist; his illuminations may have found favour with his masters, but he wanted more: he wanted to paint not only the beauty of curving plants but also human beauty. The way people looked, their expressions and movement was what excited Abdülcelil Çelebi. What he wanted to do was preserve their vibrancy in their myriad states by drawing them on paper. Everyone had an individual posture and a gaze. He constantly observed people who interested him, and planned how he would depict them.

★   ★   ★

The time had come. The young artist drew a willowy, pouting dancer swinging her hair. Her dress he coloured with the softest lilac of springtime, the shadows dancing between the folds of the fine fabric envying the iridescence of a bird's wing. Her slender wrists he garlanded with pearl bracelets, row upon row, and her white neck with a chain of golden balls. Finally, he placed a variegated red carnation in her hand. Shyly, he showed this picture that looked alive, just too bashful to leave the sheet of paper, to his master who, in turn, hid neither his surprise nor his envy. He knew it would be inappropriate, not to mention impossible, to rein in this fresh talent who daydreamed from time to time, picked his friends sparingly and exuded such an inexplicable air of appeal.

And thus Abdülcelil departed from his previous path of 'reeds', no longer decorating book pages with infinitely elegant flowers that didn't really exist, yet looked as if their fine dagger-like leaves and petals interleaved. He began to depict real people as corporeal beings possessing three dimensions, instead of the more conventional flat figures.

His colleague Mehmed Mümin was also well known for his highly skilled drawings, yet he always avoided depicting his human or floral figures as having volume, almost as if he feared it. He approached Abdülcelil one day when the two were working side by side and asked timidly:

'My valued friend, you ought to know that there is something in this human face that you are drawing that makes me suffer, that has such a bad effect on me. The more I look, the more I want to draw my eyes away from this freakishness, for it gives the impression of being alive, of following me persistently. No sooner does this thought come into my mind than I have to repent. Is it permissible for a miniature made by man to look so lifelike?'

Mehmed Mümin noted how the others suddenly pricked up their ears, dropping their work. Encouraged by this silent support, he raised his voice:

'What is the reason, *çelebi*, that you reject our tradition of drawing creatures who know their place, who don't look like they're about to leap off?'

Abdülcelil Çelebi had been expecting this from any one of his colleagues. His reply was gentle, yet firm:

'I have long wished to depict thus, pictures with volume. My dear friend, you must have known this is what I had long been striving for. 'Tis the human race that inspires me, and that is why I have endeavoured to illuminate the likeness of humans as lifelike as I could.'

The artist paused for effect, suddenly aware how this conversation enthralled the entire studio. He looked into his friend's eyes first and then the others'. Some averted their gaze, some stared, but none spoke.

'I believe that giving life to the likeness of humans on the surface of this sheet, without ever striving to compete with the reality, opens the permissible route to eternity allowed to an artist.'

Abdülcelil's determined voice impressed everyone in the studio, which was deathly quiet.

'I am aware that many will oppose this innovation, as they do every new idea. But I am convinced that this art will find favour with those who appreciate it. I will press on, undaunted.'

This short, courteous, yet defiant speech erected an invisible barrier that was a mixture of respect for his courage and diffident pity for his foolhardiness.

In truth, the artist rejoiced, having found his reason to live. When the figures were finished, their movement on paper and their smiles pierced the viewer. That was when he poured his joy into poetry. The lovers in the dreams intermingled with those in real life, the figures on paper almost came to life, almost spoke, painting and poetry finding life together.

Colours were the sun in artist Abdülcelil Çelebi's world – and this sun never retreated behind clouds. In each and every picture he painted, he juxtaposed colours in ways that others never had: cerise and lilac, lightning blue and coral, orange and turquoise, pistachio green and purple, aubergine and chickpea. What joy there was in the colours that reflected on illuminations, that joy of living!

His friends called him Levnî, meaning 'multi-coloured, varied'.

Inspired immediately by his new name, the painter composed a poem that refreshed his soul:

Poets have given me the nom de plume Levnî
My collections seen by experts
Never applaud chance works, if they be merely two or
    three,
'Tis not worth a penny if entirety not known.

Abdülcelil Çelebi was known as Levnî from this day on, and thus he would sign his work. A new name, a new identity, a confirmation of his unique art with this singular epithet! A nom de plume, an alias, as donned by countless artists in Ottoman history!

Yet few so befitted their bearers.

Gülnuş and Ahmed
A mother's legacy

Sultan Ahmed III stared at the small wooden canister in his trembling hand and, sighing, wished with his entire being for the impossible: that he could replace what had come out and forget it.

Gülnuş Valide – Queen Mother – Sultan had been interred in the mausoleum next to the mosque built in Üsküdar in her name; born to the Verzizzi family of Crete, captured by Mad Hüseyin Pasha, the Commander of Crete, and presented to the Ottoman ruler, she had enjoyed twenty-four years as the beloved Chief Wife to the sovereign and a further twenty years as the magnificent Queen Mother thanks to her two sons, who ascended to the throne one after the other. Perchance death would afford her the peace that had eluded her in life.

Sultan Ahmed had never broken a single promise to his mother since his accession twelve years back to the imperial seat, when he replaced his elder brother Sultan Mustafa. Neither Mustafa nor his father had ever failed to indulge Gülnuş; Ahmed followed in their footsteps. So it was this one last time.

Obeying her instructions, he sent everyone away: his ministers, companions, servants, in short, everyone around him. And so, unobserved, he opened the canister. The ruler knew his mother – whom he had adored – would never have asked for such measures without good reason. All the same, he never expected to read such shattering lines.

Mother Gülnuş must have decided, after many a year, when she herself was beginning to grow old, that the time had come to put down on paper the truth about the child whose life she secretly would continue to interfere in. She returned to that September of 1679 in her letter, to those days she simply couldn't forget no matter how hard she'd tried, and thence to eight years after. The addressee was unknown at the time she took her pen in hand, when she knew no scribe could be trusted to write it but her; harem denizens were most skilful in discovering the required document at the right time or making it vanish.

She sealed by her own hand the canister enamelled with red tulips and purple hyacinths that contained a rolled-up sheet of paper.

The canister was given to her son Sultan Ahmed, with instructions to open it after her death and immediately burn it once he'd read the contents. True, it was cowardly to ask her son, the Emperor, to learn the truth only after her death; she had not liked the thought of confrontation, of confessing in person.

Even this unscrupulous woman had baulked at the possibility that she would lose the love, devotion and – most of all – admiration of her emperor son.

No one could speak or think ill of the dead in any case.

Levnî and Salonika
None that remembers them

Although the Enderun was now home for Abdülcelil Çelebi, his own family had never quite vanished from his mind. He always remembered he had come from a village near Salonika, but the memories of an eight-year-old boy can only stay fresh for so long. No one of his age at the palace or at the Enderun had hailed from his village.

His circle of friends grew in time as he rose higher in the studio. When he had risen high enough to merit the epithet of Levnî, he believed the time had come to seek out his family and cheer them up. He had not forgotten their names, and he vaguely remembered his village; yet all the discreet envoys he had despatched in the past had returned empty-handed. It was as if his entire family had vanished or never existed; there was none who remembered them. They must have come into a great fortune and left the area. Levnî knew they'd have no means of living somewhere else otherwise. Many other families had also left the village for other places after he was recruited.

Previous searches had been conducted exclusively through other parties up till then, as he bided his time until his own standing justified the courage and influence to seek out and enquire about the place where he was raised.

★ ★ ★

Arriving in Salonika town for the summer
Having conversed all winter long

Sainted helper turned up with our daily bread
There did we spend springtime ...

The poet sought his distant roots in Salonika. Although he found not a single trace, the temptation to spend an entire winter and spring in Salonika's gardens was too great to resist when everything was going so well for him: his poems piqued Sultan Ahmed's interest, his depictions found favour and he himself gained the ruler's confidence.

And the Ottoman court had just altered its practice: encouraged by his son-in-law Nevşehirli İbrahim Pasha, the ruler had all but moved permanently to Konstantiniyye, leaving Edirne Palace, where he used to spend a good deal of time. Sultan Ahmed desired this gentleman, poet and artist in one, to stay in Konstantiniyye with him all the time, displaying his talent here. He could work in the art studio at the seraglio if he wanted to or in the studio at home, creating his distinctive work. Had the artist not accompanied the Emperor in the past few years, ever at his side?

However the ruler may have resented this return 'home', he knew to keep his silence. He knew Levnî well enough that forcibly trying to rein in this obsession with Salonika would only inflame it all the more, so he had given the artist leave to go for an indeterminate length of time, and suddenly at that. Noting how his lackeys found this tolerance a huge indulgence yet never dared mention it amused the ruler.

Levnî was a houseguest at the mayor's home, a rare honour from the man responsible for law and order in the city. A chance to display his illustrious visitor made him feel a little closer to the capital. What if the feasts were costly? Surely it was all worthwhile! Entertaining his visitor – one who had breathed the same air as the Emperor – and the leading citizens of his town would only elevate his own standing amongst the latter!

Levnî Abdülcelil Çelebi was looking for an old acquaintance; that much was certain. Sadly, not even the mayor had been able to find a trace of the family by the name

Levnî had supplied. There were very few left in the village who knew them; none knew where they went. The artist came close to believing they only existed in his imagination. Come evening, when leading scholars gathered, he talked of little else but these people who had lived in a village nearby, trying to conceal his disappointment.

The gentleman from the court did not require the mayor's company on these visits to the surrounding villages. This wasn't all that astonished the host: his only special request was for a vase of jasmines in his room. But be that as it may.

Abdülcelil Çelebi's return was as abrupt as his arrival. One early summer evening, he informed his host of his decision to return to the Seat of Felicity. The poet would be returning empty-handed from Salonika but for the sweet memories of new friendships made.

An imposing sailing ship was to take him home to Konstantiniyye. The huge vessel raised anchor on a sparkling early summer morning, as the passengers waved goodbye to those in the port. A tempest nearly wrecked the boat on the way. Levnî accepted his deliverance as an omen of great portent. Every passenger had prayed to God in his own fashion, offering who knows what in a covenant should he be spared.

The first familiar sight that greeted him was Topkapı Palace at Sarayburnu – that foreigners called Seraglio Point – and the second, the *yalı* called Şerefabad Mansion, was twinkling like a jewel on the Salacak shore opposite the port, the newest and most dazzling of all waterfront villas. A warm welcome for Levnî, even if neither was his own home. The course of his life had already been determined by the times he spent in the company of their owners: the head of the Ottoman dynasty and his son-in-law Grand Vizier İbrahim Pasha.

No longer would Levnî resist the force that bound him to the Ottoman court.

İbrahim and Davud
Summer, fire season; winter, fire season...

News of the great fire raging through Konstantiniyye reached Edirne just when İbrahim Pasha was in the middle of peace negotiations with Austria and Venice.

True, overturned braziers were the main culprits in winter fires, but summer in Konstantiniyye was open season for fires: couple sun-scorched timbers with a shortage of water, and the fires crackle all the faster.

Victims would thank providence if they succeeded in rescuing a few chattels before settling down to watch their homes burn like torches, almost relieved at having no choice but to succumb to inevitable fate.

On this occasion, the flames had sprung up from a single house on the Golden Horn shore near the rifle works, growing rapidly and swallowing up a large portion of the old city, the houses leaning upon one another on narrow streets easing the way. Scarlet tongues licked night into day; the fire went through one of the gates in the old city walls and returned into the heart of the city, twisting and turning, breaking into two branches, finding ways around blockages, now uphill, now downhill, before finally running out near the southern shore of the city, about halfway between the Seven Towers Castle and Sarayburnu.

When, after twenty-seven hours, this avalanche of flames finally died down, thousands of homes, shops and schools, hundreds of mosques, palaces and mills had been burnt to a cinder.

İbrahim Pasha took this fire as an omen; once he overcame his present troubles, he would focus on this problem that consumed Konstantiniyye. Success would mean that the people – their lives thus directly improved – would be better prepared to accept other changes, other innovations.

★   ★   ★

'Davud Agha: gather ye men of strength about, that they may be ready to intervene in a fire wheresoe'er it may start. Allow no delay in organising this fire-fighting force worthy of our name, that our name be remembered with gratitude in every corner of the Seat of Felicity!'

İbrahim Pasha had gone out to Edirne as Second Vizier and returned as Grand Vizier. Battling the fire monster was to be one of his first acts. His engineer was a converted Frenchman; David, now Davud, Agha set out to form his fire-fighting brigade. He handpicked his men from amongst the janissaries: big yet also brainy men with no signs of idleness who won't tire of running, ready to attack danger without hesitation.

★   ★   ★

History would make Damat İbrahim Pasha infamous for his extravagant lifestyle as an imperial son-in-law, yet he remained a relentless seeker of innovation and lasting reform, his quest never stopping until the very end.

Davud Agha's State Pump Squad did not have to wait long for their inaugural call: the fire that began on the 8th of July 1721 would be forever more known as the day a water pump was used to put a fire out for the first time.

Four men who addressed one another as 'shoulder mate' carried a wooden water tank. A lantern-bearer lit the way as the team's steps reverberated through the streets. At the site of the fire, their chief ruled supreme, the team obeying as one man. The system was very simple; everyone knew precisely where his place was. The hose-man sprayed water at the fire, the stem-man directed the hose and the pump-man worked the hand pump.

The rescue tariff was weighted in favour of the pump-men. The fire-threatened homeowner had little choice but to come to a speedy agreement: it would be unthinkable to refuse the fee on the grounds of its being too dear!

İbrahim and Hüseyin One-Eye
The agreement

The Fire Chief Hüseyin One-Eye contented himself with slitting the ears of the fatted sheep at the site of the fire. This sacrifice was a gift from the homeowner; the Fire Chief smeared the blood on the slats of the water tank and then the door of the house they had rescued from the flames.

Were they to slaughter the sheep then and there, they would pour the blood into the tank and then pump it, blood and all, yelling for good measure as they did so, but Hüseyin favoured a more elegant approach. Neither did he recognise any that could be a match. Hüseyin One-Eye and his team's legendary brawls left none unmarked.

> Whe-heey! Stronger than lions and tigers
> The scourge of two-and-seventy nations
> A-thundering we come, a-thundering we go;
> Hüseyin Agha's champions are we, rescuers of the country, whe-heey!

The narrow streets of Konstantiniyye frequently rang out with similar cries. These displays of bravado owed more to their desire to appear the hardest team of pump-men around than a concern with rescuing people's lives and property. These people were the embodiment of the simplest expectations from life: self-interest and a swagger.

★ ★ ★

Hüseyin knew that his closed eye – lost a while back in a street brawl – rendered his hulking mass even more daunting, and the epithet 'One-Eye' pleased him in a bizarre way.

Grand Vizier İbrahim Pasha, desirous of satisfying himself of the excellence of the newly founded fire brigade, honoured his commanders with an unexpected visit, intimating that he would ever be informed of every single step taken.

İbrahim Pasha knew not when he and these thugs would ever cross paths again. Yet he was crafty enough to hold them at a comfortable arm's length; these men might come in useful one day. The Grand Vizier was not ignorant that his lifestyle irritated many, and that many sought the slightest pretext to take him down; so, he cultivated 'friendships' in unexpected quarters.

Hüseyin One-Eye intimated to the great man during this inspection that they both came from the same part of the country. He was prepared to become a loyal servant to İbrahim Pasha. This would not remain unrewarded; of this he was certain.

The statesman, for his part, knew the man would be useful, though discretion was clearly more appropriate on this occasion. Why not secretly befriend his fellow Nevşehir pump-man, the fire-fighter Hüseyin One-Eye? He sent word a couple of days later, commanding Hüseyin to his seafront villa in Beşiktaş.

'What, pray tell, would guarantee your eternal loyalty, Hüseyin Agha?' The statesman came straight to the point, bidding Hüseyin – who had flung himself prone at the vizier's feet – back to his feet. 'Your reward will be very great indeed, provided your constancy in performing flawlessly remains unabated!'

A short conversation was all it took to conclude the agreement: Hüseyin One-Eye would be İbrahim Pasha's covert aide, his eye and ear in hard-to-reach places, his envoy to be despatched to strange destinations. Confidentiality was crucial to this agreement, as was, of course, keeping the bruiser's purse ever full.

İbrahim and Ahmed and Nedim

'Just see Şerefabad once, My Majestic Sovereign'

Üsküdar's Salacak quarter had a particularly merry time in 1718. The Grand Vizier's splendid new *yalı* – waterfront mansion – left everyone in awe. The grounds backed onto a wide swathe of cypress woods and the gardens were graced by bijou gazebos, spray fountains and flowerbeds in a rainbow of colours. This truly was a palace on a small scale. The water distribution point built nearby supplied not only the district of Üsküdar but also the mansion and its vast gardens.

No more *plus ça change* for the new Grand Vizier İbrahim Pasha; a new and brilliant lifestyle was his pleasure. Surrounded by the finest things in the world, sophistication would elevate his lifestyle, the challenges of the innovative and experimental making it all so very worthwhile.

The mansion named Şerefabad had been constructed with the singular aim of pleasing Sultan Ahmed, playing host being İbrahim Pasha's foremost consideration. The verses inviting the Emperor had to come from the celebrated poet Nedim; beholden upon the statesman was rewarding the man of letters handsomely:

Every breath, its water and air add life to life
Your arrival imbues the universe with teasing and restraint

Which day will My Sovereign honour us, all a-flutter,
Come, see Şerefabad once, My Majestic Sovereign.

Master of racing words as his pen flourished elaborately,
Nedim had delivered once more: Sultan Ahmed did honour
the mansion his son-in-law built with such attention to detail.
The imperial caïque delivered the Emperor up to the landing
stage; he rested briefly first in the main room of the over-
adorned mansion and then moved to the wooden garden
gazebo by the waterfront. He praised his son-in-law's fine
taste in selecting this site, tasting the delicacies placed before
him, whilst enjoying the view: Leander's Tower that looked
close enough to touch, his own home at Sarayburnu, the port,
and Galata on the other side of the city.

This was the first of so many more: *yalıs* would line the
banks of the Bosphorus, all competing with one another,
each more flamboyant than the rest, each bearing a more
pretentious name than the rest, each staging more dazzling
shows and each receiving ever more exaggerated praise.
Çırağan Gardens in Beşiktaş competed with countless others
in splendour, including Şerefabad in Üsküdar.

Yet there was one whose grandeur would remain unrivalled:
Sadabad in Kağıthane.

Mary and Ahmed
Coming face-to-face with the Grand Signior

I WENT yesterday with the French ambassadress to see the Grand Signior in his passage to the mosque. He was preceded by a numerous guard of janissaries with vast white feathers on their heads, as also by the *spahis* and *bostangees* (these are foot and horse guards) and the royal gardeners, which are a very considerable body of men, dressed in different habits of fine lively colours, so that at a distance, they appeared like a parterre of tulips. After them the Aga of the janissaries, in a robe of purple velvet lined with silver tissue, his horse led by two slaves richly dressed. Next him the Kilar Aga (your ladyship knows this is the chief guardian of the seraglio ladies) in a deep yellow cloth (which suited very well to his black face) lined with sables and last his sublimity himself, in green lined with the fur of a black muscovite fox, which is supposed worth a thousand pounds sterling, and mounted on a fine horse with furniture embroidered with jewels. Six more horses richly caparisoned were led after him and two of his principal courtiers bore one his gold and the other his silver coffee-pot, on a staff. Another carried a silver stool on his head for him to sit on. It would be too tedious to tell your ladyship the various dresses and turbans by which their rank is distinguished; but they were all extremely rich and gay, [...] that perhaps there cannot be seen a more beautiful procession. The Sultan appeared to us a handsome man of about forty, with a very graceful air but with something severe in his countenance, his eyes very full and black. He happened to stop under the window where we stood, and, I suppose being told who we were, looked upon us very attentively, that we had full leisure to consider him and the French ambassadress agreed with me as to his good mien.[1]

Profoundly impressed by the Ottoman lifestyle and the people she met, Lady Mary Wortley Montagu, wife to the British Ambassador, wrote to her friend back home. Wrapped in a cloak and a veil, she visited every corner of the city, being particularly partial to invitations from the princesses. The more she got to know, the more her admiration grew, her letters giving animated accounts of Edirne and Constantinople.

Sultan Ahmed had also heard of this Englishwoman who had been tramping up and down the city. His curiosity aroused, he instructed his valet that he wanted to see her.

Arrangements were made for the encounter to take place at a Friday audience. The Emperor and the Western woman locked eyes briefly. Lady Mary stared, for the first time and with a good deal of curiosity, at the 'Grand Seigneur of the Orient', the image that had either intimidated or enraged the West, yet never failed to intrigue. Sultan Ahmed, for his part, stared at a noblewoman from the 'other' world. He wasn't quite sure what to expect. Someone totally different? A striking beauty? A plain infidel? The Englishwoman's pale white skin and regular features were appealing, but she was just an ordinary woman. Was there in her gaze an indecent degree of uninhibited curiosity, almost a challenge? The Emperor thought this Frankish woman's stare was indeed different from his own women's.

---

[1] Lady Mary Wortley Montagu, *The Turkish Embassy Letters*, Virago, 1994, pp. 66–67.

This brief encounter affected them both. Sultan Ahmed realised that a woman who wasn't submissive still could have the power to attract him, wondering willy-nilly what a woman who hadn't been raised for the harem could offer him.

As for Lady Montagu, she had found it difficult to resist the appeal of power. She had been raised to believe this man to be a barbarian, but here was a man who was attractive nonetheless.

Their paths never crossed again. Yet they each had just had an epiphany.

★ ★ ★

In the short time she spent here, Lady Montagu penetrated the world of the Ottomans in a way no other European woman had. This world had deepened the more she dug. The English Ambassadress began to compare this one with her world, becoming more critical of the latter. She gave a full and sincere account of her observations of this country that she had so easily got accustomed to in her letters back to England. Her compelling writing made the reader breathe in the air of Edirne or Constantinople.

No sooner had she alighted in Constantinople that Lady Montagu heard about a European painter who worked in a studio in Pera and whose work was very popular with the foreign legions: Jean-Baptiste Vanmour.

First, she made sure he was the best. Then she knocked at his studio door. It was not for her to content herself with being some random ambassadorial wife whose passage through the Ottoman capital would go unnoted. Oh no! She was going to stop time in her portrait.

The Englishwoman posed for the painter in the elegant outfit of an Ottoman woman fit for a fabulous harem: a crested aigrette on her cap, a red chemise displaying a generous décolletage, silk crêpe harem pants, a dazzling jewel clasp, a loose floral frock gathered with a belt low on her belly and a long fur-lined kaftan.

No one knows if Vanmour painted a copy, or if the Emperor ever saw the portrait. Lady Montagu declared her ease as she posed in the costume of an Ottoman lady; what she never envisaged was that her letters were destined to become a lasting testimony to this period in history.

Lady Mary Montagu left Constantinople before the year was out, like a breeze, leaving behind indelible traces of her visit.

Levnî and Ahmed
Can you build a palace out of poems? Or a country out of paintings?

Sultan Ahmed III and artist and poet Levnî Abdülcelil Çelebi stared at each other, neither drawing his gaze away, like friends who communicate without speech. They had clearly come to the end of dreams and memories for the day; they rarely looked at each other when disclosing their dearest dreams. The relationship between the Sultan and the artist had its own rituals.

'My Noble Sovereign,' Levnî had begun one day, 'begging your immeasurable indulgence, 'tis my wish to propose that you and I, when the servants are sent away, when 'tis only you and I, with none near enough to observe or listen surreptitiously, that we distract each other with the most precious memories and dreams in our hearts. This may yet be a rare liberty for a ruler.'

Sultan Ahmed embraced this incredibly daring proposal calmly. He was already well accustomed to Levnî speaking his mind. Censure or chastisement would only upset the wielder, and Levnî knew it. The artist also knew his own value, but prudence stayed with him; he never overplayed it.

★ ★ ★

The Emperor and his companion often spent many an hour conversing in hushed tones, a fact that never escaped the attention either of the court or of Grand Vizier İbrahim Pasha.

Yet none was intrepid enough to refer to this friendship out aloud, not even the mighty, noble Grand Vizier himself, though married to the royal family he might be.

A totally uninhibited friendship between a ruler and his servant, even if the servant were the grand vizier himself, was unthinkable, yet Sultan Ahmed's admiration of his first minister went far beyond what the position would traditionally merit. All the same, İbrahim Pasha was discomfited indeed by how easily the ruler and the artist shared confidences. Sultan Ahmed truly opened his heart up to this artist-poet companion, talking not like a ruler but a simple person with a burden to share, when the two were alone. Had the statesman heard what Sultan Ahmed had to tell Levnî today, he would have been sorely troubled indeed.

The Emperor had decided that today, instead of being distracted by an entertaining or thought-provoking tale, he would narrate one of his own experiences. This was the tale of how he had, in the second year of his reign, dismissed his brother-in-law Grand Vizier Damat Moralı Hasan Pasha:

'I had appointed Moralı Hasan Pasha, known as Brother-in-Law Moralı Hasan Pasha, with the full expectation that he would give us useful service. But instead, when it came to my attention that he had been defying some of my commands, and even spoke disrespectfully of his benefactor, I was sorely distressed. I finally decided to dismiss this ingrate servant.'

The Emperor may spend a brief moment in taking a decision, yet this decision had the power to alter someone else's life radically.

'There was a strapping fellow known as Bald İbrahim, whom I entrusted with my life every time I went incognito in the Seat of Felicity. He would take me around in his skiff. One day, I got up like a humble merchant and arrived at his side; none knew the august ruler but for my guards watching from a distance.'

Sultan Ahmed had returned to those old days as he spoke from the heart; now he was no different from a young man bragging to a friend about his exploits.

Listening to him without interruptions, Levnî saw an ordinary servant of God sitting opposite, instead of a ruler who had no idea of the size of his wealth, a ruler whose servants stood, heads bowed, hands clasped respectfully. Levnî had sworn never to misuse the royal confidence he had been blessed with; the ruler clearly longed for the informality of ordinariness. The tale was none too special, just one of hundreds of tragic-comic events that had taken place in Ottoman history. The Emperor enjoyed continuing his tale like many ordinary people whose feigned ignorance of their superiority – be it in craftiness or intelligence – rarely fails to amuse:

'So I handed the new imperial letter of appointment to Bald İbrahim, for him to covertly convey to the vizier Kalaylıkoz Ahmed Pasha who was in Kandiye. Bald İbrahim got dressed as a merchant, loaded a trading ship with timber and set off from Konstantiniyye. The winds were clement; he reached Kandiye and handed the consignment to Ahmed Pasha. They set off for the Seat of Felicity and arrived at Küçükçekmece. This at a time when my brother's deposers – who'd elevated me to the throne in his stead – considered themselves mightier than all, so it was essential that my brother-in-law knew nothing of my plans until the last moment. Ahmed Pasha arrived at the palace at dawn, and passing through the imperial gardens, he hid in a room in the valets' dormitory.'

How ironic, that the man known as the ruler of the world, the man who held absolute power in his hands, had to resort to such machinations to appoint a new grand vizier ... Mystery and intrigue, was this to be the inescapable fate of the palace since the Eastern Roman Empire in this unique city?

Levnî had inured himself to all manner of peculiarities; still silent, he continued to listen to his benefactor.

'When Grand Vizier Hasan Pasha of Mora arrived at the council on that day, I commanded he and his wife, my sister Hatice Sultan, prepare a feast for me at the Ayvansaray villa.'

The Emperor had, evidently, desired to brighten up his brother-in-law's day one final time – the brother-in-law he was about to sack. The honour of hosting the sovereign! The Sultan may well have appreciated the cruelty of his plan, and even decided that it was appropriate to punish this servant who had gone too far, who had threatened him, with an abrupt disappointment and fall.

'The pasha left my presence, well satisfied. I sent the Lieutenant of the Gatekeepers Veli Agha after him to take back the ministerial seal. His culpability could hardly have escaped him; he bowed his head, I'm told.'

Such a dismissal would have meant a complete upheaval in his and his family's fortunes – if, that is, he would be allowed to live.

'Be that as it may, I moved into the Baghdad Pavilion, one of my favourite sites in the Great Palace, bade Kalaylıkoz Ahmed Pasha come, entrusted him with the ministerial seal and saw him don the robes of office.'

That's how simple it was: the passage between reaching the summit of power and toppling. This held true for everyone, with no exceptions – not even the absolute ruler, the august Emperor, the ruler of the seven seas; it was obvious he never felt himself completely secure. Levnî couldn't stop wondering: How was it possible for the great Emperor to be intimidated by his own brother-in-law the Grand Vizier? How was it possible for him to have to resort to such intrigues to appoint a new grand vizier? How was it possible for him to avoid dismissing his former minister in person? And was it a flaw in his character that he had narrated this tale like a thriller, or was it shrewdness?

'Hasan Pasha's punishment would have been death, but Hatice Sultan had already been widowed with four children. I took pity on my virtuous sister and spared her husband's life. I know 'tis not the custom for princesses to live in the provinces, but I sent the entire family to a palace in İzmit.'

Cowardice and courage, mercy and cruelty, attention and apathy, passion and acceptance – all this combined to make up a human being. Even if his title was Emperor, it wasn't up to him to determine in what proportion. What mattered was which of these would prevail, and when.

★   ★   ★

It was a late winter afternoon, the light cold, in 1719 when Levnî heard this strange yet familiar tale in his Emperor's presence, a tale that quickened the blood, yet was pathetic.

The Emperor had allowed the artist to sit on the embroidered cushion opposite as if he were an equal to the owner of the vast Ottoman Empire. True, the artist never failed to present anything less than complete respect, but he did not stand submissively, hands clasped before him. Moreover, his kneeling position was quite relaxed as he listened to the Emperor attentively, occasionally asked questions of the ruler of the universe, or even commented upon the tale.

Levnî brightened up the sovereign's life; this distinguished courtier was one of the most valued companions of all time in the Ottoman court. Ottoman rulers had for hundreds of years assiduously selected their companions, their conversation partners, for their intelligence, knowledge and talent. Those elevated to such lofty heights made good use of the privilege of accompanying God's shadow on earth. One such man was Haydar Captain the mariner, also known as Nigârî the painter. Süleyman the Magnificent's companion was a formidable portraitist who shirked custom in choosing to live in Galata, the infidels' quarter. Nigârî had depicted sultans uninhibited, painting Selim the Sot (later Sultan Selim II) as a crown prince with a wine goblet in his hand. He had presented a Venetian friend, a connoisseur, with a fabulous set of portraits of the dynasty.

Being an emperor's companion was no guarantee of unchallenged universal esteem. When Mustafa Han, Sultan Ahmed III's predecessor (and elder brother), was deposed, his four companions were arrested and exiled to Egypt, charged with addicting him to the pleasures of hunting in Edirne and thereby keeping him from the business of state, as if the great Emperor could so easily be swayed like a child and as if a hedonist could be made by outside influence. The culprits would ultimately be sought amongst the nearest and the dearest.

The potential for unexpected changes in the fortunes of those closest to power never spared the Sultan's conversation companions; the border between glory and ignominy was a very thin line indeed.

Companions were close to the Sultan, true; they wielded influence on him, also true. All this power made them somewhat daunting in the eyes of many courtiers. Levnî, however, was different; he was highly selective in his choice of friends. He posed no threat to the court. Still, he commanded a great deal of respect – the sincere respect shown to a peerless artist. Few companions attained such privilege with so little effort.

★ ★ ★

Levnî knew precisely when the Emperor singled him out: in autumn of 1715, soon after the death of Gülnuş Sultan, surely the mightiest and most majestic of all queen mothers, whose death shook the entire harem to the core.

The illustrious Queen Mother's deathbed agonies proved to be prolonged. Her good deeds were numerous, to be fair, but her sins were no fewer, whispered unnamed lips. Surely the length of her torment was attributable to her trespasses. Was she fearful of facing her own deeds? She finally departed one Tuesday night. Her age was known as five and seventy, yet she was still handsome; death had ill become her.

Gülnuş Sultan had for years applied all manner of unguents on her face and body, of herbs, seaweed and who knew what other unmentionables. Perhaps it was those thick potions, perhaps it was her desire to live that caused the wrinkles on her face to be no more pronounced than those of a woman in her early forties. The physician who had been called as a last resort would never have believed the true age of his patient – whom he had to examine under covers, with special dispensation given by the Emperor – if he hadn't known her identity.

Her funeral procession went through the Gate of Felicity. The coffin was placed on a coach in front of the Procession Pavilion at a ceremony attended by the entire cabinet, theologians and religious leaders. The carriage reached Türk Mehmed Pasha, the Deputy Grand Vizier. The following day, the coffin was taken to the Davudpaşa Palace and greeted by the mayor of Konstantiniyye. The Koran was recited at her head all night long. The coffin was then carried back to the palace through the imperial garden and by the Yalı Pavilion at Sarayburnu. Thence it was placed on the imperial caïque and rowed over the strait into Üsküdar. Gülnuş Sultan's will asked for interment not next to her beloved sovereign Mehmed the Hunter but in the open-air mausoleum in the garden of the mosque she had endowed in Üsküdar.

The artist had believed at the time that Sultan Ahmed, having lost his beloved mother, was seeking solace in the company of an equally colourful personality.

Levnî and Mirza Mehmed
The shadow of the past

'Blessed be your sacred morning, Levnî Çelebi!'

Salih Agha's greeting did not please Levnî. Too courteous to withhold this, however, he responded without breaking step. But Salih Agha was determined to chat. Steward to the former *Kul Kethüdası* Mirza Mehmed Pasha, One-Armed Salih Agha of Karadağ fell into slow step beside the artist as the latter was making his way to the seraglio. Levnî had been circumspect in his treatment of Salih Agha's previous attempts at winning his friendship. Instinct warned him that this man would seek out skeletons in cupboards and smile at you as he knifed you in the back.

'Mirza Mehmed Pasha is desirous of offering a master artist like yourself a cup of bitter coffee, Levnî Çelebi. He's not got long to go now; as you will be aware, he sits in his corner and counts the days, deeming himself fortunate for good company. And 'twould be an honour to converse with the companion of Our Noble Emperor.'

The elderly man in question had served as a recruitment officer in his time. Some inexplicable distaste had made Levnî keep his distance all this time, but refusal would have offended.

'The morning of the Thursday after the morrow, if that is suitable, Salih Agha, I shall come.'

*   *   *

Mirza Mehmed Pasha, endowed with a dichotomy of self-confidence and mistrust after years in service of the state, was a man who selected his words carefully, attempting to understand the mind of the man before him first.

He had served Mehmed the Hunter as *Zağarcıbaşı* – Master of the Hounds – a full colonel in charge of the 400 janissaries of the 64th Battalion. Surely a promotion to this post would have given any officer a clear run, in particular if his sovereign's epithet was 'Hunter'!

At any rate, Colonel Mirza Mehmed Agha was next honoured with the additional commission of recruitment officer in the latter part of Mehmed the Hunter's reign and had given a good account of himself there. His reward, upon return to the Seat of Felicity, was another high appointment to the provinces. Two years after that, he had risen to *Kul Kethüdası*, second only to the Commander-in-Chief, responsible for the discipline of the great janissary hearth and also a member of the aghas' council, the most influential of all. His uniform was almost identical to the top man, the only difference being the colour of their fur-lined gowns: the Commander-in-Chief wore white silk, the *Kul Kethüdası* green.

It was memories such as these that warmed the heart of the retired officer. Most were sweet memories indeed. The only fly in the ointment was that strange fire in which the *devşirme* logs had burnt. Just after that event, he had been promoted from simple Mirza Mehmed Efendi to Mirza Mehmed Pasha and had been posted to the provinces, to the centre of Anatolia as a guard. Life flowed at a more comfortable pace in the provinces, but it wasn't a patch on the Seat of Felicity for someone who had been accustomed to – nay, was addicted to – its vibrancy and colour. His following promotion had been to Governor of Tunis, a more agreeable post altogether, but retirement meant a return to his beloved Konstantiniyye, however much power he would have to forsake in return for living his final years there.

The amber-eyed boy he had recruited in April 1687 visited his dreams time and again, that angelic countenance perplexing him.

Mirza Mehmed's part was done. His commander made it very clear upon receiving delivery of the boys – no more questions.

Yet in time, Mirza Mehmed wondered about those odd coincidences that had led him to draw bizarre conclusions. Had that boy grown up into the person he thought of? At this late stage of his life surely he could ask the questions he did not dare earlier – yes indeed, this was his intention.

★　★　★

The news came just as Levnî was about to set off, albeit reluctantly, for his visit to Mirza Mehmed Pasha. The old general had just passed away. 'He passed so suddenly,' panted the messenger, 'yet last night, he was in such good health and cheer. There was a huge party at the mansion.'

Levnî and Ömer, Levnî and Love
A world of poetry

The act of painting filled Levnî with an irrepressible enthusiasm. A top-floor room with the best light was converted into a studio just like that of Master Vanmour, the artist who'd been living in Pera for years.

His friends, in particular the poets, couldn't wait to see how lifelike people appeared on paper in his paintings. Whenever he thought about their thrill, he remembered a painting he had done years ago.

The portrait of Aşık Ömer – who had once given in to envy and fallen out with Levnî – with his cap on the ground, his belt loosened and a wine glass in his hand had become the topic of the day. It was almost as if Levnî had sought to reveal the passionate relationship between them, render it undeniable. Either the painting had mirrored Nedim's poem or the poem had mirrored the painting: 'Belt loosened, your cap fallen to the side.'

Levnî always wanted to paint love, for that was what he was in love with. Yet it was only those he loved he could paint easily. Possibly, all his paintings were love itself. Levnî held himself to account so many times, yet no victor was declared in these contests.

Who knows how many lovers told their lovers, 'It is like you're beside me when I close my eyes'? Yet Levnî had no need to close his eyes; he was painting his beloved, who so appeared on paper, as near as could be.

To Levnî painting was like making love, with similar pleasure. When he picked up the brush, especially that very fine one, or began to mix the colours, the sensation that filled him was the same as the anticipation of erotic fulfilment. One never knew at the beginning how the lovemaking would progress. Would passions rise after gentle caresses, to leave a deep mark behind once the anticipated moment had come and gone? Or would the union be followed by that unbearable aftermath of an ordinary, monotonous coupling?

A colour could arise that he had never before discovered, yet he would continue to seek, always on the trail of new, hitherto unseen hues. Could he capture the colour of the Judas tree branch, darkening towards the tip, either on paper or on the lips of the beloved? Could he convey the scent of the fresh mint leaf on the gold-embroidered throw in the picture or on the lover's breath?

The concept of 'lover' in the illuminator's heart was unconventional. For Levnî to fall in love, he had to be convinced that the object of his passion was a match in talent, whether in poetry, painting or music.

Sometimes admiration would be mistaken for love, such as the attraction between Ömer and Levnî. A kind of rivalry, a contest between lovers, was what spurred him on. Was this a desire to prove oneself by overcoming the dearest, the one most desired? Was this a reaffirmation of self-confidence? Perhaps it was mutual admiration and envy towards each other's art and passion, a desire to own or to become as one mentally, as though if they were to enjoy this love to the end, they would reach the beauties within each other's minds and unite on every dimension through an emotional exchange of hopes, aims and goals.

And then what? Apparently a void would follow; not even Sultan Ahmed was able to find an answer during their conversations, despite having considered it time and again.

The love Levnî had for all things beautiful over-shadowed all. He painted those he loved, and he sometimes fell in love with those he painted, as true love only came about for him whilst he was converting the talent God had blessed him with into lines.

It may have been easy to see what the paintings described, however superficial that might be, but would the admiring viewer appreciate the meaning of signatures? Who could guess that each flower that decorated the Levnî signature had a specific meaning or how relevant sometimes even the position of the signature was? The signature he drew with flowers symbolised Levnî himself in the painting, particularly those he placed by the feet of the subject of a portrait, as if he himself was standing there at the feet of this model he knew so well.

Every signature held its own secret; those he placed on the portraits of lovers or people he had close emotional connections with were special, but he kept one to himself so that nobody will ever decipher it. The distinctions were in the curl of a petal, in a leaf or in a colour.

In that affectionate portrait of Aşık Ömer, Levnî's signature was placed right on the ground, below Ömer's heart – surely no random choice? Only Sultan Ahmed would have appreciated this, and that is why Levnî can be found right at the knees of the ruler's portrait with his signature under the feet, placing himself at the feet of his ruler out of pure devotion, not because Ahmed was the mighty ruler of the August State. Of the multitude of portraits he painted of his emperor, he signed only one so that his identity may not remain entirely concealed.

Ömer and Levnî had a passionate relationship, yet unconsummated. Both men had dreamt of an emotional and physical union, but never quite got around to it.

And perhaps it was this that guided Levnî's hand to create such an indulgent portrait. That's how inviolate this love was: only the good aspects remained in the mind, and any possible unpleasantness avoided. Purity remained sacrosanct. Here stood two individuals totally in awe of each other. Levnî thought he had quite naturally surpassed traditional concepts, whether acceptable to those around or not.

Levnî depicted Ömer in an imaginary post-coital state, after, presumably, what might have been their first lovemaking, stretched out blissfully, dishevelled, as a record of his love and a reflection of his dreams. The engraved wine bottle in Ömer's hand was a mere symbol of Levnî's forbidden love. Ömer's open collar, loosened belt, bare feet, cap rolling on the ground, dishevelled hair, head resting on one hand and eyes clearly closed in daydreams made him far more attractive in this fully clothed state, evocative of love, than any naked figure. He is clean-shaven, too, just as Levnî's spirit viewed him: innocent, fresh, handsome, in love.

Even the floral motifs on the wine bottle had been rendered meticulously, like the gently curled toes of the man. Levnî painted this picture as if he knew every single detail on that body, someone who could read its language.

Which was the more blissful, he hadn't yet decided: the glow of a passionate session of lovemaking or the thrill of anticipation. Anticipation might have been more satisfactory, as there was no end to it! Levnî and Ömer felt much more than sexual attraction to each other: a deep passion and admiration, fragile emotions; it was better not to risk giving in to their desire – far more preferable it would have been never to see each other again!

Those who examine his portrait of Ömer would never quite know whether the poet had been depicted in the dreamy anticipation of love, having a drink to relax the butterflies in his stomach, or glowing with that peerless languor that follows love fully enjoyed. Even Levnî himself had not yet made up his mind about which of those two imaginary love scenes he had picked.

The artist placed his signature not, as would be customary, at the bottom of the painting, but right under the heart of the reclining figure. Close to the red cushion nestled the name Levnî, encircled by tiny leaves and flowers. Did he hope this minuscule distinction would belong to him alone? The sharp eyes of Sultan Ahmed silently – and immediately – pointed to the placement of the signature. Levnî did not deny it; no shame in love, but this was private, not to be shared with all. He had deliberately chosen not to articulate the love, limiting his expression to painting, his own symbols. Thus was born a Levnî masterpiece.

Levnî had hesitated about including this painting in the album he was about to present to the ruler, yet the painting had already been seen by several visitors in his studio by then. To the extent that another poet friend, Şevkat, had expressed in his verses the joy he had felt when he saw the painting, how skilfully Levnî had drawn Aşık Ömer in his 'dishevelled' state and how easily he was recognised:

See here, artist, what Şevkat has guessed
That dishevelled shape you have drawn on the flat
Those looking would guess the portrait
Aşık Ömer, you have sat for one master such as Levnî ...

Even when Levnî and Ömer fell out they exchanged poems, and they made up again with poems.

Love, desire, hunger and dreams ... Levnî knew he would never be able to define the boundaries of these concepts or analyse them completely, but what he did know was that he was fortunate indeed, being able to express himself in painting and poetry.

The bad blood between him and Ömer – all due to envy – would have caused for Levnî no end of regret had he but known how little time they would have together.

I have fair turned into Mecnun in countenance, weeping
    miserably
Favour for the sake of a thousand and one words, O
Celil
Separation has constricted my world, once so vast
O Ömer, the elixir of severance on my side

The acrimony clearly hurt Ömer equally deeply, but it took another poem, asking for the cause of their anger, to heal the breach:

Ömer's counsel would suffice for the wise in the world
Futile friend does not thank the heart
Let's make up, grudges ill become the faithful
Tell me, I beseech thee, my dear, why this sulk?

Levnî responded with a *nazire*, a poem written in the same metre and style, using the same words, repeating the desire for reconciliation:

Where did I offend, O king, that thou sulkest?
I merely prayed for thy favour, thou stopped talking
Passionate I may have been in thy love, yet no sinner,
Thou payest back thousandfold my one fault with thy
   sulking

* * *

Aşık Ömer – Levnî's great young passion – had been gone for many years, and the illuminator's overwhelming and apparently endless grief continued unabated. However, Levnî tried to forget Ömer, to stop seeking him in others; it was as if Ömer appeared before him time and again, his forceful personality standing firm. Levnî had enjoyed brief love affairs with women, and now there was a youth, Selim by name, who was infinitely dazzled by the illuminator's art – and intimating he was none too loath to welcome closer contact, both in skin and in spirit.

For Levnî to fall in love, he had to admire the object in total; this was the first condition, and none too easy, yet when he did meet one such, his first instinct was unequivocal resistance.

Apprehensive at the prospects of his resistance buckling, of diving headlong into a love he could not enjoy openly and of possibly suffering again, Levnî wrote a song wherein he hid the consonants in Selim's name.

The song might have helped release his own soul and lay his troubles before his beloved Emperor:

The heart has alighted on a fairy-faced renegade
The heart has alighted on a tempter of the world, a
    youth
The name of that siren, Levnî will state in letters,
Only the self-confessed speller can work it out ...

One is S, and the next L, and an I and an M
The heart has alighted on a youth, owner of these four
    letters

Brief love affairs were quite exhausting, just like those well-favoured tulips. Yet it was they that fed his poetry and painting; he couldn't give them up, for little desire did he have to pick up a pen or brush with no love in his heart.

He was about to taste the inimitable delicacy that was the dream of possessing instead of the act of possessing; he had to abandon this adventure before embarking upon it, to grasp onto something before he was carried away doing what he always did. He had to overcome his desire ... Levnî suddenly felt as if a whirlwind had abruptly appeared in the desert and, leaping a step beyond it, he had saved himself; however, his eyes might have stung from the searing sands.

★ ★ ★

Levnî enjoyed a degree of privacy outside the court rarely afforded a man in his position. Sultan Ahmed well knew any restriction on his beloved companion could alienate him. The Emperor may well have identified with the artist; as Levnî basked in his freedom, wandering on the convenient paths of ordinariness, it was as if the Sultan was meeting strange people in strange coffee houses, engaging in strange conversations and – who knows? – maybe even fancying someone.

Finally, he decided one day that he would make these dreams a reality and enjoy the distinction of ordinariness. Sultan Ahmed would go in mufti and venture outside the palace, certainly without a word to İbrahim Pasha, once the summer was over and the *yalı* parties done with.

İbrahim and Fatma

'Whether she teases you out of love, that would be for you to comprehend, My Vizier ...'

'Crown of my life! Fair light of my eyes! My Sultan, my angel, see how I rub my face against the earth; I am drown'd in scalding tears.' So wrote the great İbrahim Pasha after he wed his young bride, before they were united.

The statesman was fifty years old when fortune finally smiled upon him: he had been deemed worthy to become the son-in-law of the Ruler of the Seven Climes, Emperor Sultan Ahmed III; the Sultan's beloved daughter Fatma was his great prize. Clearly his promotion to Deputy Grand Vizier, his wedding present, was not going to be his last.

Fatma Sultan, only thirteen years old, had not yet reached puberty, but this was already her second marriage. She had been married off to the Silahtar Ali Pasha at the age of five. A silver coach had taken her to the Queen Sultan's Palace in Eyüp, where the wedding was to be held. Celebrations had gone on for days. What delighted the child bride most were the colourful sweets she had received. As for the man they called her husband, well, she'd not even seen him once. Ali Pasha rose to Grand Vizier in 1713 and built a majestic palace for his wife in anticipation of happy days to come. But he fell at the Battle of Peterwardein before the marriage was even consummated. She was a widow at the age of twelve, the young wife Ali Pasha had not even managed to see with his own eyes. The commander of the Austrian forces, Prince François Eugène de Savoie, had unwittingly altered the fate of two men: one died and the other won the first's position and wife.

★ ★ ★

İbrahim Pasha was the key player in the 1718 Passarowitz treaty with the Austrians. He had, in fact, refused the post of Grand Vizier that had been offered during the war, thereby initiating the appointment of his friend Mehmed Pasha to this highest and rather slippery post. Fatma Sultan was the Emperor's daughter by his Chief Wife, Emetullah Sultan. With this favoured princess, now his wife whilst he was the Second Vizier, he had already reached the dizzy heights of being an imperial son-in-law. Here was the key to his future advancement.

Skilful manoeuvring during the peace negotiations won Nevşehirli İbrahim Pasha the Grand Vizier's seal; true, concessions were given, but nonetheless he emerged as the victorious commander of the relaxing atmosphere of peace. He had been raised as the perfect clerk, not as a soldier. He had learnt calligraphy from Hafız Osman, just like his benefactor Sultan Ahmed. And he indulged in the popular pastimes of the time, excelling at riding and archery, just like his benefactor.

'İbrahim Pasha was wed to Fatma Sultan. The Emperor presented them with a delightful necklace, of a plate of gold with a solitaire diamond in the centre, eight smaller ones surrounding it, fourteen rubies around those and seven and thirty diamonds on the outer rim, and yet so many more other jewels.'

That's how a chronicler noted İbrahim Pasha's rising star.

The Grand Vizier placed great value on history and historians; a copy of *Naima's History* never left his hand. He always tried to learn from the past. History would show just how successful he would be in practising what he had learnt.

His influence and wealth grew by the day. One of the most powerful of all time, İbrahim Pasha attracted more and more envy in the court. Also noteworthy was his ability to win over that gentle aesthete, Sultan Ahmed.

★ ★ ★

İbrahim Pasha did all he could to nurture his Emperor's fondness and trust, although he suffered from the rise of – in his view – insurmountable obstacles between the two from time to time, especially when it came to the Emperor's favourite daughter. The statesman knew he merited the hand of the princess thanks to the sovereign's trust in his kindness and generosity, but above all because the Emperor believed he would be a good husband. He would never jeopardise this belief.

'My majestic, miraculous, imposing, powerful, fortuitous benefactor, My Lord, My Emperor, the cause of my good fortune,

God willing, we have discharged our duties commanded by imperial edict. My mistress the Sultan came back from the palace, but did not favour your servant with her blessing. She had not told me so herself, but it appears some have claimed, "the Pasha has been accustomed to concubines, he would not have forsaken them". What calumny is this? An insane man would I be! My former station was different; to act this way now would be blasphemy. I swear that nothing of the sort has even occurred to me, Your Imperial Highness will be well aware. Our august Chief Wife will need to forbid those who would upset our august Sultan, Liege Lord.'

The great İbrahim Pasha wrote this plaintive letter to his father-in-law. Her fondness cooled by rumours of İbrahim's womanising, she had gone to visit her father. The problem was that they were all true. He had to find out who had been telling tales.

Until his wedding to Fatma Sultan, he had taken the most delectable concubines to his home, and his bed, until his fiftieth year; his first wife, who had given him two daughters

68

and one son, had never complained. But when the wife in question was a princess, things were very different indeed. Like all imperial sons-in-law, he was forced to divorce his present wife first, an unarguable rule of the game.

'My Vizier,

We have discussed this matter with Her Royal Highness, the princess; we can assure you that no one has said anything to her; she may well have unfounded concerns of her own. She was very well yesterday. She wished to return home in the afternoon, ordered her coach and mounted it happily. We even accompanied her to the coach and sent you our greetings. She greeted back, responding, "Tell him not to worry, I would not have anyone speak such unpleasantness". She wished to get back home; whether she missed her home, or wished to tease you somewhat, that would be for you to comprehend.'

This was a man's letter to another man, but also one from a father to a son-in-law. The Emperor not only reassured his son-in-law but also reminded him, iron hand in velvet glove, that understanding his daughter's disquiet and keeping her happy was her husband's duty and no other's.

Sultan Ahmed's letter failed to allay İbrahim Pasha's concerns. He had to watch his step as of now. It must have been the plump concubine who brought his morning coffee, who clearly had let the cat out of the bag despite all the gold he had tucked into her chemise! The risk of losing Fatma Sultan washed over his back like a bucket of ice water. This would have meant the collapse of his entire universe, this world that he had bedecked with such finery. He truly did love his spoilt and coy young wife in his own fashion, but her greatest asset was that she was the ruler's favourite daughter. And Nevşehirli İbrahim Pasha was not one to content himself with one woman for the rest of his life. A man with an eye for beautiful women would need to be very circumspect indeed, especially if he had so many enemies waiting for the slightest slip.

Festivities in Kağıthane
New beginnings

The air was redolent with fresh flowers and grass – so vibrant, so joyful after a day's rain – that overpowered the cloying sweetness of the hyacinths, never mind the barely discernible scent of the tulips. Kağıthane Stream burbled cheerfully past, a silver blade slicing this verdant blanket.

Sultan Ahmed mused that this must be the manner of the gardens of Paradise. His Grand Vizier had informed him of a small banquet he had prepared for the 15th of April and that he would be exceedingly well honoured should the Emperor deign to attend.

The sheer scale of the festivities amazed the Emperor as he approached in his imperial caïque. İbrahim Pasha had flowers planted everywhere; he had marquees erected for the comfort of the Emperor, the harem contingent, valets, countless statesmen and servants, so that none should miss the comforts of the palace. A cloth wall that stretched on and on set the harem marquee apart.

Once the delicious picnic was over, the picnic of spit-roast lamb on wood fires, whose aroma whetted the appetite, with *iç pilav* – rice with chicken livers, currants and pine kernels, cooked in the kitchen tent – apricot compote and semolina pudding, it was time for the entertainment: javelin games, people on horseback and on foot, horse races and wrestling matches, all to amuse Sultan Ahmed. The winners were rewarded generously. Legendary was the splendour of the day.

His benefactor's pleasure being İbrahim Pasha's first priority, the vizier would outdo himself each time he entertained his emperor.

★   ★   ★

The 15th of April 1719 was a turning point for Kağıthane Stream, the site of royal picnics for hundreds of years. This would become the favourite spot for the denizens of the Seat of Felicity, the brightest stage of, and closest witness to, the opulence of an entire era.

This day would be a turning point for Levnî Abdülcelil Çelebi. In the midst of those festive crowds, his eyes met those of forbidden honey: a young concubine in the service of Fatma Sultan, wife to İbrahim Pasha. Instead of running away, she gave him an almost insolent stare. Drawing a chiffon veil over her face as she sauntered back into the tent, she turned her green eyes back at him for one last glance.

The artist did his best to find out anything he could about her, the risk of disclosing his interest be damned; her name was Şebsefa and she played the tambur.

Levnî did not taste the roast meat or his favourite pudding that day, unlike everyone around him who attacked the food with relish. His soul was sated with the fresh excitement of having discovered new beauty. He might have forced himself, but not a mouthful would go down, his heart was beating so fast. Never had he been so jolted out of his wits by a beauty. This was different from all his previous fancies.

Levnî and Ahmed and Mihrişah and Şermi and Hümaşah

'What have we consumed, pleasure or regret?'

Once again the Emperor and the artist sat facing each other. It was the morrow of an herb night; last night's pudding that came from the imperial kitchens had been perfect in both consistency and flavour.

Once a year, in the spring, a large batch of paste would be boiled in huge vats: long pepper – similar to cinnamon seed in appearance – mint, the aphrodisiac herb called galangal, rose and poppy petals, sweetened to a thick, syrupy gum. Some would be set aside for the Emperor and the rest handed out to courtiers. The Chief Surgeon was particularly keen to invent concoctions to best serve his benefactor, the Emperor. The pudding shop in the kitchen got to enjoy an unforgettable night too: special entertainment was laid on for the cooks, with a string orchestra to gladden the heart, shadow puppets and clowns too. As for the Emperor – happy to have dispensed such joy to his subjects, he would savour the effects of the fresh paste with his pick of the young lovelies in the harem, experts in coquetry all.

Chief *Helva* Cook Dubnitseli Refik Agha mused on the unpredictability of the fate of objects as he ground the herbs. Take for example the fabulous porphyry mortar in his hand, originally brought to Constantinople hundreds of years ago from Egypt in the service of the newly accepted religion of Christianity, to be used when blessing the believers. This massive bowl served on, but this time in the kitchen of the Muslim Ottomans. Could it be that hundreds of years of wear had rubbed into this carved stone that had always belonged to powerful people its own might, to infuse pastes with such potency?

Dubnitseli wondered where these thoughts came from, shook his head as if to clear it, and began to think about the approaching evening's promises. He had kept it close to the chest up till now, but that blue-eyed, rosy-cheeked fresh apprentice Bright Selim had been on his mind. Refik Agha was determined to seduce the lad after the music and poetry of the evening.

Twice earlier he had caught Selim circling around Levnî, the Emperor's favourite companion. He knew this rare man, a peerless artist, was an accomplished poet to boot. Was Selim of the blond locks and languid gaze dazzled by the man's stunning poems that spoke to all – so graceful, yet startlingly insightful? What shall he do to seduce the lad? It wasn't impossible to force his suit by threats, but that was not the Chief *Helva* Cook's preferred fashion. Just like his puddings, he wanted affection to reach the right consistency gently, in its own time.

Dubnitseli knew Levnî fancied women too. What the artist liked was the alluring, whatever pleased the heart. Or did he feign love just to stoke the fire of poetry or his paintings? Neither the wife he had been married off to with no particular sentimental attachment, nor his well-known first love – of whom no one would ever dare remind him – would evidently sate Levnî's heart. The handsome youth was never going to measure up. But a new rumour had begun making the rounds. The companion had fallen in love with a concubine serving Grand Vizier İbrahim Pasha's princess wife, the ruler's favourite daughter. Dubnitseli had even heard that the artist had painted her likeness on a piece of paper, like a living human being. But who knew about these poets! Falling in love with a lad like Selim – and he was so close, still playing the game by the rules – meant succumbing to overpowering thoughts like now, and defying bans; yet how worthwhile a prize! These fancies were the only things that enlivened this otherwise monotonous life spent between the kitchen walls.

Refik Agha did know that the Emperor did not tolerate such canoodling in the palace. It was in the early days of Sultan Ahmed's reign when reverberations of the Minderkıstısı İbrahim Agha scandal shook the palace to the core. The reckless sword-bearer had taken a young lad to the palace to lie with at night. How Minderkıstısı barely escaped with his life was still fresh in memory – what audacity to carry the object of his lust into the home of the ruler of the universe! Nonetheless, the man from Dubnitse was going to find it hard to control his lust.

What precious gift would the Emperor send him in gratitude for the paste to make sure he would be grateful? A silk kaftan, a pair of coral-handled tortoiseshell spoons, or a purse of gold? The Emperor's imminent largesse suddenly outshone all other considerations.

★ ★ ★

The sweet languor of a night of over-indulgent passion still clung to Sultan Ahmed, which he was trying to shake off as he sipped his morning coffee out of a jewelled china cup and mused on the women in his life. His favourite wife, Emetullah Banu, was already into her thirties, well past her prime by harem standards, yet her experience and maturity ensured her place in his heart. That said, the Emperor's unshakeable yet ageing love for her did not – nay, could not – prevent his picking other *gözdes*. It wasn't his enjoyment of other women that bothered the Emperor. It was the fact that he had sent Mihrişah off at some hour of the night – Mihrişah, his second great love – to beckon his new latest *gözde* Hümaşah and Şermi, the two young lovelies.

Barely twenty-seven, Mihrişah Emine was basking in the glory of womanhood secured after the birth of two crown princes. Fatma Hümaşah was sixteen and Rabia Şermi seventeen. Both had been hand-picked in the snowy villages of the Caucasus as children, brought over to the harem and raised together in the thousand and one arts of pleasing the august sovereign, the refuge of the universe: two wild flowers, now fully grown into slender roses in the palace.

Hümaşah always displayed a bashful submission, turning her deep green eyes away from the Emperor's black ones as she tried to cover her pink-white skin with her golden hair cascading down to her waist, seemingly unaware of her extraordinary beauty: an upturned nose, a shapely mouth, full breasts and hips in contrast to a narrow waist, elegant hands and those two irresistible moles at the base of her neck. Her timidity thus transformed into a searing allure. Her dimpled smile, revealing pearly teeth, was frequently withheld, the better to bless Sultan Ahmed when she did smile.

In contrast, Şermi was much more daring. However, such behaviour was frowned upon in the harem; perhaps this accounted for the name that meant 'bashful' she was given upon arrival, so that she may rein in her exuberance. That names affected demeanour, everyone knew, but whether this worked on Şermi, none could say. She certainly stood out with her thick dark hair, arched eyebrows, eyes set wide apart and naturally outlined with curly dark eyelashes, her aquiline nose that gave her face a noble air, clear skin and willowy figure that enabled her to look the Emperor eye to eye when they stood up. Unconventional was her beauty, virtually exotic, and she was quick of intellect too.

It was this contrast that so inflamed passion in their benefactor, seeing them side by side, loving them side by side, like eating tahini and molasses together, finding the perfect flavour in the blend.

The two young women hid their jealousy well, if indeed they were jealous. Hümaşah and Şermi were more comrades than rivals. Sultan Ahmed had favoured them with pendant earrings, which he insisted they wear each time they visited him: large emeralds swinging from amongst small rose-cut brilliants for the blonde Hümaşah and blood-red rubies flowing from a bed of huge white Yemeni pearls for the dark Şermi.

These earrings bore witness to the Sultan's refined taste. He had personally described the designs to the imperial jeweller in minute detail. Unrestricted by the conventional limitations of his sex, he had an intrinsic appreciation of the sparkle of precious gems that created the most flattering combinations. What guided all his lovemaking and saved it from monotony was the beauty of the detail. He might ask one of his women to release her painstakingly pearl-strung braids one by one, slowly, and then he would kiss her hair strand by strand. Or he might reward the slow unbuttoning of small gold-thread balls from the breast down to the navel by throwing a single gold coin into the silk harem pants, the sensation of cool metal against warm skin a joy to be savoured by the Sultan and the *gözde* alike. The newly minted coins were ideal for this purpose, even in their name: lover's gold.

Sultan Ahmed had long ago discovered that women were much more generous if they too enjoyed lovemaking, however much they might suppress expressing their own pleasure. He knew he had to prepare them beforehand so that he might repeatedly warm their hearts for this matchless act. He sought not a simple selfish pleasure hunt but to acquaint himself with women's secrets, to read into their souls in those most intimate moments. If only a single woman would express her own desire and ask him to do things she wanted! But imperial pride stopped him from asking.

And now he regretted breaking Mihrişah's heart, surely an irreparable hurt: driven insane by the paste, he'd switched women in the middle of the night. And what about Fatma Hümaşah and Rabia Şermi? Did they really enjoy being loved together? This thought that occurred for the first time astonished him. The worry that he might have upset his women was one he could only share with Levnî. As for the harem folk, well, he had only discharged his duty as Emperor, after all.

He knew all too well that tales of legendary sexual exploits would make the rounds on the morrow of an herb night, tales of various pastes prepared in the *helva* shop of the palace, tales echoed in mansions and coffee houses by men both high-born and lowly, tales exaggerated beyond all comprehension and relished, giving their imaginations full rein. Even his opponents would smack their lips at accounts of his masculine prowess, repeat and even identify with them; moreover, they would take pride in being ruled by such a mighty male – so what if he was profligate or cruel? Any intimation that Sultan Ahmed believed otherwise would have caused great dismay. How could His Imperial Majesty regret having offended one of his precious women?

Sitting opposite, deferentially, was Levnî, little different from his companion in that he too had enjoyed the benefits of the paste. Neither of the sated bodies, however, housed a sated soul. It was as if they were both prodded by the lack of something indefinable, preventing them from inhaling the splendour of living.

Sultan Ahmed, ruler of the great Ottoman Empire, possessed all that his imagination could conceive of; but he was perceptive enough to know that his imagination was not limitless. He did give his baser instincts a free hand, nonetheless. Why would he need to check them? This natural superiority had been granted him on his day of ascension just like the sword he had taken charge of at that magnificent girding ceremony. So, the great Emperor was pensive, having yielded to his lust last night and switched his women. As for Levnî, he too introspected his own actions after enjoying every variety of sexuality in one night. Isn't it ever thus with conflicts?

'Is it appropriate for us to ascribe our inconstancy of heart – what love does to us – to the seasons, my Levnî? Why would spring affect our minds so deeply? What have we consumed, pleasure or regret?'

The Sovereign was ready to attribute his excesses to the season, but Levnî was less keen to shirk responsibility.

'Surrendering even to one's own baser instincts is certain to exasperate one, My Sultan. "Overcoming avarice and lust is triumph indeed," claimed a Frankish philosopher, a statement repeated by another Frank, this one a painter friend in Pera – a statement I have oft considered. How many on earth can attain such triumph, I know not.'

The Emperor was grateful to his companion for the sympathy. This topic evidently gave Sultan Ahmed a guilty fascination. His exhausted and happy body reminded him of the previous night's events, aggrieving him all the more: excesses defied attempts to forget, emotions more befitting woman, not a man and certainly not a king. No one would call him to account; none could. All those women in his mind: all he had to do was send word and they would warm his bed, bearing a gentle smile on their faces. But the bed they graced would be that of the Emperor, not Ahmed's.

His companion understood. He had not long stayed faithful to anyone either. Yet his excuse was different: the ecstasy of poetry. Levnî noticed that each time he made love, it was Şebsefa who filled his dreams. That was what he had been resisting.

They discussed such intimate matters as two ordinary friends, debating how far man's baser instincts could be channelled, but steered clear of reaching a conclusion.

Ahmed and Levnî
Devşirme

'I had a curious dream last night, oh Levnî mine. I was, in this dream, a *devşirme* boy. I was all a-tremble as I walked behind the official who'd come to fetch me. Naked was I. Cold was I. It was pitch-dark around us. Crying and yelling was I, yet no one heard me. This was a nightmare. I stayed awake and pondered on't till the morning light. I thought, were I but to listen to your tale, I would understand better, perchance calm my concerns a little; at the very least, I might look upon't with your eyes.'

This was the one topic they had strangely avoided all this time. And the time had come, Levnî knew, to tell his own tale in all candour:

'I was very young then, as you know, My Sultan. There were other lads like me in the village. I was strangely unlike my elder brothers: they skinny, I plump. Mother sent me to gather wood with them at that young age.'

The companion sighed. Something must still hurt after all these years!

'Yet there was no discord in our home, unlike all the others in the village. We had a hot meal on the table every night. I vaguely remember how father would seat me on his lap every so often, how we sat with my brothers by the fire and sang and how, most of all, how mother tucked me in on cold nights, her slim white hands oft on my mind. Do you know't was her I most missed on those first lonely nights, on my thin mattress in the cold dormitory?'

The companion pretended not to notice the tears welling up in the Emperor's eyes. His intention was not to sadden but to tell the truth as he knew it. This may well have been the first time – and yea, also the last – he was voicing these thoughts since he had been taken away from his family.

'Yet nothing compares to the fear those grim-faced officials inspired. I thought my new life would be all dark, dark and unknown. I never looked back, not because I was so courageous, nay, quite the opposite. I knew were I to look back at mother, father and my elder brothers, all petrified on that little square ...' The knot in his throat surprised him, all these years later. Then he continued, mastering his emotions once more: 'Were I to look back, I, little more than an infant at eight, I would have rebelled so highly, and who knows what ill would befall my family or me. Some unknown hand guided me to seek shelter in that hapless herd of lads. There were many worse affected than I was. I looked to console them in a while.'

He would have been amazed at the thoughts flocking into Sultan Ahmed's mind if he only had the slightest intimation. The Emperor was staring at his companion as if one enchanted, yet he was seeing something else, ghosts even. How his mother had caused his brother's torment! How people made people suffer, how they had the capacity to make others suffer!

'My despair, verily like an endless well, My Beloved Emperor, brought forth acceptance. I grew to believe that all is meant for us. And I learnt how those upheavals served to open some boxes. I had to come to this palace to paint these pictures, to recite these poems and to sit before you. I had to go to Salonika to appreciate all this, as, again, you know all too well.'

Sultan Ahmed might have ostensibly tolerated that journey, but he still found the occasion to tease the artist. Levnî did know that this displeasure stemmed from the Emperor's affection for and trust in him. The Ottoman ruler may have kept his own counsel, but he had been upset. Not because he distrusted the artist's loyalty, but rather because he believed the palace – his palace – should replace any real family.

The companion added quietly:

'Yet they still appear in my dreams; who knows, perhaps one day ...'

Sultan Ahmed was feeling overwhelmed by conflicting emotions, so many of them! He was silently thinking, This I have heard is the tale of but one! And yes, he is very dear, his fate different and immoveable, but what of the others? What sacrifices are being made to perpetuate this lifestyle, this system? Or is it really only destiny that has a hand in all?

He was going to abolish the practice of *devşirme* for good if his rule lasted long enough. His viziers would disagree, but let them; this unique practice no longer was justifiable, for the days when its imposition could be defended as part of the natural order had long since gone – this much he knew.

★   ★   ★

'What if a prince of yours were to have a child of his own, My Benevolent Emperor?'

Levnî had sprung this question at one of those relaxed sessions. He had asked, knowing how it would startle the Emperor. The unwritten agreement between the two was that they could converse as two equals. This had been Sultan Ahmed's specific wish, the wherewithal to converse without sycophancy. And if he would have to pay the price, so he would.

It was the value of human life they were discussing. His companion had just reminded the Emperor of an edict of his ancestor, whose name he bore, Sultan Ahmed I: crown princes were forbidden to sire children. Should any concubine who accompanied a crown prince in the cage fall pregnant, the baby would be killed at birth to avoid future issues with the order of accession. This nature-defying edict was clearly intended to prevent confusion, any upheaval in the running of the state – but at what price?

The ruler took his time to reply. His gaze travelled over the colourful decorations of the room, the gold-work curtains and the flowers in the garden outside. Levnî didn't expect a clear-cut answer at any rate, his intention being to make his companion think; he waited, watching his ruler's handsome and pensive face. Watching him at these times presented the artist with a rare opportunity to etch in his own mind the impressions of the face, those priceless impressions that would run between hand and paper. The Emperor's gaze was locked in the distance when he spoke:

'Thank God all my princes are very young yet, Levnî mine. Little can I say whether I could implement this law, condemning my own grandson to death; I know not.'

Sultan Ahmed shook his head, as if rejecting the images that appeared, and then looked into the eyes of his companion, now more confident.

'I would break with custom in all probability.'

And so Sultan Ahmed was inspired to contemplate how much right one man had to interfere in the lives of others, and to what extent.

His companion was turning into a confidant, and that made concealing the single greatest secret about him increasingly difficult.

Dubnisteli's *Helva*
The finest flour and butter

Chief *Helva* Cook Dubnitseli Refik Agha tipped a generous amount of fine flour – carefully sifted by his assistants earlier – into the wide copper pan. An assistant added the starch at once. Neither spoke a word, even avoided looking at each other. The *helva* cook nodded, and rice flour, in the same quantity, was also added to the pan. The mélange began to crackle in the copper pan, heated by the wood fire with fine butter melting in the heat, calming it all. The chef stirred expertly, unhurried, with his wide wooden spoon as the assistant tipped four kilos of pure honey, careful not to get any on his hands.

That delicious aroma of toasted, buttered flour mixed with honey, redolent with the promise of Paradise, instantly permeated the kitchen and went up the vast chimney, but not before it had licked all in that tableau that ever preserved its magnitude and dignity, no matter how many times it might have been repeated in the past: the copper pots of all sizes, marble bowls, china and gilt sherbet pitchers, lined up in the wooden cupboards and on the shelves and all polished to a goodly shine, the broad expanse of the pristine worktop and the stone floor washed to a shine countless times a day. The young assistants swallowed surreptitiously lest they be branded 'greedy' – a lapse that had no place in palace etiquette.

The assistant who had been waiting for his turn patiently lifted the pan on the next burner, where the milk had been boiling, and slowly added it to the mélange at just the right time, under the hawk-like stare of his master. The master of the kitchen finally tossed the golden *helva* exuding mouth-watering smells once more with his wooden spoon, a single flick of the wrist, as if he were carrying out the last stage in a holy ritual.

The imperial *helva* had all but reached the right consistency. Dubnitseli murmured gently, 'Good enough for the holy mouth of Our August Emperor!' Was there a plaintive note in there or had his infinite respect guided him? He removed the dessert from the heat, covered it with two layers of muslin and left it to rest. As he watched his assistants clean up, he wondered how it would feel to watch the Emperor eat his *helva*. Soon he would dish it out into a splendid china bowl and entrust it to a page to carry it to the Privy Chamber, so that Sultan Ahmed may taste it whilst still warm. The page would, in turn, hand the *helva* tray over to the waiter in that room decorated with such fine paintings of flowers and fruits on the walls that they whetted the appetite.

Dubnitseli Refik Agha wasn't convinced that this water-green china bowl they called *mertebanî* would really change colour at the touch of any food containing poison. Yet he wondered, knowing full well he could never test the theory. What if someone thought he was trying to poison the ruler of the universe? Perhaps he could test it out in secret one day; poisons were not hard to come by.

Ottoman rulers had, for centuries, insisted on eating out of these fine porcelain plates and bowls that came out of Cathay. True, they did, every so often, use İznikware, their striking carnations and tulips a feast for the eyes, but the pride of place belonged to the Chinese plates. Left to his own devices, Refik Agha would have preferred the İznik dishes to serve his Emperor. These lovely plates were underrated in his opinion. If clumsy kitchen hands broke a china plate, they trembled – nay, were petrified – far more than if the broken piece was an İznik. Yet even the İzniks were running out. Replacements were nowhere near as good these days, and this was a state of affairs that did not please the Chief *Helva*

Cook. The Nevşehir cooks who had inundated the kitchen since the ascendance of the Grand Vizier, being from that part of the world himself, had no appreciation for İznikware. They couldn't even pronounce Nevşehir: to them, their hometown was still Muşkara. The Grand Vizier may have elevated his hometown, changing its name to equal his own elegance, yet people took longer to accept change.

Dubnitseli's thoughts wandered deep, too deep for the imperial kitchen, and the path to the Emperor's Privy Chamber was not all that short. No more delays now. He lifted the muslin, stirred his masterpiece once more and served into the cool of the celadonware. The imperial *helva* was ready to be served to His Majesty.

Dubnitseli was confident that the secret of delicious *helva*, a *helva* worthy of that ambitious name, lay in stirring correctly at the right time. True, the ingredients were important, but that they would be the very best the breadth and length of the Ottoman lands produced went without saying. The true culinary skill lay in how adequately they were blended. He was most pernickety about the flavour of honey and so chose a variety that bore the breath of Black Sea pines, clear and intense. For the Chief *Helva* Cook, the thousands of bees that toiled for days to fill those tiny containers with a delicious liquid were like the hundreds toiling in the kitchens to feed the Emperor of the Seven Climes. He, of course, was the indisputable ruler of these kitchen workers. He felt most important when he went to the Egyptian lands every year to purchase supplies. Treated like the dignitary he was, bathed in flattery and gifts, he savoured his position as he picked the produce of one, and disappointed the other. And, oh, those little escapades!

Dubnitseli suddenly came to his senses. He had nearly forgotten to accompany the *helva* with the luscious lemon sherbet he'd decorated with fresh mint sprigs. He had soaked Yemeni ambergris in the sherbet and then sieved those off along with the lemon peel. He topped the drink with clean snow from the high mountain peaks. He caressed the cool surface of the gilt sherbet pitcher lightly, over the fish-scale pattern and the spout lid's birds, whose curves belied the hardness of the metal they had been carved out of. These little, shiny birds were just like him in a way: wings opened out in preparation for flight but never daring to fly.

Ahmed and İbrahim
Lantern time in the gardens

Grand Vizier İbrahim Pasha's waterfront palace gardens in Beşiktaş had, for many days now, been the site of much excitement. Painted wooden galleries had been set up, facing each other, resembling miniature amphitheatres, narrow shelves going down in steps. Palace folk tried to determine their purpose, the master's plan having been revealed only to the craftsmen building these structures, who were sworn to strict secrecy.

It was the middle of the most promising month in the year: April raises hopes and brings joy to the heart. The *yalı* was preparing to entertain the Emperor of the Universe that evening. The host didn't want the surprise show to be spoilt. He would take such delight in amazing Sultan Ahmed, and a pleasant treat it would be.

Countless tulip vases, made of glass and silver, had been carried outdoors as the evening drew on – a slender flute, only wide enough to take a single tulip stem, and with a broad base for balance. They were too many to count. Each carried a single tulip, picked from only the rarest and freshest buds.

İbrahim Pasha personally oversaw the arrangement of the tulips in colour harmony and commanded many to switch places with others, so the bright flame-red tulips were followed by shades of red that became lighter, all the way into the corals. Tulips from the palest pink to the deepest fuchsias were ranged on a different shelf; all the colours waved in shades deep and pale. The shelves facing those bore tulips from the palest lilac to the deepest purple, and in between were the yellows, from the most searing sun-bright to the coolest metal. The statesman had the purples and the yellows arranged in the middle to best display the divinely contrasting harmony of these two colours. Lace-like variegated tulips marked colour changes. Those precious white tulips called 'unique pearls' lined up on the bottom and top shelves.

Coloured crystal globes hung from the shelves on fine chains between the tulip vases to reflect the light of the lanterns on the bottom shelf. Coloured lanterns hung from the trellises in the garden.

It was beginning to get dark, and the hour set for the arrival of the most valued guest approached. Kaftans lined with sable would stave off the evening chill. The wind was but a light breeze. İbrahim Pasha bade the lanterns to be lit.

As the imperial caïque drew up at the pier, Sultan Ahmed stood up in the royal box of carved and gilded posts and a velvet baldachin. Eager to enjoy the feast İbrahim Pasha had laid out, he felt no need to hide his impatience.

The Emperor of the Universe couldn't believe his eyes when he stepped onto the garden, once appropriate responses had been given to the florid phrases of welcome, and walked through his crowded entourage. It was as if the gardens of Paradise had alighted on the earth, tulips sparkling in the descending dark. A thousand and one beams of light splintered off the cut crystal to reflect on the flowers nestled in brilliant silver vases, creating a scene that defied instant comprehension. The light breeze gently swayed the tulips and the crystal globes, heightening the effect.

The Emperor slowly walked between the rows of tulips and reached the high seat in the small, open-fronted tent erected as protection against the evening chill, and the music began. The princes who had been allowed to accompany their father were most delighted by the goldfinches, canaries and nightingales in silver cages hanging from the branches.

Sinuous dancers would come on once the delicacies in the gilt bowls were consumed. Grand Vizier Damat İbrahim Pasha had created a fresh, lively and sparkling world for his master.

A thousand and one lanterns illuminated Sultan Ahmed, whose seat, being higher than all present, cast a very long shadow over the tulip beds, very like an imposing and unknowable giant that had settled on the flowers.

The Emperor had been quite delighted with the entertainment.

'My Precious Vizier, your efforts are praiseworthy indeed, and the trouble you have taken has pleased me very well. This fantastic lantern show, the illumination of the tulips and the crystal shining like the sun – all this is the mirror of your accomplishment, very much like the skies had descended upon the earth.'

'My Emperor, the light of my eyes, the crown upon my head, 'tis you, the presence of our benefactor, that lights these gardens so! I will give an account of the tale, if you permit.'

This exchange of compliments was of a calibre that made the other viziers envious, but so well accustomed they too were to flattery that none would risk missing one single word. İbrahim Pasha continued, upon the Emperor's nod:

'This, in effect, My August Sultan, is a custom that goes back to Chinese kings. They used to hang a multitude of lanterns on trees with many branches in Peking to turn night to day. Skilled Chinese painters made toys to decorate the grounds. The Abbasids likewise held similar festivities come springtide.'

The Grand Vizier had picked all this up in a book that was prepared by a flower fancier, not that he felt any obligation to divulge his source. The Sultan was well impressed with the depth and breadth of his Grand Vizier's knowledge. His son-in-law, whom he had entrusted with running the country, knew very well how best to prove his value. The man sitting in the imperial caïque at the end of the night was thoroughly satisfied with himself and his choice of grand vizier.

This was the first of many festivities that would mark an era, festivities that would always be known by the most fabulous aspect of the entertainment, the illuminations – 'lantern festivities'.

Ahmed and İbrahim and Levnî
Pleasures

You are my torch, and My Witty Vizier
None to match you, your loyalty is famed the world
over

So, fondly, Sultan Ahmed addressed his son-in-law after a festive night. If he wondered whether he had overdone the compliments, none can say.

'The pleasure of the latest lantern night my son-in-law organised still lingers, Levnî Çelebi.' The Sultan sighed a little as he talked of the night: 'I was so enveloped in the harmony of the music, as if the multitude of lights thrown by the lanterns around us, the incredible movements of the fair dancers and the brilliance of the crystal cups all combined to transport me to a peerlessly happy universe, wherein I leave all my troubles behind, convinced life would continue in this vein. But as dawn breaks, I grow pensive, concerned by how addictive it all is.'

The Emperor was trying to justify his enraptured state during the previous night's fabulous lantern festivities. Levnî courteously pretended to tolerate this bizarre, nay, ridiculous state; still, he could hardly forbear a gentle warning:

'Your loyal servant and all your servants are pleased, My Fortunate Sultan, when your heart is gladdened with pleasure. Good diversion is your right, true; yet I am humbly given to muse that this much extravagance shown by İbrahim Pasha is more to his own ends than to please you, Our Majestic Emperor. Your loyal servant also partakes of wine and ever delights in music and dance, yet prefers to keep something more for the imagination to delight in.'

★   ★   ★

The invisible rivalry between Levnî and Grand Vizier İbrahim Pasha never ended; rather, it flared up and waned from time to time, enriching and balancing Sultan Ahmed's world. True, Levnî also enjoyed the dizzying entertainment held in the captivating aroma of the flowers surrounding them, countless delicious dishes, elegant verses exchanged to the singing of the nightingale and the intellectual debates and discussions, despite his efforts to hold back. A sense of endless rivalry stemming from his surrounding himself with the most elite artists flattered his artistic pride regardless of how flippant he might be, enkindling and enriching both his poet's quill and artist's brush.

Yet the artist also took great pleasure in diverting himself with visits to coffee houses frequented by folk bards. There he shook off the mantle of the courtier and joined a different world, one which he enjoyed completely. This was how he and Ömer the Bard had met years ago.

He also knew that the songs he wrote inspired by these meetings were much plainer, much less elaborate and so much sharper. This was akin to living not one but two lives.

Levnî only talked of this life if Sultan Ahmed asked.

Neighbours in the East

'Your Majesty, we have received news of Afghanistan. Mahmud Han has defeated the Persian armies that had marched against him. He has taken Kerman, Yazd and Mashhad. Our men on the ground inform us that his power is mighty indeed.'

The Grand Vizier wanted to inform the Emperor personally. İbrahim Pasha was never enamoured of the practice of war, even if it took place elsewhere.

'Wasn't this Mahmud Han's father the chief of the Kılcılar tribes? The warlord who became the Chief of the Afghanistan State, revolted in Kandahar, killed the Governor of Persia and declared independence?'

İbrahim Pasha concealed well his surprise at how accurately informed his Emperor was and how deep his interest was in the matter.

'Precisely as you give an account of it, Your Majesty, that is the man. Now it is said he will besiege Isfahan.'

Sultan Ahmed may well have enjoyed the benefits of living in peace, yet he could not ignore the potential for change in the balance of power presented by a tribe of Turkic origin standing against Iran.

Ambition and belligerence could so easily spread; being prepared and monitoring closely would be expedient indeed, all the while avoiding interference – quite the best course of action.

Or None Will be Able to Stop This Madness!
Tulips

There were flowers everywhere.

An Edirne clockmaker's labour of love for his Sultan found favour in the palace: a clock decorated with roses, tulips and many other flowers besides. The outwardly cool bright yellow metal face was encircled with the warmth of a slender, gilded wooden hoop, like a waving golden stream. Roses covered the green-painted wooden housing: red, blue and yellow, then poppies and in between them all, the tapering petals of red tulips.

The master enameller Ali Üsküdarî had painted thirty different flowers on the pages of a poetry book to present to the Emperor. There were so many flowers: yellow tulips, blue delphiniums, pink roses, purple columbines, orange lilies, double-flowering buttercups, double-flowering lilacs, azaleas, Judas tree blossoms, pink star-thistles, grape hyacinths, red carnations, double-flowering daffodils and periwinkles.

But tulips commanded a special place. This graceful, alluring flower had created its own mania. There were 239 varieties, each prettier than the rest.

'The tulip they call "enamoured" sells one bulb for five hundred gold pieces, My Sovereign! Yet some high-ranking people still fall over themselves to purchase them.'

'This "enamoured", you call it, My Pasha – is that the one in the centre flowerbed?'

'As you so rightly declare, My Noble Sovereign, it is that diamond white tulip that finds such favour.'

'Then place a cap on its price, My Grand Vizier, that none may demand more than one thousand kuruş, or none will be able to stop this madness!'

Beneath the Golden Vault

They were sitting in the Breakfast Gazebo, one of the Emperor's favourite spots in the imperial palace. Built by Sultan Ahmed's grandfather, Sultan İbrahim, originally as a fine site for breaking the Ramadan fast on summer evenings, the gazebo usually hosted holiday greetings. It was also called Moonlit: Sultan Ahmed, his father and grandfather all having enjoyed the panorama of Konstantiniyye illuminated by the calm waters of the Marmara reflecting the image of the full moon.

It was not customary for an emperor to sit here with a companion.

The little gazebo was in effect a small, canopied balcony overlooking much of the palace and Konstantiniyye, a little jewel that enchanted those looking up at the palace from the city. Four slender, fluted copper pillars supported a vaulted canopy, topped with a high finial, the gilding so fine that the entire structure looked proudly golden. Sultan İbrahim's insane antics had been legendary, his frequent flinging of cold coins at his numerous *gözdes* one of them. How was it that he had come to commission this gazebo of the Chief Imperial Architect? Had it been he himself who had selected the spot, with a specific shape in mind? Or had it been the noble architect transforming this small projection into such a splendid site, fearful of displeasing – and determined to impress – his Emperor, whose penchant for ostentation was widely known?

Sultan Ahmed raised his eyes up to the cradle vault and re-read the inscription that encircled it, his eyes now fixed in the distance. He always contemplated the details of the buildings his ancestors had left behind. What he wanted most was to create a legacy that would keep his name alive. Take for example this dazzling site: it was not known by the name of its founder. Baghdad and Revan Pavilions had been named after the military victories of Murad, İbrahim's elder brother – Murad, whose name had struck fear in the hearts of all in all four corners of the earth! Would their founder's name be remembered always or would these jewel-like pavilions maintain the names of far- distant cities conquered once, so long ago?

He stared out towards the Golden Horn stretching beyond the palace gardens, deeply blue as if illuminated from below. Sultan Ahmed turned his gaze to the New Mosque a little beyond, whose cemetery safeguarded the mortal remains of his grandmother Turhan Sultan, his father Mehmed the Hunter, his brother Sultan Mustafa and his own children, whose numbers changed all the time – and some of whom for one reason or another died young. This place would in all probability house his own body till eternity when his time came.

Whenever his Emperor fell into a pensive mood, Levnî waited, perfectly still; his presence being the only support he offered. Even the great sovereign turned into an ordinary human being at his most vulnerable from time to time, wishing to seek solace in the existence of another human being. His sovereign suddenly broke into a soft hymn, which did not surprise Levnî in the least – a hymn that could have been written on a day of reckoning. Necib, the Sultan's nom de plume, bewailed his own lack of urgency at reaching out for God's secret, mercilessly accusing his own heart of ignorance of hidden treasures and reluctance to overcome his own weakness.

Oh ignorant heart! Have mercy, I wonder why
You never sought to hurry to comprehend the divine secret

Oh heart, like Necib on the brink of arrival,
You never accepted the divine knowledge in the corner
of the prayer rug.

Converting his confession into verse had almost cleared perplexing thoughts. Sultan Ahmed felt that indescribable relief that always followed at these times. Levnî knew that the affable man within, the man who took such delight in the diversions of this world, would not be long in returning. He bowed his head silently. The poem was elegantly composed. The companion was grateful that the two men could, when required, understand each other without speaking. He knew this was no time for comment. They sat in silence for a while, gazing at the white and blue hyacinths in the garden below, inhaling their wonderful scent carried forth by the light breeze. The companion finally drew upon his experience and asked the one question that would please the ruler:

'The hyacinths must have been recently planted, My Noble Sovereign. Where do the bulbs come from?'

Sultan Ahmed replied enthusiastically, just as Levnî had known he would.

'These are the white and sky hyacinths that have come from Maraş. Each year these beauties are planted with painstaking care!'

Sultan Ahmed could equally be referring to coy concubines as he gazed at his rare hyacinths, his eyes sparkling. A cloud had come and passed; now was no longer the time for despondency – the moonlit party of the previous night had inspired the Emperor to write another song. He must write it down forthwith, and then beckon the musicians. A certain note of melancholy in the song was essential, of course; of that there was no doubt.

Levnî and Ahmed
Counselling the sovereign

'My Majestic Emperor, 'tis very difficult to proffer you work that is worthy, I know. I have attempted with these modest verses to combine some good advice with my own opinion. I hope any errors of judgement will find tolerance.'

And thus did Levnî present his latest work, another extraordinary undertaking – composing an epic, blending proverbs with his own watchwords. And how differently it read from other divan poets' work, with plain, unadorned language, the language of the people, thoroughly befitting a folk bard. The poet had not stayed his hand: the prose spared none, not even the Emperor himself. This elegant epic gently prodded all manner of human folly. It was Levnî's own ideals that found voice.

True, these verses that bared a sharp soul tormented by evil could have arisen at any time in history; that they did when extravagance and bribery was commonplace as men longed to attain the most refined of pleasure and diversions, however, was no coincidence.

> Heed ancestral counsel, pure of heart be
> Heart reaches out to heart, 'tis said
> Temper your fury, generous of spirit be
> Sharp vinegar harms its vessel, 'tis said
>
> You know downward runs water
> Says the wise man to the fool
> Heed your words, eschew idle chatter
> Avowal and faith are one, 'tis said

Mind you don't covet every gain
Your last push grows into a vane
And on lakes, their heads forgotten
Foolish ducks dive arse first, 'tis said

Worldly goods: do not be fooled
Momentary adversity: do not be troubled
Leave not today's job till the morrow
The cliff only bedusts on the day it collapses, 'tis said

I, too, have sacrificed a sheep on this field
Come, then, prepare to show your skill
None can forestall fate
Force spoils the game, 'tis said

Fate plays by its own rules
Eschew undertaking all sorts of trouble
Take a lesson from the bird of prey
Ere measures, then he swallows, 'tis said

Many are that would waste time
Some that know and others that do not
'Tis an old custom: mountainfolk descend
And displace vineyard folk, 'tis said

Whomsoever I have asked cautioned
Never ask the uncharitable for counsel
Chew ash and coals but not the scoundrel's morsel
Time will come he'll bang on, 'tis said

In vain do some run hither and thither
Now straight, now bending
Never mind cry, those who fall of their own accord
May yet lose both eyes, 'tis said

Take this advice to heart:
They smile that seek to flatter:
Take no offence at friend speaking the truth
Truth spoken does needle, 'tis said

Work with ancient wisdom
To equal saints in esteem
The fool ignores rhythm
Plays the drum badly, 'tis said

They that lack a learned guide
They that ignore sage counsel
They whose words won't bear proof
Are like an empty store, 'tis said

Rein together the donkey and the horse
And see their natures grow close
Only serve a good man if you must
Water flows, 'tis the way of it, 'tis said

Fortune's bazaar is in uproar!
He that bides his time has much to gain
Fairly negotiates the merchant of honour
The scoundrel spoils the market, 'tis said

'Tis the way of it, ever and evermore
Man needs man, oh troubled heart
Wish to help the pauper?
He that handles honey licks his fingers, 'tis said

Should you hold malice in your heart?
Invite not envy into the deepest part
Suffer your patron, covet less profit
The buyer trusts the seller, 'tis said

Agree in word and deed?
Lose not even if you make no profit
Avoid avarice, be content with less
He who sells cheap, sells quick, 'tis said

Mind you hold firm contentment's ring
Should you wish to hold firm the helm
The camel wanted fine antlers
And lost both ears, 'tis said

Oh, heart! Mud can't cover the sun
The sage stands out, even if mute
'Tis the fool who only likes himself
He dances to his own tune, 'tis said

Should effort demand skill
The maverick horse is sure of foot
The poet needs voice, strings and words
A lone stone makes no wall, 'tis said

Take heed, avoid deceit
Be known as a true man
Steal a stranger's door
A stranger will steal yours, 'tis said

Should you pay a visit to your beloved
Keep your eyes peeled
Walk on snow, leave no track
Strangers will hear of it, 'tis said

Nothing for it; God's will prevails
Heartache rips the heart apart
Whatever it takes to reunite lovers
One reunion is worth a thousand gold coins, 'tis said

Be it sung or spoken
The sage disowns not his wisdom
Never lose hope in God
Mysteries are revealed ere dawn, 'tis said

Take heed, Levnî, of the wisdom of sages
Say these proverbs in verse
Maintain your dignity on the field of skills
The heavy press down to raise the light, 'tis said

Birds of prey are short of life
Two acrobats can't dance on one tightrope
Dig no well deeper than your height
Who knows when you might slip on the road?

The Emperor listened with an imperceptible smile upon his face, his dark eyes sparkling. He then got up and kissed Levnî on the forehead. This was the highest accolade a subject could hope for: imperial endorsement. Further proof was a purse of gold Sultan Ahmed sent the following day, the most precious material gift Levnî had received to date.

As for the large oval emerald ring the Emperor removed from his own finger to place on Levnî's left hand, on the little finger, the artist would treasure this as his most valuable memento all his days.

Levnî and Ahmed

Who is the Emperor in reality? What is it that he can and cannot do?

Sultan Ahmed could hardly be described as steadfast. It was not for him to confront real problems, so disrupting the peaceful atmosphere İbrahim Pasha offered would have been the last thing he would ever do. His precious son-in-law and Grand Vizier ruled the empire, the palace, the people, the treasury and even the Sultan himself. The vizier had been endowed with extraordinary intelligence and talent. The endless powers he had been equipped with helped. Yet, when the Emperor of the World, Sultan Ahmed, was left alone with his conscience, he was crushed under the weight of having given in to his weaknesses, of having chosen the path of least resistance. His companion, his dear friend Levnî – oh how deeply he understood the ruler! – had offered a solution almost as if the artist had been following the ruler's train of thought. Training his willpower at times when there was no obligation and of his own choosing was not insufferably onerous, and it provided satisfaction.

The Emperor and the artist elaborated this game, Ahmed and Levnî, two ordinary men. True, Sufi ordeals had provided the inspiration, but since these two could determine the time and measure, testing themselves was not intolerable; they didn't have to suffer excessively like dervishes did. Thus began the sport of testing themselves, checking their lust or fury being a favoured test of self for Levnî and Ahmed.

Sultan Ahmed wasn't to know that it was his destiny to succeed in checking his fury that would swell like the sea or his frustrations that would sink as deep as ravines.

The Emperor's love of earthly pleasures was legendary, but his determination to master his desires was known to Levnî alone.

'My Sovereign, there is so much Your Majesty is capable of that no one else is; this is known far and wide. As for me, I often think upon all that others may do, but you may not, and the more I think, the more their excessive number makes me think.'

Levnî expected the Emperor to find something to complain about, but had to bite the inside of his cheek to stop himself from laughing at the reply all the same.

'There are too many valets in the Privy Chamber who never leave me alone for one moment wherever I go. For instance, say I'm putting on my trousers. Have you any idea how many pairs of eyes watch me? I had to write to İbrahim Pasha the other day to warn the sword-bearer in suitable language to dismiss most, leaving only three or four! Now I can finally don my trousers in peace!'

★   ★   ★

The limitations on the Emperor's life most impacted the one aspect of his life in which everyone believed him to be most free: women. He could not select the women to join his own harem. This honour was reserved for girls selected by the Sultan's mother or sisters, presented to the Emperor by a general as spoils of war or purchased as a very young girl by some official at certain parts of the empire. In that last instance, the girl would then have to excel at something during her education first. True, he was at liberty to pick whom he liked to bed, but he could never be left truly alone with his choice: the lady steward had to stand behind the drapes of the bed, both for his own safety and the proof of paternity for any issue of the coupling. So, there were no secrets concerning whom he had bedded. It was possible to get accustomed to all this, certainly – provided one did not examine it all that deeply.

Another limitation concerning his women was that they could not be present at entertainments attended by his male friends – and all his friends were male.

Neither could he ever enjoy being truly on his own: everything, including washing and dressing, he was expected to do with the assistance of servants whose sole aim was to serve him.

In contrast, when he ate, he always ate alone. All those who circled were there to serve and not to accompany.

'That being said, My Sultan, there are things that you and you alone can do, none other. To give an example of this: only you can cross the Second Courtyard and enter through Harem Gate on horseback. The only coins that are minted in the Ottoman lands are in your name. You can call for a subject to be beheaded when you are angered.'

Silence fell. Neither voiced the obvious: that the Emperor was the only man allowed to make love within the boundaries of the palace, that he could do this with a different woman every day and could sire countless children.

'Opening the treasury, delighting your subjects and giving leave for great festivities to be organised, also only you.' The companion finished with the greatest privilege of all in his own esteem: 'And you, My Sultan, are also capable of boundlessly encouraging all manner of artists, architects, calligraphers, poets, musicians and illuminators that they may create the most matchless buildings and new works.'

Sultan Ahmed smiled as he listened. Clearly this little game was to his liking.

'There also are actions I would not do, that would not be appropriate even if I were to wish them, my dear Levnî. However much I might wish to, I cannot travel abroad, unless it is on military campaign. I cannot walk around unaccompanied, even if in mufti, in my own country; I'm always followed by guards, albeit discreetly.'

Levnî decided then and there to give his Emperor a typical Konstantiniyye evening as an ordinary man. Sultan Ahmed continued to complain:

'And I will never know what anyone truly thinks of me. Don't deny it, my precious companion, I would not wish to enter such a debate! As you know, no one can argue with me.'

'With your kind leave, My Sultan, I don't know if I might displease you by mentioning another thing you may not do, but this may be truly the price of your position. You may never forge truly close friendships with your brothers or nephews, since they are your rivals for the throne.'

Those last words of his companion pierced the Sultan to the quick. Little did he think it likely, but nevertheless – could Levnî possibly have an inkling?

Levnî and the Likeness
of Şebsefa

'Were Ferhad alive now
wouldn't I wish to be tested so'

Levnî had succeeded in spying on the fair Şebsefa on a few more occasions, always from between curtains, and here he had set her playing the tambur, at the front of the picture whereon he depicted musicians. After that first encounter in Kağıthane, he had come across her once at İbrahim Pasha's Beşiktaş palace and twice in the house she went to for music lessons. The concubine was one of many whose job was to serve and entertain Fatma Sultan. The maiden went to the old master Salih Efendi – accompanied by eunuchs, of course – from time to time to take lessons. Levnî had visualised her sitting down with other musicians for this painting.

In the painting Şebsefa looked as graceful, as fragrant and as ephemeral as the four o'clock flower she was named after: she would easily slip through the fingers if one were able to touch her. It was her poise that made her all the more alluring: modest, understated – yet striking, like a variegated flower unaware of its own beauty. She stood apart from the other three girls as the only one whose eyebrows met in the middle and the only one who wore a single tulip in her hair, in contrast to the crowns of carnations on the heads of the other three. A fleeting smile danced on her tiny lips, and her neck was drawn plumper and longer than the other girls'.

The lovely young girl sitting next to her, playing the tamburine, had fixed her eyes on Şebsefa with disguised admiration or even respect. Her red outfit contrasted with Şebsefa's diamond white dress, its plainness even more striking. A translucent silk crêpe chemise fell upon her finely striped pants, emphasising her charms. The other girls were in high-necked dresses, all the way to the neck, but Şebsefa's plump, rounded breasts looked to almost overflow her collar, as if completely unaware. A mysterious eroticism was created by the rings on her thumb and fingers, so elegantly strumming the strings with the plectrum and the gold balls of the bracelet on her white wrist. Her henna-coated fingers played the tambur expertly yet casually, this delectable Şebsefa, fluttering the single scarlet tulip in the gold-embroidered scarf on her head.

Time had stopped in this picture that begged the viewer to reach out and touch. It would last for hundreds of years, speaking of Levnî's love to all that might view it. In the protective arch that framed the musicians, the veins in the marble gathered in two globes on either side: the world of the artist and the world of the concubine, constantly moving – similar, yet totally separate. Some of the refinement in the painting was for the artist himself and none other, yet the artist within still hoped for understanding.

Sultan Ahmed gazed at the painting for a long time, and then looked Levnî in the eye as if he had read beyond it.

'The effect this fair tambur player has on your heart is clear, Levnî. I wish to know her story.'

'It is difficult to reply, My Sultan. I must confess this beauty is proscribed to me. I first saw her at the Kağıthane picnic and then created the opportunity to see her again elsewhere. Yet the rose-faced fairy in the picture owes as much to my imagination as my memory. Were I to seat her down before me like Frankish painters and capture her likeness on paper, I would not have disclosed the secret of my heart so.' The artist and the poet became one: 'What I have learnt to appreciate, My Sultan, is that true happiness comes from seeking unattainable love, painting the angel-faced beloved I will never possess; yes, taking Ferhad's test, he that guides lovers everywhere.'

Levnî: ingenuity is what the path of love grants us
Raising mountain upon mountain
Were Ferhad to be alive now
Wouldn't I wish to be tested so.

Levnî's reply concluded with his latest verse and pleased
the Emperor, driving away the strange gloom in his soul.

Levnî and Şebsefa
Does true happiness hide in dreams?

Levnî lifted the heavy silk curtain and entered. Facing him stood Şebsefa, whom he had painted but a day previously. It was as if the image had come to life. Levnî was left alone in Fatma Sultan's palace with this fair damsel, this beauty who had sprung from the painting. Either the Emperor had made this possible to test the man, or perhaps he had simply offered her as a precious gift.

She had green eyes, almond-shaped and set wide apart, eyebrows that met in the middle in contrast, tiny red lips, long black hair that framed the plump white neck, plump pink dimpled cheeks and slender, almost fragile white hands. And most enchanting of all was the way those eyes looked at him, innocent and seductive at the same time.

Levnî thought back to his conversation of the previous night with the Emperor. Was it possible to control one's desires whatever the circumstance? Or was this not a sin but perhaps a miraculous blessing bestowed upon man by his God? He almost regretted having mentioned it to the Emperor. Just then, the young woman leant forward a little, as if she wanted to present her assets – that seemed on the point of leaping out of the décolleté of her shift – and tidied up her skirt, demure as you please and yet so seductive. Then she threw back her transparent headscarf edged with gold embroidery. Levnî admired this feminine ritual in all its countless ways, his knees almost going weak. That the girl was accustomed to obeisance was all too clear, but he knew not what she expected of him. To take her away?

The damsel clearly awakened the man calling out in him. He couldn't resist it any longer and stroked her white neck, the coolness of the emerald earrings – the same colour as her eyes – startling him. This cool contact, this light touch broke the intensity of the moment, bringing him back to his senses. He made his mind up then and there: he would resist, disappoint Sultan Ahmed. He would defy both his own body and the elegant test set by his Emperor.

He turned and left the room. Neither had spoken a word to each other, yet Levnî sensed her recognition and even approval of this emotional struggle. This sharp emotion heralded more to come.

Levnî appreciated once more that unrealised dreams made for the truest happiness. Still, it was good to chase unattainable dreams, to rejoice when one closed the eyes and to relish the distinction, thanks to the gifts bestowed upon man.

The artist was impatient to get back, prepare paints and brushes, and paint Şebsefa again upon a sheet of paper, never to be lost again, having found the best excuse to paint yet: love and the pain of love. Reunion could wait. Who knew when the time would be right?

Levnî and Ahmed
The Emperor's likeness

The irresistible beauty and the week-long lifespan of the tulip symbolised the irresistible brevity of human life. Those who appreciated this fact viewed life as a banquet where all that destiny offered deserved to be relished to the last drop. It was as if both İbrahim Pasha and Sultan Ahmed chased the finest moments as they advanced towards the inevitable end that awaited every mortal, and so trying everything was permissible.

The Emperor knew no taboos, either in sex or in splendour. Perhaps that was what inspired him to seek the pleasure of defying other boundaries. Levnî's paintings broke through unacknowledged prohibitions. Until that time, book illustrations had merely represented the outward appearance of people and landscapes, whereas his art gave them life. Sultan Ahmed's enjoyment of such works of art challenged convention and rejected these unnamed taboos; he was a man of refined pleasures, in any case.

Levnî had earlier presented his emperor with his *Portraits of the Great Genealogy*. Sultan Ahmed III carefully examined, one by one, the twenty-three portraits of the emperors of the Ottoman dynasty, beginning with Sultan Osman Gazi and ending with him. True, there were other depictions of his ancestors in his treasury, but Levnî's portraits were different. They were so lifelike: the great Mehmed the Conqueror, a gold ribbon around his turban, sword at his side, like he had taken Konstantiniyye but the day previous. Selim the Grim's fierce gaze petrified all that viewed his likeness, whilst the grandeur of Süleyman the Magnificent upheld the burden of victories and years.

As for Mustafa Han, elder brother to Sultan Ahmed, teasing as he looked out from the sheet of paper, his sparse, golden auburn beard and blue eyes twinkling as their mother Gülnuş Sultan's smile taunted, as if he were saying: 'There, brother, they toppled me and put you on the throne. Are you easy? Are you happy? Or has that pesky lover, that power, begun to consume you too? Will Levnî depict you as lifelike on paper as he did me? Take heed: he is far too loyal; whether he will be as assiduous with your portrait, I cannot say.'

The ruler of the August Ottoman Empire, whose reputation made the four winds tremble, the Grand Seigneur of the East, the magnificent sovereign of the fabulous city of the two continents, the potentate of the harem and the generous patron of artists, Emperor Sultan Ahmed shivered a little and rested his gaze on the room to flick away these troublesome thoughts. He remembered the day his brother had handed over the throne. The possibility that he might face the same ignominy one day was daunting. Levnî had painted this portrait and all the others when Sultan Ahmed was still in the cage and his brother reigned as the famed Sultan Mustafa Han. Both Mustafa and his father Mehmed the Hunter had been depicted differently from all the rest, sitting before a striped curtain, in subtle deference to his own loyalty to the father and son. The resemblance between the two men was unmistakeable: portly, proud and clear-faced. Sadly, Levnî had not been able to present his painting to Mustafa Han, who was deposed by the rioters on the pretext of his lack of interest in the affairs of the state. It was the same rioters who then elevated Ahmed, sentencing the toppled Sultan and his sons Mahmud and Osman to the cage. How tranquil Mustafa appeared in Levnî's portrait, as if he were completely unaware of the evil ways of the world!

With a start, the sovereign returned to examining his own portrait, a later addition to the collection. Ahmed had not seen such a powerful depiction of an emperor in the others.

And more, he had been portrayed with his beloved Prince Süleyman, the first time an emperor's portrait included his son.

The colours of the garments demanded attention and the Emperor was pleased by the artist's wit. Well aware of Sultan Ahmed's preference – despite the weight of the gold and silver thread in the deceptively plain garments – Levnî had dressed him in two kaftans, the inner in gold and the outer one in silver, and reversed the colours in the prince's outfit! The Emperor took this to indicate that his son would continue his bloodline. Would he yet rule?

Levnî's comments in this selection of colours did not end there: the same colours in reverse meant the Emperor was unique, inimitable. The Crown Prince had manifested the same thought in his stance: hands clasped in front, face devoid of guile, not prepared to outshine Sultan Ahmed, a mere continuation of the line, no personality needed in this element at this time. So many pieces had to fit together before a crown prince could accede to the throne, primogeniture notwithstanding; the hardest of them being staying alive until his father the Emperor released his own soul or was deposed.

Laying aside these thoughts of the continuation of his bloodline, the Emperor's gaze slid to the three fabulous aigrettes on his high turban in Levnî's portrait, pinned in a row as he liked to wear them on ceremonies. The court jewellers who had presented him with these aigrettes one holiday had been amply rewarded with purses full of gold. The golden mounts were shaped like flowers and adorned with large diamonds, rubies and emeralds. A line of rubies and one of the pearls topped each. Black heron feathers fanned out, rising above the pearls and between the fine branches decorated with diamonds seemingly waving before the viewer's eyes.

Levnî had seated him on a throne that did not exist in his treasury, a mystery that Sultan Ahmed enjoyed solving quickly: decorating with flowers real and imaginary created the illusion of combining other worlds. Sultan Ahmed knew this symbolised the throne in Levnî's heart.

What decorated the throne was not precious like gold, emerald, mother-of-pearl or tortoiseshell. Plant motifs in a myriad of colours, reflecting the refined Ottoman taste of hundreds of years where flowers and leaves stood out individually or intertwined with others, washed over the back, headrest and the sides, each creating a universe of colour and shape. The backrest for the blessed back of the sovereign was bedecked with small posies set within suns, fresh as on the day they had been picked: roses in bud on one side, hyacinths and tulips on the other. Levnî's flowers had made him famous. The Emperor wondered idly whether these plump flowers outshone his own figure or not. He smiled at the sight of the double-flowered pink rose and its buds – yet another Levnî wit! The very same flowers decorated the ceiling of Sultan Ahmed's private chamber in the harem, the small wooden room that was graced with depictions of the most striking flowers and fruit. The artist had transposed the ceiling of the Sovereign's favourite room onto the throne.

What about the carnations on the coral rug that the throne stood on? Like the foaming waves of a river poised to leap off the surface, those motifs that ran from one side of the painting to the other and the gold step that the Emperor of the Universe rested his foot against, right in the middle. *Tempus fugit*, that is what that stream of carnations under his feet seemed to be saying.

He then returned to his elegant figure: his dignified seat on the throne, at ease. The shoulders appeared even wider with the fur collar, from which rose the head proudly; the pensive expression in his almond-shaped black eyes rendered his face even more evocative with the shadows of the dark beard grown upon his accession according to the custom; the slender fingers grasped the armrest, adorned with the emerald and pearl rings on his little finger; and his jewelled belt buckle matched his aigrettes amidst the soft folds of his fur-lined robe. He examined all this and was very well pleased.

Almost as if he knew his image that looked into the distance well past the extent of the sheet of paper was destined to be quite unique, it would transport him hundreds of years into the future and leave many in awe.

Levnî and Ahmed
Family

Little could Rabia Gülnuş Sultan guess that the child named Abdülcelil after his recruitment and raised at the Enderun would turn out to be one of the finest of all Ottoman artists despite his turbulent life. All she wanted was to ensure a good life for the unfortunate prince despite the way she denied him his birthright. It never occurred to her that this young man and his elder brother, Sultan Ahmed, would become such close friends, almost as if they set out to prove blood ties.

Sultan Ahmed constantly resisted the temptation of disclosing this secret to Levnî; each time he thought about all that he had endured prior to his accession, before reaching this position, his life in permanent danger. The possibility that truth might out always filled Ahmed with fear, the one emotion his mind set upon for a good long time. Eventually this jumble of feelings gave way to a type of strange joy, one Ahmed couldn't explain to himself. The idea that Levnî Abdülcelil Çelebi, whose unique artistic talent he was in awe of and whose unassuming disposition he liked well, was a blood relation – this was a thought the Emperor found very pleasing indeed.

And how refreshing it was to be able to become friends with a brother from the same father, with no risk of fighting for the throne, no fear of assassination, no malice aforethought! Watching him as they conversed, listening to his voice, looking for traces of their father or ancestors in his face, Sultan Ahmed was both bewildered and content – at least for the time being. He would have to ignore the multitude of perils this situation presented. No one shared the secret to remind him in any case. Fraternal emotions that any ordinary person should be able to enjoy, but that were denied a ruler, had been awakened. Moreover, he was a father who doted on his own children – in his own fashion. His relationship with his daughter Fatma Sultan was truly affectionate, for instance.

★ ★ ★

'My Noble Sovereign, your fine stature is almost the same as mine, your majestic nose resembles my humble one, and what's more, when I look into your blessed eyes I feel a strange sensation of looking into the mirror. What a peculiar set of coincidences!'

Noticing the facial and spiritual similarities between his Emperor and himself, Levnî wondered how he, an artist, took so long to observe the resemblance. Since their game – a gift of their friendship – was to speak every thought as if the two were of equal rank, he had no misgivings about voicing this revelation.

The Sultan kept his composure, but he was shaken. Apparently unmoved by this remark, he pretended to take it as a compliment and moved on.

Sultan Ahmed knew not when he might be called upon to disclose to his closest companion the secret he had not forgotten once since the death of his mother. He waited without knowing what he was waiting for. He knew Levnî well, and the latter's efforts to discover more about his past did unsettle the Emperor, however infrequently might the artist bring the topic up. Yet he was unable to tell his dear brother why he toiled in vain, why he followed the wrong trail and what the truth about his roots was. So many times he had attempted, and so many times his courage had failed him.

As for Levnî, he too waited, without knowing what it was he was waiting for, growing ever more irreverent of his station in life. Although he knew the matter to be distasteful to his Emperor, for years he continued to search for members of his old family, sadly all in vain. All he could tell was that every trace had been obliterated, down to the logbook that was destroyed in that small fire that only damaged a few rooms. He returned empty-handed from Salonika. That terrible tempest on the way back could have been a warning that altered his outlook on life, but it failed to make him forget.

Ultimately he chose to rejoice in what the day brought, without knowing what the future would bring. He disclosed his thoughts to his Emperor: 'Always consider many steps ahead and not just the one, and you could be condemned to miss this moment.'

*　*　*

When he was left on his own, Sultan Ahmed tried to visualise the outcome if the roles of emperor and artist had been reversed. Ignoring the curious stares of courtiers and forgoing the entertainment planned for that night, he went to bed early: he even declined a *gözde*'s company. By early morning, he had come to a decision to solve this question in his own way, the question that spread in his mind and erased all other concerns. Next time the two got together – alone – they would exchange roles. Levnî would become the Emperor and Ahmed the artist and poet. This was not quite as challenging for Ahmed as might at first be feared; he was an accomplished poet, after all, one who relished his poet identity. His life might even have been much easier, much happier if he had been a simple poet and not the Emperor of the Universe – a thought he dispelled as quickly as it had come – a thought that countless rulers in the past had similarly chased away.

*　*　*

As they talked of their dreams, Levnî looked startlingly imperial, which Ahmed both enjoyed and found intimidating at the same time. He decided then and there to end the game before too long.

Sultan Ahmed had suddenly remembered the pretender event of many years ago. A young man had turned up on Chios with an incredible tale. His mother had been one of Mehmed the Hunter's countless *gözdes*, he claimed. She had incurred the Emperor's wrath – no one knew why – and he had banished her to Egypt without knowing she carried his child. It was unthinkable for a woman who had shared the ruler's bed to be exiled: only her body could ever leave the palace once she was strangled. Yet he claimed otherwise. The mother had been taken, he continued, to the King of Spain when her past was revealed, she had borne her child in Spain and gone thence to Morocco first, then Algiers later. This so-called crown prince had now arrived on Chios, bearing some forged firmans and only able to speak Arabic and Frankish, pressing a claim on the Ottoman throne. It was clear that he intended to cross to Anatolia, take some brigands behind him and declare his sovereignty. The necessary was done immediately: the young man and his so-called vizier lost their heads, and the heads were despatched to Konstantiniyye to be displayed outside the palace gate.

Sultan Ahmed visualised the severed head of Levnî on display outside the Imperial Gate and shivered, erasing this thought immediately. He came to a decision: the only way to protect his precious friend was by concealing the truth. Only under the gravest of conditions might he change his mind.

Prinkipo
The things this isle has seen ...

Spring arrived in full glory on Prinkipo Island. The deep green of the pines and the cypresses provided the backdrop for the blossoms: the dazzling white of plums and the deep-to-pale pink of the peaches. Judas trees were in bud, impatient to break out. The wisterias were next; they would adorn arbours or simply climb cypresses. Even the dust on the road had turned its face to the colours of summer, taking its cue from the rest of nature awakening once more.

The islanders had set to spring cleaning in their insouciant cheer as only Greeks can. The aroma of cooking emanating from the houses wafted in: stews enriched with wine, freshly gathered herbs and spring onions; golden courgettes fried in olive oil and drizzled with fresh garlic yogurt; stuffed vegetables redolent of generous handfuls of mint and pepper; and most of all, grilled fish garnished with rocket leaves or simply wrapped in fresh greens.

A handful of shabby taverns on the seafront joined in the spring rush to redecorate. The largest of the islands in the archipelago facing Konstantiniyye on the Marmara Sea relished its proximity to the capital of the great empire, yet still delighted in being so far away from the chaos and intrigues. What life lacked in big-city blessings was more than made up for in the beauty and peace. Life here was as clear as water and as deep as the sea, a state of mind specific to islanders alone. Islanders always dreaded the possibility that city folk might catch on and move to their beloved island – lock, stock and chaos.

This was no longer the wearying, melancholy exile of hundreds of years ago, that terrible site of the deepest, darkest Byzantine history. How much of the island's beauty had registered with the exiles, none could say. The difficulty of getting to the island coupled with the ease of monitoring had made it an ideal spot for exile. New arrivals initially breathed a sigh of relief at finding their necks and heads still on their persons. This was true of sad princes, over-reaching clerics, military commanders fallen from grace or a once-powerful empress. But all too soon they accepted that far from the city meant far from power. Their next act invariably was to seek ways of regaining lost power, their ambition knowing no limit. The players changed, but the game remained the same.

The ancient monastery in the island's most remote spot known as Maden ('mine', for the dense strain of iron ore mixed with layers of lime) was well known to have housed countless unfortunates or those of ambitious mien who had created their own misfortune. The island was named Prince's Island for a good reason: Justinian II of the Eastern Roman Empire had erected a palace here in the 6th century. The island's infamy, though, owed much to the monasteries where exiles spent their remaining days on earth.

As the armies of Mehmed II marched resolutely towards Constantinople, his fleet commanded by Baltaoğlu Süleyman Bey claimed the archipelago for the Ottoman Empire, a month before Constantine's fabulous metropolis fell. It was an April day in 1453 when a warm breeze caressed the trees in blossom and the sunshine failed to allay the islanders' fears. Intrepid mariners grateful for terra firma under their feet – after Marmara's enervating south-westerly – had only faced token resistance: both sides already knew that destiny was immutable. Yet, the island would not yield its unassailability that easily, regardless of who claimed ownership.

Thus did Prinkipo stretch out languidly into the sparkling waters of the Marmara, confident of its own beauty and untouchable for hundreds of years. Time slowed down here and rarely allowed the monotony to break. The most exciting incident in the life of the island in recent history occurred in the first year of Sultan Ahmed's reign, eighteen years ago. The Governor of Konstantiniyye and the Imperial Imam, who had been found guilty of conspiring with the rebels, were made to await word of their fate in the Manika Hüseyin Bey galley moored off the island until, that is, the command to execute the exiles had arrived.

The only thing that upset island life was a south-westerly storm churning the seas, but years of experience had taught the fishermen how to stay on its good side. So, it was inevitable that a vessel drawing close on such a day, when the south-westerly demanded obeisance, all boats were beached and that mysterious creature called the sea had to be left to her own devices, yea, the arrival of a vessel on a day such as this was bound to incite curiosity.

Jacques
Buried treasure on Prinkipo

'If fortune is with us, we'll reach the island safe and sound before the afternoon, before the south-westerly rises to whip up the sea, but if a sudden tempest were to blow, then we'd be shaking constantly on the boundless main – I've no idea what we'd do!'

The big sailboat captained by the grizzly Genoese set sail from Karaköy to constant grumbling by its Turkish sailors. His efforts to dissuade his passengers from sailing on this day – the large fee offered notwithstanding – had failed. The Frankish passengers insisted, and proud of his credentials as a seasoned sailor, the captain ultimately yielded – not to mention the fee, the like of which he had never earned to date. And he loved being proven right; his frail passengers would suffer so in the coming tempest. Truly, the anticipation of that sight gave him great pleasure!

This foppish Frenchman, the Embassy Secretary, had to command considerable wealth, since he had immediately accepted the fee demanded: three gold coins. He informed the captain that it was his wish to pay his respects to the ancient Greek monasteries on Halki. Three monasteries stood on the island resembling a sack on the ground, which gave rise to its Turkish name of Heybeliada, 'isle bearing sack'. Travellers were frequently attracted to these monasteries and to Hagia Triada in particular, nestled amongst cypresses and pines. The pretext of visiting these monasteries would raise no eyebrows. At the very worst, the captain may have been puzzled as to why a Catholic would want to visit Eastern Orthodox sites, but not enough to question his passenger.

The mysterious passenger intended to inform the captain that he had changed his mind when they approached the archipelago, that he wanted to visit Prinkipo first. He hoped that they would be viewed as nature-loving, somewhat eccentric foreigners.

Jacques, the rising secretary at the French Embassy, was certain he had discovered the nine-hundred-year-old secret of buried Byzantine treasure. This had been the work, prayer and promise of years.

He no longer remembered the first day he'd heard of the treasure; it was as if the knowledge had always lain in the corner of his mind. He had taken countless paths and had fallen into profound despair time and again. Now, so many years later, what he offered the one man who knew was highly audacious. But the desire to reach the treasure had become all consuming; it wasn't about the value of the hoard – solving a mystery that went back hundreds of years was paramount in the Frenchman's mind. Seduced by the history of the Eastern Roman Empire through his years of service in Konstantiniyye, he was driven by the desire to touch the jewels of a powerful Byzantine empress, jewels that had not seen the light of day for centuries, and to possess those jewels. Like all men driven by ambition, his actions were permissible to his mind.

The Frenchman had planned every step, ostensibly taking 'nature' voyages for some time now to points on the Bosphorus and on the Marmara and Black Seas, voyages that didn't interest him in the slightest, but were essential in establishing his credentials as a nature lover. Before he chartered this boat, he had chartered many others. He could never forget how the boat that had almost capsized was salvaged by a rope thrown from the shore off Akıntıburnu in the Bosphorus. It had all been worth it, though: his voyage to Prinkipo – and even spending a few days on the island – should arouse no suspicion. Except for this south-westerly, drawing attention to his insistence on setting off regardless, ambition prevailing over caution, rushing him! The Marmara Sea seemed determined to resist: that incredible tempest could upset all his plans – which was not a possibility he would entertain. His longer-than-planned stay on the island could easily be attributed to the tempest; he couldn't have returned however much he wanted! Once he held the riches of Byzantium in his hands, in any case, what anyone else thought would cease to matter.

It was as if an invisible force was preventing him from reaching the treasure quickly. The south-westerly cleared the air into sharp focus and the unexpected vessel battling the frenzied waves for hours offshore, failing to come any closer and providing the islanders with hours of diversion. Not that anyone could have helped.

The sailboat was creaking, and the last thing Jacques's poor valet saw was the toppling mainmast. The faithful man had served Jacques for years. His crushed skull continued to pump out blood long after the soul had departed. Jacques thought fast, ever proud of his composure: returning in this storm was out of question, so they would have to take the body onto dry land for burial. This would certainly give him the opportunity for a survey. Better yet, how about burying the body in the monastery grounds? Oh, yes! This strange request could easily be carried out, provided suitable gifts were distributed, and his loyal servant could be laid to rest on hallowed ground.

Some on board did wonder if the loss was not a warning, but Jacques was not one to say die. Buried treasure was an irresistible force that continued to exert its attraction on hunters blinded by ambition.

Cantemir
The Moldovan Prince

The mere mention of his contact's name would have imperilled the Frenchman, so Jacques took special pains to keep his correspondence with Dimitrie Cantemir a secret. And now he was preparing to receive his reward for having secreted the prince into Constantinople. It was late springtime. All that Konstantiniyye wanted to talk of was the lantern festivities İbrahim Pasha had held to amuse the Sultan. The tulip craze had reached ordinary people, who now flocked to picnic grounds. All troubles and concerns postponed, it was time to bless the spring like in the olden days, to bless and to celebrate – an ideal time for the audacious effort that would have drawn much unwelcome attention otherwise.

The former Moldovan Voyvoda, the glorious Dimitrie Cantemir – son of the Voyvoda Constantin Cantemir – had no choice but to flee to Russia after siding with the Russians and thus betraying the Ottomans at Prut in 1711. Yet his desperate longing for Konstantiniyye never waned. Nothing could make him forget: neither the Princess Anastasia he married after the death of his first wife nor the Ottoman costume he wore to the masked balls held under the auspices of the Tsar. He wanted to see the peerless city he called Tsarigrad once more before he breathed his last. He knew certain execution awaited him in case of capture, but he thought it was worth a try all the same.

The most colourful and unforgettable years of Dimitrie's life had been spent in Konstantiniyye, witnessing the reign of four emperors in his twenty-two years, nothing to be sniffed at! He was accustomed to the Turks, their manner of living, their art, and they, in turn, had held him in flatteringly high esteem.

The prince had arrived in Konstantiniyye as something of a hostage in line with tradition: whilst his father served as Moldovan Voyvoda, the son resided in the capital. Dimitrie later served the Emperor as a diplomatic envoy. Needless to say, he too had taken his share of hypocrisy in all this time, but warm friendships left deeper traces in his memory. Isn't this always the way when one has to leave a part of one's life behind for good – only the good memories stay?

Dimitrie Cantemir spoke eleven Eastern and Western languages and was familiar with the three great cultures: Graeco-Latin, Italian humanism and Islam. He was a composer, musician, historian and philosopher. This extraordinary man had two palatial residences, where his musical evenings were all the rage for Konstantiniyye's élite. He had recorded Turkish music in a notation of his own devising. Listening to him playing the tambur was a true delight.

And one of his closest friends was the artist Levnî Çelebi. He was also on good terms with the Russian Ambassador Pyotr Andreyevich Tolstoy, a friendship that would alter the course of his life. Amongst close friends were also the French Ambassador Ferriol and famous poets of the time. It was he who trained several great musicians, he who had a particular interest in Sufi hymns.

Dimitrie Cantemir had left Konstantiniyye in 1710, when he acceded to the position of Moldovan Voyvoda. He had spent years here and left in glory.

The newly appointed Voyvoda had achieved another first with the full consent of the Emperor: he had performed his latest composition on the tambur before the Emperor in expression of his gratitude. Grand Vizier Baltacı Mehmed Pasha was thoroughly content with his choice, recommending this extraordinary man for this vital post.

The very same Baltacı was destined to realise the magnitude of his error and quite soon: it wasn't a year before the imperial army was locked in battle with the Russians in Prut. That Dimitrie Cantemir in whom he had such confidence had knifed the Ottomans in the back, showed the Russian commander the way and even supported the man with his own troops. The day had been Baltacı's, and he wanted to know at once the whereabouts of the Voyvoda to punish the traitor who, he was told, had vanished.

Whether Baltacı believed the Russians or pretended to in order to conceal his own disappointment at having been deceived, no one knows.

Cantemir and Eirene
Beyond the centuries

Dimitrie Cantemir was a true polymath, and he had a particular interest in Byzantine history, which guided his quest into trails overlooked by others in those happy days in the imperial capital, the aroma of that peerless thrill in his taste buds, of chasing after the unknown as he delved deeper into the dark passages of that fabulous civilisation, Eastern Rome. Living in Konstantiniyye provided him with the ideal location. Dimitrie knew how to press an advantage.

His father the Voyvoda's influence opened countless doors to Dimitrie, and the younger man chanced upon some documents in a forgotten place of interest to no one else, one of many such sites that no other soul troubled to seek out. Nestled inside the binding of a manuscript in an unkempt library in an old church waited an unexpected discovery: documents concealed in haste. Documents written in a crude code, referring to a treasure Empress Eirene had secreted in the Prinkipo Convent, treasure she had not had the opportunity to recover later. And a sketch!

The text must have been written by a loyal servant to the Empress in the year 802 when she and her lady were banished. The parchment had survived all this time and fallen into Dimitrie's hands. Virtually illegible, grammatically poor, yet in the prestigious Attic Greek of the educated classes, the writing gave an account of the inconceivable treasure buried below the floor of one of the nuns' cells in the convent on Prinkipo, on the command of the Empress herself. It was as if the words on the parchment spoke of the writer's conviction that the Empress would never see those fabulous metals and jewels again, and neither would the writer, yet she was loath to consign them to the earth for all eternity. The servant must have believed that leaving this document behind might vindicate her own life.

Dimitrie Cantemir wondered about the fate of the writer when he read these lines. History took count of the masters and mistresses as it – all too often – consigned the servants to anonymity.

No one could tell if the treasure this sad tale referred to truly existed, and even if it did, whether it still lay undiscovered. Three huge, round emeralds and a wine-dark ruby, fine enough to be set in the centre of a crown: these gems were described hastily, yet vividly. The writer must have liked them best.

The story of Eirene, Empress of the Eastern Roman Empire, was not a terribly long one. When she was in power, she had exiled her beautiful granddaughter Euphrosyne – daughter of her own son Constantine VI – in August 797 to the convent on the island. But the day came that turned the tide: although Eirene was once supported by power struggles, only five years later she fell out of favour, and in 802 the cruel Empress herself was exiled. The first act of the new Emperor Nikephoros was to despatch Eirene, head now shaved, to Prinkipo first and later to Lesbos. The deposed Empress died on Lesbos and her body was brought back to Prinkipo in 803 for interment at the convent. So, the ambitious Empress had found a way of getting back to her treasure, although not in her lifetime.

The treasure Eirene secreted away in the hope of returning to power had become her companion in the grave. Cantemir frequently wondered about this bizarre turn of events.

The strange information in these documents meant far more to Cantemir than the possibility of wealth. He was much more interested in reaching out to the past, touching ancient lives even if only for one breath. He regretted having boasted of this find at a wine-fuelled home party – heavily wine-fuelled! His was the thrill of a scientist, flushed with a new discovery, impatient to share this with his guests. True, only one person had pricked up his ears at that late hour, when most of the company were too inebriated to care much about the conversation: the young Assistant Secretary at the French Embassy, but just one person had sufficed.

Cantemir knew he wanted to slink back into Konstantiniyye, the city where he had spent the best days of his youth. He would disguise himself as a recently appointed low-ranking French diplomat. Nine years had passed since his departure; this Frenchman who had been pressing him all this time would assist, thanks also to Cantemir's flawless command of French. The French Ambassador would never set eyes on him, either: the secretary had recently taken up a lot of work at the embassy and convinced his ambassador that a long rest at the dam in Belgrade Forest village was just the thing.

Levnî and Ahmed and Cantemir
Old friends

'I dream of a treasure buried on the Great Island, My Sovereign, dating back to the Rum infidels, a sizeable treasure,' said Levnî softly, relating the story of the events on Prinkipo as if these were nothing more than his dreams.

Telling the Emperor what must not be voiced was tricky but pretence of fiction might avoid invoking royal wrath. They had granted each other limitless rights when it came to dreams, so Sultan Ahmed couldn't chastise his companion even if he wanted to. Had this information arrived through the official channels, however, his position would have necessitated raining punishment on scores of people. That indescribable pressure would have been very difficult to resist. So, the Sultan rejoiced silently and the two men communicated by eyes alone.

Sultan Ahmed considered such buried treasure inauspicious in the first place. Were someone to take it away from his land, he would have been relieved, not perturbed.

'At the time of the Roman Empire, Empress Eirene, a woman of infinite might, had jewels the like of which had not been seen: globes of pearls and other gems besides that overflowed from trunks. This Eirene fell from grace, after much finagling against her, and was exiled to the biggest of the islands. But those who banished her from Konstantiniyye were unable to check her influence, and this crone had her loyal servants secret the rarest gems in her treasure out of the palace and conceal them in a corner of the convent. Her intention, of course, was to dig it out at some later date, the crone was that certain of regaining power. But her plans came to naught; she was buried in the same place and her blood money served no one for centuries.'

Sensitive to the doings of the city's previous owners, Sultan Ahmed was impatient to learn more; although he understood that these bloody tales benefitted no one, here's another inexplicable conflict! Levnî knew his Emperor was captivated by this tale; gazing into the distance, he took a deep breath, as if whipping up his audience's interest. In fact he was scrambling for courage to voice a name, however reluctant he was to admit it. He picked his words very carefully:

'This Dimitrie of the Cantemirs – yes, I know his name is repugnant, My Fortunate Emperor – as you know, was a very inquisitive man and a scientist also; he was intrigued by all manner of bizarre things and followed their trails. He found some scratchings in some places along these lines: words that spoke of this colossal treasure. All these travails stem from this information.'

Although he was shaken, Sultan Ahmed concealed it well; moreover, his curiosity was aroused now. Dimitrie Cantemir was a wound in his side, a man he had once trusted and whose friendship he had enjoyed. All that made the betrayal even worse. So now the Moldovan nobleman reappeared on the stage, so long after he had been supposedly consigned to memories. The Emperor knew his companion wouldn't have brought up this name in vain, the name of this traitor, who had escaped after the battle of Prut.

As Sultan Ahmed mused thus, Levnî also rolled back the years: suddenly he was standing at the familiar entrance to that palace that looked out at the Golden Horn in Fener. It was as if the servant was about to bid him enter that splendid reception room, for the artist to savour the sight of the simple yet tasteful furniture: cupboards brimming with books, gilt tables topped with elegant vases and sparkling crystal chandeliers illuminating the room. He would examine the folds of the Frankish drapes framing the windows with their gold-tasselled tiebacks, but most of all, feast his eyes on the Vanmour paintings hanging on the walls. Entering this palace always promised so much beauty, and never disappointed.

Suddenly he would hear Dimitrie jest, 'My precious Levnî Çelebi, always a little early; I was beginning to worry!' The voice would come from behind him, the Moldovan servant of the Porte.

'No need for worry, My Lord; I even bring some good news.' Levnî unrolled the sheet in his hand. 'Noble Dimitrie, I know you liked the portraits of the august Ottoman emperors I've been working on. The collection is close to completion and I've brought you a copy.'

Cantemir was delighted; he had been waiting such a long time for this, but had been biting his tongue lest he intimidate his friend. 'I am fortunate to be blessed with such a talented friend!'

A knock came; perhaps Nef'i the poet was at the door, eyes sparkling with excitement, asking whether Cantemir would be kind enough to compose the music for his latest poem... Levnî sighed. All this was in the past. How quickly one dipped into dreamland! He was almost certain he could smell the apple wine that accompanied the meal and the poached pears with almonds and the violet sherbet that followed.

The Emperor's fury had been compounded by the fact that the Moldovan's critics had been vindicated; hence, the unwritten taboo of mentioning the traitor's name before Sultan Ahmed. Yet Levnî had spoken in such a manner that Sultan Ahmed was all ears. And he knew Levnî would not have brought this subject up without reason, just when it had all been almost forgotten.

'Continue, my gently spoken Levnî.' Sultan Ahmed was equally soft-spoken, almost fearful of defying his own ban.

'It appears that the young secretary to the former Frankish Ambassador Monsieur Ferriol heard something. However it happened, he was the only one to have heard Cantemir's secret, and whatever he did to learn the precise location of the treasure from Cantemir, he failed.'

Levnî passed over the fact of his own attendance at the wine party where Cantemir had spoken of the Roman Empress Eirene's buried treasure, words he had chosen to ignore. Enjoying the Emperor's full attention, he continued:

'Every effort this secretary made on his own to discover the site of the treasure failed, but according to my friend, whose ears reach far, he never gave up. Now, he says, the time is ripe: Dimitrie Cantemir is desirous of visiting the city of Konstantiniyye, taking advantage of springtime. Secreting him into the city, dressed as a Frankish man, had its own price, clearly: the location of the treasure, information a fair price for all the trouble, surely.'

The Cantemir that Sultan Ahmed visualised was a different man entirely. Not the powerful Cantemir of old time, possibly conscious of an approaching end, desperate to see the city where he had spent the best days of his life just once more, sneaking in like a thief. This ignominy was to be paid for by information that only he himself had, in exchange for getting to the Seat of Felicity as little more than a quivering fugitive. Sultan Ahmed trembled silently at the Moldovan's soft spot for his capital, whatever Dimitrie's transgression.

The ruler and his companion sat in silence for a while, both lost in the events of the past. The treachery of a well-liked, trusted friend wounded like hot iron.

'True, he was an extraordinary personage, but nothing can excuse treachery!'

* * *

In time, the clandestine treasure hunt became one of the Sultan's favourite tales. He listened to Levnî as if the tale came from a different land. He had no intention of pardoning Cantemir or his companions should they be captured; nevertheless, if they were successful they might deserve to escape unpunished. The single-mindedness of human pursuit evoked approval from Sultan Ahmed, even if the goal was only wealth – he may even have silently envied their perseverance. He also knew that Cantemir's goal was to bid farewell to the place where he belonged, however much he might serve another's ambition on the way.

Games within games, and so few spectators! That was life in Sultan Ahmed's view:

'What really lies below the ground is the sum of the pains and tribulations of those who lived above it. All that they will succeed in unearthing from the red soil of the island is trouble! Yet hope springs eternal; suffer no one to check it.'

İbrahim and Hüseyin One-Eye
Information

'So this tale of treasure is true after all?'

It was a rare quiet night at İbrahim Pasha's Beşiktaş palace. The Grand Vizier was listening to his informant, admitted into the male reception room from a side door.

'I paid Bald Yusuf of the crew of the galleon that took the infidels to Prinkipo. I gave him one gold coin for the information. These geezers were impatient to get to the island despite the great south-westerly storm that was brewing up, like others had also heard of the treasure.'

İbrahim Pasha's personal informant was reliable: Hüseyin One-Eye could get to places the great statesman could not, blend in and make friends easily. The fireman had so far served his fellow countryman patron well, and generous had his reward been in return. The Grand Vizier would then decide which piece of information deserved to be passed on to his patron the August Emperor, and which to save for himself, for use later or simply to let be.

The matter of the treasure buried on Prinkipo was one he would save for himself for the time being. What he hadn't counted on was that Levnî, who was equally comfortable in the company of bards and hoodlums, had his own sources of information in the coffee houses.

Whether the information would serve a purpose was as yet unknown.

Eirene's Treasure, Jacques's Treasure
In the old convent on Prinkipo

Prinkipo's convent had survived into Sultan Ahmed III's time hobbling, more derelict than solid: the dome had collapsed entirely, and although some of the truncated pyramidal capitals still topped the columns, quite a few were carved with plane tree leaves and now lay on the ground. The islanders still referred to this place as 'camares' but few of the nunnery cells had survived. The ancient convent built at the bottom of a gentle slope covered with cypresses had seen proud days, head held high, and suffered much.

The convent owed its existence to the munificence of Justinian II, the Eastern Roman Emperor – for that's how the Byzantine Empire was known at the time, a time when the empire was young. The Emperor's wish was to erect a palace on this, the largest of the Paradise Isles near the capital, the isles of gentle climes. Two hundred years later, Empress Eirene – as if she had a premonition about the part this convent was to play in her final days – had the convent repaired and extended. Had she known this modest building would be her future tomb, whether she would have done more, who knows? But the nunnery's own destiny was revealed before too long: the place of exile for Byzantine empresses, to be repeated time and again, beginning with Eirene herself.

The building, set in a quiet corner of the lovely island, its only neighbour an uninhabited islet opposite, had much misfortune to contend with. In 1204, Latin crusaders sacked the convent, enslaving the monks and nuns. In 1302, it was the Venetians' turn. What ensued was a determined decline, step by step. Yet it continued to protect Eirene's treasure, those ill-omened pieces of rock and metal in its red-earth lap – a strange loyalty, perchance a will to protect others from harm. The islanders were reluctant to approach the convent at any rate; those simple folk knew all too well what was good and what brought evil.

*   *   *

The monotony of island life was broken abruptly: all eyes were on the galleon that managed to battle the crazed south-westerly and make it to the ancient pier on the island, albeit in a sorry condition. It had been years since such an exciting vessel had moored at Prinkipo. Leading citizens of the island ran to the dock to assist, and a number of well-dressed passengers alighted carrying a body wrapped in tarpaulin, the cloth ragged, unable to conceal the blood.

As the sea around the island turned into that unique deep blue in preparation to greet the evening, the settling darkness was beginning to obscure the bright light of the May south-westerly. The Frank, apparently the leader, declared his intention to inter his poor servant who had died on board. The site he chose was the ancient convent and he would do all that was necessary – not excluding a hefty donation to the island's church. Thus were the inhabitants of this Konstantiniyye: the awful chaos that was the big city rendered all residents somewhat strange. The Frank knew how to spread money around; his will would be humoured, but there was little room for haste on the island; they would wait for the morning, the body laid out in a suitable cellar and the guests accommodated elsewhere. The duty would be discharged at first light, since it was quite hot they wouldn't tarry, and the priest would also be able to attend.

Jacques had succumbed to greed and so must have lost almost all caution, but he still reserved sufficient presence of mind to appreciate how a burial without a priest would have aroused unwelcome suspicion. He would send the priest on his way immediately after the funeral and get on with his work. If things went badly and the priest grew suspicious – well, then, he would have to be prepared to sacrifice the man, wouldn't he?

Jacques was convinced that he wouldn't sleep, yet it wasn't long before exhaustion and the sweet wine offered at the meal did their work. He laid his head on the pillow and went out like a light.

They all awakened early on the morning of the 14th of May 1719 and hastened – without breaking their fast – towards the soft soil at the southeast where the convent was located. They noticed neither the fresh island breeze, redolent of wisteria and laurel, nor heard the chirping of the early birds. Volunteers from the island who helped carry the makeshift coffin and the tools were struggling to keep up with the hurried pace of the city man.

Stone blocks covered in moss startled this bizarre funeral procession when they reached the ruins of the convent beyond the shadow of the cypresses. Jacques, now completely accustomed to the role of the chief, was convinced that nothing could stand in his way. He didn't even need to consult the sketch that he knew by heart. Pointing towards the spot he had ostensibly picked for the grave, he directed the dig. It was only when a solitary horse suddenly reared up and neighed pitifully behind them on the path that they noticed just how eerily quiet it had suddenly grown. The sweetly singing birds had all fallen quiet, as had the childish cries of the seagulls. The sea they looked down upon from a little height was like glass, not the same sea that had boiled and frothed so only a day previously. The men who had been happily wielding their pickaxes, fired up by the promise of generous fees, looked petrified at the sight of all manners of insects and creepy crawlies abruptly pouring out of the soil, falling over one another. The creatures of the earth were running to escape from an invisible foe.

Jacques felt icy water flush through his veins; he was close to something he couldn't name. He wanted to run, dropping everything, but his feet felt nailed to the red earth, the earth he had been so impatient to dig and which was now determined not to let him go. That thundering howl drumming up from the depths, that infernal noise – was that the grumble of an uncontrollable monster?

Unexpected or Ever Predictable
Earthquake

'My Noble Emperor, the violent quaking of the earth that occurred in the morning has caused grave damage in our lands!'

The Emperor was impatient for the information Grand Vizier İbrahim Pasha hastened to convey, which he did as soon as his despatch riders returned with the names of the epicentre and places damaged.

'The city of İzmit, many of its villages, half of Yalakabad and all of Pazarköy and Karamürsel have been razed to the ground. There is serious damage to İznikmid, Kazıklı, Sapanca and Düzce, and many of your subjects were killed.'

İbrahim Pasha usually avoided communicating bad news if he could help it. He would solve the problem first and inform his benefactor later, if at all, which explains – at least in part – his Emperor's high regard. But even İbrahim Pasha would struggle to conceal the extent of nature's wrath simply to spare his Emperor's feelings. He added comfortingly in response to the pain on Sultan Ahmed's face:

'With God's grace, there is not much more damage elsewhere on either the European or the Anatolian sides.'

Sultan Ahmed commanded that the numbers of dead be determined in the fine communities of Yalova and İzmit, and the extent of the damage, so that everything possible could be done without delay:

'What's happened cannot be undone. Wailing will help nothing. Make sure to bandage wounds swiftly, My Great Vizier, make sure to erect tents for the survivors, and feed them!'

Sultan Ahmed had been awakened from his sweet sleep in the arms of Mihrişah by that awful trembling. Her screams had frightened the dozing lady steward at the foot of the bed and the yelling of two women roused the entire palace. But as loud voices were eschewed by seraglio manners – regardless of the situation – most of the residents bit their lips. The majority congregated in the courtyards and on the patios, the evacuation of the women and children supervised by the eunuchs, who also calmed down those crying in fear.

Her composure flawless, Chief Wife Emetullah Sultan moved in the crowd and soothed palpitations. Sultan Ahmed had enquired after her well-being first and then the rest of the harem, his attention to protocol providing her with a degree of satisfaction.

The youngest concubines were most in need of mothering and reassurance. A gentle chiding was called for at times: 'Don't scream so, girl! All we've had to worry about was a little fright, but consider others elsewhere who've lost so much! Save your grief for them!' Her own daughter was close to her heart as she calmed them down, but she was sure Fatma Sultan would be well looked after by her own husband.

Hümaşah looked smaller than ever before cuddling close to Şermi as usual. Her friend's lack of attention she attributed to fright; even at a time like this, she was prepared to give everyone the benefit of the doubt. As for Şermi, her mind was occupied with Mihrişah being in the Sultan's bed at the time of the disaster: could she somehow twist this to her own advantage, linking Mihrişah with ill omens? Şermi's gaze wandered as she considered the subtlest ways of exploiting the situation. Utterly unaware of the malice aimed at her, Mihrişah sat with her two sons, holding the nine-year-old Süleyman by the hand and hugging the two-year-old Mustafa. Little did she remember of donning her pants and shift and leaving the Sultan in haste, running in the dark corridors of the harem to reach her sons.

Nearly calmed down, the harem had moved to one side of the garden when the still-hungry ground under their feet shook again and again. This time, the women's terror was hard to allay. It was only when the sovereign appeared in front of his black eunuchs that calm was restored in the garden. Their master and benefactor was here; he would share this terrible day. Sultan Ahmed had come to look after his large family and his people.

★　★　★

The seraglio had not escaped unharmed: there were cracks in some walls, dislodged window casings, a couple of the boathouses collapsed at the Yalı Pavilion side and countless items of china now lying in countless pieces in the kitchens – all of which was minor compared to what the country had suffered.

Disheartening news flowed in relentlessly, from all parts of the city. Only a few houses had been spared; the very least was fallen chimneys. The mosques were in a sorry state, with cracks in the domes of Fatih, Bayezid and Edirnekapı Mihrimah mosques and many collapsed minarets. The ancient battlement by Galata Dungeons had tumbled over the adjoining bookshop and buried four people; only one had been rescued alive many hours later. An arch had fallen down at the Yağlıkçılar Arcade, crushing ten, it was said.

Days later a full inventory was made: forty mosques and twenty-seven minarets had been razed to the ground and there was grave damage to the land walls stretching from Yedikule to Ahırkapı. Thrace had not escaped the effects of the earthquake either.

The estimated number of dead in İzmit and Yalova was over six thousand, six hundred having been buried under the mosques alone. Four-fifths of İzmit was devastated. The bonded warehouse at the shore had sunk into the sea, together with the Chief Customs Officer and his staff. The horror of the witnesses to this catastrophe would ensure the tale survived through the ages. Kazıklı to the east of Karamürsel in the bay had almost disappeared altogether. The Grand Vizier was determined to comfort those who had suffered in the earthquake.

★　★　★

The aftershocks continued to shake the land for days afterwards, yet life went on.

Ten days after the earthquake, İbrahim Pasha entertained the Emperor at a fabulous party in Kağıthane. The party had been weeks in preparation, as not even the great earthquake was going to dim the Grand Vizier's yen for fun.

A fortnight later Sultan Ahmed moved to the Aynalıkavak Palace at the Imperial Shipyard Gardens to enjoy the new summer, taking his favourite women along.

Festivities, Despite All

The Golden Horn shore was preparing for the summer. Gardens were painted by tulips and fragranced by roses as Aynalıkavak Palace filled with anticipation to greet the Emperor. The former Shipyard Palace had been transformed by the gift of colossal mirrors from Venice: mirrors of poplar, that is, *aynaları kavak*. Another rumour pointed to archery targets known as *ayna*, 'mirror', at the range nearby.

Aynalıkavak was a particular favourite of the Sultan for the summer months, well liked by those picked to accompany him, far from the crowds of the harem. Emetullah Sultan, Chief Wife to the Emperor of the Universe, had the place of honour regardless of which young lovely happened to be the flavour of the day. The others did have to exchange places from time to time. But now they were all set to forget those terrible hours of the earthquake.

The knowledge that distant victims had been housed in tent towns and provided with food was consolation enough that the court might now focus on enjoying life here.

The Emperor could, with a relieved heart, look forward to pleasant hours at the domed reception room reaching over the waters of the Golden Horn. He could easily get to the archery field nearby and erect range stones marking the furthest his arrows had flown to better etch these feats into one's mind. Or, he could dress up in the colours of the tulips illuminated from below by tea lights reflected in the calm waters of an evening and lose himself in the music played by virtuosi. Poems would naturally follow.

Dimitrie
The final farewell

It took a few days for news of Jacques's death to reach the former Moldovan governor (and new fugitive) owing to the earthquake that had brought everything to a virtual halt. Despite Cantemir's affinity with Jacques over their shared passion for history, he had always found the younger man's avarice distasteful. But hearing about how the man changed one world for the next, he quite forgot his own troubles briefly, whiling away in bizarre dreams: the French secretary was now in a different world, the glitter of Eirene's jewels in his hand, and him in rich purples, the colour only obtained by crushing the rarest of rare thorny seashells. Very likely he was on the back of a fine horse, galloping below a banner of the same purple fluttering in the breeze. He had travelled through time and joined the haughty ranks of Byzantine nobility.

Cantemir chose to shrug these dreams off. Now there was no one left in Konstantiniyye who would conceal him and ultimately sneak him out of the city. All that remained was the chaos of the earthquake.

And possibly his old friend, the artist Levnî Çelebi?

* * *

Exactly like he did after the battle of Prut – when Grand Vizier Baltacı Mehmed Pasha sought Cantemir high and low to mete out punishment until convinced by Russian insistence that he had vanished – so now he disappeared once more. The earthquake had created sufficient chaos, and he had never officially been back.

No one asked Levnî what he had been up to at the time, least of all the Emperor.

Levnî and Prinkipo
Reunion with the isle

A young mariner assisted Levnî to alight. No longer merely ramshackle, the pier was all but unusable since the earthquake. Gathering the skirt of his robe, Levnî picked his way carefully on the odd board, the few that remained of the decking. The only sound on the shore was the gentle lapping of the waves.

The red sand spread over the path crackled under his feet as he climbed up from the pier towards the largish town square. The red islands, Levnî thought, aware of the wealth of iron ore in the soil; to an artist, though, scientific explanations rarely did justice to the wealth of secrets behind colours.

Roof tiles lay scattered on the ground outside the two-storey stone houses giving way onto the square, and the walls were cracked. Some looked uninhabitable, and they would have to be demolished and rebuilt from scratch or would require extensive repairs at the very least. The owners must have been sleeping outdoors. Strong aftershocks still shook the ground from time to time and no one dared to enter a building even if the damage was limited to cracked window casings or dislodged doors.

It had never crossed his mind that Levnî would one day visit Prinkipo for such a purpose. He was informed there were countless injuries, but relatively few fatalities on the archipelago: a few fishermen on the open sea and some folk at the ancient convent.

The sad cause of the visit notwithstanding, why was it that he enjoyed being on Prinkipo? Was it the refreshing air of the island, the true beauty of nature here, or did it somehow relate to his imagination, identifying the island with something within himself? Memories and dreams fused together. He remembered how as a young child, well before he had any inkling about the turbulent future that awaited him, the family had visited Salonika a few times, and how these visits had been his happiest days to date. Above all, it was the jasmine pots that had made such an impression on his young mind, still fresh all these years later.

That gently persistent scent of jasmine never left him. Edirne Palace – whose art studio he had worked in, the palace that had determined his fate – was blessed with a profusion of jasmines. Mehmed the Hunter's skilled gardeners jealously guarded their precious jasmine bushes in massive planters from the bitter cold of Thrace, these favourite flowers of the ruler. It was this strong scent that the artist had so hungrily inhaled on unexpected visits of the majestic Gülnuş, the Queen Mother, when he was such a young artist. Years later, he had found jasmine trees on this island, and somehow this flower had come to symbolise the unattainable for him. Yes, he could get up and look out of the window towards the Marmara Sea whenever he felt bored. That gaze in the direction of Prinkipo somehow alleviated his heavy heart, forging a bond between his soul and the island. Yet there were times when the pain within became unbearable. Then he closed his eyes to visualise himself walking on the streets of Salonika as a child, or in Edirne Palace as a young man, or on the island paths. So practised was he in this daydream that he could convince himself that he had moved, that he could smell those scents from his youth and feel the breeze in his hair.

But here he was now, at this place he had not visited for so long, and for a terrible reason – an earthquake. His earlier musings weighed on his conscience. A disaster had occurred here, and he had been despatched by the Emperor as a result of the bizarre events immediately preceding it. He was here to investigate the death of the strange visitors to the ancient, deserted convent where islanders eventually going for help had discovered the inconceivable buried treasure that the slipping soil had spat out.

* * *

It was quite a shock for the islanders to find the buried treasure immediately after the great earthquake. True, a few of their number were far too ready for a discreet distribution to fund new lives, but their prospects should they ever be discovered would not be worth risking. Yea, some might have pocketed a few smaller items, but the greatest items had been safeguarded: three huge emeralds, a massive ruby and heavy gold items, all worthy of the great Emperor's treasure, as well as the gold coins bearing the head of the ancient Empress; selling them without attracting curiosity would have been impossible. The original arrival of these gemstones gave rise to several speculations. The only point of consensus was the bad luck attached to the treasure. Since the island folk wanted to get rid of it as soon as possible, they were delighted to greet the man who arrived to take charge, accompanied by imperial troops. The Emperor was sure to reward their loyalty generously.

The precious charge was no longer at the convent where it had been found. It had been entrusted to the priest. Levnî insisted on going to the convent first, however, to take a gentle stroll to the place where so much had happened and see with his own eyes the guardian of the treasure that had benefitted no one, the treasure for whom so many had died.

* * *

For such a long time he had stayed away lest the reality disappoint, preferring to confine the island to his dreams. As the longing grew, so did the unattainable appreciate in value. That was no longer a place on earth: Levnî's dreams transformed the island into a place whose distance was indeterminate, a place that perpetuated the beauty of the melancholy within Levnî's soul, beyond the reach of any vision.

The artist walked on, forgetting the situation he was in and heedless of those speaking to him – albeit at a respectful distance. All his senses focussed on the essence of this small piece of earth surrounded by the sea; he hardly noticed the collapsed buildings. Everything was clean, calm, beautiful and unthreatening, just like the city of his childhood so powerfully etched in his mind. The visitor was enveloped by Aleppo pines, junipers, mastic trees and olive trees, the calming and now-woebegone air of the plants that adored this island.

The island was like a wounded beauty.

At the ruins of the convent Levnî returned to his own world, once again the man trusted by the August Emperor, the man who faced exaggerated deference as a result. The spot where the dead and the treasure were dug was pointed out. Levnî remembered that night many years ago, how animated the Moldovan Cantemir was as he related the story of his find. In vain he wished he never knew about that evening, and that the accurs't buried treasure was still under the ground.

The only fatalities had been the burial party. How this awful cataclysm spared everyone else would always remain a mystery.

Jacques had come so close to the goal of his life. He may have even died happy, feeling the treasure just beyond his reach – who knows? For one brief moment, his fingers might have brushed something beyond time, just as he had dreamt of for years and years.

The Emeralds and the Ruby
The prophecy

'What I see is blood-red matchless rubies, deep red like wine and merciless as the crater of a volcano, and emeralds transparent as seaweeds, dark as cemetery cypresses and ruthless as snake eyes.'

The old soothsayer rarely spoke so definitively. His usual preference was for much rounder expressions, open to a variety of interpretation; that was a more certain method of filling his purse. On this occasion, however, the words just flew out from his mouth:

'It was like armies go past these stones, raising dust wherever they go, and grief-filled hearts battle greed-filled ones. Ancient, these stones are, and mighty too. They were sent to the seventh depth of the earth as if the high skies had flung them in a thunderbolt and then flowed out again like lava – none could stand in their way. They adorned an imposing crown for a while, then were prised off and buried in the ground from where they had originally sprung. But the earth rejected them, refusing to hold them in its lap for a long time! They sprouted out of the ground, covered in blood once more.'

The soothsayer was struggling to catch his breath, the burden of the images that appeared on the divination water so heavy as to make him forget in whose presence he spoke. He was on the verge of collapsing on the floor then and there. He collected himself and continued in a gloomy voice:

'Curse. Curse and pride and greed enveloped these stones. They dragged down the woman who buried them here in secret, like they punished the woman who banished them from daylight, who put an end to their dazzling as marks of power, to their being admired, and condemned her to the underground.'

What he heard sickened the imposing man listening to him from his elevated platform. He had no wish to listen to more, yet was unable to deny his own curiosity. He nodded to encourage the soothsayer, who had paused.

'There was no concept of time where they were. They wished to reach daylight again and so attracted the greed inside mankind like a magnet, and they succeeded. And now they are in very noble hands, and are mighty pleased to be so admired, but their curse continues unabated.'

The soothsayer's force was beginning to wane; it was time to speak of the future. His exalted listener frowned attentively without breaking his silence. The soothsayer got ready to reveal the crux of the matter:

'Emanate evil now, they do not, the stones, but it is certain they will not bring joy to the fortunes of their new proprietor.'

With a sudden tremble, the old soothsayer waved his hands before his face as if to dispel a ghostly image. He paused, opened his mouth and shut it again. At long last, the lord and master spoke:

'Stop your mumbling, soothsayer! Will they bring ill luck to their present owner? He never asked for them!'

Yet the gems wanted him. These gemstones consider themselves worthy only of a ruler, thought the soothsayer, but what he said out loud was different:

'There is no need for concern, Your Grace. What could a few stones dug out from seven layers of earth do before your infinite might?'

The soothsayer was gratified by this powerful man's need for the consolation he offered. The torment of his own soul, however, did not escape his horrified notice, as if watching from outside his own being. How chaos overwhelmed his mind, and then out arose something refined, clarified! It was as if someone else had entered his head and used his voice to speak out. He shut his eyes after a brief pause and reached out into the future in a soft voice, as if murmuring to himself:

'Tis on the hilt of a splendid dagger I see these three large emeralds, years from now.'

The man before whom all but one bowed down reached out to the dagger in his belt, almost instinctively, and then recoiled; the dagger had singed his hand. The soothsayer ignored the incident and continued:

'They voyage on a big caravan, far from here, towards the land of the Persians. The dagger is wrapped in red velvet, carried close to the heart of a glorious Ottoman general, but it does not belong to him. This emerald-adorned dagger is entrusted to his charge by the Majestic Sovereign.'

İbrahim Pasha thought the old man's prediction might have some traces of truth, and yet – to believe that such a long-winded and bizarre story could fit into a bowl of water? No, he found it difficult that morning. Never could he have imagined what lay in wait for the emeralds: that another Emperor would commission a magnificent dagger with these emeralds on the hilt, a dagger he would send to the Persian Emperor as a gift – the Persian Emperor who would cause his benefactor's and his own downfall, no less – that the intended recipient would himself fall to an assassin before the gift ever reached its destination, that the jewelled knife would return to Konstantiniyye, where it belonged, that it would console its owners for a brief period but would overthrow them too, taking offence at a perceived slight – not enough admiration? – and that ultimately people would flock from all four corners of the globe to view these emeralds on the hilt of the dagger. What he could and did believe was that these gemstones would bring anything but good fortune to his benefactor.

The soothsayer knew the Grand Vizier to be generous, yet he was rewarded with a purse much heavier than he could have ever imagined. Surely this was a purse meant to seal his lips! As the old man left, İbrahim Pasha turned one thought in his mind over and over again: There must be a way of ridding ourselves of these accurs't stones.

★ ★ ★

'My Blessed Sovereign, I must confess, when these three cabochon emeralds flowed out of that worn-out old leather purse and into my palm, they quite took my breath away!' Levnî said in all sincerity.

Sultan Ahmed indulged İbrahim Pasha's request, odd though he deemed it: his son-in-law had wanted to hear the story of the gemstones that came from the Red Isles once more, from the mouth of Levnî, and the three men convened in the Privy Chamber.

Whilst Levnî related all that he saw on the island, including his own impressions as vividly as possible, he silently wondered about the Grand Vizier's concern, especially when İbrahim Pasha listened to him so attentively.

Then it was the great man's turn: the statesman related the soothsayer's predictions, ill at ease as he did so.

Sultan Ahmed had no desire to add these infernal gemstones and gold into his treasury. Curiosity ruled, and he examined them anew. The gold coins bore the image of Empress Eirene on both sides. This was totally unheard of, an eccentric manifestation of the Empress's desire for uniqueness. On both sides were inscribed her title, simple and mighty: *EIPENE BAΣIΛIΣΣA*. Eirene stared out of the gold coins useless for a toss, strings of pearls hanging down from either side of her face, wearing chequered embroidered robes and holding the imperial sceptre, as if she had finally found peace looking out from 900 years ago. The emeralds and the ruby could well have adorned the crown on her head.

What to do with the gold coins didn't trouble the Emperor in the least: melt the lot down to fund public kitchens, channel this gold into charity. The unfortunate image of the cruel Empress who had suffered so would vanish.

As for the stones, though, now that was a little trickier.

These gemstones had passed from hand to hand for hundreds of years, like symbols of lust for power, and brought bad luck to their owners. From whence had they come to Byzantium in the first place? Was there no way of protecting oneself from their curse? The Emperor, his son-in-law and his companion looked solemn enough to be discussing a matter of state.

'It is certain that the treasure of the maid *y'clept* Eirene will bring no good.'

The solution proposed by İbrahim Pasha was truly ingenious. Even Levnî was moved enough to bow. The Grand Vizier convinced the Emperor to retain the gemstones until such a time that a gift could be made of them to the ruler of an eternal foe. The Emperor would command a dagger to be made for the Emperor of Persia, the hilt encrusted with these three emeralds. A suitable occasion to send this dagger would come, given time enough. And a dagger was the most appropriate item to bear these stones.

Not that İbrahim Pasha would have given credit for his inspiration – the soothsayer he ostensibly doubted, yet in his heart believed utterly – but he knew commissioning the dagger would be the next Emperor's destiny. İbrahim Pasha concluded with humility appropriate to a selfless servant:

'If you would be generous enough to present the ruby to your servant, you would have separated these gemstones, and so be rid of them. I, your servant, am prepared to undertake the risk instead of endangering you!'

Sultan Ahmed had other ideas, though. He agreed separating the stones was the right course of action, but had no intention of handing the ruby to his son-in-law. He would have a new aigrette made out of that large ruby and he would wait until someone came along that swept him off his feet.

The Library
New horizons for the Enderun officials

Erecting a new building in the middle of the Inner Palace called Enderun, in this Third Courtyard of the imperial palace that only admitted the Emperor's closest, was no mean feat. Erecting a new building with an entirely new purpose just behind the majestic Audience Chamber – as if in competition with it – and on the foundations of the Pool Pavilion that had been demolished especially for this purpose, that most certainly was no mean feat. The library was but one of the innovations of 1719, that most dynamic year.

Dedicating an entire building to books was unheard of; true, books had always been precious and the most priceless of all belonged to the sovereign himself, but those books had always been safeguarded in the treasury. And here was Sultan Ahmed venturing to spend a fortune on a building specifically for books alone so that Enderun officials may read.

Theological and literary books would fill the cupboards, as would books on sciences, medicine and history. Enderun officials were also known to be partial to books on dream interpretations. Poet Nedim – whose verses rejoiced in the finer things in life – would be appointed as Curator, rumour had it, thanks to his tireless praise for the Emperor's innovations.

The Chief Imperial Architect raised the building over a semi-basement so that those priceless manuscripts, plain and illuminated, would be properly safeguarded from humidity.

This building combined the unassuming splendour of antiquity with the cheerful insouciance of its own time.

The drinking fountain in front, set between the twin staircases, was as innocuous and inviting as the library itself: it had a heart-shaped gilt handle on the tap and carved tulips bending elegantly on either side. The staircases led to a porch, slender columns supporting arches, a veritable portal for the supplicant to enter a hallowed chamber. The Emperor had been pleased, and the Chief Architect's reward reflected the favour.

* * *

Levnî climbed the stairs, passed under the porch and entered the library, enjoying the bright warmth that enveloped him. The companion was here on his own in response to his Emperor's request for an honest appraisal, for a full impression.

The gilded and painted dome was like a reflection of the rich world contained under it. The colourful flowers in the rows of vases looked eternally fresh, the tulips in particular. Soft daylight, not dazzling, streamed down onto the readers from the clerestory windows of the bays on three sides of the central chamber.

A deliberate quiet spread from the golden hexagonal flagstones on the floor to the veins of the porphyry columns and from the tranquil repetition of the blue-and-white tile patterns on the walls to the subtle sheen of the silver screens and the mother-of-pearl built-in cupboards. These fabulous tiles, produced 200 years ago when the Ottomans enjoyed the peak of their power, had previously graced the walls of other imperial pavilions: as those other buildings succumbed to the effects of time, so were these priceless tiles painstakingly prised off to serve their new purpose. And here they were, stuck to mortar with the pride of yet another emperor's taste.

Levnî mused what attacks he would face if some folk were to have the slightest idea that he cheerfully depicted inanimate objects as if they were living creatures, not satisfied with breathing life into the images of individuals – life eternal, at that; little can they conceive of the wealth that is imagination, of anything beyond the plain truth. To him, the tiles on the walls combined into an enchanting creature that came alive once all the pieces were in place: the head, the arms and legs. Just like a book that came into being only once all the pages had been glued and bound together, or a pavilion when its walls, roof, doors, and the rest came together, the library needed curtains and rugs before it could begin to breathe.

As for the chandelier hanging down from the centre of the dome, nothing about this unashamedly vainglorious fixture could be defined as modest! Overcome with the generosity of his Emperor, an officer in the gardeners' corps put all his skill in paper cutting to work to create this matchless chandelier that it may hang in the library for hundreds of years, to expand like the joy in his own heart and spread light.

Sultan Ahmed rewarded the talented officer with a gift of fifteen kuruş.

Is it coincidence that these thoughts always rush into my mind in this library? wondered Levnî; perhaps it was wiser to let some mysteries rest, in just the same way unattainable ecstasy shone brightest of all.

Figures trapped between the pages came to life, thought Levnî. This chamber encouraged stories harking back to 1,000 years; either they told one another or addressed listeners imaginative enough. That's how the figures I create will live on, hoped the artist.

Sultan Ahmed, too, wanted his works to survive his own lifespan. This library- building had pleased him well; everything had been selected carefully and implemented with precision: its site, dimensions, materials and decoration. It had been wise to strike the foundation with his golden pickaxe, the very same pickaxe his ancestor, the very first Sultan Ahmed, had used in the foundation-cutting ceremony of that fabulous mosque. The third of the Sultan Ahmeds may well have realised that he would never outdo his ancestor in the endowment of imposing mosques.

Fabulous fountains and a grand library now were more fitting reflections of the colour of his spirit, more appropriate vehicles to ensure his name lived on.

İbrahim and Ahmed
The Cabbages and the Okras

'Vizier mine,
I have seen naught of you since yesterday. Nothing holds pleasure without you. I have commanded of my Enderun officials a match of *cirit*. Join me so we may watch together. May the Good Lord never draw us asunder! Send my daughter if she will come.'

This sincere letter flowed from the pen of a father looking forward to watching a sports match with his son-in-law and wishing to see his daughter; yea, a father and an emperor besides. The Emperor was as keen on sports as his son-in-law was, his particular favourites being watching *cirit* and shooting firearms.

Sultan Ahmed settled on the soft cushion on the throne facing Gülhane Square; the game was about to begin. The marble throne in the palace garden was a relic of Sultan Murad IV, himself an accomplished horse- and marksman. İbrahim Pasha was seated on the stool next to (but lower than) the throne. Levnî stood behind the Emperor, along with a number of viziers and officials.

First to file out onto the field were the Enderun officials in the Okra team colour, red, followed by the harem's black eunuchs in the green velvet outfits of the Cabbages. Both teams looked determined to win, to earn the generous reward the Emperor was certain to hand out. That he favoured the Okras was no secret. Could it have been due to his companion's influence? The Grand Vizier, rather unpredictably, supported the Cabbages on this occasion, and not the Emperor's team.

The rivalry between the two teams was 300 years old, going back to the time of Çelebi Sultan Mehmed: the Sultan whose cavalry school in the plains between Amasya and Merzifon was legendary – Amasya was famous for its okra and Merzifon for its cabbage. A recruit into either team would be apprenticed to a master cavalryman, to excel both in horsemanship and in swordsmanship – broadsword included. The hardest test of all required the cavalryman to slice through a roll of wet snow-coloured felt wrapped round thirty wires, which required a slow approach and a quick change into a gallop before attacking the roll in a single move.

The field held the full attention of the spectators. The cavaliers paraded first to the music of the *mehter* band, the finery of their steeds displayed to best advantage. This was the challenge stage. Then started the game in earnest, both teams throwing sticks across the field. The Cabbages nimbly evaded the sticks aimed at them, as fleet of gait as a dark cloud; their equestrian skills were formidable indeed. The Okras yelled, 'Whoa, you black agha, you!' defending with a red fury that radiated from their outfits. The match got more and more heated, with little quarter given to the opponents. Neither team lost a man to injury: wounded players continued regardless. The umpires ultimately decided that the Cabbages had prevailed, hitting their opponents more frequently than the Okras.

Sultan Ahmed was well pleased with the match, despite his team's loss: the match had been well fought. The number of purses filled with gold coins he distributed to both teams bore witness to his satisfaction.

İbrahim
Eating one's cake and having it

An insignificant village until the early 18th century, Muşkara stood in Ürgüp, the Central Anatolian district renowned for its bizarre geological formations. There a young man of twenty-seven left the village of his birth to seek his fortune in the Seat of Felicity and entered the court as a *helva* cook, progressing to halberdier, clerk and, all too soon, to the dizzy heights of serving the Crown Prince Ahmed.

Now the time had come for Grand Vizier Damat İbrahim Pasha to bless his hometown like the Seat of Felicity itself – his munificence practically rebuilt Muşkara village: it now had two mosques, a *medrese*, a public kitchen, a school, a library, a bathhouse and a *caravanserai*, as well as numerous fountains and shops. All these new edifices renamed the enlarged town: Nev-şehir, 'new-city'.

It was not for him to let the grass grow under his feet, to waste time. High on his list was entertaining his Emperor day and night, of this there is little doubt, but he did far more. Not a day passed before he introduced some new, improved fashion of ruling the empire. Although Sultan Ahmed's support was indisputably essential, the ideas all originated in the Grand Vizier's mind.

'Many a vessel passes by Leander's Tower, My Noble Sovereign. They all require light. We shall light a torch at that site if that be your will.'

'A worthy notion, Grand Vizier mine. What will it cost?'

'My High-born Sultan, your servant had taken the liberty to commission some rough calculations: eleven pounds of olive oil will be required each night.'

'Make it so!'

* * *

Grand Vizier Damat İbrahim Pasha's work reached far and wide, and pleased as many as not: regulating the silver content of coins in circulation in order to raise the value of the currency, dedicating a school, a library and his own mausoleum in Şehzadebaşı, repairing the Masjid-al Aqsa in Jerusalem, ridding the army of the useless so-called suicide troops and raising taxes to fund the construction of a new arsenal foundry as well as a multitude of other public buildings in the Seat of Felicity.

İbrahim and Levnî
Secret rivalry

İbrahim Pasha took special pains to invite the Emperor's favourite company to his lantern festivities and Kağıthane parties. This was a *sine qua non*, a necessity that made Levnî a regular at these parties, whether İbrahim Pasha liked it or not!

In fact the Grand Vizier admired Levnî's art and found little fault with his disposition. It was the Emperor's extraordinary affection and – strange, but true – something akin to reverence for Levnî that this most powerful of all the pashas found so disconcerting. At times he likened Levnî and himself to two acrobats on one tightrope competing for the Emperor's attention. Moreover, he knew the artist did not care whether he led or fell back in this contest. The insouciance he occasionally saw in Levnî's gaze infuriated the great Emperor's son-in-law, who lived in fear of losing his position.

One day, when the two men were waiting for the Emperor – a very rare occasion, when these two men were left alone – the Grand Vizier took the bull by the horns and asked what the secret of Levnî's constant good cheer was and of his ability to easily placate the Emperor.

The companion's response astonished the statesman, who wasn't expecting an honest answer in the first place:

'The key to counting our blessings, My August Pasha, is to view our time now from an imaginary future, a time when we no longer shall walk this earth!'

İbrahim and the Ambassador
Dazzling opulence

The *yalı* projected out over the sea, propped up on graceful angle braces; the red sienna of the walls painted the sea a flickering red, brushing afresh with each breaking wave. İbrahim Pasha had deemed the Köprülü family waterfront villa – commanding the finest Bosphorus view – appropriate to entertain his distinguished guest.

The Grand Vizier's seven-pair caïque glided over the water and moored first, followed by the massive galleon carrying Virmond, the Austrian Ambassador, and his entourage; *mehter* music greeted both sets of arrivals. Coffee in cups nestled inside jewelled holders and sherbets presented in silver goblets heralded the hospitality to come as the party watched the coloured musky smoke emanating from gilt censers at the Grand Vizier's Beşiktaş palace before setting off. The Ambassador had yet to recover from the elegance of that reception. They walked along the coloured pebble path, flanked by bonsai trees in marble pots, and relaxed in the garden a while. The guest managed to cast only a fleeting glance at the wide-eaved high buildings extending to the rear of the garden; he knew one to be the harem, and that overt curiosity would be considered improper. Eventually, moving slowly as in a procession, they entered the reception hall at the waterfront, feigning indifference to the sumptuous decorations at the embankment.

The Amcazade Hüseyin Pasha *yalı* near Anadoluhisarı had been adorned like a wedding venue. Flowers greeted the visitors first, late summer bounty all: ripe apricot-coloured roses, bright pink variegated double-flowered carnations and slender jasmine behind them all in long-necked crystal vases. Cut flowers competed with the floral decorations on the walls, the hyacinths and tulips that wanted none of the vibrancy of the real ones. It wasn't tulip season at any rate, so the painted image commanded the entire field.

Windows defined three of the walls on the reception hall. The spray in the marble fountain right below the gilded vault created its own rainbow as it caught the dying light of the day. Virmond was dazzled.

He walked, inhaling the fragrance of the flowers, and sat down where he was shown a Frankish chair with gilded, fine carvings. The Ambassador's efforts to maintain his composure before this grandeur failed; he couldn't prise his gaze away from the peacock-embroidered red velvet upholstery, the gold-thread purple and yellow silk kaftan worn by the Grand Vizier sitting opposite him, or the skilfully carved ivory picture frames on the wall, even if he resisted the Bosphorus vista opening up before his eyes. He also knew that by tradition he too would be presented with a similar kaftan once the meal was over.

The servants lined up small, covered silver bowls – too many to count – on the high silver dining tray before them, their movements unhurried, graceful, harmonious. There were no knives at the table, knife jobs being delegated to the hand, but there were mother-of-pearl spoons with tortoiseshell handles and peculiar forks. The Ambassador knew not to be astonished by the number of dishes, as since their arrival on Ottoman lands they had been fêted very well indeed. Yet what the Grand Vizier laid out outshone even the description of a royal feast. This was an ostentatious display of huge wealth. Hit its mark it did: the haughty Austrian envoy tried, and failed, to conceal his shock.

The dragomans standing to the rear conveyed the Ambassador's admiration as Grand Vizier İbrahim Pasha smiled surreptitiously. The Ambassador had already suffered much amazement during the presentation at the imperial palace a month earlier: the opulence of the Audience Chamber was unsurpassable, but it was unlikely that the man had much opportunity to inspect his surroundings whilst in the presence of the Ottoman ruler. That had been payday for the servants of the Porte. Hundreds of menacing-looking troops lined up in perfect stillness to receive their just rewards before attacking the meal of chicken, *pilav* and saffron pudding specially prepared in the imperial kitchens, which all had been an unforgettable sight indeed. This had been followed a few days later by a formal parade on the occasion of Şeker Bayramı, Eid al Adha, when the Sultan and his retinue proceeded to Blue Mosque for holiday prayers in a staggering spectacle. The Ambassador, watching from a pavilion to one side of the Hippodrome, couldn't take his eyes off the Emperor's steed's emerald- and diamond-encrusted harness whose shining was fit to equal the morning sun, the Emperor himself sitting upright regardless of the jewels weighing him down and the halberdier guards wearing their tall headdresses of brush aigrettes surrounding him. What is life, in any event, if not a show?

İbrahim Pasha brought his attention back to the present: the reception room now played host to the sinuous undulations of three dancers to the music coming from the drums and strings at the door. These men, so carefully made up to look like women, danced as if they were on the verge of a trance, exceedingly intriguing the Ambassador and his entourage. There was no doubt that these sights would remain etched in their minds for all their days. As sunlight faded and the sky darkened, the show moved to the sea. The Ambassador saw that the reception hall that projected over the water was now surrounded by lanterns on row barges. The sea provided a captivating, moving, dark background for these lights, as he noticed there was no light inside the building. He could have been on a raft afloat on a sea ablaze with innocent fire. He gazed back at the Grand Vizier, awed by the man's artistic talent.

At the end of the party, the Ambassador was presented with a kaftan lined with Croatian sable, a kaftan like a silken flower garden with tulips, hyacinths and roses encircling golden cypresses. The material was the colour of the sun, that inimitable pink that spreads as the sun begins to sink below the horizon. The dragoman explained that this colour was called *gülgûnî* in Ottoman: 'roseate'.

The Austrian Ambassador's commission had been to convey his Emperor's good wishes. He returned, bearing the reciprocal goodwill of the Sultan but also much more: impressions of a fairy-tale world that defied his imaginative powers.

Circumcision Festival

'None has ever seen such a festival
Never has there been such merriment'

'As per your orders, My Lord, men have been despatched hither and thither to collect supplies: 10,000 wooden dining trays from İzmit, 1,000 ducks, 8,000 chickens, 2,000 turkeys, 3,000 spring chickens and 2,000 pigeons have been obtained from Mount Tekfur, İnecik and Hüdavendigâr districts.'

'Well done, Halil Efendi. Your efforts will not remain unrewarded! Know you, too, that this festival merits the finest, the grandest in both music and dance.'

'My Fortunate Pasha, the Chief Singer Hook-Nose Hasan Çelebi has already gathered eighty singers and musicians, who will begin imminently. Countless gipsy dancers have been presented with gold-thread frocks, and acrobats have hailed in from all corners.'

'Take special care to ensure public order during the festival, Halil Efendi!'

'Public order officers are trained and ready: in the event of any disturbance, troops dressed up as clownish shepherds will make funny faces to lighten the mood. They will also douse the perpetrators with water they carry in bags. Please rest assured, My Lord, that any brawl that might erupt could thus be placated sweetly, without causing injury to the spectators.'

September 1720 would be one of the most joyous, most vibrant months ever to be recorded in Konstantiniyye's history.

Kitchen steward Halil Efendi, he of the far-reaching reputation for honesty and capability, had been entrusted with the arrangements for the circumcision festival for the Sultan's four sons: Süleyman, ten, Mehmed and Mustafa, both three, and Bayezid, two years old. And here he was, reporting back to the Grand Vizier, whose express wish it was to be kept apprised of every single step, that the festival might be a success.

İbrahim Pasha's own son, the Emperor's grandson, would also be circumcised alongside the crown princes; this honour – that no vizier had achieved to date – had created such a sensation! The son of the Commander-in-Chief of the Janissaries would also join the royal boys. The occasion merited the charitable act of circumcising 5,000 poor boys. The chief surgeon supervised the 150 surgeons commissioned for this purpose.

The noblemen, viziers and governors of the empire all considered in great detail what gift they could present to properly express their gratitude at the blessings they had received from the August State as soon as their invitations arrived. True, Sultan Ahmed had shown generosity in deleting the customary circumcision gift list, leaving the quantity, value and type of present to the guests' taste and purse. Yet this might prove to be more of a challenge. What presents would best suit these dukes and generals, to leave everyone else reeling with astonishment at these displays of loyalty to their benefactor, yet not reveal the extent of their wealth perilously?

★ ★ ★

The festival would take place in Okmeydanı and the Golden Horn. Every single profession would participate in the guilds' procession, displaying their finest wares or skills before the Emperor and the guests, and presenting their gifts. Breathtaking displays of acrobats, wrestlers and dancers, accompanied by skilful musicians, all manner of fireworks and generous amounts of food and drink would all increase the opulence of the festival.

The diplomatic corps were also invited, along with the residents of the city: the splendour of the celebrations were partly planned to actually celebrate the auspicious event and partly as a manifestation of the solidity of the Ottoman State – for its own subjects – and as a show of force for the representatives of foreign nations attending.

Ten sheep were sacrificed as the Emperor's tent was being erected in Okmeydanı, and seven for the Grand Vizier's. İbrahim Pasha's extravagance continued to amaze all.

Court officials, kitchen workers, surgeons and guests all were allocated their own sky-blue tents. Small, brown tents would serve as toilets. The loge erected for the Emperor was modelled on the Justice Tower. Thirty cannons had also been placed on the square to greet the arrival of the morning, the afternoon and the Emperor. It was as if the entire imperial court had been transplanted to this site.

★   ★   ★

Sultan Ahmed looked well pleased with his life as he sat on the high-backed gold throne placed under the tent's gold silk baldachin. The diamond aigrette that resembled a large tulip bud on his turban could have captured the entire light of the day. His Grand Vizier stood to one side and his princes to the other. The boys were all dressed in fur-lined silver kaftans with gold clasps. The palace officials lined up according to rank behind the Emperor, like his shadow, to protect him as well as carry out his slightest wish immediately.

Those presented to the Emperor walked in a single line over the tulip-patterned carpet on the ground, between the palace officials, and kissed the skirt of his robes. This particular ceremony preceded the displays. No one was in a hurry; extraordinary times were meant to be savoured.

The statesmen paid their respects to the Emperor and retired to their tents to relax with coffee and sweets. A surprise feast awaited the janissaries in addition to their twice-weekly meals served by the imperial kitchens: 200 rams and 300 sheep were roasted, with live pigeons hidden within their bellies, and followed by 4,500 trays of *pilav* and saffron pudding. Poet Vehbî likened the troops flocking to the food to a partridge making for the canary. The first few morsels of meat plucked from the roasts liberated the birds, which flew off in a flutter, delighting and astonishing the crowds.

İbrahim Pasha left the Emperor and went into his own tent, bidding his festival steward to come to his side.

'Our August Emperor has commanded a game of foot *cirit*. Call my officials on stand-by. They've not waited in vain for Our Lord's pleasure!'

'Your word is my command, My Noble Grand Vizier!'

'And bid the band strike the big drums, Halil Efendi! Let there be nothing lacking!'

'As you wish. May our benefactor enjoy the day!'

And finally the fun began. The first show, predictably, was the foot *cirit*, the Emperor's favourite – everyone knew how frequently he asked for *cirit* matches. The lads started, urged on by the beating of the drums and tamburines and the stentorian yells of the gatekeepers, and sticks began flying in the air. The players were trained by İbrahim Pasha's men. The cut-throat rivalry on display fanned the flames of support in all present, the Emperor and the crowd alike. The match became so heated in such a short time, with both teams setting upon one another with such vigour that the gatekeepers had to intervene. The Okras were on the verge of defeating the Cabbages, but spilling blood at these celebrations would have been unseemly. As a rule, these matches witnessed little quarter given, but an inexhaustible degree of aggression occasionally ran the risk of taking the game beyond the boundaries of sport.

Clowns dressed up as Persians softened the atmosphere next. They battered one another with huge maces made out of coloured paper and regaled the crowds as they feigned injury, making silly faces as they did so. At the same time, a life-size ostrich puppet was pulled before the Emperor, the giant bird's wings flapping. Alluring puppet dancers played the tamburine and shimmied as their cart passed before the Emperor, a veritable tribute to the puppet master's skill. The power of the imagination was finally allowed to run riot.

Now 'cavaliers' wearing models of horses below their waists rode onto the field, making a great show of heroically attacking a castle on wheels. The castle sustained a hit and blazed into an immense firework, sparking and exploding. The band continued to ring heavens and earth with their loud music. The crowds were beginning to get into the spirit.

Along came death-defying acrobats, a gift from the Governor of Egypt: fully meriting their title, they grabbed everyone's attention. One placed the iron spike at the bottom of a lit torch between his eyebrows, leaping to the right and left as he then spun the torch; another poured himself through – like water! – in a series of hoops of ever-decreasing diameters. This last acrobat finished his act by slipping through a narrow hoop made of swords pointing inwards, again, like a thread going through a needle.

The waiting staff had begun to lay out the supper, placing red silk cloths over the gleaming silver trays. Leading Ottoman statesmen were being entertained in the Grand Vizier's tent.

At the end of the first day of the festival, the Emperor gave leave for present giving – the part of the festival so many anticipated the most. The Grand Vizier's offering to his benefactor took the place of honour, as expected. Poet Vehbî would later describe just one of the great man's presents, the diamond in the centre of a sash of rubies and emeralds: 'clearer than the double-flowered rose bearing a dew drop and brighter than the crystal ball of the moon that is the chandelier of the heavenly firmament'. The Grand Vizier lined up more before Sultan Ahmed: showy jewels, Chinese porcelain, trunks adorned with gemstones, 300 phials of scent, clocks, heavy gold-thread fabrics, matchless fox, sable, lynx and ermine furs, silver-plated rifles and thoroughbred horses bedecked in jewelled harnesses. To the princes and their mothers he gave priceless Korans, books, clocks, fabrics and steeds.

The governors and viziers also presented their gifts as proofs of their loyalty to their master: rare books, jewelled items, fabrics and furs. The Emperor expressed his satisfaction with them all, to their communal gratitude, and then the gifts were laid out on the display stands before the big tent.

★   ★   ★

Prince Süleyman couldn't take his eyes off the tightrope walker. The Egyptian acrobat had lashed three swords to each leg. The swords passed between one another with every step, the clearance between them negligible. On his feet were high-heeled wooden sandals, not soft-soled slip-ons as one might expect. Süleyman pointed to the acrobat, gently pulling at the sleeve of his younger brother Mustafa, who clapped, delighted. A crown prince was rarely allowed to act like an ordinary child, but his own circumcision festival might just be the exception.

The boys normally watched these breathtaking displays alongside their father, their backs protected by the army of servants and guards. They might never be as free, and as joyful, for the rest of their lives. Sultan Ahmed kept glancing at his sons from time to time, quietly delighting in their joy.

Once night descended, it was time for fireworks. Each successive night's display – each with a different theme – outshone the previous: Catherine's Wheels that split the darkness of the night with golden sparks, colourful sailboats that abruptly exploded into a thousand pieces and ascended to the heavens, fountains spraying silver waters and emerald-hued fans that opened up in the firmament. It was difficult to believe these were only fireworks, so convincing they appeared. Each time the fireworks flared up, the spectators regretted their destruction. Yells of admiration mixed with the music, the festive atmosphere now fully established.

Conspicuous amongst the spectators were veiled women in large numbers, who had been granted leave to watch the festivities alongside the men before the Emperor, that all his subjects may enjoy the fun. The women had enjoyed the *cirit* game the most, that bizarre match between men who nearly tore one another apart. Who knew when they might ever approach such a public display again?

The Strongmen
Festivities ever, astonishing festivities

'Bid a mug be placed atop that tall pole, Vizier mine; have it filled with silver coins. Let us see which daredevil will take it up there and which can bring it down! Let us test their skill this way, that they may display their best!'

'Your wish is my command, My Noble Sovereign.'

İbrahim Pasha asked for a silver mug and had it filled with silver coins worth 130 kuruş. Now all he needed was a man who could scale this pole standing in the middle of the field, with neither a tree nor tent nearby. No one risked climbing up this high pole devoid of a single handhold. Eventually someone thought to build a scaffold so that the Sultan's wish may be executed, and the shipyard slaves were fetched for the construction. Captured at various campaigns, these were men sentenced to row on the galleons. They moved slowly, their legs in chains and necks in irons tied to one another. Suddenly, one of the slaves turned to the dragoman accompanying them and spoke in excited tones. The dragoman, having sought and obtained permission to speak to the Grand Vizier, quickly conveyed the man's proposal: there was little need for a scaffold; the slave could ascend unaided, and would carry out the task. In return he asked for his freedom. The Grand Vizier accepted immediately and even prepared the manumission papers there and then, to encourage the man further. The shackles removed without delay, he lashed himself to the pole with one of the mohair bands at his waist, and the other band he flung as high as he could on the pole, making a loop whose ends he clung to. The entire arena held its breath watching the young man. He hoisted himself as high as he could, and then re-looped the second band higher still. When he reached the top, he dangled a slim rope down, to which he asked the mug be tied; he drew it up, reverently kissed the silver vessel symbolising his freedom first, then, after placing it securely atop the pole, he climbed down as easily as he had climbed up. To the people on the ground, the cup now resembled a turtledove atop a cypress. Now a multitude of young men would struggle to get their hands on the mug and its contents, and provide much diversion for the crowd.

İbrahim Pasha kept his word and set free the slave who had so deftly carried out the Emperor's request. He also gave the man a handful of gold coins. The former slave in turn, grateful for the new lease of life, recited the credo and converted to Islam then and there. His reward was promotion to Captain and the command of his own galleon; he proceeded to the circumcision tent to fulfil this pillar of faith. The spectators had just witnessed a fairy tale with a happy ending.

* * *

'This firework you will now observe, My Sultan, is nam'd the 'Mausoleum of Aurangzeb'; in fact, it is a barbican filled with 1,200 fireworks.'

'Was this the idea of the festival steward, Vizier mine?'

'That is so, My Noble Sovereign; were this to please you and provide agreeable diversion, with your kind permission your servant would reward the man.'

Sultan Ahmed watched the fireworks display from his loge resembling the Justice Tower with its pointed tent.

Fireworks flared up like cannons being fired from the battlements of the massive model. The incredible sight concluded with the crane puppet nesting atop the spire sneezing fire from its beak. The firework next to it was in the shape of a seven-headed dragon. This contraption moved with the flow of air, spewing out scarlet sparks 'like a demon out of hell' for one hour. Poet Vehbî would later note that all this had 'regaled the dead with laughter and healed the cripple.'

★ ★ ★

The Emperor had moved temporarily to the Aynalıkavak Palace during the Golden Horn–side shows. This was where he spent the night once the day's entertainment was done. He was sitting in the reception hall bay projecting over the water. The soft cushions on the sofa below the wide windows provided ample room for the Emperor and his sons. A magnificent tent had been erected in the garden for İbrahim Pasha. Slow-moving rafts on the water provided the stage for the displays.

A two-storey structure topped a broad raft. The musicians on the lower level struck up a lively tune. Right before them were male dancers dressed like women, undulating their entire bodies and sliding their heads, flicking their pleated skirts. But most of the spectators were focussed on the top level: fireworks were flying off into the air, now making a golden cypress, now stars, now Catherine's Wheels. The giant puppet finally caught fire: first its streaming beard, then the sparks flew at his garments and the mace in his hand and he suddenly turned into a multi-coloured fireball, making the children scream with delight mixed with fear. The Emperor joined in his children's joy, laughing out loud. The pages standing before them turned to one another and smiled: conditioned to hold their master's happiness truly dearer to their hearts than their own, they were more attuned to his spirit than their own. They were genuinely grateful to the people who so delighted their master.

A great wheel, swings and a merry-go-round were set up on rafts made all the more appealing by gigantic puppets the following evening. But denied the permission to participate in this colourful ride on the water, the little princes sulked.

★ ★ ★

Hacı Şahin the Strongman walked into the centre of the square and lay on his back.

The festival was in full swing. The Emperor, the princes, the court, the viziers and the people of Konstantiniyye shuttled back and forth between Okmeydanı and the Golden Horn, not that anyone complained. Fun and energy had overtaken the entire city and suspended troubles.

A heavy-set donkey was brought to the square. The strongman hugged the donkey, waited for his assistant to tie the animal securely with ropes and man and beast went through a small hoop held upright, like a thread through the eye of a needle. The next act came immediately and his ties were loosened: Hacı Şahin leapt nimbly onto the shoulders of his assistant, then leant down and picked up an urn filled with water, taller than himself, and placing this urn atop his head, he straightened up. He looked as relaxed as if he were taking a walk in the garden as the two men progressed around the square, Hacı Şahin's arms akimbo. But the most thrilling of all his acts was the one where he bore two drummers drumming on a single pole, balancing this weight on one shoulder as he wandered around the square. There was no doubt that he would be well rewarded after this show.

Next in line was the artillery show. A frightening model elephant, covered in colourful embroidered cloths, tugging a spinning castle of two storeys, and gunfire emanating from within! Three model horses and troops firing back at the castle completed this act. The dwarfs clowning about to entertain the Emperor stopped to watch. Who knows? Perhaps they were imagining themselves as those brave fellows in the artillery.

Standing close to his Emperor, Levnî constantly visualised how he would depict these scenes, each and every one, as he watched this bizarre display. Rather than re-create an exact representation, he would in all likelihood paint scenes that appealed to all the senses, that conveyed something of the colours and movement that he could almost smell and taste. He was getting impatient to experience in paints the smoke greys emanating from the field guns and rifles in all their variety of hues, the whites and the pale and deep blues of the skies and the clouds, the folds of the yellow and coral cloths on the back of the gigantic elephant. He was getting impatient to endow the heads and bodies turning this way and that with new life on paper.

★   ★   ★

Something new was in the offing before Aynalıkavak Palace. A pair of ropes stretched between the tall plane tree on the embankment and two galleons on the water had intrigued all who were watching, not least the Emperor himself. Countless row barges, filled to the gunwales with spectators, had come as close as they could. European diplomats invited to attend the festival from the beginning till the end were also present in a row barge. Even Grand Vizier İbrahim Pasha himself was getting ready to watch at the bow of a large vessel moored at the shore.

Breaths were held – it was so still that the movement of the fishes in the deep blue waters were nearly discernible. The musicians in the two skiffs moored below the ropes struck up an upbeat tempo at a sign from the maestro. Suddenly a horse coach carrying a veiled woman, fan in hand – all puppets and models – emerged from under the furled sails on one of the galleons. The coach was commanded remotely! The wheels slid true on the ropes, and the puppet horse moved with a perfect gait, truly miraculous! The coach moved slowly and boarded the second galleon. The director and the engineer had given a good account of themselves, achieving the impossible. The spectators, in perfect silence until that moment, broke into cheers of appreciation. What would the Emperor say?

The night's festivities continued on the theme of equilibrium. Small, round platforms, weighed down with poles for balance, were fixed to other ropes stretched similarly. Male dancers with angelic faces had been awaiting their turn. As soon as the coach boarded the galleon, the music changed, and the terpsichoreans began to dance to the rhythm of their finger cymbals. When the tightrope walkers concluded their acts, the dancers unlashed themselves from the poles, swan dived into the water and so proved their proficiency in swimming too.

★   ★   ★

Professional guilds were an essential part of the festival. Every single guild in Konstantiniyye paraded before the Emperor, and this colourful river ran for days and days. Tent-makers, cobblers and fine shoemakers walked together; the grocers and greengrocers passed in one group, the coppersmiths, jewellers and tailors made up their own; candle-makers with barbers, and quilters with cap and skullcap makers – each guild passed by, proudly bearing symbols of their work or samples of their products on coaches or palanquins, accompanied by actors, clowns, dancers and fireworks. At the conclusion of the parade, they presented their own gifts, each one more impressive than the previous. This was an unnamed, yet merciless contest. Which would outshine the rest: the shoemakers' finest kid-leather boots (two pairs adorned with pearls and emeralds, worthy of the Emperor's feet) or the sheen of the lightweight Circassian slippers, embroidered with gold thread and pearls? The silver candlesticks, the gilt trays, the towels embroidered with gold thread, or the silver-thread fabrics?

The resplendence of the jewellers' palanquin would cause talk for days after the festival. The large gemstone aigrettes bearing plumes of flamingo feathers hanging from the sides of the palanquin had dazzled everyone present, as poet Vehbî wrote: 'Like the drops of the Pleiades, like pearls, the sun and the moon.'

The grocers and greengrocers made up a game of firing Sinop apples from cannons and medlars from rifles, amusing the sovereign hugely and so making all the other guilds jealous. In any case, the greengrocers' canopied litter was a visual feast in its own right: all types of fresh fruit, their colours ranging from yellow to pink, blood-red tulips and pink carnations in vases set between the fruit, bright yellow quinces hanging from the sides and the immense watermelon. Obtaining all these fruits fresh at this time of year, in late September, was a veritable feat.

The parade of the cattle-dealers, shepherds and butchers was something else again: the shepherds led, wearing their mohair capes and carrying their long pipes, the biggest rams of their herds, horns gilded, the huge sheepdog pacing at their side baring its fangs. The butchers followed, freshly slaughtered and neatly skinned carcasses hanging at the sides of their cart, not the most appetising of images, but that was the only skill they could display; but the gigantic puppet drawn by well-fed oxen that followed was funny, its comical face female on one side and male on the other. The travelling kebab cook had set up a stall in the middle of the square and the mouth-watering smell of barbecued meat on skewers spread forth. This particular procession concluded with the tanners, their finest cured and dyed leathers on show, the last link of this professional group.

Then came a very refined trade – the candle-makers. The apprentices walked, bearing slender gilded tapers as tall as themselves that burnt with golden fire, whilst their master presented a massive, decorated and heavy silver candelabra bearing a scented candle to a palace official. But all eyes had turned to the barber's coach that followed; a small barbershop had been set up within, flower-embroidered flannels hanging from the sides. A handsome young barber, rosy of cheek and wearing a pink outfit, was washing the head of his customer with unhurried expertise, drawing water from a sack that hung down from the canopy, the water pouring into the basin held steady by the customer as the flannels hanging from the sides waved gently. This was such a natural-looking scene that one could be forgiven for thinking he had opened the door of a real barbershop and gazed inside.

*　*　*

The people who enjoyed the festival most, without missing a single act, were the poor children circumcised as part of the celebrations. All wore the fine robes and red caps donated by the palace. As they walked around in a herd, the elder boys knew this would be their finest hour, since in all their lives never would they enjoy such attention again. The younger boys, on the other hand, were dizzy with the entertainment and a surplus of sweets.

Games
Cut-throat rivalry

First came the crack, and almost immediately the red clay urn blew up into a thousand pieces, then the next and the next – İbrahim Pasha's rifle didn't stop until all the urns lined up had been smashed. Spectators braving the rain shouted heartily. The Grand Vizier did have a formidable reputation as a marksman. The statesman continued, proud now, his servants loading the rifles tiring long before he did.

The day's programme had begun in defiance of the black clouds gathering in the skies, but once autumn's downpours took hold, the show had to be suspended for the day. The Emperor had retired to Aynalıkavak Palace. But İbrahim Pasha had no wish to stop the fun. He had too much energy to stand still. In any case, this was an opportunity to demonstrate his skill in marksmanship using this complicated contraption called a rifle, to such extent that the chronicler would describe the Grand Vizier's proficiency at some length, mentioning 30 as the number of urns thus shattered, yet the artist never depicted these scenes for some reason. But wasn't target practice in the pouring rain a kind of defiance anyway, when one could have been relaxing in the tent instead, enjoying the soothing harmony of the music and the undulations of the dancers? It was a challenge issued to life, to both friend and foe.

That Sultan Ahmed was equally fond of firearms, just like his father Mehmed the Hunter, was well known, to the extent that the younger Emperor's marksmanship merited a plaque at the range in the early years of his reign. But the Emperor favoured *cirit*, horse racing and *matrak*, a version of foot *cirit* in which a large number of combatants tried to best one another's hitting.

*   *   *

The *matrak* players entered the square from two sides, and all the other shows came to an end. The big drums of the *mehter* band overwhelmed all other sounds – deep, resonant, like the accelerated beating of a heart. The pipes and cymbals had dimmed to merely supporting that martial rhythm. These big bruisers first greeted the Emperor, then their opponents, before lining up in two ranks facing each other to wait for the starting signal. Each and every man of them was well muscled, taut like coiled springs, their biceps straining the fabric of their sleeves, baggy trousers on their legs and comfortable shoes on their feet. They stood firm, sizing up their opponents surreptitiously whilst feigning disinterest. This was an opportunity for which they had all been training for many a year, and this was the grand occasion when they could give it their best.

The *matrak*, a long, polished club made out of boxwood, could become a deadly weapon in the hand of an expert player. If it hit the target, which was the head, and hit with savage force, blood was sure to flow. Avoiding being hit was equally crucial.

Cynical moves began almost as soon as the match did. Any faulty move, such as hitting below the shoulders, resulted in the offender being eliminated immediately. A player who felled an opponent, having hit him on the head ruthlessly, suddenly found himself suffering a similar fate. The low cracks heard when club met club was accompanied by the music. Some clubs broke. One player, who was swinging his club above his head like a mace, was caught unawares and lost his advantage, falling to the ground. The game proceeded along these lines. The Emperor, the pages, the viziers and the common folk – everyone was captivated by the merciless rhythm of the game. When it came to an end, the players raised their hands up in prayer, thankful for having given a good account of themselves. The winner was announced to cheers and boos; clearly, not everyone was delighted with the outcome. Those who were delighted were the players themselves: the Emperor had despatched purses filled with coins, purses adequately heavy.

★ ★ ★

'When are we going to watch a polo match, Grand Vizier mine, I am desirous to know?'

'Your wish is my command, My Noble Sovereign. Your servant will send word to the festival steward forthwith that he may prepare the field for the morrow!'

The steward despatched the water-bearers; the beaten earth surface of the square was swept and sprinkled liberally with water in preparation for a polo match. The arena for expert horsemen was ready. The mallets – slender sticks with curved heads – and the boxwood ball were gilded and polished. The goals were set up: stone columns embedded in the earth, five metres apart, the gap measured painstakingly. The steward bade the water-bearers shake the posts as hard as they could and breathed a sigh of relief when none moved an inch; sunk quite securely, no impact would dislodge these posts. The following morning would open with a great polo match, and the Emperor won't be able to sit still.

This game was called 'bolo' in south China, though everyone knew it was first played in the land of the Persians. Was it the expert horsemanship required that made Turks take this game to heart so? It was rumoured that the game had been played 2,000 years hence in the land of the Turan king and that the Byzantines and the Arabs played their versions in the past. One of the favourite books of Sultan Ahmed depicted a dazzling polo scene. Each time the Emperor sat down to flick through the pages of this book, his companion by his side, the

16th-century book would open up to this particular section. The accompanying legend was equally enchanting: the 8th-century Muslim commander had captured the jewelled ball of the Alexandrian nobility using nothing but the sleeve of his robe and so rose to the position of Governor of Egypt.

Expert horsemen entered the square in a slow gait and bowed before the sovereign. These finest riders in the land of the Ottomans were monuments to grace, half in the greens of the Cabbages and half in the red of the Okras. Each and every man feigned disdainful ignorance of his superiority and yet was so obviously conscious of said superiority. And it wasn't just their inimitably upright seats; their distinction manifested itself in how naturally they held the reins, man and animal a single unit. Not everyone could become an expert horseman; the training was incredibly demanding. The horses, finest thoroughbreds each, were equally haughty and exceedingly well-trained – ready to do their riders' every bidding.

The *mehter* band struck up and the music rang from the earth to the skies. Well accustomed to these passionate melodies, the steeds barely stood still. Their riders were little different, but they had to comply with the rules, for this was what they had been taught. So, they checked their impatience, reined in their steeds and waited for the starting signal. The winds suddenly overpowered the drums and the cymbals; the pipes signalling a rider from each team to come forward and reach for the gilded ball in the centre. The objective was to hook the ball with their curved mallets and send it into the opponents' goal. The way the mallets clashed, they could easily have been the players' souls! The opening gambit was followed by the other riders entering the game, reaching for the ball, their horses extensions of their bodies. The ball was sent spinning this way and that, flashing between the legs of the galloping horses and the mallets that smashed against one another at great speed. Each time the ball passed between the posts was a goal; the Emperor fidgeted, the crowds waved and the *mehter* band continued to strike as impressively as at the beginning.

The match ended with the Okras triumphant. The Cabbages had played equally well, but the winners had the run of luck this time. The winners were rewarded, and the losers not forgotten either. İbrahim Pasha was well satisfied with the outcome; his team lost to the Emperor's, so his benefactor would be greatly pleased.

The Grand Vizier commanded his festival steward to organise horse racing within a few days. The magnificent horse race held for the circumcisions of Sultan Ahmed and his elder brother Mustafa in the Edirne Palace still occupied the memories of some, as did the fabulous gifts generously handed to the victors by their father Mehmed the Hunter. İbrahim Pasha was determined to outshine their predecessor's bounty in this festival.

The Grand Vizier personally selected the racehorses; this was not a job to be delegated. Sixty-six made the grade, each more imposing than the others, each speedier than the Prophet's holy steed. Even the Emperor himself was unable to conceal his admiring sighs at seeing these elegant, slender-limbed horses and their expert riders in ranks of six. They raced, neck to neck, rein to rein, in six lanes, as if flying; each race was won on a nose alone. The final race was breathtaking, as were the winner's prizes.

Sultan Ahmed also enjoyed wrestling, again, to the music of the *mehter* band. Whether he identified with the wrestlers, no one knew, yet Levnî had often noticed how the sovereign gritted his teeth, opened his hands into claws, grabbing the cushion below him or the one at his back when the match got going. The stronger proving his superiority and crushing his opponent must have awakened indescribable emotions in the spectators, an inimitable satisfaction. Rigid rules dampened the excitement of the moment at some times and offered deliverance at others; these rules were there to check man's infinite capacity for blind violence.

The Emperor was a dedicated spectator, one who never withheld praise well merited. Any wrestler who quickly, deftly and indisputably pinned his opponent down knew a great prize awaited him that was generous enough to secure his future for some time to come, especially at a festival such as this one. The wrestlers, encouraged by the music, provided some of the most unforgettable scenes in the entire festival.

The festival's conclusion was even more resplendent than its opening. The tents in Okmeydanı had already been dismantled by the time the court marched back to the palace. The paper trees with confectionery gardens and animals made in the princes' honour paraded in a grand procession through the city were a sight that gladdened the eyes and made the mouth water.

The paper-and-wax palm trees that were an indispensable part of any Ottoman festival required some engineering: some buildings on the route back to the palace had been subjected to compulsory purchase – and their oriels demolished – to make room for these immense and colourful structures tugged by thick ropes to travel through the narrow streets. The confectionery gardens were very heavy; only strapping shipyard lads could carry them on trays. These impressive gardens had everything, and it all was made of sugar: gazebos in the centre, a fountain and sprays, all surrounded by orange, quince and pear trees, cypresses and flowers. The soil in the garden was of musky ground sugar, the pebbles made of sugared almonds in a myriad of colours. Huge trays carried on the heads of shipyard workers displayed sugar animals: game birds, pheasants, parrots and lovebirds; peacocks, a pair of turtledoves, a cockerel, a ram, a lion, a leopard and a pair of deer – each one so intricately detailed that they could have been real, able to leap or take wing any moment. Would the princes really bring themselves to ruin these masterpieces merely for a sweet tooth?

Levnî and Seyid Vehbî and Ahmed

'Woe is you, you smarty, if you missed this festival!
Lend an ear to my account of the moment'

Levnî laid his brush down, pulled back and cast a critical eye
over the illustration he had been touching up. Yes, this was
just what he had wanted – a living picture. The people within
looked as if they would force their way out of the frame. The
opium addicts were flinging themselves hither and thither,
desperate and clumsy; the brown of the bearskin dominated
whilst the garments of the addicts resembled so many
coloured stains on the yellowish background of the soil. He
had depicted the opium addicts flinching from the bears and
snakes let loose upon them.

These souls called 'wretches with lives in their pockets' had
been lured with the promise of opium and coffee to entertain
the crowds. Terrified as they already were by the fireworks,
once people started flinging coins at them they lost all control.
This was a cruel trap well beyond the domain of playful
teasing. Their demented scampering as they tried to save their
lives regaled the crowd to uninhibited laughter; their torment
had become part of the festival fun. Some had tripped and
fallen down, some bent double and others were caught in the
huge paws of the bears or struggling with the snakes. The
officials sauntered between them, ramrod-straight, wielding
sticks.

The artist had worked on the facial expressions in the
picture one by one: terror, shock, fury, sulking, cruelty,

pleasure and apathy. Every individual displayed a distinct emotion. The charity circumcision boys were amongst the spectators, a surgeon supervising them. They were holding hands tightly, just the way they had been told to; the one at the front was holding the hand of the janissary in charge of public order. The boys were dressed in their distinctive outfits of red caps and long, colourful robes, their faces so innocent. In Levnî's depiction, they were not watching the bizarre, intimidating scene, eyes wide open; that would have been too predictable. The artist knew that was the moment the charity boys would be taken to the circumcision tent and so apprehension dominated their faces, as did anticipation – for here they were, on the verge of yet another step towards manhood in the eyes of society. The flailing buffoons were not their concern just then.

Flocks of birds flew in the skies dotted with white clouds, far in the distance. Why had the artist included these creatures? Was his intention to indicate the variety of events that take place on this earth?

Letting bears loose upon opium addicts and then finding entertainment value in watching how the wretches scuttled away or even got caught and mauled – and all this at a circumcision festival – was a testimony to the prevailing attitude towards nature's own cruelty. Few at the time would have found this uncommonly strange. Levnî's illustration re-created this scene in all its vibrancy. Here was a manifestation of contradictions; how the mighty proved his own power by oppressing the weak, and yet failed to see his own frailty!

Similarly enthralling were the tumblers eliciting loud cheers from the crowd. But would they not create even more attention if one stumbled and fell? The Turkish word for acrobat is *cambaz*, from *can*, 'life', and *baz*, 'wielder' – so, one who takes his own life into his hands. They appeared well aware of the peril, and every move they made was a challenge issued not only to the laws of physics but also to the spectators. Levnî, for his part, had sought to indicate this defiance in every frame, the reactions of individuals in that legendary kaleidoscope, in the midst of the splendour of the celebrations. He derived immense pleasure, each drop of paint a source of gratification, for the end result must be totally different from all that had preceded it.

The artist had not kept a chronological order; that would have been out of character. What he had to do first was capture on paper the fusion of what remained in the memory and what the imagination embellished. He had to express his emotions as he had observed the events as sincerely as possible. He had grown impatient to draw the scenes that had thrilled him personally: the audience with the viziers and clerics, for example – how he toiled to render this ceremony extraordinary! The festival book would be cleaned up by the calligraphers in any case, the illustrations then inserted in the correct order before binding carefully. So, the fireworks wouldn't take precedence over the clowns. Levnî had enjoyed working on the crowd scenes, making sure some figures bled off the page, just like he had observed in the paintings of master Vanmour, as if the movement continued beyond the confines of the page.

* * *

Levnî had stayed close to the Emperor throughout the festival, etching every moment into his memory; immortalising the festival was going to be his duty, his mirror on the events. He knew from the start that he and he alone would be commissioned to illustrate the festival; anything else would have been unthinkable. The honour of writing the chronicles of the celebrations fell to Seyid Hüseyin Vehbî, a poet much in the Grand Vizier's favour, so naming the resulting volume *Sûrname-i Vehbî*, 'Vehbî's Account of the Festival'.

Vehbî did refer to himself and his own experiences during the celebrations on a number of occasions in the 175-page book; yet he never once mentioned the illustrator. Well, Vehbî may have held the pen, but Levnî held the brush. People looking back on this fabulous festival hundreds of years later as they flicked the pages of the book came across not Vehbî's portrait, but Levnî's, riding his horse in a crowded scene, gazing into the distance, lost in thought. The artist had signed his name on only two frames out of the total of 137: once at the start of the festival, at the foot of his beloved Emperor sitting on his throne, holding an audience with the viziers and scientists, and once at the end of the festival, on the scene depicting the return to the palace of the Enderun officials, that interminable procession. This second signature was placed below the hoof of one of the horses. None of this was arbitrary: these signatures were placed deliberately, subtly symbolising loyalty and pride.

Levnî had drawn people from all walks of life, savouring the joy, exuberance and tolerance of people who were enjoying a break from the monotony of everyday life; his art brought back to life the atmosphere of those heady days. The action moved from right to left in an unbroken line; the artist zoomed out at times to show more people and zoomed into great detail at other times. Occasionally everything stood still, showing the viewer a crucial moment, and then speeded up again; but continuity never faltered.

People of every type – that was what Levnî focused on the most: the Grand Vizier, his splendour outshining everyone else; palace pages gossiping; janissaries keeping an eye on things; viziers anxious to please; cheerful water-bearers dousing troublemakers in the crowd; strongmen expecting a hefty tip; frowning guards; acrobats completely engrossed in their act; women relishing these crumbs of liberty, yet chattering all the while; pale-faced princes in their finery, with their affectionate footmen; European diplomats trying to suppress their astonishment; and dancers giving it their best. And again, in nearly every frame, the Emperor in his finest, most enviable robes in the softest colours of nature: the colours of lightning and ice, diamonds and roses, chickpeas and cinnamon, saffron and walnut, pistachios and lemons, and coral and lilac. Even the face of each animal was unique; every creature the artist's eyes had captured stood apart. Some carried on with their own concerns, completely absorbed in that moment that goes on forever, oblivious to the viewer flicking through the pages; others hold the viewer's gaze undaunted, forging an inimitable connection, ignoring his surprise. There was one singular feature, however, whose secret none could decipher, known to the artist alone: the face of Aşık Ömer, the poet, showed up in every crowd scene, either on a spectator's head or on one of the artisans.

One of Levnî's favourite characters was the conjurer. Overturned cups and small balls his tools to display his sleight-of-hand skills, he delighted his audience as he deceived their eyes; this illustration is so lifelike that viewers couldn't take their eyes off it. He had a pointed, sparse beard and upturned moustache below a huge nose. He had rolled his sleeves up and loosened his cummerbund, which was what allowed his hands to move so fast. A tamburine player accompanied him, more to distract the audience's attention than anything else, but no one paid him much heed. The conjurer's conical cap was spangled with countless symbols; the tinkling of the tiny bells at the tip of the cap, as he moved his head, was almost audible to the viewer.

★   ★   ★

Lunacy... Lunacy and the ecstasy presented by the muse combined now and then. It was at those times that Levnî found unprecedented harmony in juxtaposing colours, colours that flew this way and that in hard-to-believe combinations, the illuminator's energy rising as he painted, the fervour manifested in every corner of the picture. That's what happened in the last miniature of the *Sûrname*: the dazzling scene where his beloved Emperor scattered gold coins before the gilt-vaulted Breakfast Gazebo. The four princes – Süleyman, Mehmed, Mustafa and Bayezid – had finally been circumcised at the conclusion of the festival and were lying in their beds set up at the Baghdad Pavilion. The Chief Surgeon was standing by the princes and clearly reassuring İbrahim Pasha that all was well. The beds were covered in the finest cloths available, each in a different colour and pattern, possibly even in no known pattern, existing only in the artist's imagination. Heavy drapes hung down on either side of the beds to protect the princes from the autumn cold, making the boys look tiny under the weight of all this fabric. Each bed's canopy had been decorated with a pair of aigrettes, pink flamingo feathers fanning out, diamonds and emeralds dazzling.

This was the only occasion when all four boys had been depicted together; Bayezid, only two years old, had not been able to attend the festival alongside the others, and now there he was, plunked in the middle of a massive bed, unable to understand what was going on, frightened and bewildered. The princes, sons of different mothers, lay coddled by the innocence of childhood under the decorated vault of the Baghdad Pavilion, knowing not what life had in store for them: power and happiness, or deprivation and hurt. Two were Mihrişah's sons, her place in the Emperor's heart unquestionably secure, and one was of Ümmügülsüm, not a particular favourite. The fourth boy had been sired with a little plump girl the Emperor had entertained only once; she merely happened to have been at the right time in her cycle. The boys all shared one purpose, however: the continuation of the dynasty.

Sultan Ahmed had told his dear Grand Vizier that 'twas the time of scattering. Levnî didn't place himself in the frame, but he clearly had witnessed this with his own eyes, possibly from the roof of Revan Pavilion, looking down at the pond-side patio. The picture draws the viewer in: the firearms officers and equerries flanking the Emperor as always, and those flanked by the servants in turn – all wearing their high, gold-embroidered caps, plaits hanging down on either side of their faces all the way to their chins, their robes in the softest of oranges, greens or yellows, all tied with gold-embroidered sashes. Sultan Ahmed had one hand in the pocket of his yellow robe, and gold coins were falling upon the ground from the other hand, which he held high as his walnut kaftan skirt flapped in the wind. He looked calm, as if carrying out an ordinary task, his outfit plain, wearing no jewellery, with the satisfaction of a job well concluded on his face, surrounded by his closest aides. There were too many coins to pick up – some might have even dropped into the bottom of the marble fish pond. Some of the servants were scrambling on the marble floor, greedily picking up coins. Others stood immovable, staring at their benefactor unblinkingly with their hands respectfully clasped before their abdomens, too dignified even to stare at their colleagues crawling on the floor.

The artist gave life to the fabulously bountiful autumn time in the bunches of grapes, in every shade of purple twinkling between the vine leaves pale and deep on the vine wrapped around the railings. Those shameless deepening pinks of the skies, just like the Chinese clouds in miniatures of yore, testify to Levnî's own name, 'multi-coloured': the pinks had settled upon the sheet at a time when the muse had entered his soul, quickening his lunacy. The birds flying in a V configuration before the clouds were the only connection the artist had with the real world in a scene where the sun will never set nor the colours ever fade. The eyes fix upon Levnî's Emperor standing in full glory, ramrod-straight, in the centre.

Levnî's illustrations were to be the last of a particular genre. There would never again be such magnificent books illustrated in so resplendent a manner, or such splendid festivals meriting dedicated chronicles – or, indeed, another emperor of such extravagant scenes. Over time pictures would desert books in favour of canvas.

* * *

Sultan Ahmed carefully picked up the heavy bound volume that was the *Sûrname*, his demeanour one of receiving a priceless jewel. He rewarded the writer and the illustrator with the most splendid of prizes, not forgetting the calligrapher, the binder or any of the art studio workers who had contributed.

This would become his favourite book. The Emperor inspected every single scene at every possible opportunity; it was like reliving those moments each time.

İbrahim Pasha too had ordered his own copy; he also wanted to preserve those precious moments in pictures. Yet he had selected one of Levnî's apprentices for the illustrations. Levnî refrained from commenting about this strange choice; he contented himself with remarking to his friend Yirmisekiz Çelebi that such a mammoth task would have taken up too much of his time. He even guided the artist working on the Grand Vizier's copy, but that's not to say he did not resent the decision İbrahim Pasha had taken without consultation. He resented it very much indeed.

★ ★ ★

The Emperor frequently bade Levnî come to his side and turned the pages in his company. Levnî relished those moments, as any artist would whose work is appreciated. Sultan Ahmed loved Levnî's wit, and since he knew the personages depicted very well he inspected the expressions on the faces of each man, smiling surreptitiously at some of the antics and laughing out loud at others. The scene showing the janissaries at the meal, for example, had amused him hugely, human nature being his particular interest: there was one greedy man, running at the *pilav* and saffron pudding, whose tall hat tumbled off his head whilst another, witnessing this ignominy, clutched his own as he too ran.

At times Sultan Ahmed questioned the artist on nearly every single line.

'What guided you to depict my library so, Levnî Çelebi? Know you not that the exterior is in the finest marble available?'

For some reason Levnî had chosen to illustrate the library clad in shiny Kütahya tiles in wheel patterns matching the steel blue of the domes in those fabulous final pages of the book. Yes, he did know the library was clad in plain marble, and yes, he had taken pains to illustrate everything as factually as possible, but perhaps in his imagination this library was much more colourful.

'Forgive my presumption, My Noble Sovereign, yet in my imagination I wished to depict that modest building in so decorated a fashion. Suffer it to remain if it pleases you.'

'So the most precious work in the library will for ever depict the library as different from reality!'

Noticing the Emperor's tolerant and even amused gaze, Levnî gave free rein to his imagination:

'Even as the ideas in our mind frequently overrun the capacity of our vocabulary, My Sultan, my brush similarly repudiates the accustomed rules of depiction!'

And so remained Levnî's colourful world in the depiction of the library, puzzling viewers for many years.

What impressed Sultan Ahmed most were the final two frames in the book.

'How well you have conveyed the affection in my gaze, companion mine! I am touched. This must originate from the composition of such a mature man as yourself!'

The Emperor was watching the return to the palace of his sons, a fabulous procession, before the boys would submit to the surgeon's scalpel. A silk-cushioned throne had been set up before the window on the first floor of the art studio on the Divanyolu. Sultan Ahmed had chosen to observe his sons – the raisons d'être of this festival, the apples of his eyes – from the art studio, accompanied by Levnî. İbrahim Pasha had been astonished at this insistence on sitting behind a small window of iron railings instead of a much more appropriate seat, but had failed to convince the Sultan. The Emperor's favourite companion had ousted the Grand Vizier once more. Sultan Ahmed appeared very happy looking out from behind the railings in Levnî's picture.

Levnî successfully fitted the entire story with countless little tales into these frames.

Sultan Ahmed best appreciated the illuminator's attempt at portraying what lay beyond the immediately visible.

True, the symbols of power dominated the picture: guards whose white feathered hats resembled gigantic fans were everywhere, Prince Süleyman on horseback and his younger brothers in a coach, tiger- and leopard-skin saddle cloths under the jewelled harnesses. But a loving father watching his sons with pride was the key feature. Levnî had deliberately divested the sovereign of his royal trappings; this was what pleased the Emperor above all. Neither was his the only affectionate gaze: the artist had portrayed such genuine fondness and protectiveness in the eyes of some of the valets, footmen and guards surrounding the young princes! The ten-year-old Süleyman looked tiny on horseback. In the moment following the one frozen by the picture, the boy would kiss the doorstep of the building his father was watching from, the unexpectedly deft move raising cheers from the spectators and reducing his father to tears. Yes, there was much in these final pictures that tugged at the heartstrings.

Yirmisekiz Çelebi and Ahmed
Return from Francia

Sultan Ahmed laid the pocketwatch depicting a flawlessly executed lakescape in enamel down on the gleaming rosewood writing desk. The desk stood on slender wooden legs, its carved flowers dazzling. The Emperor wondered how convenient such a high surface was to the act of writing. He, and everyone around him, always wrote sitting cross-legged.

He moved to the tall chest of drawers in walnut, pulling the drawers out, sliding them back in, again and again, holding the gilt handles shaped like wreaths. And look at those tiny naked babes on the carvings of that gilded seat, so plump, so lifelike! The very same infants, but this time as cherubim, had leapt to the frame of the crystal looking glass. These glasses were highly sought after by the harem women; any who received such a glass styled herself privileged.

The Emperor was inspecting just some of the countless objects Yirmisekiz Mehmed Çelebi had brought back; the diplomat who bore his janissary battalion number as an appellation had been charged with forging a good relationship with the French king.

Mehmed Çelebi hastened to the palace upon his return on the 20th of October 1721, the journey's dust still on his feet, in response to his Emperor's command. Sultan Ahmed was impatient to listen to the Ambassador's account of his experiences, of what he had seen. The Ambassador had departed immediately after the conclusion of the circumcision festival and spent one year in the lands of the infidels.

★ ★ ★

'The women are held in higher regard in Francia than the men, that they do as they please and go where they wish to. The finest nobleman shows more respect to the basest than she deserves, and their will is done in all counties.'

Yirmisekiz Mehmed Çelebi's account had inspired an avid curiosity in Sultan Ahmed. He was certain he knew the women in his world very well, but had always wondered about others. In any case, that Lady Montagu, wife to the British Ambassador, had kindled a burning desire in his heart to visit faraway lands, to meet different people – how very odd! Since that time, he had frequently thought of far-off lands and other people. Who knew but he might yet, one day, visit these places of the infidels! And so he had finally decided to send a trusted envoy to the land of the Franks, to see and visit, not to do battle. He personally might not be able to go where Yirmisekiz Mehmed Çelebi did, nor see what the envoy saw; yet this loyal servant would give him a detailed account of all that he had witnessed – and new worlds opened up before him as his returning envoy recounted his tales.

Yirmisekiz Çelebi had described the Frankish women so well, down to how their hair fell upon their faces as they participated in the king's hunts and war games:

> The king's men and wenches of his kin had gathered at the place where the city ends. We, too, stood with them. Once the king himself arrived, we all mounted our steeds, and that was the same time when the wenches got out of their coaches, decked out in men's garb, and yet with diamonds too, and began cavalry practice, all riding, yet feminine wiles a-plenty, their fringes strewn hither and thither.[2]

---

[2] Yirmisekiz Mehmet Çelebi, *Yirmisekiz Mehmet Çelebi'nin Fransa Seyahatnamesi*, Tercüman, 1976, p. 149.

His astonishing account brought the free and seductive Parisian women to life before Sultan Ahmed's eyes:

> The maids are constantly on the street and visiting house to house, never do they rest in their own homes. Men and women stand together on the streets, fair making the cities look very crowded. 'Tis the women who do the shopping, and sit about, so they do.

The fascination was clearly reciprocated: these women were equally curious about the Ottoman men. Sultan Ahmed felt he too could have been there as he listened.

The Ottoman Ambassador's night at the opera had to be the most astonishing experience of his time in Paris:

> There is a play they call *opare* [sic], this is particular to the city of Paris alone, where they show odd arts. This palace was constructed specifically for this opare. Though enclosed on all sides, yet they illuminated it with hundreds of wax tapers and countless candles on crystal chandeliers. The women were decked out in silks and gemstones, that they created such a dazzling brilliance in the candle flames that it defies description ... A big, embroidered curtain hung before us, where the musicians sat. Once everyone sat down, this curtain suddenly rose up and a large palace came into view behind it. The players in the palace courtyard, and a score of angel-faced damsels all in spangled garb and frocks, encrusted with jewels, emanating brilliant light over the entire congregation, began to sing, accompanied by the musicians. The essence here is to represent a tale like reality. The congregation we went to were told this story: there was an emperor who fell in love with the daughter of another ruler and wished to marry her. Yet the maiden was enamour'd of the son of yet a third. They showed all that occurred between

these people as if it were real. Say the emperor wanted to despatch himself to the princess's garden; the palace before us vanished, replaced by a garden that appeared suddenly, with lemon and orange trees.

The more Yirmisekiz Çelebi narrated, the more Sultan Ahmed was filled with the indescribable feeling of having missed out, anger and resentment growing. Why was the Emperor of the Seven Climes so enthralled by the oddities that took place in far-off lands of the infidels, places he would never see unless on a military campaign? Was the appellation of 'the Ruler of the Seven Climes' before his name, the title of an Ottoman emperor, wanting somehow, or even invalid? Or was its validity confined to the minds of his loyal servants?

In short, they showed astounding skill that defies description. They showed thunder and lightning, on display were oddities and bizarre occurrences that none could believe short of actually witnessing them at first hand.

The ambassador continued, gratified by the interest his words aroused in the great ruler:

They have also constructed in the king's palace a dance hall dedicated to the opare society, this one being even larger than the previous, its walls of porphyry marble, bedecked with bizarre pictures in gilt frames. When we arrived, the noble wenches mostly had come dressed in garments festooned with gold and gemstones, all sitting in boxes. The crowds were greater than in the opare in the city. The king then arrived and sat down. A decorated curtain was hanging in the front, suddenly this curtain was raised and behind it came into view the stage where supposedly a bright sun had risen and the stage filled with angel-faced damsels. The size of that sun was that of a large dining tray and fashioned so skilfully of golden material that candles burn behind it to create the illusion of the divine rays of the sun emanating. The dancers were all noblemen and women, sons of princes, and generals, and dukes; these were the only dancers at a royal congregation. And these dancers wear special dancing costumes, covered in silver thread embroideries on silken cloths. And on their heads do they bear wide headgear, fair like crests, and adorn themselves with scented black kohl and rouges to better define their beauty.

A place where men and women have fun together, and no marriage contract required, either! The women have equal say, none with a sole purpose of pleasing her man, their own happiness, comfort and joy paramount. This was an entirely different order. As these thoughts blew through his mind, Sultan Ahmed noticed with surprise that, true, he found them strange, yet he did not reject them out of hand. He had no problem with the happiness of women. He was certainly much more considerate of his women than many a previous emperor. And yes, he did have some idea of how Frankish people lived, but such a candid account stemming from the heart of this life was the first of its kind, and so he gave his imagination free rein as he listened, all ears.

Emetullah and Ahmed
Took my fancy!

Sultan Ahmed settled back, laying the embroidery frame down on the sofa to inspect his work from a distance. The fine, diamond-white silk stretched to facilitate embroidery now bore floral motifs with pointed petals, picked out in the pale and deep hues of lilacs and hyacinths; a few gold threads twinkled like dewdrops in between, not too many, so that beauty may lay in simplicity. The leaves drawn on the fabric awaited the petrol-green thread.

His Chief Wife and lifelong companion Emetullah Banu Sultan watched her man, the depth of her love shaking her to the core. She bore one of the names of the Emperor's unforgettable mother, and the pride that accompanied this knowledge.

Sultan Ahmed's passion for women wasn't confined to the sexual gratification they offered – not that a woman who failed to give him pleasure would have interested him in the first place – but he genuinely attempted to cultivate the finer aspects of the fair sex in his own life. Emetullah discovered this in time, a priceless treasure she safeguarded: what made her indispensable in the Emperor's esteem was the way she confided in him, voiced her desires and explained, to the best of her ability, her observations on life. Still, how wholeheartedly he had embraced embroidery! She was surprised at first, but had grown to recognise that look of achievement on his face when he was pleased with his progress, like a child who had carried out a task well. Those were the times when they became a true couple, an ordinary man and an ordinary woman sharing a pastime they both enjoyed, talking of whatever came to mind just then, helping each other, smiling or simply communicating without words. These were the most precious moments in Emetullah's life; she wouldn't even exchange them for passionate nights of love when the Emperor's desire honoured her. This need to share not just love, but life in its totality, was the thought that repeated itself in long nights she spent in the ruler's arms.

They were sitting in the Emperor's Privy Chamber, that marvellous, splendid, exuberant, stunning, surprising, joyful, ebullient, bewildering, seductive, peerless, attractive, appealing room; the room that invited the occupant to share in its own happiness, the room of the dizzying colours that reflected the spirit of its imperial founder, this wonderful space that is all those adjectives and more, that small room decorated with the refreshingly vibrant paintings of flowers and fruits. It was hard to decide what name to give this room – Fruit Room, Flower Room or the Room of Delights? Ottoman rulers had been living at the seraglio at Topkapı since the time of Mehmed the Conqueror; the harem – that is, their own home – was the section each did the most to improve and build upon. The palace was the heart and brains of the great Ottoman Empire, the headquarters of the administration and services, true; but the harem was where the Emperor and his family lived.

Sultan Ahmed had long wanted to build a room different from those of his ancestors' works, something reminiscent of the Edirne of his childhood days, clad not in tiles but in the comforting warmth of wood and in Edirnekâri gilded painting work – a cosy room, not an overwhelming one. This room was accessed through the Privy Chamber of Murad III, an ancestor as artistic as he himself was, although the larger chamber was fabulously big and tiled, with a massive fireplace and an ornamental fountain. Ahmed's room, on the other hand, offered an entirely unexpected domain: on his command, the entire room had been panelled in uplifting depictions of flowers and fruits. He was only thirty-two years of age at the time, a mere two years into his reign, and yet early on, it had been apparent that a breath of fresh air, a refined taste had come to rule the palace.

Emetullah gazed in awe at the paintings of fruit on the wooden panels below the gilded arches every time she came into this room. Most intriguing were the purple grapes – wouldn't their frosted glaze dampen the hand were one to reach a hand out to touch them? Those big bunches strained to escape the rarest of blue and white china bowls they had been placed in, only remaining in place by the painter's art. The tulip and rose paintings had been drawn painstakingly; now they were arrogantly aware of their beauty, standing beside the fruits. Their only raison d'être was beauty, not filling stomachs.

Tiny drawers were concealed amongst the paintings on the walls, just like the jewels that suddenly appeared for Sultan Ahmed to clasp on the neck or the ears of his latest favourite. Emetullah Sultan shook off her reverie, this last thought rather more startling. She would occasionally dream of being the only Sultan of the great ruler's heart, yet reality would crash down all too soon, just as it did then.

Her eyes settled on the tiny cupboard in the corner. A concealed door in this cupboard opened out to the wide antechamber to the rear, and a looking glass hung over the door. This was the ideal vehicle for jesting, yet Emetullah's memory of it was not a fond one. A year before, still glowing from the previous night's passionate lovemaking, she had believed her beloved Emperor to be alone and silently made her way to the room in the hope of a repetition. The Chief Black Eunuch hadn't warned her, thinking the Emperor had summoned her, but when she entered the room, she realised the Sultan wasn't alone. Alerted by the stirring lady steward, the Sultan had silently sent the other woman off, down this passage, and opened his arms to Emetullah. She had later found out that the other woman had been Şermi. Sultan Ahmed was gallant enough not to offend Emetullah, however much he might be entitled to all the women in the harem. Emetullah never forgot, but she was accustomed to pretending her heart was whole, not broken.

* * *

Emetullah had long been aware of Sultan Ahmed's interest in handicrafts, and embroidery in particular. When he invited her at night, he always noticed the colours, patterns and embroideries of her garments, frequently complimenting her fine taste as she loosened her sash to remove her silk robe and gauze chemise: 'How well these red roses on your chest flatter your cheeks, my fair one, and these gilt branches are so becoming to your abundant locks!' Still, she had hesitated for a long time before daring to suggest that they embroider together – such a feminine task! Thankfully, the sovereign had eagerly embraced the suggestion instead of flying into a rage.

Emetullah bent down to her work whilst Sultan Ahmed was engrossed in completing the shape of the slender petal; at times the sovereign enjoyed the moment in silence. She was so accustomed to viewing her man's slightest whim as the purpose of her own existence that some things came to her naturally. Emetullah was the perfect example of a woman who relegated her own personality to the background and offered full use of her love. She could have existed in any time or place throughout history, yet she would have remained the same. And so she would enjoy the distinction of staying by the ruler's side to the very end.

* * *

The opportunities for doing things with his women other than making love were limited: Sultan Ahmed could sit in the garden, perhaps, but there was no question of sharing the *helva* chats or poetry evenings. These were evening parties during which the Emperor would be surrounded by his precious son-in-law İbrahim Pasha, some of his favourite companions, occasionally a favoured vizier, as well as hand-picked poets and theologians, all to entertain him whilst they too enjoyed a good time and even, perchance, learnt something, benefitting from the highly intellectual conversation.

Yet eunuchs were the only men who could be present where harem women were. When she thought about all this, her mind did go back to the accounts her sovereign related to her about Frankish women.

It was after one of their lovemaking sessions, longer than ever before; Sultan Ahmed had lain his head on her warm breast, like the bliss that violently frothing waves, exhausted by the deep sea, feel once they reach the shore and spread over the soft sand. He began to speak softly of those far-off lands and the people who lived there, almost as if he were talking to himself, maybe of his own dreams. He had told her how women and men have fun together in the lands of the Franks; his tales had overpowered her, and she never forgot:

They promenade on the flower-flanked paths of the gardens, arm in arm, and dance before the musicians in the palace, and watch representations of musical tales in immense chambers decorated with curtains.

The enthusiasm with which he had related these odd customs of the Franks had made Emetullah realise that he too wanted to share his diversions in the company of his women.

'Just visualise this, Emetullah mine,' said Sultan Ahmed, raising his head from her breast, and propping himself up on one elbow, 'they showed odd arts in this location in Paris town they called opare. The king and the noblemen and their wives all went to see. They lit the chamber like the day with hundreds of wax tapers and crystal chandeliers; its interior, all the posts, walls and ceilings gilded. And the women, covered in silken fabrics and jewels, sat next to the men.'

This was evidently the most intriguing aspect for the Emperor, this status of the women. How was it possible that these infidels lived so differently, in such complete contrast

226

to his own life? Wondering how it would be to live in that
fashion was impossible to resist, however difficult this might
be to accept.

Sultan Ahmed noticed that Emetullah was listening, eyes
wide open, not just to please her master, and so he continued
to astound his woman and to illuminate her:

> The embroidered curtain by the musicians is suddenly
> raised, revealing a great palace behind, they tell
> me. Some twenty damsels with the countenances of
> angels, all immersed in shining garments that spray
> light everywhere, begin to sing, accompanied by the
> musicians. The essence here is to recreate a story. When
> the emperor in the story arrives at the garden of the
> maiden he is enamour'd of, the scene suddenly changes
> into such a garden that it was filled with lemon and
> orange trees. Then descend from the heavens clouds,
> and yet men too, and they display games of fire. They
> show such startling things that included thunder and
> lightning. As for the times of love: well, they enact those
> like real ... Then the wenches pass their arms through
> those of the men, all leave laughing, to go and partake
> of a myriad of delicacies set out on high tables, and the
> king with them.

Emetullah tried to visualise all this, but too extensive were
these scenes, too fantastic for her imagination to embrace.

Emetullah wished silently, too, that the Emperor did not
wonder so much about the women in the land of the Franks.

Yirmisekiz Çelebi and Ahmed
Breezes from Paris

Never one for solitude, Sultan Ahmed took special satisfaction in sharing the good times: listening to music, watching dancers and savouring delectable desserts in the company of his beloved son-in-law and Levnî – who topped the list of the Emperor's conversation companions – and poets. Yet as he did these things neither his beloved Chief Wife Emetullah nor any of the other women in his harem could be present. The closest they could come would be watching concealed, behind some impenetrable cage in the distance. And conversely, where his women were, his male companions could not be. He knew breaking these rules to be beyond his power, Emperor though he may have been. Sultan Ahmed had listened to Yirmisekiz Mehmed Çelebi's account of how women and men had fun together in Frankish lands, and that those women were not regarded as prostitutes – quite the opposite! He had been astonished at first, but the more he thought about it, the better he understood.

Sultan Ahmed was determined to widen the boundaries of his own life at the very least. He would bid his son-in-law İbrahim Pasha to carry out those plans they had long been discussing: erecting pavilions and mansions that soothe the eye and heart in the delightful valley of the Kağıthane stream of the famed sweet waters. His son-in-law well liked creating new recreation sites and did this exceedingly well. Those palace gardens in the books Yirmisekiz Mehmed Çelebi had brought back from the lands of the Franks, those gardens would pale into insignificance beside the beauty of his Sadabad. Hadn't he long been yearning for a new site for fresh air outside the palace grounds, in any case? A place where water splashed like in a waterfall, a paradise where flowers vied with one another for supremacy... neat gardens where the women could also stretch out in their own section.

Everything Yirmisekiz Çelebi spoke of captivated the Emperor:

> During the month of Ramadan, whilst we were fasting, the field marshal arrived and asked, 'We plead and entreat our ladies wish to observe you breaking your fast. You would make us exceeding happy were you to consent, and our king may even desire to attend.' We had no recourse but to agree, 'Their wish is our command; pray bid them welcome,' we had to say. Some half an hour before evening, two hundred wenches immersed in gold and jewels and diamonds arrived, and sat at chairs facing us. Our mansion was transformed fair into a women's house, and overflowed. The following day, another two hundred wenches and damsels arrived, all bringing some manner of confectionery or pastries. We broke our fast and ate. They would not leave, still sitting at three o'clock; it appears they were waiting to observe our prayer. Nothing for it, we washed, and prayed, and finishing the prayer, we sang hymns, and recited on beads, and the women watched us all and were much admiring.[3]

This admiration was undoubtedly mutual, not only an arrogant curiosity about 'the other' and a covert approval but also carnal desire for the unattainable. Sultan Ahmed may well have understood this mutual yet secret attraction

[3] Yirmisekiz Mehmet Çelebi, *Yirmisekiz Mehmet Çelebi'nin Fransa Seyahatnamesi*, Tercüman, 1976, p. 124.

far better than the diplomat who had been there in person. And so Sultan Ahmed lifted all the veils in his imagination and there appeared before him a seductive Frankish woman, possibly a good deal more attractive than any in real life. He would not rest until he possessed one of these Frankish women, however much of a commotion this would cause in the harem.

★ ★ ★

The ruler's most trusted men were despatched to find a suitable candidate. It would be no easy task to find a French virgin who would consent to entering the Ottoman Emperor's harem, in this time of peace, of her own free will, and she had to be of exceptional beauty. There were many beauties in the harem who had been born in Frankish lands, but all their ties with their past had long since been severed. The Sultan knew not the number of the concubines in his harem, yet he now desired a Frankish woman to teach him the ways and manners of the Europeans in the most intimate congress possible, in his most intimate harem, not a woman who had been brought up in the Ottoman manner from a young age.

The sovereign's desire surprised Faik Efendi most. As customs steward, it was his office to purchase young Circassian, Georgian and Abkhaz concubines for the imperial harem. On this occasion, however, diplomats with European credentials 'instead of Faik Efendi' had been entrusted with the charge. Great skill and tact were required to accomplish the task, lest any risk of friction arise between the two states. The Sultan's men were confident they could locate such girls ready for this adventure: boredom and the irresistible attraction of the image of the Orient would undoubtedly help.

The fantasies of oriental eroticism – real or imaginary – must have secretly attracted European women as much as they did the men.

İbrahim and Ahmed
and Tulips
Sadabad

'Vizier mine,

My daughter is in fine health and sends you her greetings. When will the complex named Sadabad be completed? Inform me of what task you are at present engaged in, and that occupies your mind.'

The period of time that would much later be named the Tulip Era continued to present Sultan Ahmed with one refined diversion after another. The festivities and banquets were stunning in their variety, for they all celebrated life. Outstanding creativity was essential to prevent monotony. The moving light provided by candles on the backs of tortoises was livened up by the happy laughter of countless dancers, their eyes smouldering. The spirit of lanterns had to spread to the entire city in Sultan Ahmed's and İbrahim Pasha's view; this happy tune that seemed to have no end should be sung by the populace of the city known as *Mahruse-i Konstantiniyye* – Constantine's capital – and *Dergâh-ı Selatin* – the Court of Sultans. This was a life of pomp and circumstance.

The settings changed all the time: banquets grew more frequent and were laid out in the gardens of waterfront villas and mansions along the Bosphorus, the Golden Horn shores and Kağıthane, those residences that virtually waved with the wealth of their decorations.

Kağıthane had been something of a mirror for the empire for hundreds of years, sharing its fortunes. In the time of Süleyman the Magnificent, it enjoyed a dignified majesty, proudly staging the fabulous conventions and processions of, say, the jewellers. During the reign of Sultan Ahmed – and so the premiership of İbrahim Pasha – began the setting for an entirely different splendour: refined tastes, yes, but extravagant ostentation too, a place for flighty women and Lotharios, fully compliant with official policy yet curiously staring at the West, a place where Parisian palaces and gardens were re-created, albeit Ottomanised; but the relationships with Western modes fell far short, and later it became the symbol of the abrupt collapse of a splendour that was raised on weak foundations, though many efforts at revival followed – its star dimming unstoppably, possibly even mortified at the wretchedness that lay in wait.

★ ★ ★

The Emperor's ceremonial arrival, his relaxation at the pavilion whose walls were decorated in the European manner and before which tiny waterfalls burbled, ostentatious festivities and endless feasts had rendered Kağıthane the obligatory venue in the city.

Sultan Ahmed and his beloved son-in-law gathered around them the best poets, musicians and scientists, day in and day out, and their presence made beauty all the more visible. That graceful flower called the tulip had grown to symbolise all that was refined; eulogies composed for the flower elevated the value placed on its varieties, to the extent that possessing different types of tulips became a craze. Suddenly no effort to view and obtain the bulbs of the latest cultivar was too foolish. The two cultivars lovingly developed by one of the most famous tulip growers of the time, Şeyhülislam Veliyüddin Efendi (who also happened to be an accomplished calligrapher) caused much envy.

The Master of Flowers was responsible for the monitoring of tulip growers, tulip gardens and tulip trade, and for punishing those who sold blossoms and in particular tulips at prices above the state-imposed cap. İbrahim Pasha even issued an edict on impounding the flowers of those who broke the law.

A French merchant was to note one day, 'Turks place less value on human life than they do on horses or tulips.' This was a double-edged sword, no doubt: a European mercilessly judged Turks to be merciless as he illuminated tulip mania.

Levnî and Yirmisekiz Çelebi
Heady dreams

It was close to mid-morning, just the right time for coffee, when a hand knocked on Levnî's door. The visitor was his friend Yirmisekiz Çelebi Mehmed Efendi. 'I greet you on this auspicious day,' said Mehmed Efendi, smiling.

'I bid you welcome, Mehmed Efendi!' replied Levnî, genuinely delighted. There was little need for a more florid exchange between the two old friends. The artist had always been surprised by this elegant man's penchant for his old appellation harking back to the janissary battalion he had been raised in, instead of styling himself a much more elaborate one.

The artist was not at the palace, nor was Mehmed Efendi inundated with work, affording a rare occasion indeed for two friends to spend some time together. True, they did frequently attend the Emperor's gatherings, chat and even debate, but as Levnî said, 'When the two of us are together, we hold the looking glasses of our hearts to each other, and with words agreeable do we make real earthly dreams.'

Yirmisekiz Çelebi Mehmed Efendi had been promoted to Ambassador when he was serving as a treasury official. Upon his return from his mission in France, he had been rewarded with the post of Chief Imperial Accountant, a position that the Emperor would entrust his closest friends with. There was a lot to learn from this man upon his return from Paris! Levnî frequently found himself feeling jealous of the time his friend spent with his beloved Emperor. Now he wanted to know all that was possible to learn about that 'other' world, and in particular, about the art of representation.

Yirmisekiz Çelebi told Levnî that immense likenesses of people were hanging on the walls in the land of the Franks, that when viewed from a distance, these likenesses were deceptively realistic, that in some the kings and in others entire battlefields of warriors looked to have frozen in mid-movement. These were all painted on canvases stretched on wooden frames, said Efendi, and the paints were an oily mixture. He too was fascinated by all that these Frankish people did. Levnî asked his friend to describe in detail the portraits hanging on the palace walls in Paris again and again, and his friend repeated patiently, boasting a little:

'We went with the king to view these strange paintings hanging in the palace hall. There the king told us their names, one by one, each like real people, their gaze fixed on us, watching us haughtily.'

The envoy's account of his impressions at the tapestry studio captivated the artist. His friend's admiration for the depictions on wall hangings inflamed Levnî's desire to create similar works.

'Observing the rugs on the walls, more numerous perhaps than a hundred, our jaws dropped in surprise. Take flower embroideries, for one: the more you gaze at them, the more realistic they appear in their vases. The way they have shown the eyes, eyelashes, eyebrows and even the hair on their heads and beards, yea, 'twould be impossible to find art of this scale to depict them on paper – even Kamal-ud-Din Bihza'd would find himself powerless.'

Strange emotions battled within the heart of Levnî as the diplomat compared the greatest Persian artist of the past with contemporary Frankish painters. But most of all he knew he was envious of – not just in awe of – those facial expressions that reflected the subjects' inner worlds like mirrors in those depictions!

'Some are shown laughing, to convey joy, others look pensive for their sadness, some are frightened, some cry, some look to be grieving so deeply that one look suffices to indicate their disposition. However much I may speak, none can visualise it all.'

'Wrong, wrong, Yirmisekiz Çelebi – I can visualise it, oh, so I can!' Levnî insisted each time, trying to suppress an irresistible and unintelligible yearning. At other times he indulged in this yearning, totally submitting to it. His friend's impressions of Paris recounted in gentle words each time they got together not only surprised Levnî but also carried him away into a colourful world of dreams:

'The streets in the town of Paris are exceedingly wide. Whilst they accommodate five or six coaches side by side, there were some neighbourhoods where the crowds were so dense that three men on horseback could barely make their passage. It appears that the entire townsfolk had come to watch the procession. Their houses are of four or five storeys, with windows looking upon the street. Each was crammed full with more men and women than could fit. The wenches here are held in high esteem and they are exceedingly inquisitive. Women and men both were desirous of watching us dine, some for visiting, some just to observe. They would send word, "this is the wife or daughter of some eminent personage, wishing for your leave to watch you dine" and so we would have no recourse but to acquiesce.'

Levnî
Quest

Levnî studied the works of past masters in order to understand individual characteristics, to relish those distinctions and to admire as well as dissect. A degree of vanity was an essential element in his nature, as it has to be in every artist's. Yet he also was tolerant. He saw no issue with drawing inspiration from the work of others. In his quest, he had tried, to the best of his ability, to learn about the history of world arts from the incredible illustrated books and albums in the Emperor's treasury. But what Yirmisekiz Çelebi brought back had opened new worlds before Levnî's eyes, feeding his unlimited creativity, making him feel he was in those lands of the Franks from time to time – oh, how these books had even occupied his dreams!

The Sovereign had placed most of the books in his treasury into his precious new library in the Third Courtyard, so that all Enderun members might benefit. This was such an unprecedented deed, like his many others; just in the same way Sultan Ahmed praised Levnî's pictures that looked so realistic, and so encouraged the artist.

* * *

Levnî had secretly exchanged paintings with a Venetian artist who passed through Konstantiniyye: the Ottoman gave a few of his own illuminations and a portrait of his beloved Emperor in return for some pictures that so well displayed depth, all but flesh and blood. As for the incomparable image of the Ottoman Emperor – oh, how it had quickened the Venetian's heartbeat! He had seen oils and black-and-white engravings of ancient Ottoman emperors made by another European artist, but those paled in comparison to owning the contemporaneous portrait of a living, regnant grand seigneur, made by someone who knew him well. The Grand Seigneur was depicted sitting cross-legged on his throne resplendent with all the glitter of the Orient. The Venetian had been thrilled to note every last detail: the majesty of his posture in contrast to the slender facial features and elegant hands, the black beard, the diamond aigrette adorning his turban, his fur-lined, gold-thread-embroidered kaftan and the emerald-encrusted dagger at his belt – but above all, his superior gaze commanding the entire world.

In return, the Venetian had presented the Ottoman artist with a few landscapes depicting colourful vessels, banners fluttering and tall, pink palaces, along with a number of portraits. One of these Venetian sitters had been a courtesan who had entertained the artist in the past. This particular painting had impressed Levnî the most. The woman looked so realistic, so lifelike and so relaxed. She was almost entirely naked, her shiny dark hair covering her shoulders and breasts, her eyes unashamedly inviting. She seemed on the verge of leaping out of the textured surface of the canvas, roughened by the layers of oil paint. The artist decided to keep this picture to himself, not show it to anyone else. He knew hanging these pictures on his walls was out of question; true, he heard Europeans did just that, but were he to try such an outrageous break with custom, to liven up his small house in the Seat of Felicity thus, instant censure would be his lot. His own illuminations were almost too realistic as far as religious fanatics were concerned, in any case. Thankfully, his Emperor and Grand Vizier both supported innovations, and none dared to criticise Levnî's work openly. There was yet time before depictions could free themselves from the pages of books and rise to the walls.

He thought he would talk to the Emperor about all these paintings except the portrait of the Venetian woman. He might even show them. He knew Sultan Ahmed to be very interested in European painting. The Emperor's open-minded attitude to all that was new was amazing, yet Sultan Ahmed appreciated how politically inexpedient it would be to demonstrate this attitude overtly, lest he become labelled 'infidel emperor', a term all too easy to affix. His interest in the West despite his traditional appearance, his commissioning of a diplomatic mission headed by Yirmisekiz Çelebi with the sole aim of establishing friendly relations with France, his interest in the books brought back and taking hints from those books even – yea, all this had already attracted a great deal of criticism from fanatical quarters. Conservative elements had long marked him thus. Expediency required a policy of appeasement for the time being on the part of the Sultan and his Grand Vizier.

History had already taught Sultan Ahmed that a ruler had no freedom whatsoever; however all-powerful he might appear, invisible boundaries checked that power at all times, and everything hung on a fine thread.

Vanmour, Levnî's painter friend, was another scintillating treasure. The Frank's studio in Pera was akin to an oasis in the illuminator's eyes. They all used to enjoy such wonderfully long conversations, when their common friend Dimitrie Cantemir also lived in Konstantiniyye. However different their origins might have been, these dazzling minds understood one another well, bright ideas and interests binding them together.

İbrahim and New Delights

'Dragoman Efendi, make sure there be no depictions of people on those wall tapestries you will bring back from the lands of the Franks! As you know all too well, those tapestries called *gobelin* will adorn the walls of our master's Sadabad palace. Landscapes of numerous trees, lakes, rivers and depictions of flowers in pots will all be appropriate.'

'Your wish is my command, My Lord; please rest assured, your wishes will be carried out to your satisfaction.'

'Mind you forget not the wines, Lenoir Efendi. Bring back one thousand bottles of the sparkling wine they call champagne, and five hundred of the kind they name Burgundy!'

This extraordinary Grand Vizier was also rumoured to have favoured women who had caught his eye from afar at the Kağıthane outings with a twenty-four-carat gold coin they called 'lover's gold', his advanced years and dread of offending his august father-in-law and imperial wife notwithstanding.

★　★　★

And so it transpired that he met Mehtabe on one of those little clandestine outings at Kağıthane: a very brief trip it was indeed, and for once he was not accompanied, as he usually would have been. The Grand Vizier had sought anonymity in the excuse of monitoring the final preparations for the festivities scheduled for two days thence, a party that would amuse the Emperor. A few ladies had relaxed on the silk rugs laid out on the grass, clearly to welcome the arrival of early summer. Evidently they intended to enjoy the scenery before the heat had set in: the carnations planted to replace the fading tulips and violets and fresh roses, all against the silver ribbon that was the stream. True, they were accompanied by their servants and slaves, but İbrahim Pasha could not afford to come too close; it simply would not have been appropriate. But rules were made to be broken, provided the right people were involved.

The Grand Vizier dismissed the flapping black eunuchs trying to guard their charges; the women, in contrast, had loosened the ties of their cloaks and veils, revealing their fringes and tresses. The women – and their servants – knew full well who this distinguished white-bearded gentleman was, strolling by so close. That was how Nevşehirli İbrahim Pasha locked eyes with Mehtabe, wife of the Chief Judge of Konstantiniyye Zülalîzade Arnavut Hasan Efendi. The statesman's innards were set aflame – how was it possible to forget those violet eyes or the flick of an auburn strand of hair that fell over them? And hadn't those eyes promised something immediately perceived by the seasoned philanderer?

It was no problem for the Grand Vizier to find out who this alluring young belle was. The Chief Judge's wife's beauty had long been legendary around the Seat of Felicity, in any case. So this delectable thing was she. He was determined to possess her; he would risk it.

This was nothing less than forbidden love.

The Winds of War in the East
Restless neighbours

'Mahmud Han has besieged and conquered Isfahan, the capital of Persia, My Sultan. Our messenger despatched by Hasan Pasha, our Governor of Baghdad, further informs us that Mahmud Han has also enslaved Shah Hussein and placed himself on the throne of the Safavid dynasty. Hussein's son Tahmasp has saved his life by escaping to Qazvin.'

The ordeals of the Persian Shah were of little concern to Sultan Ahmed; this powerful neighbour was always a threat. Yet peace was always preferable to war.

Whilst an unprecedented degree of lavish party-making continued in the Seat of Felicity, whilst a hitherto unseen proliferation of music, poetry and flowers nourished souls, and whilst the languor of peace had settled over the hearts, it was difficult to determine to what degree, if at all, the Ottoman Empire had to intervene in the affairs of its eastern neighbour.

The Emperor and his Grand Vizier held long conferences, consulted with the other viziers and finally came to a decision: war. The objective of the campaign that would set off against Persia was twofold: to recapture those former Ottoman holdings and as a show of force.

And so the Ottoman Empire opened three fronts in April 1723: Iraq, Azerbaijan and the Caucasus. None were commanded by either the Emperor or his Grand Vizier.

Şermi and Ahmed
On the shores of the Marmara, one fine summer eve

'Know you that not even the slightest flaw will be tolerated in the evening's festivities! Gather ye the freshest, sweetest-smelling rose petals from the rose garden at the top, that we may sprinkle the dining tray before our benefactor with these petals! Not too early, not too late – just in time, before the roses begin to lose their bloom! Then bring ye them to me forthwith, that I may pick over with my own hands before sprinkling them!'

Gözde Şermi was clawing herself into a slightly more elevated position in the complicated world of the harem, emboldened by the interest she had evoked in the Emperor of late, and so she emphasised his favour at every opportunity as one of the women whom the Emperor took up more than the others, but she wouldn't stop until she reached *Kadınefendi*, that is, Wife, or even – who knows? – *Başkadınefendi*, Chief Wife. Here she was, ordering the lady steward about, already giving herself the airs of a chief wife. She did have a plan; tonight was the night for the paste whose secret she had jealously guarded. She fully intended to bear the Emperor a child.

The Emperor had indicated he wanted to party with his women at the Pearl Pavilion this night. He usually preferred the coast palace he had commissioned at Sarayburnu, but on this occasion Sultan Ahmed had commanded his ancestors' favourite venue to be prepared. He thought the gentle breezes of the Marmara would refresh the steamy languor of the hot summer night. It wasn't always the easiest task to move the massive contingent that was the harem to one of the palaces on the Bosphorus, but on some nights, the Emperor wanted to see all his beloved women about him.

The 16th-century Pearl Pavilion that projected onto the Sea of Marmara had been so named after the pearl-strung pendant that hung above the inimitable throne in the reception hall. These ceremonial pendants had decorated thrones and halls from time immemorial, and their long tassels were lavishly strung with pearls, large rubies and emeralds that caught the sun's rays and held them, and other dazzling items besides, but none had been so famous as to name an entire building except for the pearls here.

Twelve generations of Ottoman rulers had enjoyed life in the braced projection that reached out towards the sea. In return they had maintained the pavilion in good repair, occasionally adding an extension or two. And so the Pearl Pavilion had almost been a friend that witnessed their glory days.

Word that the Emperor was on his way caused a final rustling in this large hall that so embraced the sea, and then everyone settled in their places, following protocol. Those in charge of the countless types of fruits and sherbets cast their eyes over the fine porcelain bowls one last time, to make sure everything was as it should be. The musicians and singers took their places, and the black harem eunuchs, the only men in the vicinity, clasped their hands before them.

All that moved now were the curtains billowing in the gentle breeze that came in from the open windows. The sea had barely turned to indigo from the day's blue; not a single rowboat lantern was visible. Making sure there was no one at sea was but one of the items on the list of preparations. In any event, it was well known that any curious male eyes that might dare look upon the scene of the Emperor and his women together would never see another sight.

The cypresses on the shore opposite looked like an unfinished page layout, a very carefully designed layout not quite complete: slightly different was every single tree, their colours all faintly dissimilar. The mosque minarets rose up into the heavens, as if they were pens that would write upon the skies. The sparse lights of Üsküdar succumbed to the mist settling upon the waters one by one in the darkening hour. The bright lantern of Maiden's Tower had already begun to pierce the darkness. The islands in the distance, those isles witness to every memory the Marmara held, were but lonely blurs.

The musicians wore translucent chemises in a diamond-white gauze; the collars were very generous indeed, and when they waved around to the rhythm, losing themselves in the music as they blew their wind instruments or strummed their strings, they revealed the eternal conundrum that what remained concealed was indisputably more alluring than what was overtly on display.

Şermi had been unable to sit at the feet of the Emperor as she had hoped, yet she had been so certain all day long! Weren't the unexpectedly tender caresses that Sultan Ahmed had bestowed upon her the night before – how he had lain his head on her tiny belly and fallen asleep – weren't those a secret invitation to Şermi after all? Thankfully the *gözde* he did beckon over was not Hümaşah. Şermi knew the flicker of jealousy clouding her dark, beautiful face would not escape Hümaşah's attention for a moment. Her friend would counsel her not to indulge in impossible dreams. Friend, indeed! Nay, she is a co-wife to me, she scolded herself silently, and immediately regretted this uncharitable thought. Şermi was unable to check the ambition that overwhelmed her; the self-control exercised by Hümaşah, and the ease with which she did so, never failed to impress the darker concubine.

Ambitions hesitated briefly when a prince was born in the harem – until, that is, the women realised that the mother of the future emperor would rule absolutely, and so each would stop at nothing to eliminate the others blocking her path. Emetullah Sultan, who had ruled for so long as the Chief Wife, had only borne a daughter; but all knew that her place in the affections of the Emperor was inviolate, higher than anyone else's. That's what Şermi wanted: to be as high as Emetullah – or to displace Emetullah. Perhaps she would apply this delicate paste some other night; she would bear the sovereign a male child, as the midwife whose loyalty she had secured with a pair of diamond earrings had advised – oh yea, most certainly one day.

Levnî and Ahmed
Tavern delights, Konstantiniyye delights

'Set ye a fine table for this evening, Master Yorgakis, as you excel, for my distinguished guest tonight comes from afar.'

'Rest easy, My Lord, none has ever left my shop less than satisfied!'

'My valued friend is a silk merchant from the city of Bursa; he is not familiar with the Seat of Felicity. I don't want to let him return before visiting this tavern, and I know you will do me proud.'

Levnî did fuss, as he wished to entertain his best friend to the best of his ability. He was concerned; there was no room for the slightest mishap tonight. The most important concern was to conclude the night without revealing the true identity of the guest. True, the guest in question knew little of the Seat of Felicity other than the palaces, mansions and mosques, yet it was detail that made the city great, made it unique. So, here was Levnî, preparing to share with his dear friend what he himself enjoyed, in one of the oldest taverns of this Konstantiniyye, one of the richest details in the fabric of the city.

Old Yorgakis ran a tavern located on the ground floor of a stone building in Galata, on one of the streets that opened out to the tower square. The soft light emanating from the tinted oil-lamps in the niches showed the simple wall decorations to the best advantage. The hall was large, high ceilinged and well ventilated, although less than adequately illuminated;

the rows of huge wooden wine casks ranged along one wall were surely promising to the wine lover. Tiny bottles lined up on the narrow wooden shelf – finely carved and decorated in a myriad of colours – alongside the facing wall: different grades of olive oils, vinegars, pomegranate syrup and lemon juice. Huge slabs of coloured stone on the floor, laid out like a gigantic chessboard and now stained with years of splashing drinks, had suffered the tread of countless pairs of feet, the only sign of movement on the otherwise bare floor. Low stools were set around sparsely placed large dining trays raised on wooden stands, awaiting the evening's custom.

'You have honoured us well, My Noble Lord, you have brought us joy! You are early, the Good Lord be praised; nothing I could offer you would be adequate for you or your valued guest, but please come this way!'

The artist and his friend – wearing everyday clothes, of middling height, a dark beard framing his lower face – moved to the table shown: it was already set for the twosome. The beaten-copper dining tray was quite plain, as were the crystal glasses and pitchers and the plates on which the *mezes* were served. What was going to impress was the food and drink. The table was resplendent with colours and aromas. The entire bounty of nature on the cusp of autumn had bedecked the table, alongside the last of the summer produce.

The colour of the wine from the Aegean isles competed with the ruby on the finger of the precious guest. And its bouquet – oh, yes, the sunshine on the vineyards and the shade cast by the grapes themselves, and the thousand and one scents of the earth: the resulting combination, tired of waiting in casks, relaxed and spread, wafting in the air. A world was concealed in this translucent liquid, a world that came into sharper focus the more one drank of it. Yorgakis would also insist that the noble gentlemen taste the white wine that came from Tekirdağ; its tart nose remained long on the palate and transported the drinker to another world.

The grapes brought along after the arrival of the guests were still cool, fetched from the bucket hanging deep in the well. The black grape bunches showed the frost of the cool best, plump and juicy, jostling one another.

The deep yellow of the melons, last of the season, that thick yellow of summer sunshine, looked even more intense next to the fennel-white cheese. A pomegranate – first of the season – had been cracked in the middle and set in the centre of a plate; every single gemstone of its seeds sparkled alluringly, promising resistance to the melancholy of the cold weather approaching, at the very least in the insouciance of this dimly lit tavern.

Spring onions varying from nacreous white to deep green were sprinkled between the tiny *meze* plates set on the round tray, an appetising decoration, like pointed knives in a round frame. The pale matt-green of the broad bean paste on an oval plate whetted the appetite.

Was it the slippery purple of the mussel shells that enhanced the promise of the delicacy? But Levnî had specifically asked for stuffed mussels, certain that not even the palace kitchens could provide the same flavour.

The spiciness of the fresh dill sprinkled liberally over the pickled mackerel nearly overpowered the scent of the wine vinegar. The old tavern-keeper had wrapped the sardines in delicate vine leaves – gathered in the tiny back garden – prior to grilling and painstakingly laying them out on a tray. As the leaves were separated, the skins peeled off, and the now-bared sardines watered the mouth even more. Yorgakis didn't intend to offer any more fish; overdoing it was not his style, and offering competing tastes, never. The one thing he would not forget was livers, Albanian style: finely diced, tossed in finely sliced onions and sprinkled liberally with flaked chilli. Little bread rolls, toasted into a golden colour, were placed in the centre.

Unsalted almonds and shelled walnuts had been placed in small bowls, their colours mingling, and sprinkled with snow, so difficult to get at this time of year as it was usually gathered in large quantities in the winter and kept in snow-stores. This was the rarest of all that was offered tonight; not every patron was so honoured. The tavern-keeper had thought this would impress the guest from the provinces; how was he to know that his guest commanded dedicated snow-stores of his own?

Yorgakis himself had shelled the pistachios from the south.

The Greek tavern-keeper's delight was apparent as he greeted his valued patrons with riddles of his own devising, all of which led to names of his *mezes*: 'So then, short of stature, velvet knickers; apron in front, felt cap atop, purple robes, green kaftan?'

It took a refined man to appreciate these subtle witticisms; seeing the provincial guest's eyes light up pleased the tavern-keeper. The man was clearly in the know, for the answer had come immediately: 'Aubergine!'

Yorgakis had laid down the fried aubergines garnished with yogurt, subtly flavoured with garlic, indicating proudly he would not charge for the dish.

The tavern-keeper, delighted at the reaction of the provincial guest to his food and accompanying riddles, sensed a good tip was forthcoming. He prepared another dish, remembering the recent words of a poet, and approached the precious guests: 'What is this that had turned black/its skin broken up into pieces/they hanged it by the leg/it sprays blood whomever dares touch.'

These gruesome lines startled the guests, and so, failing to elicit the correct answer, he raised the lid triumphantly and left the dish of black mulberries before them. The noble patrons laughed, reaching out to the mulberries, and so the source of mulberries and the riddle both retreated. Yorgakis wasn't keen on the ill-bred, people who couldn't hold their drink; any such customer would be turned back if he ever returned. But customers like these two, who knew how to enjoy a drink, and appreciated the effort he himself had gone to – that was the type of customer to nurture, whose loyalty was worth cultivating.

Just when the patrons were beginning to enjoy the effects of alcohol, the musicians arrived. Tayyar Civan, a regular, also made his appearance at the same time, a toughie who loved his wine, who lived on who-knew-what, but whose reputation had spread to the darkest streets of the Seat of Felicity. He was best known for flamboyant sartorial affectation. His greenish turban was loosely wrapped around his red cap and his black fringe fell upon his brow. He had no beard, but sported countless scars, proof of his escapades into the realms of brawling. He wore a short purple jacket, a salmon-pink shirt and a baggy pair of blue trousers with a very low crotch; a grey scarf with a silver fringe was flung over his right shoulder; he also wore lilac gaiters with silver studs, red shoes and an ivory-handled dagger tucked into his pistachio-green sash. All this combined to create an equally extraordinary and daunting image. He was one of Levnî's unusual friends. He made for their table when he spotted the artist and his companion, heavy eyelids evidence of his already inebriated state.

Levnî's look of concern was countered by Ahmed's authoritative head shake; the 'provincial guest' clearly wanted to know more about the real inhabitants of the city in their natural setting.

'I bid you good evening, my lords, and good appetite!'

'Pray join us; let us continue together!'

Levnî's guest it was who had anticipated the host and invited Tayyar Civan, already bearing down upon the two; there was nothing for it now. Master Yorgakis fetched a stool immediately and the thug grumbled something in thanks as he settled.

'Yorgakis, what is this feast? 'Tis more like the Emperor's meal; when do ye ever do me so proud? You rascal, see if I don't get my own back!'

This, in Tayyar's esteem, was sufficient compliment for the hosts he had selected and so he set upon sampling the *mezes* and the wine without being bidden. Thankfully, he had already consumed enough not to notice how strangely reserved his poet friend was tonight. Having bolted down enough of the food before him, he gazed at the pair and let loose as usual, with no by-your-leave:

'Is this bloke a brother of yours then, Levnî Çelebi? The two are so very alike, except that his get-up is much fancier, lest ye miss it!'

The fancier man didn't let on just how these words had cut him to the quick (the plainer one's discomfiture was limited to embarrassment, that's all). It was the former who replied:

'I hail from the county of Bursa. Abdülcelil Çelebi is a distant cousin on my father's side. He is a courteous host that he leaves me not unaccompanied in these strange parts.'

The thug wanted to impress the guest, now established as a stranger, and so leapt in, his munificence knowing no bounds:

'So, now I understand why I knew ye not. Dader Banu has many belles in the establishment, go, were you of a mind to seek such gratification, and give her my greetings. She will see ye well.'

Levnî strove to suppress a smirk, wondering how this ignoramus would react, were he only to have the slightest idea of the number of belles who graced the harem of his table companion! His guest thanked for the offer, courteous as ever, and stated they would pay that establishment a visit by and by.

This time had turned out to be much different from the previous occasions when he went in mufti, chatting to a few ordinary folk and wandering around a little in the skiff of Bald İbrahim of Serez before returning to the safety of his keep. He was experiencing the city to the utmost, and wasn't this what he had truly wished for?

Once the night was over, safe and sound, his companion decided otherwise; it would take an awful lot for him to repeat the experience. When they reached the palace pier, collected by the secretive imperial guards who had followed them at a discreet distance all night long, the illuminator's face reflected the exhausted relief of someone who had successfully passed a test. On the face of the Emperor was the delighted surprise of a child given a brand-new toy.

İbrahim and Mehtabe
Forbidden love

'A note has arrived for you, madam, this time borne by a man, answers to Hüseyin One-Eye. I've hurried it over, and not been seen.'

'Thank you, my precious steward. What I would do without you, I know not.'

The steward giggled, unexpectedly girlish in her advanced years; she viewed herself as an essential element of this fabulous escapade, one that she herself would never experience. And the warmth of being appreciated, augmented by hefty tips, as her lady did! Mehtabe gazed impatiently at the roll the steward drew out of her wrinkled bosom; she hurried to break the seal and read through the note in one breath.

She had feigned disinterest and timidity at İbrahim Pasha's advances at first. Yet she was well ready for an affair of the heart. She believed this to be finally the love that she deserved. The bland life she led, married to a man who wholeheartedly continued the sobriety required of a sharia judge in his home, had finally been livened up, and at such an unexpected moment!

Mehtabe's background was unassuming – nay, poor. When she was a slip of a girl in that small Western Thracian town of her birth, neighbours would proclaim that this little coquette was destined for greater places. Brains and beauty arrived early, too. One look into her eyes, and the gazer would have to look again. Finding her way into the imperial harem was an early ambition, yet the *Kadı* heard of her beauty well before the Sultan ever had the opportunity to, and her milkman father hadn't hesitated for a moment. Particularly fond of moonlit nights, the *Kadı* had renamed his fourteen-year-old bride Mehtabe, 'moonlight lady'. The girl found herself in the bed of Zülalîzade Arnavut Hasan Efendi. Unable, initially, to believe his fortune in possessing such a precious treasure, the man had grown complacent in time, and more interested in the newly arrived petite concubine.

And one had to concede that Grand Vizier İbrahim Pasha had pursued her relentlessly, from the day following their first meeting at Kağıthane, with a single-mindedness specific only to men who are used to getting their own way. The infrequency of their meetings despite the statesman's relentless pursuit kept the flames of this forbidden relationship alive. The statesman sought the right opportunity; his time was all but filled with his wife and his Emperor. But where there's a will, there's always a way to be found, and a place.

Mehtabe remembered the first present he gave her – a sapphire ring, the exact colour of her eyes, like a protestation of love shining in the deepest of blues. Every subsequent meeting had been similarly generous, give İbrahim Pasha his due: a jewellery box encrusted with diamonds and rubies, a pair of twisted gold bracelets, pearl-and-emerald drop earrings, soft slippers embroidered with pearls and a few of the rarest tulip bulbs. So, she had to conceal the jewellery from her husband; but there was nothing to stop her wearing them at the gatherings of her closest friends. Mehtabe took great delight in displaying her precious jewellery until rumours spread too far and wide to be ignored. The tulip bulbs given by the Grand Vizier were even finer in meaning than the jewellery, and he had named each and every one in reference to his mistress: 'scarlet sparrow', 'coquette', 'pleasure giver', 'rosy cheeks', 'dawn's mist' and 'ruby dagger'.

★ ★ ★

Fatma Sultan presented İbrahim Pasha with a son at this time. Sultan Ahmed was in seventh heaven. He named his grandson Mehmed after his own father, the glorious ancestor of them all. The dazzling presents he sent his daughter were the talk of the town for days and days. Life went on at its accustomed pace in İbrahim Pasha's *yalı*.

Tidings of Victory from the Front
War, on the other hand

'The commander of the Iraqi front has captured Kermanshah, My Majestic Sultan. The King of Lorestan, Ali Merdan, who answers to the man who proclaimed himself Tahmasp II in Tabriz, has also been vanquished. Sine, the capital of Erdelan, has surrendered willingly.'

Sultan Ahmed rewarded the messenger with a purse of silver; the man had summarised the news before reading the written report.

After observing the divan council in his usual place – behind the grille in Justice Tower – he issued an edict towards ensuring public order.

The said commander of the Iraqi front died immediately. Afterwards, his son was appointed in his place. The new commander outwitted the Safavid Mahmud Han's move to annex Hemedan next to reinforce his rule and conquered the town. It was the Ottoman Empire that consolidated its position with the capture of Nihavend and Hürremabad soon after.

The war in the East had turned into a ruthless battle of interests, a massively chaotic mêlée where only the swiftest triumphed. The Ottoman Empire battled both Shah Tahmasp, who led some of the Safavids, and Mahmud Han, who had captured the Safavid throne, whilst recapturing former Ottoman holdings one by one.

Life carried on in extravagant splendour at the seraglio.

Marie-Geneviève-Marguerite and Ahmed
The sovereign's new love

The Emperor had commanded young Marguerite to come to his bed wearing Parisian clothes. He knew the Master of the Girls found this an eccentric request, but he didn't care. The only thing he did insist on, however, was that the girl would wash thoroughly in the palace baths, in Ottoman fashion. What Yirmisekiz Çelebi recounted about the hygiene habits of the Europeans was not only revolting but also horrifying. Now he waited impatiently for the arrival of the Frankish girl.

Marie-Geneviève-Marguerite was not only a formidable beauty but she was also one of those adventurous souls that arise in every society, in every period. She came from a noble yet impoverished family and might have ended up scampering to keep her head above the others in palace intrigues as a lady-in-waiting or at best married a rich man seeking aristocratic blood and bred a handful of children. But the maiden had fabulous dreams, and she knew herself to be highly sexual too: no shrinking violet was she, instead impatient for the treasures of love and lust. The rumour that spread in Parisian parties and many had found hard to believe, namely, that the Ottoman Sultan had despatched his men to find a young Parisian belle for his harem, reached Marguerite's ears. She found that this rumour quickened her heart, and the same heart grew cold towards her inexperienced young lover, who counted a stolen kiss a major triumph.

Marie-Geneviève-Marguerite had observed the Ambassador and his men during their diplomatic sojourn in Paris on a number of occasions and pretexts; she did not find them alien at all. If anything, their stately and proud bearing, distinctive behaviour, masculinity, yea, even brutality – all these were traits she had admired. The idea of submitting as a love slave to the mighty ruler of the East, the grand master of them all, was heady indeed. The lightness of her eighteen years needed but a spark to take wing.

The allure of the unknown had blinded Marguerite to the darker implications of becoming a slave in a harem. She was sure she would become the queen of them all – even, oh, yea, transforming the ruler of the East with her love, making him into a new man. By the time she learnt that reality bore little similarity to dreams, it was too late.

And finally, after an escape from home, which it had been politically expedient to present as a simple case of elopement, a journey whose details had been suppressed, and long preparations – some she found highly agreeable, others terrifying – here she was, before the gathered curtains of the Grand Seigneur's bed.

★   ★   ★

She came out of the Turkish bath – her first ever – glowing pink; never would she forget this bathing episode, this violent clash of cultures. The bath mistress, an assiduous member of her profession, had set out to prepare the Emperor's squeeze in the proper manner. Depilation of the entire body with sugar wax was an inescapable part of this routine. The peevish Frankish damsel had resisted as soon as she realised what the intention was; she had screamed at the top of her voice, resisted with all her power and finally succeeded in getting away from the bath mistress. The experienced servant had decided not to force the sovereign's latest favourite. Were this oversight to infuriate the Emperor, her own defence was ready.

And now the Frankish damsel was confident of her own beauty, wearing for the first time a gown she had ordered in

Paris: pale blue taffeta, adorned with creamy lace at the chest, sleeves and skirt. She had also rejected the scents the lady steward had tried to douse her in; she would have neither the sharp lavender nor the heady rose. Her own seductive perfume she had brought over from Paris, the blend of orange-blossom and lily-of-the-valley in the crystal phial would do very well, thank you. She had applied it liberally wherever she thought appropriate.

The huge bow on the deep décolleté of her blue gown bore Sultan Ahmed's first gift brought by the harem eunuch: a showy brooch, depicting a bird on a branch. The bird's body was of a large turquoise, its eyes emeralds and pointed wings of diamonds. The branch it had perched on bore leaves made entirely of diamonds. A slender spring behind the jewel shook the leaves with the slightest move of the wearer; the startling blue-green of the jewel flattered the colour of her eyes. Marguerite was finding it hard to believe that the Emperor had gone to the trouble of commissioning a jewel specifically to compliment her assets; her own fairy tale of a thousand and one nights had already begun.

She had to style her hair in Parisian fashion herself, in coils that piled up into a high bun; the hairdresser mistress, who normally did the harem ladies' tresses, was unfamiliar with this style.

Ahmed greeted her by getting to his feet, having learnt from his envoy that women were treated with surprising deference. He wore not his usual lovemaking outfit of fine nightgown and cap, but a thin silk kaftan bearing an intricate pattern of tulips and a jewel-clasp belt. The ruby aigrette sparkling on his turban had been selected to accent the red of the kaftan, however much the Emperor would deny giving in to vanity. Never had it been seen before that the sovereign of the Ottoman State would go to such lengths to impress a Frankish damsel.

And so suddenly here they were, not an emperor and a concubine, not the chooser and the chosen, but instead, a forty-nine-year-old man, his youth long gone, and an eighteen-year-old girl, the freshness of her young days all too obvious. Both tried to impress the other, ignoring the pathetic or ridiculous conflicts of their situation. Neither did the girl appear to have made much effort to 'adorn herself with scented black kohl and rouges to better define her beauty', in the words of the imperial envoy; instead, it was the Ruler of the Seven Climes himself who had gone to such lengths!

Ahmed held Marguerite's trembling hand and gazed into her eyes; seeing excitement, but also curiosity, defiance – and above all, desire – in those sea-coloured eyes, he was shaken to the core. Sultan Ahmed had only seen an infinite submission on the faces of the women he had selected to bed; the best he could hope for was delight in having been picked. Yet Marguerite bore the insouciance of Paris; she was entitled to sexual gratification, this could not be the monopoly of men, even if they be the Emperor, said her artless innocence. It seemed both had much to learn from each other, and learn they did.

Untying the intricate lacing of her corset was a first for Sultan Ahmed, an arousing new experience. The layers and layers of lace underskirts that were revealed beneath the gown were another surprise. Her shocking willingness to undress aroused him as much as the avid interest with which she watched him undress.

* * *

It had been no longer than a fortnight since the arrival of Marie-Geneviève-Marguerite at the imperial harem. Her command of Turkish was limited to a few words at best. Sultan Ahmed had attempted to learn some French, but it was impossible for the two to hold the simplest of conversations. So, they tried to communicate not by not talking but rather by not worrying if neither understood what was being said. The Parisienne had followed a dream of happiness in the powerful arms of the mightiest man of the East, a man she viewed as the symbol of sexuality. Sultan Ahmed was all too ready to indulge her dream, and so he willingly gave pleasure as he took his own.

The Emperor quickly got the hang of kissing and lovemaking in the Frankish fashion, and Marguerite, for her part, soon learnt what pleased her man. The only predictable thing about their lovemaking was its unpredictability; they changed the rules constantly. What these two people enjoyed was one of the rare, truly passionate love affairs in the history of the great harem, that fabulous place of dazzling İznik tiles, painted decorations, ornamental fountains, silk throws, splendid jewelled hangings and unbelievable sorrows, many of whose rooms were used for living in and for loving in by the Ottoman emperors; but none ever knew how long the sovereign would continue to be in love.

Meylidil and Ahmed
No return

Marguerite's hands caressed Ahmed's closely shaven skull, then followed down to his wide shoulders; stroking the Sultan's powerful body – witness to years of riding and archery – pleased her well. She felt grown up, part of a very exclusive, highly superior world, at such times. And she was rewarded well each time.

The Emperor had stretched out on red tulips and blue carnations – almost too small for the naked eye – embroidered in the style known as 'sand needle'; this cool white linen sheet had turned into a veritable flower garden. Marguerite was familiar with Parisian refinement, but the attention paid to detail here far surpassed her expectations. She returned her gaze back to the man. Sultan Ahmed had little patience with interest in anything but himself when in bed.

The French girl's entreaties had finally borne fruit, and the lady steward, whose usual seat was by the foot of the bed, had been demoted to the door. This was the singularly most horrifying thing for Marguerite, the presence of the poor creature whose duty – or was it punishment? – was to observe what Sultan Ahmed did with the woman in his bed. This was for his security. He was inured, hardly noticing the steward's presence when he made love. He might at best drop down the curtains around the bed for privacy so the lady steward would not see, but imperial lovemaking would be audible to her in all its detail all the same. Once, when the Frankish girl raised her voice, she and the lady steward had come eye to eye when the latter had to put her head through the curtains, alarmed for the safety of her master; she cared not a whit for anything else. But Marguerite did, and so avoided a similarly mortifying situation ever again at all costs.

*　*　*

Ahmed had renamed this fabulous girl Meylidil, meaning 'the desire of the heart, heart-snatcher'. This name meant much more than the obvious. It symbolised much that Sultan Ahmed's soul yearned for but could never attain, possibly even new worlds, even their dreams thrilling on their own. It was as if a new chapter had opened up before Sultan Ahmed with the advent of young Meylidil, a new viewpoint on the world, on life, on women and men.

He and Meylidil got together once a week – other than the nights – mid-morning, ostensibly to study French. The new *gözde* talked about the palace in the pictures decorating the books Yirmisekiz Çelebi had brought back from Paris. She talked of the fun times, of parties, the feasts and shows at balls, one thousand and one shapes of water spray thrown by the fountains in the palace gardens and of unforgettable theatre shows in water. This was very different from Yirmisekiz Çelebi's account. Sultan Ahmed took notes in his own handwriting against some of the illustrations in the books.

The notion that the young woman might miss her birthplace clouded the ruler's brow from time to time. The worst was when his beloved Meylidil talked of the times when she used to dance in the arms of others. However difficult it might be for him to admit, this was the black cloud of jealousy, plain and simple.

*　*　*

The great master Antoine Watteau had included Marie-Geneviève-Marguerite in one of his delightful paintings of careless and handsome folk having a good time in the countryside. The young girls had secretly gone to the studio a number of times to pose and she had enjoyed this representation on canvas of her own beauty. The skilful manner in which the fresh pink on her cheeks, the graceful curve of her neck and cheeky sparkle in her eyes had been depicted had mollified her father somewhat, but he never stopped scolding her for posing in a crowd scene like some commoner, even if the artist was one as celebrated as Watteau. This painting now hung in the king's palace; this was the only memento her parents had of her. She grew to realise the cruelty of her farewell letter much later. Marguerite did wonder from time to time, however seldom that was: did her parents raise their heads to look at the painting hanging in one of the entrance halls each time they went to the palace for a reception? Or did they bow their heads, still smarting from the insult? Meylidil's pride prevented her from indulging in the fiery abyss of regret.

Yet each time she was left alone in the night, when darkness settled upon the harem and even the oil-lamps began to flicker, when all the other denizens of the harem – the dark-eyed Nurışems, the rose-lipped Goncanigâr, the moon-faced Hüsnimelek, plump-necked Binnaz, golden-haired Şayeste and Ferhunde with the mole in her dimple, all these women who had been wrenched from their own families at a very tender age, whose birth names had long since been forgotten and who had been raised at this majestic school to entertain one single man, to make him happy, to offer him solace and bear his children – avoided her company, this extraordinary Frankish beauty who had chosen to come here of her own will as an adult, and with whom their master was clearly infatuated, that was the time her thoughts went to the land of her birth, to Paris, to her home.

And when she did so indulge, however unwillingly, she knew a kind of insanity had possessed her, so she forced her thoughts back to this one man who was the centre of her universe, her only consolation. True, he was completely infatuated with her, yes, yet there were others he lusted after equally, hard as this was to accept. She had come here knowing this to be the case, but thinking she could somehow change things in the artless courage that stems from being very young and intrepid.

So, the Grand Seigneur was the sum total of the little damsel's life, and the little damsel was a pretty and tiny diversion in the life of the Grand Seigneur ...

İbrahim and Ahmed

'Vizier mine, more precious than my own life, my loyal companion, my Nestor, would that the Great Lord refrain from granting me another besides you as My Vizier.'

'Vizier mine,

'Your foot has been aching. This news has grieved me greatly. If the physician's medicine does not work, then you must see the surgeon; neglect is ill advised, you must see the physician. I had meant to visit you today. Would my visit trouble you? If you are unable to move to a different room without much suffering, I will postpone my visit. May the Good Lord be nigh and grant you a speedy recovery, amen.'

This correspondence was but one testimony to the Emperor's high esteem the Grand Vizier enjoyed. There was little here that could not have waited until İbrahim Pasha was well enough to personally come to Sultan Ahmed's presence. The Emperor wanted to see his Grand Vizier frequently; that was all. He had complete trust in İbrahim Pasha in matters of state as well as those of pleasure and entertainment. İbrahim Pasha may well have been the most privileged minister of all time. The Emperor was genuinely fond of him, too. İbrahim Pasha's health was his own concern, which he freely expressed:

'Vizier mine, more precious than my own life, my loyal companion, my Nestor, would that the Great Lord refrain from granting me another besides you as My Vizier.'

★ ★ ★

Sultan Ahmed acted as if he had completely forgotten, during his brother's reign, how he himself had criticised Sultan Mustafa's utter trust in, and limitless powers granted to, Şeyhülislam Feyzullah Efendi, and how ultimately those close to the top cleric had 'occupied the world', deposing his brother. Yet it was Sultan Ahmed himself who, not that long ago – then still a caged crown prince, awaiting his turn at the throne – warned his elder brother:

'My auspicious elder brother, Your Majesty! Your flattery of the esteemed *hodja* stems from your trust in him, and if the root be your respect for the right to teach and the right to learn, so be it. The exalted position of the Emperor is verily a divine light; the people's rise and fall are measured against their proximity to this light. Should your light persist on illuminating only one individual, or a group of individuals, it is self-evident that others would be offended by your partiality. By modifying your favour to a more rational level, you would reconcile your favoured servants by sparing them from the ill will or envy; this would well suit your beneficent rule. That being said, you it is who knows best.'

This outburst had astounded the viziers around them by its audacity. And here he was, the very same man who had once warned his elder brother against overindulging one servant, now endowing his own Grand Vizier with unprecedented licence.

İbrahim Pasha was blessed with a razor-sharp intellect. He also was one of the most greedy pleasure seekers that history had ever seen, to the extent that those who envied him hissed 'pleasure pimp' behind his back. He had, to be fair, earned the soubriquet: he adored luxury and extravagance. Profligacy ran through his veins and all this he adorned with his refined tastes, and yet his tireless work in supporting science and the arts and his efforts in bringing technology to the land were impossible to overlook.

İbrahim and Ahmed
Riddles

'Vizier mine,

'Devise some riddles, and send them to me; make them hard, not simple. Also send me the illustrated Frankish books seen at the *yalı* last year.'

Sultan Ahmed was so certain that his Grand Vizier would never fail him that he had grown accustomed to asking the statesman for even the things that would normally have been the responsibility of a servant. So receiving an imperial command for riddles, such a favourite with the Sultan, didn't surprise the statesman. The sovereign had also asked for the Frankish books with illustrations.

When Sultan Ahmed found the answer, 'Nail!' to the riddle, 'a tiny Arab, with a tray on its head' his pleasure was plain to see; or 'Snail!' to 'what manner of clerk is this/writes and scribbles as it heaves its basket on its back'!

The poets wrote riddles day and night for the Emperor: 'What is this thing that breaks when I tread on 't/half of it is silver, half in golden yellow/not a living creature, but takes life/brings cure to the sick man in need of life' was easy with 'Egg!' but 'The Good Lord above has created above a sceptre/ silver edges, diagonal centre a golden chalice' was a bit trickier to answer as 'Narcissus!'

★   ★   ★

Sultan Ahmed had summoned his son-in-law. İbrahim Pasha arrived in a hurry. His patron must have something of importance to share, he knew; but what he was not prepared for was a riddle his Emperor had written:

'Apron in front, felt cap atop, purple robes, green kaftan.'

The Grand Vizier wondered who had taught his Emperor this riddle, before he collected himself well enough to reply. Then he noticed Sultan Ahmed's favourite companion Levnî standing in the corner of the Privy Chamber. The Emperor had been spending more and more time with the artist of late, so it must have been Levnî who had devised this riddle. Their eyes locked briefly and the artist bowed respectfully. Never one to reveal his fury or worry that easily, İbrahim Pasha responded:

'My Noble Sovereign, pray grant me time enough to consider!'

Ahmed and Hümaşah and Şermi and Nazife and Meylidil

Bath time

The steam rose to the pierced dome, filling the caldarium of the imperial bath like an aromatic mist. It also enrobed the young, naked bodies surrounding the sovereign, transparent and alluring. The Emperor was sitting on the marble seat like a throne by the basin. He was too busy to listen to the murmuring of the water trickling down the ornamental fountain, all his attention focused on Şermi, who was soaping his feet slowly, deliberately. He feigned, at least for the time being, disinterest in Nazife soaping his back. Nazife was very young indeed, and determined to please her master. Being this close to the Ruler of the Seven Climes, touching his bare skin – surely these were rewards enough for now! There was little room for haste here; everything had to move at the viscous pace of trickling sherbet.

The joy of bathing was the ultimate finale to a busy night for Sultan Ahmed. He never bathed alone, always accompanied by as many concubines and *gözdes* as could fit behind the gilt grilles. Sultan Selim II, also known as Selim the Sot, his ancestor, was rumoured to have slipped chasing a concubine in the bath and thus met his end. Sultan Ahmed, for his part, was far more prudent: embraced by several women in the bath, there was little risk of him slipping!

These bath parties were one of the things Meylidil was struggling to accept. True, there were Turkish baths in Paris, but she herself had never been in one. In any case, those baths were more effective in their small chambers, suitable for lovers' assignations. Parisians did bathe after a fashion, if you could call dipping into a tub of water briefly bathing, but no one washed as thoroughly as people did in this country. She had taken great umbrage at being forced to bathe as she was prepared for the Sultan's bed for the first time, but eventually she had learnt this to be a *sine qua non* in the Ottoman lifestyle and forced herself to accept it.

The small section set aside for the queen mother and the chief wives marked the end of the women's bathhouse in the harem. This section was called the Queen Mother's Bath. And what truly unnerved Meylidil in the women's bath were the merciless stares of the Emperor's women, seeking the tiniest flaw: whose skin was the fairest, whose waist slenderest and whose hair longest. Things were different in the Emperor's bath, the bigger of the two baths in the harem. The race here had a different goal – to attract the Emperor's favour.

This cut-throat race sometimes quickened Meylidil's competitive spirit, but mostly left her nonplussed, even suffocated.

Meylidil and Fatma
Friendship

Meylidil never warmed to the harem women, who were her co-partners in the affections of her man. The merciless denizens of the harem never welcomed the young girl into the fold, despite the countless commands, exhortations and pleadings of the Emperor himself. She insisted on maintaining her Frenchness, an attitude tolerated by the sovereign. The young *gözde*'s life in the harem was all too soon whipped from the wings of ecstasy to the depths of despair. No one in the harem – none of the wives, concubines or stewards, not even the emasculated harem officials – had ever forgotten the sauntering of this triple-named French girl, this *Mari Jönviv Margarit*, how she had sauntered down the dark corridors of the harem, resplendent in her blue ball gown, on her way to her first night with their Emperor.

The only person not to reject her outright was Chief Wife Emetullah, this mature woman with a gentle heart. This new, young co-partner who brightened the life of her one and only beloved, who opened brand-new horizons before her man, had not upset the lady – quite the opposite: his joy gave her cause to rejoice. Emetullah never spared her friendship of this strange young girl. Meylidil was nearly the same age as her daughter Fatma Sultan, the Sultan's precious daughter, the apple of his eye, the daughter he had found a fitting bride for his cherished Grand Vizier. Meylidil was one of the first people Fatma Sultan had wanted to meet when the princess paid the harem a visit from her palace on the Bosphorus. The two young women managed to converse somehow, one speaking rudimentary French, the other struggling with Turkish.

Meylidil did envy the princess, wanting to spend as much time with her as possible. Fatma Sultan came from the world outside; she may have been a woman, but she could get out of the house to visit her father's palace, sometimes on that fabulous boat, sometimes in a coach drawn by fine horses. And she was her father's precious, spoilt daughter, whilst Meylidil was a little despondent. Yet Marguerite too had been spoilt, in that home now far behind her; she knew how good it was to be indulged by a loving family, not a lover: how carefree, how freely given it was.

'Last night's lantern party was monumental,' said Fatma Sultan, 'İbrahim Pasha had placed colourful whirligigs between the tulip vases and the lanterns, right before the musicians. We watched from the harem windows and enjoyed the sight exceedingly well.'

Sultan Ahmed usually took a few of the women from his harem each time he went to a party thrown by İbrahim Pasha, allowing them to watch the festivities from a women's section. Meylidil had also participated a few times, but she wanted to go all the time, not wait her turn. However much she might try to conceal it, the Emperor's preference of others before her broke her heart. She was impatient for the end of May to come, just like the other women and *gözdes* did, so they could move to Aynalıkavak Palace. She thought the Emperor might be more accessible there, that he might be able to spend a good deal of time in the garden. She never gave up on her dreams.

She showed Fatma Sultan the latest present given to her by the sovereign – an aigrette, a fabulous jewel in the shape of a massive tulip, made of a ruby surrounded by diamonds. A faint cloud passed over the face of the princess as she took in the size of the flawless, blood-red ruby, the clarity of the diamonds and – above all – the extraordinary elegance of the jewel, indicating the presence of an exceptionally attentive man, but she was quick to gather her wits:

'It flatters your golden hair well; may you be granted the fortune to wear it on auspicious days, Meylidil!'

İbrahim and Fatma and Mehtabe
Different loves

The latest buzz in all the parties was the tale of the two songs İbrahim Pasha had composed for his wife, his one and only young wife. İbrahim Pasha's heart, though it sang to his princess wife, was occupied elsewhere: a new love he could not forsake. The risk of discovery by his princess wife frightened the great man to death. But whenever the idea of calling it all off beckoned, his lust simply drowned his terror. The judge's delectable wife had swept him off his feet; İbrahim Pasha was utterly besotted with Mehtabe.

İbrahim Pasha did truly love his wife the princess. The poems he wrote came from a sincere heart, yet there had always been invisible barriers between the two. The aristocratic Fatma Sultan was not a lusty lover, but a tender partner he almost protected as he caressed and stroked. There were times when he wondered whether it was the Emperor's precious daughter he protected or his own existence. This was a true enigma, yet he succeeded in shooing this thought away into the farthest corners of his mind each time. The provocative Mehtabe, on the other hand, offered no inhibitions.

Levnî and
the Likeness of Meylidil
Signature

Sultan Ahmed's new experiences with Meylidil were not for him to share with anyone else. However close his friend – even a cherished companion – no gallant man could relate these things to another. But his own ideas and emotions on the new worlds opened by women – now those were subjects fit for discussion with Levnî.

Sultan Ahmed had established his repute as one who treated his women well, gentler and more tolerant than would have been customary. Discovering new horizons with Meylidil had encouraged him to go deeper with the others. He would make a real effort to understand them all better; so, he began to spend more time with all his women, and not just for lovemaking. He had already been embroidering; he now moved on to needle lace, giving rise to surprised delight in the harem, where nothing ever remained a secret. It also caused much gossip in the brightly lit mansions of the great and the good, and in the dim coffee houses of the Seat of Felicity, about yet another fad – strange Emperor, strange fads.

The denizens of the harem much admired the fineness of the lace their ruler's hands created, or at the very least appeared to do so, but none attempted to understand the sensitivity that underlay the work. Except, that is, for Levnî: his beloved sovereign had been moved by a desire to appreciate the tiny little detail at the tip of the needle that brightened this small, insulated world of his women. The Emperor had not sought, as one might have supposed, the sense of accomplishment that comes from forcing the boundaries of manual skills in creating those miniature embroideries.

* * *

'Do you understand how strange and difficult it is to lack that which is proscribed, Levnî mine? Yes, there is much that is forbidden to all of us – yea, even to me – but defying those bans does not offer a triumph over the unattainable, does it? How to tell you what is on my mind ... My ancestor Sultan Mehmed the Conqueror had his likeness painted by Italian masters; the portrait painted in the oils invented by the infidels was so lifelike that even his son Bayezid Han dared not destroy it, but had it despatched to that Italian instead. Yet how I would have wished to possess that painting in my own palace, in my own treasury, that I may imagine this noble king of our bloodline standing beside me!'

Sultan Ahmed saw how his words delighted his companion, as the illuminator's eyes had sparkled, waiting for the rest of his benefactor's proclamation.

'So I treasure those likenesses that you make, that look real, that look like they have volume. It is my desire to see more of these likenesses. If I were to command you to make the likeness of one of my women – of Meylidil, the one of Frankish origin, the one I spoke to you about – would I surprise you over-much?'

* * *

Levnî knew this to be a seminal moment. From this point onwards, his work would be much easier, no one would criticise him for too realistic a portrayal of any creature: the ruler, a tramp, a hound, or a flower, nothing he put on canvas with a brush would meet censure. He was also certain that painters who would come after him would strive to overcome even more, and would paint lifelike paintings on stretched canvas, just like the Frankish artists did.

He painted Meylidil as Marie-Geneviève-Marguerite, as an unattainable Frankish woman, wearing a gown with a deep décolleté whose lace barely covered her breasts, and a fan in her gloved hand. He inspected the signature he had placed at the bottom left of the picture. He had lavished as much attention on the flower of his signature as he had on the rest of the portrait, not that this was immediately obvious. Levnî always set out to limit access to the finer nuances of his work to a select few, else who would note that the single pink thorn apple rising above the letters *lam, waw, nun* and *ya* – that made up the word Levnî – was different from all the rest? This very fragile flower blossomed into full glory under bright daylight, as if it were laughing out loud, and then sulked into vanishing as soon as the sun moved away: did the artist find some parallel with the concubine's own disposition, next to her man, and then away from him? Or was it simply the apparently uncomplicated intricacy of the flower? Who would ever know?

Levnî and Ahmed
What the Sultan enjoys

'I wish I could lock all dreams in pictures and all words in poems, not to imprison them – no, but quite the opposite: to grant them eternal liberty, to bring them to the spring of life.'

The ruler waited a little to better savour his companion's words – how he longed for a similar ambition! To create beauty on canvas using his hand directed by his soul and to pour his soul onto those sheets!

The Emperor's art of choice had been calligraphy since he was a young prince, and now he was determined to progress. He would put to good use the skill God had blessed him with, to create beauty that would live on, that would please the hearts of those who looked upon his work. He had practised the art of Hafız Osman Efendi, had spent many hours learning from this master and finally merited a certificate from his teacher.

Sultan Ahmed III did realise his dream; he became the finest calligrapher emperor of all time. Vacillating between pride and modesty, he presented a copy each of his hand-written Korans to Kocamustafa Şeyh Nureddin Efendi and to Veliyüddin Efendi, the imam of the Hafızpaşa Mosque; he also sent two copies to Rawza-al Mutahhara, the Pure Garden that is the Prophet Mohammed's mausoleum in Medina.

Sultan Ahmed asked Levnî to adorn his finest calligraphic work with flowers. The result revealed the similarity of talent between the two men as it also concealed it. Thus, the Sultan struggled hardest to conceal the secret he harboured.

* * *

'This infidel named Aristotle has spoken such truths, Levnî mine!'

Sultan Ahmed had desired to inspect the latest translations together with Levnî.

'But then, he was the teacher to Alexander the Great, was he not? İbn Rüşd himself had referred to this great teacher, especially on matters of religion.'

His companion thought to himself that the Emperor ever did enjoy flaunting his deep knowledge:

'Just as you say, My Sultan, it was thanks to Aristo that İbn Rüşd came to the conclusion that religion was philosophy simplified to make it more accessible to the people.'

Levnî and the Emperor did indeed take great pleasure in discussing such matters.

'You showed such munificence when Spandonizade and Yanyalı Esad Efendi collaborated on the translations of Aristo from Greek and presented their work. The gold coins you handed out must have made them immeasurably happy!'

An avid reader of history, Sultan Ahmed had commissioned translations of countless books from Arabic and Persian and instructed the Greek-speaking scholars Spandonizade and Yanyalı Esad Efendi to translate the works of Aristotle. The translations of Yirmisekiz Çelebi were of equal interest to the Emperor. İbrahim Pasha shared and supported this interest, and it was he who had made it possible for a translation council to be founded. Both men preferred opening up to such vast horizons than trying to anticipate future balances of power on the heels of the battles that dragged on in Iran: the politics of war they found highly distasteful, and even vexing.

Whether Sultan Ahmed would have acted differently had he known what the turmoil in the East would cost him in the future was to remain a mystery forever.

Levnî and Yirmisekiz Çelebi
Tulips, everyone's favourite

'This one is called the 'pleasure herald', Levnî Çelebi. I know you will like these tulips. I had to bring you a few bulbs!'

'What troubles you have gone to, Mehmed Çelebi! How will I know to thank you sufficiently? These tulips will brighten up my tiny garden, and will remind me of you each time I look upon them!'

Yirmisekiz Çelebi had brought his friend a new cultivar he had been working on; the deep purple of the petals paled into lilac towards the tips. The statesman was very pleased with his new tulip. He had guarded the bulbs jealously up to now, saving one small trunkful for the Emperor.

The post of Imperial Accountant that he had occupied for a year was not entirely to Yirmisekiz Çelebi's liking – all that work with land deeds and different sizes of landholdings granted in return for military service! Yet he surely did enjoy the power this position gave him. He had further been promoted to Chief Daily Bookkeeper in the following year. Both Sultan Ahmed and İbrahim Pasha had shown sufficient trust in the man to keep an honest record of daily expenses.

The former diplomat could finally spend as long as he wanted with his precious tulips. Master of Flowers Lalezari Mehmed Efendi, a namesake, was one of his closest friends, however much this latest cultivar may have caused envy between the two men. Tulips required application, and not only for the growing. Bend onto one's knees before this fragile flower to catch its scent, so unlike hyacinths or carnations!

They spread their bouquet generously, requiring no exertion of their admirers. The rose needed a breeze, however slight, to carry its fragrance. Magnolia was the only flower reluctant to divulge its perfume; those magnificent, unique petals would blacken at the slightest touch. It tolerated no rough handling, and one had to approach lightly and inhale deeply.

Yirmisekiz Çelebi also chose the tulip.

Mosque Illuminations
Greeting the sultan of the twelve months

'I have issued the command, Levnî mine, for those hanging illuminated pictures to fly from every royal mosque to brighten up the hearts every Ramadan!'

Sultan Ahmed was in high spirits. Finding another way of adding more beauty to the Seat of Felicity always cheered him up like a child. His son-in-law İbrahim Pasha was adept at presenting innovations and bright ideas as if they were the Sultan's. The companion wondered how the Grand Vizier had gone about it this time.

Many royal mosques had begun to display *mahya* illuminations during Ramadan, in celebration of the advent of the sultan of all the months. Symbols of sovereignty, these mosques were further distinguished now by these illuminations: as only royal mosques could erect more than one minaret, so only royal mosques could be so adorned. The inhabitants of Konstantiniyye very quickly espoused *mahyas*, and their popularity spread far and wide. The Sultan's latest firman would equip all mosques with *mahyas*, costs being met out of the Sultan's own foundation.

The first *mahya* had been flown during the reign of Sultan Ahmed I, between the minarets of the Ahmediye, also known as the Sultanahmed Mosque, whose splendour outshone Hagia Sophia. Despite the universal admiration it had evoked, this expensive celebration had never been regulated.

'My August Sultan, one *mahya* consumes six kilos of oil. Süleymaniye Mosque will use up 1,099 kilos.'

Sultan Ahmed was startled at the cost; true, he loved these illuminations that transformed the Seat of Felicity into a sparkling jewel, and had asked Levnî to learn quite how they were made. Still, he had no idea that this ostentatious display that so pleased the eye and the heart could cost this much. İbrahim Pasha had not mentioned the expense.

Those were the days when life flew at a rapid pace, new pleasures discovered, the joy of living reinvented. Ramadan had begun at the end of May; people could stroll from one mosque to the next, comparing the illuminations, and debating which was the most skilful. The verbal messages on these dazzling displays gave way to pictorial illuminations nearing the end of Ramadan: mosques, mansions, Leander's Tower, flowers or boats. Konstantiniyye had always loved lights. The whole city so embraced this custom of bedecking minarets with oil-lamps that they extended from the entire month of Ramadan to the two religious festivals and the five holy nights.

*   *   *

The master *mahyacı* had written that night's message on a sheet of graph paper so he could work out the precise distribution of the lamps. He inspected the rows of rope he had prepared: the knots were spaced evenly and were firm; he also checked the leather ties at the knots. All the ropes were ready. He began by making the curve of the D, the first letter in tonight's illuminations. He worked carefully, taking delight in his unhurried pace. There was no need for haste as the entire city watched his work until the morning light.

He had worked hard to rise to the position of *mahyacı* to Süleymaniye Mosque, so he would never do anything less than his absolute best lest he lose his privilege.

He had prepared the minaret oil-lamps earlier, too. These lamps consumed twelve grammes of oil per hour. Others made the wick out of pistachio stems, but Süleymaniye's master roasted freshwater reeds and then wrapped cotton wool around them to obtain a brighter flame. He had even taught his apprentice, no professional jealousy staying his hand.

The apprentice placed the buoy into each oil lamp first and then assisted his master in putting each lamp into a large, round housing, carefully shutting the lid on each one to prevent the oil lamps breaking or going out. The master then hung the lamps from special wires inside the minaret.

Residents encouraged the rivalry between *mahyacıs*, moving from mosque to mosque every night to pick favourites and informing the *mahyacı* they nominated the most popular of the night. This was a new, sparkling contest.

The *mahyacı* of Süleymaniye got ready to fly his lamps just after the *iftar*, the breaking of fast, as he did every might.

He released the oil lamps inside the housings, one after the other, along the ropes, creating a waterfall of light the height of the minaret. The spectators in the courtyard indicated their approval by placing little sweets or freshly baked muffins into the lamp boxes. He was confident as ever, although they found tonight's inscription not exactly extraordinary.

He couldn't believe his eyes when he pulled up the lamp box to find a gleaming gold coin at the bottom. It was too late to identify the donor.

Sultan Ahmed sped away, disguised as he was in a worn kaftan, a simple turban on his head, no aigrette. Beside him walked his companion as the two men mingled with the crowd. The inscription shining out from the Süleymaniye Mosque *mahya* still burnt bright in the eyes of their mind, though they had left the vicinity of the mosque named after the Sultan's world-famous ancestor: 'Don't succumb to your baser instincts!'

Ahmed and Tabriz and Tbilisi and Yerevan

War rages on far away

'The siege of the city of Tabriz has concluded with a triumph, Your Majesty! Your servant Abdullah Pasha has taken the city!'

Welcome news indeed; and Sultan Ahmed rewarded their bearer generously.

Things were heating up on the Azerbaijan front. The Ottoman commander had to battle the support forces of Shah Tahmasp as well during the fight for Tabriz, after which he had entered Erdebil.

The Caucasus front was led by the Governor of Erzurum, who took Tbilisi and claimed the region of Guri for the Ottoman Empire.

All this had disconcerted the Russians: neither the collapse of the Safavid dynasty nor the division of Persia served their interest. Negotiations with the Ottoman Empire over the future of Persia dragged on. By the time the Ottomans declared Shirvan to be under their protection in those turbulent times, the Russians had already occupied Baku. The region continued to seethe.

'We have annexed Nakhchivan, and then Yerevan, for the Ottoman Empire, Your Majesty!'

The Ottoman Empire enjoyed military glory harking back to the old days, and even regaining some of the former landholdings.

* * *

News of the Persian Mahmud Han's insanity reached the seraglio; clearly all the stress had proven too much and his cousin took over.

The new Persian ruler sought recognition by the Ottomans; refusal made war inevitable – a war destined to rage on for another two years, only coming to an end with the Treaty of Hamedan, under the terms of which the Ottoman Empire held territories so gained.

İbrahim and Mehtabe
One assignation after another

'Strange men, whose faces indiscernible in the dark of the night, come to the reception hall of the mansion, My Sublime Pasha; my husband, the judge, never tells me who they are. Yet I am certain these men are after our benefactor the Emperor, and you. A great fear overcomes me, My Precious Lord, and causes me anguish.'

'Have no fear, my coy Mehtabe, my pudding-white-necked beauty. We can prevail over our foes, and know how to guard ourselves!'

Their assignations took place in someone else's house. Grand Vizier İbrahim Pasha tried to extract all out of every moment together, few and far between as they were, and he had begun to live for them alone. Feigning disinterest in what he heard, he drew Mehtabe to his chest, stroking her auburn locks and then snuggling his head against her white breast. The statesman was not going to frighten the woman who had done so much to please him; nor would he endanger the fireworks in his heart, one more day's delight for his life. But the woman's tale corroborated other rumours he had been hearing. There was now little doubt that he was concerned indeed.

Marie-Geneviève-Marguerite and Meylidil
To die, but as whom?

After another violent cough, Meylidil looked at the red stain spreading in the handkerchief she put to her mouth indifferently. She had been terrified the first time, well beyond surprise. The aches in her chest and back and the night sweats should have warned her, yet the young woman had supposed herself immune to the disease, thinking instead she had contracted a cold after the garden party, with those Bosphorus breezes! The experienced lady steward had diagnosed the ailment immediately, quarantining the girl from the others and from the Emperor. That was the worst: not being able to see or reach the man for whom she had changed the course of her life.

Yet another sad harem tale, one of countless tales of sorrow, approached the end. Meylidil was about to die after not even three years in the harem of the Ottoman Emperor, leaving Sultan Ahmed to her rivals, though she should have enjoyed so many more days and nights of passion yet! She still hadn't decided whether she was the lover, mistress or proprietress of this man, even as she lay dying.

Chief Wife Emetullah nursed her, commanding her own concubines, on this bed where she had suddenly collapsed during one of those endless fits of bloody coughing. Emetullah forbade her daughter Fatma Sultan from approaching the dying girl in her final days; everyone knew consumption to be infectious. Emetullah herself was not one to shirk danger.

The care she showed one of her youngest rivals was utterly untainted with any concern of self-interest.

'Your Majesty! As you are aware, your woman Meylidil is gravely ill, and wishes to see Our Noble Sovereign one more time. I know we must protect you from this disease, but if you were to pay this desperate soul a visit, whilst safeguarding every precaution? This is my humble opinion.'

Emetullah rarely called upon her influence over the Sultan, her awareness of it notwithstanding. And yet here she was, almost forcing the Emperor, just to indulge her young co-partner for one last time. Sultan Ahmed, for his part, had been waiting for just such an excuse to visit this strange woman, whom he had failed to understand completely. It was not for him to worry about rules, yet his feet had gone backwards up to now. He knew what devastation this illness – oh, so common in the harem! – wreaked. He had been reluctant to see the once beautiful Meylidil in this state, and even refrained from replying to her pitiful, short letters. He had avoided the name and even the idea of fear; this would have been totally inappropriate for a man, much less a ruler! Now there was no escape. He nodded, without looking at the face of his one true wife. He got to his feet and signalled Emetullah to follow.

The nurse was stunned to see the Emperor, as it had been unheard of for their benefactor to visit someone suffering from such a contagious disease, but hers was not to speak out. As she walked backwards, wilting under Emetullah's stern gaze, she was already planning how best to tell the tale to her confidantes in the harem later, a little bit of colour in her monotonous life.

Meylidil gazed at the man first, but then long and hard, her eyes full of gratitude, at the Chief Wife. Emetullah left the room silently, her eyes brimming. Sultan Ahmed reached out to the hand he had until so recently held in passion, but this time held it gently, trying to avoid hurting the girl. He didn't think crying inappropriate. He was not accustomed to farewells, nor such grief or discomfort. The hand looked as if it could break at the frail wrist. It had grown translucent;

even the fingers looked insubstantial. He kissed the tips of the fingers lightly and left the room.

When Ahmed left, never to return, Meylidil was transformed, for the final time, back into Marie-Geneviève-Marguerite. She returned to her past in the little room given to her in the harem infirmary, the room with the painted walls. Her first ball appeared before her slowly closing eyes: the elegant necklace of semi-precious stones made by the celebrated Parisian jeweller Strass on her collarbones, not the real rubies and emeralds of the new life she had chosen; the light of thousands of candles in the chandeliers hanging from the high ceilings; the sparkles that blended in this light; the splendour of the jewellery, silverware and gilt frames on the walls; the whispering of the taffetas and laces as bodies dancing flung the fabrics hither and thither; and finally, in the front, a man in love with her and only her, a man who had no other woman – and then the chorus of a familiar opera at the Versailles Palace. Was it Jean-Baptiste Lully's melodies that enchanted the kings or Handel's Aggripina that was on stage? It felt so close, and yet she was so very far away!

★　★　★

'Her lungs couldn't cope with the damp of the harem, nor could her heart withstand the crowded solitude of the harem,' said Emetullah Sultan to her daughter Fatma Sultan. Meylidil the *gözde* had given the Ottoman ruler pleasure and joy, but she had been unable to give him a child that would remind him of her, in whom their traces would live on.

As for her portrait that Levnî had painted with painstaking care, on the unprecedented orders of the Emperor, it lay hidden for a long time, perhaps awaiting rediscovery by one who appreciated his art.

Vanmour and Konstantiniyye
This city's painter

Konstantiniyye was the spring that gave Jean-Baptiste Vanmour life. This city welcomed him with open arms at his arrival, a timid painter still blessed with the courage of youth; he in turn abandoned himself in this inescapable love. He had no inkling that destiny might have swept him here – quite the opposite: he used every excuse to extend his sojourn. He stayed on good terms with the French Ambassador, whom he had accompanied on his way out, and cultivated good relationships with the locals; as a result, commissions followed one another, and he delighted in settling into the chaos of this enchanting city.

The cream of Ottoman society recognised and venerated him as the celebrated painter equally expert in depicting the remarkable outfits and landscapes and the 'portrait-worthy' dignitaries of their unique land. As time passed, he grew to appreciate that he would have become a stranger anywhere else, and he never left Konstantiniyye for long – other than the occasional visit – as if he had always lived here. He never strayed too far from his circle of friends, that elegant society of the Bosphorus.

The painter had been born in Valenciennes, then Flemish, now in French Flandres, close to today's Belgian border. Included in the retinue of Charles de Ferriol, appointed French Ambassador to the court of the Ottoman Sultan in 1699, the then-twenty-eight-year-old painter was expected to record for posterity this exotic, mysterious, colourful, eerie and rich country and its people. The album of outfits Ferriol commissioned of the painter was later published to great acclaim in Paris, and even prompted Louis XV to bestow upon Vanmour the title of *Peintre Ordinaire du Roy en Levant*. The young Vanmour had surpassed expectations in this collection that depicted Ottomans from all walks of life: the Emperor himself, court officials in ostentatious outfits, soldiers of every rank, bashful and seductive women, all manner of merchants and even the lowliest beggar, all expertly reborn in the book and on canvas.

Thus must have *le Comte de Ferriol* regained some degree of royal favour. The eccentric diplomat never achieved an audience with the Emperor, his refusal to obey the one unbreakable rule standing in the way: he would not remove his sword. What he must have lost in failing to present his credentials to the Grand Seigneur, he must have gained – at least in part – in the eyes of the king thanks to this fabulous album.

The painter's patrons in the main were European diplomats and their personnel who wished to take back something of Konstantiniyye when they returned home. Vanmour even succeeded in accompanying a diplomatic delegation to the palace so he could depict the Sultan's audience ceremony on canvas. He couldn't believe his luck when this privilege came his way, even when he found himself in the Audience Chamber of the Grand Seigneur, accompanied by palace officials.

The first thing he perceived when he entered that wondrous Audience Chamber in the centre, nay, the heart of the seraglio, that reception hall adorned with stunning decorations that turned it into a fairy-tale venue, was the breathtaking, insane fusion of red and gold. He forced himself to stay still briefly lest he fail to follow protocol.

Unnoticed by the dark-bearded man sitting on the wide throne over which hung a pearl-embroidered baldachin, the painter cautiously etched on his memory every single detail without appearing to do so. The owner of the Ottoman Empire did appear sufficiently magnificent, befitting his repute. The robe on his back was woven of gold thread and silk; that delicious blend had been lined with fur, and the two sides were laced with emerald-studded gold straps. The fourth finger of each hand bore a ring, one of emerald and one of ruby. The hands rested on the knees, as if to overpower the boredom of the lengthy ceremony. Vanmour wondered if the Emperor ever did sit back to rest against the huge gold-embroidered cushions. The stool the ruler rested his feet on was as heavily decorated with jewels as the throne itself. The aigrette on his turban radiated the peerless light of that diamond, the one whose acquisition had caused such incredible effort, and the long heron feathers stuck into the jewel made this oriental headwear even more alluring. The two turbans placed next to the Emperor, on a cushion, were equally decorated with aigrettes of similar brilliance. The painter had found this strange, despite having spent such a long time here in Konstantiniyye. Evidently the great ruler had no objection to the presence of items whose only purpose was to dazzle foreign emissaries with a display of wealth and power: two turbans and a jewelled escritoire.

He then cast his mind back to the disgraceful antics at the French court not so long ago when as the Ottoman Ambassador Yirmisekiz Mehmed Çelebi presented his credentials to the then child king Louis XV. The marshal entrusted with the education of the eleven-year-old king, it appears, had asked the Ottoman Ambassador to pull the boy's golden locks, to prove the health and beauty of the young king – perhaps that these lovely tresses were natural? Then the boy king had been told to run to the centre of the room, to display the strength of his legs! Vanmour visualised again the discomfort of the diplomat, he who could only approach his own ruler close enough to kiss the hem of his robe, no closer. Ever courteous, however, the diplomat simply murmured, 'Masha' Allah, masha' Allah!'

The painter smiled at the recollection of Yirmisekiz Çelebi's tales of bizarreries of his time in France, tales he told Vanmour and Levnî. Sultan Ahmed's display was much more refined and noble in comparison to the French show!

He began painting as soon as he returned to his studio. The Grand Seigneur sat dignified, grave and calm, in a manner that emphasised his superiority. The Ambassador and his retinue – dressed in heavy kaftans and divested of their weapons, as per court custom – were escorted by countless officials in order to eliminate any possible threat to the Sultan's well-being. The Ambassador at the head of the delegation, clearly honoured with the most elaborate kaftan, still had to stand many paces away from Sultan Ahmed. He had handed over the King's letter to the Chief Bookkeeper in charge of foreign affairs, who in turn had bowed before the Sultan and presented the letter to Grand Vizier İbrahim Pasha. Sultan Ahmed observed all this quietly, splendidly majestic.

This was a painting that accurately depicted the ceremonial atmosphere of the Audience Chamber.

* * *

Konstantiniyye found its way to every one of Vanmour's paintings, beauty and conflict stretching out together as he ultimately became assimilated with the city. His studio in Pera was a meeting point for the city's intellectuals. Levnî Abdülcelil Çelebi, close companion and portraitist to the Emperor, was a close friend, as were Yirmisekiz Mehmed Çelebi and his young son Said Efendi – points of pride for the painter.

They were blessed to live in an exceptionally flamboyant era, where not only the imperial Ottoman palaces and gardens shone like the sun but also Pera itself glowed with the glory of the French court. Vanmour was something of a guard of honour at this congregation of constantly changing diplomats, he being the only permanent fixture. The frequent visits of French ambassadors and officials at his studio raised no eyebrows, as the studio had become the ideal venue for diplomats who didn't necessarily wish to publicise whom they were meeting.

The painter wore out five French ambassadors in his time in Konstantiniyye; some highly intelligent, others vain or ostentatious, each passed through the palaces and the gardens. He, on the other hand, never left the city, and like the true Konstantiniyye man he had become he would be buried in these lands.

Levnî and Ahmed
The Sultan has one final tale to tell

Sultan Ahmed preferred storytelling to listening, so long as he had a deserving audience. And there had been such a lot to tell throughout his reign, each and every one a tale of ambition or rage that exacted its toll on the bearer.

Commanded to the Sofa Pavilion, Levnî hastened to the palace on foot. Accompanied by pages, he would cross wide courtyards and finally reach the presence of the Emperor. It was a rainy day; on days like these, Sultan Ahmed gave in to despondency, his tales growing correspondingly morose. The artist wrapped his wide-collared waxed cotton coat. It was these thick coats that protected everyone from Konstantiniyye's damp.

He looked at the huge chimneys of the imperial kitchens to his right as he walked down the tree-lined path in the Second Courtyard of the imperial palace. Smoke came out of each one. Who knew what delicacies the cooks were busy preparing for the ruler of the universe, and all those servants who worked to ensure his comfort and safety? Levnî always loved cooking and eating, which explains why he occasionally sought permission to call upon the kitchens. He had forged friendships in the kitchens, but now was not the time to tarry; the Emperor awaited him and haste was called for.

Sultan Ahmed smiled at his companion who stood at the door of the reception hall, hands clasped, waiting for a signal:

'No need for hesitation, my cherished companion. Pray hasten to my side!'

The Sofa Pavilion faced the Bosphorus. Floral decorations on the walls, red mattresses on the wide sofa that went all the way round the walls and silver-thread-embroidered cushions all lifted the heart. The emerald and ruby drops of the fantastic canopy hanging from the centre of the ceiling usually caught the light, and then flicked the rays to all four corners, this time in colour. But there was no light to spread on this day. Every wing of the floral silk curtains that usually framed the Bosphorus view had been drawn back, yet it was still quite dim inside. Evidently the Emperor had been contemplating the darker aspects of his own reign and wished to share them with a friend. Who was more trustworthy than Levnî?

'I know you relish reading about history as much as I do, you poet, but there's nothing like listening to a first-hand account, is there?'

Whenever the Emperor felt guilty about some transgression or other, and sought exoneration in Levnî's esteem, he called upon the artist's poetry, as if this shared gift would raise the level of understanding between the two men. Poets were renowned for their tolerance, however unlikely for an emperor to feel the need to explain his own wrongdoing. Sultan Ahmed's question may well have been rhetorical, so Levnî mumbled something that might pass for an affirmation.

'I had talked to you in the past of the oarsman Bald İbrahim of Serez, you will remember. Now I wish to tell the entire tale, Levnî mine.'

When, much later, Levnî remembered this conversation, he wondered whether Sultan Ahmed's intention was to imply something else, but no answer presented itself.

'This water-man İbrahim, having given a great account of the task entrusted to him, I rewarded by promoting him to the Captaincy of a galleon, and in time further elevated him to the Admiral of the fleet. He was known as the son of a famed wrestler and also by the moniker Crazy Master İbrahim. He had captured fifteen galleons in the Mediterranean until he reached that position, and took one thousand slaves. He was one mean fellow, for sure!'

The Emperor had become the storyteller once more.

'In time, of course, the number of his enemies grew. All manner of foreign emissaries living in the Seat of Felicity set traps for him, too many to count, and he escaped every single one. The Grand Vizier was Süleyman Pasha at the time and he had turned out to be far too trusting a soul, and so I deemed this duty to be more appropriate to this İbrahim.'

That Sultan Ahmed wanted to exonerate himself was evident, although no one had called him to account. Who could question him, in any case? What he wanted was to listen to his own conscience by opening up to a man he had complete trust in and trusted to understand him too.

'They were discomfitted as they told me the story later. They prepared him in a room of the Imperial Pavilion before bringing him to my presence. When the stinking cap was removed off his bald head, the felt cracked and disintegrated, it was that filthy. They had to burn handfuls of amber to dissipate the stench.'

The Emperor couldn't bring himself to admit that his choice had been wrong, yet he was honest enough not to blame another.

'This Bald, Mad İbrahim sadly revealed himself to be unworthy of this post all too soon. Dropping inappropriate hints around sycophants like "I am an unmarried man; it is truly very cold, I do love a squeeze," etc., he filled his – hitherto empty – harem in three days with concubines presented to him. He spent his entire time in the arms of these beauties day and night.'

The Sultan had no desire to tolerate lasciviousness in his servants. They were selected to serve, not to seek pleasure.

'He was a brave man in essence. He had much to attend to that needed speed, yet went and forged too-close ties with the janissaries on some pretext, and spread fear around. The dimwit then carelessly let slip in my presence, "The janissary

308

commander now does my bidding; we're one tongue and one
front together." I had to order his neck be severed, lest he turn
upon his benefactor. His premiership lasted no longer than
twenty-two days.'

Seated on the sofa next to the window, Sultan Ahmed
showed only in outline. An immovable outline, whose majestic
stillness defied even that strangely disproportionate shadow
caused by the long face and massive turban, the width of the
shoulders notwithstanding.

'I have no more wish to see another Grand Vizier's head. I
never want to encounter the eyes staring into eternity on the
bloodied face of a man I chose myself, a valued statesman I
entrusted with the seal of premiership by my own hand.'

The Emperor waved his hand violently as if to brush off
a nightmare. The rubies on his fingers sparkled briefly like
droplets of blood in the gloom.

'I appointed my son-in-law İbrahim Pasha after many
a bitter experience. I chose this equable, peace-loving man,
being myself desirous of eternal peace, deciding that, yes, he
had his faults, but his virtues were more numerous. And I
honoured him in a manner no other grand vizier before him
had been deemed meritorious: I gave him my own emerald
seal as the imperial seal.'

Then he added in a heart-wrenching moment of candour:

'He will be my final grand vizier. God grant that his only
resemblance to Bald İbrahim of Serez be the name and not
their destinies.'

Şermi and Abdülhamid
Prayers answered

A forty-one-gun salute announced glad tidings, the birth of another child for the Emperor. The people of Konstantiniyye were accustomed to such events as births and deaths of princes and princesses. All that they could be asked to do was to pray for longevity for the new arrival, that he or she propagate the august bloodline.

Sultan Ahmed named his youngest prince Abdülhamid, an unprecedented name in the dynasty. The dark baby with black hair, eyes and eyebrows had arrived at such a golden age of military triumphs and festivities – the norm, not the exception – that his father gloried in naming this new prince he believed to be auspicious.

The astrologers predicted good fortune and a high star for Abdülhamid. His mother, the now palpably self-satisfied Şermi, believed all this; her son was sure to reign for a long time. The most senior astrologer's pronouncement, 'The number three surely holds great importance on his fate line; this ought to be interpreted favourably,' concealed what he had actually foreseen: that Abdülhamid would be secluded in the cage during the reign of three emperors to precede him, and the final three generations of the dynasty would come from his sons and grandsons in return.

No one would dare pronounce the word 'last' in connection with the dynasty.

Şermi had dedicated herself to consoling Sultan Ahmed with great gusto after Meylidil's death. Other women had also inevitably tried, but Şermi was determined to entice the ruler of the universe in one thousand and one ways, not releasing him from her clutches until she reached her objective – she fell pregnant.

The midwife's affirmation, when it finally came, lifted her to the top of the world with delight. Except, in her case, the world was limited to the four walls of the harem. No matter – she could now take her place amongst the powerful women in this world.

Refik and Selim
Death in the kitchen

'So skilful he was, and charming too – poor thing must have attracted the evil eye!'

'The apple of his master's eye, he was!'

'So tall, blue-eyed – and golden locks to boot; he was such a heartbreaker!'

'So many hearts he broke, and carelessly too, the tart!'

'I heard Levnî Çelebi was informed immediately, and hastened to the *helva* kitchen, beside himself!'

'Better not repeat everything you hear!'

The death of Bright Selim, Assistant Cook, was the talk of the palace kitchens, neither master nor apprentice being indifferent to a little gloating. Few were genuinely sad, less concerned for the dead man and more curious about the survivor: the Chief *Helva* Cook whose every command was law in the kitchen and whose pride knew no bounds.

It was mid-morning when the rosy-cheeked Selim suddenly sickened and collapsed on the spot, his mouth frothing and his skin growing green, just like the china bowls his hand broke as it swept over the worktop when he fell.

The Chief *Helva* Cook Dubnitseli Refik Agha had asked Bright Selim to sample his latest concoction, a Seville orange pudding – in the hope that his name might be attached to a new dessert, perhaps? – but stopped the lad from pouring it into a small *mertebanî*. Refik Agha spooned a little into an İznik bowl instead and handed that out, slapping his other apprentice, the greedier one who would taste of everything given half the chance, scolding him, 'Learn to wait your turn!'

As befitted his dignified fame amongst the kitchen folk, Selim gracefully took the bowl from his master's hand and dug his spoon into the translucent orange pudding with relish. A sudden convulsion of his body and young Selim embraced death in the same instant.

The greedy apprentice nearly lost the power of speech when he noticed the pudding spilling over the worktop and on the floor, altered its curious green as it splashed a china bowl. Thankfully everyone attributed his peculiar state to the deep grief caused by witnessing the death of a colleague. What he *did* know was that *mertebanîs* changed colour when they came into contact with poison, which explained imperial preference for hundreds of years. Yet he had no intention of telling anyone what he had seen in the depths of the kitchen. An idea had occurred to him, perhaps to somehow use this knowledge to secure a position higher than his master's?

He was to be disappointed, however: Chief *Helva* Cook Dubnitseli Refik Agha walked out of the palace courtyard behind Selim's funeral procession. He spoke to no one, neither Levnî Çelebi, nor any other; nor did he bother hiding his grief.

No one ever saw him again.

The Queen Mother and the Sultan
Records obliterated

All historical records on Levnî were meticulously obliterated, first by Gülnuş Sultan, and later by her son Sultan Ahmed, heir to the secret. The expunction from official chronicles was achieved with great ease, and no one any the wiser.

Researchers much later might be puzzled by the dearth of information on this, the most celebrated artist of his time, except for his works. The only written reference outside the Ottoman court's scope of influence was the history of the Ottoman Empire written by Dimitrie Cantemir. The former – disgraced – Moldovan Voyvoda had to seek refuge in Russia. Despite his close friendship with Levnî during his stay in Konstantiniyye, Cantemir only mentioned Levnî in a snippet, referring to the 'imperial painter'. The puzzle was beyond his grasp in any case.

Let historians write what they will after both mother and son are long gone. Levnî too would have departed by then, in all likelihood. Nothing post-mortem could have been as reliable or detailed as chronicles taken at the time. Obscuring Levnî's identity partially countered the injustice done to him: leaving him shrouded in mist could hint at something more than a mere artist or a conversation companion.

İbrahim and Hasan
Impossible to relinquish

İbrahim and Hasan, two rivals, weren't playing on a level field. They had locked horns long before İbrahim Pasha fell in love with the blue-eyed beauty of auburn tresses, proscribed to him – and prescribed to Hasan. The sharp İbrahim had always succeeded in staying a few steps ahead of the judge. The Chief Judge of Konstantiniyye enjoyed a high-ranking position, yes, but it was no match for the office of the Grand Vizier, and the brightest of the grand viziers at that. What brought them head to head this time was somewhat more serious than mere power politics.

The judge had always indulged his beauteous wife, refusing to listen to rumours, turning a blind eye to her newly acquired finery. No one knew for certain whether he did all this to hang on to his position, as maliciously suggested by some. What was certain was that Zülalîzade Hasan Efendi bore a deeply entrenched grudge against the Grand Vizier and by extension the Emperor behind the statesman. Another secret he would take to the grave was his oath to avenge himself before he left this world.

★ ★ ★

'My Noble Pasha, your blessed name is ever linked now with that of the wife of Zülalîzade Hasan Efendi! His wrath is said to know no bounds, that he is mad with anger and that he enjoys some support too.'

It took all the courage he had for Hüseyin One-Eye to utter these words. This was mortifying. He knew his limits; he wasn't used to discussing such matters with Grand Vizier İbrahim Pasha. No matter how deep his loyalty to his benefactor, this transgression was one he could ill condone. True, he would carry out his orders without question. Warning his benefactor of the threat posed by the judge had relieved his soul somewhat, the judge who for so long had been in cahoots with the Grand Vizier's enemies.

The Grand Vizier's reaction was nothing like Hüseyin had feared. Quite the opposite – he bowed his head. He was a desperate man in love, a man who couldn't give up the woman he loved, knowing full well he was walking towards a precipice.

The poor harvest of 1728 led to a minor famine in the city of Konstantiniyye, creating further unrest. It was customary to place the blame on some misfortune or other. On this occasion the shortage of food was attributed to the Judge of Konstantiniyye. A clearly feeble charge, but things had gone well beyond the struggle between two men. The Grand Vizier recognised that universal acclaim did not greet his every action, not that he had cared up to then. Opposition – to him and his council – was only to be expected; frequent administrative reshuffles would normally suffice. But if the Chief Judge of the capital was involved in secret plots, perhaps the time for concern had arrived. İbrahim Pasha's conscience was clear.

Thus, historian Raşid Efendi – who enjoyed the Grand Vizier's confidence – replaced Zülalîzade.

And for the time being, the story of the ousted Zülalîzade Hasan Efendi was relegated to the collection the Emperor might wish to relate in the future.

Levnî's Dream and Ahmed's Fountain
Premonition

'I see a tree just before I awaken in my dream, My Emperor, just as in Osman Gazi's dream, which he interpreted to mean he would establish the great Ottoman Empire. In those wondrous moments when dreams take the reins, that tree with the bright trunk bears not leaves on its branches, but tulips in many colours instead, tulips that hang down, not reach up, as if they sulked somehow. I also see my humble likeness on this tree. Then all the tulips wilt, but the tree trunk shines on, strong as ever, only the colours change.'

Levnî's recurring dream of the past few days took some courage to recount, but he was determined to tell his Emperor without hesitation, alteration or decoration.

Sultan Ahmed remained still for a good long while, long enough to convince his companion that the Emperor was lost in thought. He then got to his feet and commanded Levnî to follow.

★   ★   ★

Konstantiniyye folk were not accustomed to seeing the Emperor exit from the Main Gate, except for Friday prayers. He would normally take the sea route on his way to summer palaces or to visit his daughter and son-in-law in their *yalı*. It was unheard of for him to emerge from the gate on horseback, with only a companion by his side and a few imperial guards on foot, with no pomp or circumstance.

His barely audible murmured musings reached Levnî's ears, but no further:

'How much longer will this fountain run after I'm gone? Even if it doesn't run, will passers-by still admire the delicate tulip and rose carvings, the blues and greens of the graceful tiles? And will they do as my couplet inscribed thereon asks or will they pass by heedless? How one would wish to be a seer at times like these!'

Sultan Ahmed III had been full of enthusiasm when he commissioned this ornate fountain, more like a set of public drinking taps in the Ottoman fashion, a year earlier. The couplet inscribed on the fountain came from his pen, a desire for acknowledgement and to etch his poetry on minds at the same time:

'Turn the tap on in Allah's name, drink of the water, pray for the King Ahmed,' they entreated.

All agog at this unanticipated prize, passers-by soon gathered into crowds chanting, 'Long live My Sultan!' Their voices rang out as the Emperor of the Seven Climes, standing before Hagia Sophia, turned his steed's head back towards the Imperial Gate. He acknowledged exuberant cheers with a faint nod, then gestured to his Grand Vizier – who had hastened to the site, having heard the news – to distribute a few purses of gold coins.

His unexpected venture caused much comment. The most popular was his desire to prove fearless in the face of growing opposition by venturing all but unaccompanied in public. No one could have imagined the real reason: his companion's dream suddenly opened his eyes and, overcome by an insane desire to settle accounts with his past and his future too, he chose this fountain to symbolise his pleasure and his life.

Levnî, for his part, sensed everything to be slipping from his fingers.

This proved to be the last chat Sultan Ahmed and Levnî would ever enjoy in peace.

The Ottomans and Persia
Face-to-face with the
Persians... face-to-face with fate

Shah Tahmasp was astonished and delighted at the same time: so the great Ottoman had yielded to all his presumptuous demands!

Assisted by Nadir Han of the Khorasan Afşar Turks, Tahmasp had regained Esfahan and Kandahar from Ashraf Han – whose head was despatched to Tahmasp as the latter settled into the Persian throne. Now the time had come to regain territory back from the Ottomans, who, intoxicated with victory celebrations and festivities, regarded the Persian issue as resolved.

Shah Tahmasp chose to incite the locals against the Ottomans as the most convenient method, and that was how he found the audacity to demand the return of Tabriz, Kermanshah and Hamedan.

★　★　★

Sultan Ahmed had lost his taste for war.

Grand Vizier İbrahim Pasha had lost his taste for war.

The Persian Ambassador was well aware of this state of affairs.

Persia regained Kermanshah, Hamedan, Erdelen, Lorestan, Hoveyzeh and Tabriz with the treaty of June 1730 and the Ottoman Empire held Tbilisi, Erevan and Qaht.

★　★　★

Nadir Han, Vizier to Shah Tahmasp, saw the opportunity to wrench even more. Emboldened by Konstantiniyye's desire to avoid war at all costs, he entered Tabriz.

The Grand Vizier proposed, albeit unwillingly, 'It is fitting and appropriate to take action against the traitor; yours is to command, ours is to execute!' Sultan Ahmed finally declared war on Persia. He announced to his enraged subjects that he personally would lead the campaign.

Sultan Ahmed foresaw neither quite whither the disturbances that had begun in Persia eleven years earlier would lead, nor what they would ultimately cost him.

Levnî and Ahmed
Call to arms

By the Grace of God oh, My Shah,
News spread all around
This is your glorious name,
Dignity lies upon the ground

Levnî says that all the world
Prays for you as one
Go to the eastern lands, My Shah,
Time to set forth has come

Levnî's poem issued a candid entreaty to Sultan Ahmed, voicing the people's wish, that they saw no other way. Sultan Ahmed had to set forth, lead the army to the eastern lands and solve the Persian problem once and for all. The people expected nothing less than a victorious return.

Upon his command, Sultan Ahmed's flamboyant campaign tent was erected in Üsküdar on the last day of July in the year 1730. The janissary, artillery, armoury and cavalry battalions also set up camp on the Anatolian shore. Konstantiniyye's army of merchants constantly supplied the armed forces.

United in their preparations to show those Persians the might of the Ottomans!

İbrahim and Hüseyin
One-Eye
Too late now

'My Lord, it is rumoured in the dark corners of Konstantiniyye that our forces at Tabriz Fortress retreated on your orders.'

Hüseyin One-Eye avoided preamble, as was his custom, losing no time to convey the information he had been gathering. Accustomed to his brusque manner, his patron nodded him on.

'They're all grumbling, saying that our Emperor, the Ruler of the Universe, only intends to go as far as Bursa, and you, my benefactor, are planning to winter at either Tokat or Amasya! Some smart arses even claim that you'll go no further than Aleppo; all you'll do is appoint a commander-in-chief to lead the army, that's all.'

İbrahim Pasha had no intention of disturbing his ease, not that he could ever explain this to his man. Leaving Konstantiniyye, this paradise, for a long time, even – who knew? – forever, was not a decision to be made in haste. That his hesitancy would cause him great grief one day was no secret to the Grand Vizier, yet here he was, still reluctant to forgo his comfort.

'The worst is the rabble-rouser Albanian Patrona Halil of Horpüşte, a bath attendant of the 17th Battalion! His swarm of hoodlums grows by the day!'

'Rest easy, Hüseyin Agha, we shall do the needful forthwith. Keep your eyes open, that you may inform me speedily!'

The precariousness of the situation was finally dawning upon Grand Vizier Damat İbrahim Pasha: what they faced could no longer be soothed with bribes or simple strong-arm tactics. The merchants supplying the forces at great cost – the forces that were expected to depart, and yet were still tarrying – could not be kept waiting for payment forever. That could so easily tip the balance. The Grand Vizier decided to call his steward – also his son-in-law – for consultation.

Levnî and Ahmed
Where the lifeline veers off

The ruler's voice was extraordinarily soft; was there even something of a tremble there?

'Here is the toughest test of all, my precious Levnî. You and I have debated for years about the limits of self-control, but what I am about to tell you is beyond your wildest imagination, so bear this in mind.'

Sultan Ahmed had finally decided to disclose that one single secret he was determined not to withhold any longer. He would not leave this world without telling Levnî. And moreover, he had come to this decision very quickly, at a point in his life when he knew his own lifeline had veered off inexorably, when he knew his reign was slipping away.

'I broke the seal on the letter left to me by my mother, Paradise be her domain, after she passed away, believing it contained her last wishes. But reading that letter infuriated me first so much I could scream that a woman, even if she be my own mother, had so deceived the Ottoman sovereign. Then shock overwhelmed me that such vital information had been kept from me, the master of the universe. Sorrow then took over for Lady Afife, who had lost a life out of her own, and my *pater* Mehmed Han, who had been denied a healthy son, and of course, for my precious companion, whose life had been altered into an entirely new course. And finally, I was powerfully troubled.'

The Emperor appeared to have dismissed any thought of the dark days that awaited him. His entire attention was now on telling the truth – as he spoke, Levnî thought the ground was crumbling under his feet.

'Your partiality for jasmines had always broken my heart, Levnî; this was the favourite flower of our *pater*, Paradise be his domain, this you must know, as if this were a secret connection between the two of you.'

He had sighed as he spoke. It was getting harder to keep up the monologue.

'We shall have time enough yet to consider all this. None can disregard the present tribulations our state faces. I'm resigned to abdicate, but an unexpected war of succession would cause irreparable damage. Just imagine the rest!'

Sultan Ahmed hesitated.

'And I also fear for your safety, brother.'

That last word was all but whispered, yet it thumped the hardest.

The companion was unable to speak immediately. Conflicting emotions had overwhelmed him: joy, fear, fury, pride, euphoria and caution, settling one upon the other, yet emotions that were not mutually exclusive.

'My Most Precious, Saintly Sovereign, 'tis too late to lament the misfortune of my poor mother. As for me, just knowing that I belong to this glorious bloodline is sufficient. Have no doubt that I shall continue to act as you expect of me, that I shall guard this secret until eternity. God Most High preserve the August Ottoman State, My Majestic, Noble, Benevolent and Blessed Sovereign!'

Inspired by something from deep within, Levnî waxed lyrical like a court sycophant in a style he would normally avoid for precisely that reason.

'Your mother Lady Afife was a gifted poet, Levnî; I hope this knowledge alleviates your grief and enables you to see your own poetic skill in its rightful place.'

★　★　★

Maintaining the Levnî of old was no longer possible, after this long tale and short conversation; this much he realised instantly. The answer he had sought all his life looked to be the end of it, at least the end of Levnî Abdülcelil Çelebi, artist and poet. Sultan Ahmed was right: this tale outranked any speculation on self-control they had considered up to that day, but harbouring this secret was the greatest challenge either of them could issue to themselves. Yet, disclosure would constitute a death warrant for Levnî; however contentious the claim, the existence of another contender for the throne, two years senior at that, would present a new threat to Mahmud Han, the emperor-in-waiting, as well as Crown Prince Osman, three years younger, awaiting his turn in the cage, and even the children of Sultan Ahmed himself.

Not even for a moment did Levnî consider making a bid for the throne. Having solved the mystery of his past, he felt greatly pacified. This was one secret he could easily take to the grave. All his life he thought he had come from far distant lands, and now he learnt he had never, in fact, strayed too far!

This was the last time Sultan and favoured companion met.

İbrahim and Hüseyin
One-Eye
'No, not such an end!'

'Hüseyin One-Eye desires an audience with Your Noble Lordship.'

İbrahim Pasha's magnificent Bebek *yalı* always greeted the new day bright and early, but it was far too early to awaken the statesman, especially after such a busy night, with the day yet to break. The world was calm as the waters gently lapping at the landing stage awaited the first light of day. The new day concealed very well the nightmares it was preparing to unleash.

İbrahim Pasha leapt out of his mattress so quickly that the housekeeper – fully expecting a tongue-lashing for such an early alarm – could hardly conceal his shock, but the statesman had no time to waste with trivia.

'Fetch him at once, and wait outside the door until I call!'

Forced to suppress his curiosity at this unequivocal command, at least for the time being, the housekeeper shut the door behind the massive bulk of Hüseyin One-Eye.

One glance into the single eye of the burly fire-fighter indicated the gravity of the situation to the fortunate, dignified Grand Vizier and son-in-law to the Emperor, Nevşehirli İbrahim Pasha. Wasting no time on pleasantries, One-Eye launched into an account of the gunpowder-like atmosphere in the city, the angrily seething troops and how they no longer wished to safeguard their benefactor, the report liberally sprinkled with gutter language that was his inimitable style.

As the fire-fighter chief spoke feverishly the statesman weighed various probabilities, his mind working at lightning speed, on how he could leverage being always the first to be forewarned – be it good tidings or bad.

★   ★   ★

The Grand Vizier and his loyal servant talked for a long time. The bleakness of the situation darkened İbrahim Pasha's heart, as the morning light advanced deeper into the large room projecting over the sea, illuminating the full glory of the plain yet elegant room: the red silk duvet of the rumpled bed, the walnut side-tables with the rosy mother-of-pearl inlays, the thousand-and-one-coloured flowers on the wooden covings and the gilded Edirnekâri cupboard. The statesman briefly entertained a crazy idea that he would swap places with these costly, yet inanimate objects that held no further value for him as of this moment.

'No, not such an end!' he mumbled to himself; a strange calm had settled on him in spite of everything. 'We have overcome such tribulations in the past. What others may do, I know not; what I do know is that my end should not be thus, not like this, this is not what I deserve.' A voice piped up from within fuelled by a childish rage, still arrogant: 'We have not recited all the poems that await reciting, or sung all the songs.'

The housekeeper was accustomed to İbrahim Pasha's eccentric commands, but even he found it inexplicable that he himself, and not one of the footmen, had been charged with fetching the Chief Furrier Manol Efendi from his home at this ungodly hour. Even more puzzling was how the statesman despatched his favourite ring, the dazzling one he never took off, the one with the twin rose diamonds on one single hoop.

Patrona Halil and Ahmed
'Naught but what must be, must be...'

The rabble-rousers were the Chief Judge of Konstantiniyye Mad İbrahim and Bald Mehmed, a janissary commander. There was one more person, one working behind the scenes to mastermind the uprising: the former Chief Judge of Konstantiniyye Zülalîzade Arnavut Hasan Efendi.

What had disconcerted, astonished, angered, infuriated, crushed and incited resentment – concealed or overt – nay, openly fed their envy was the sybaritic lifestyles of Sultan Ahmed and his Grand Vizier Nevşehirli Damat İbrahim Pasha, purses of gold so liberally spread as they burnt thousands of oil-lamps and embraced hundreds of concubines.

Not for the hoi polloi were all the works of art and science, nor the prospect of a better life facilitated by innovations: fires put out by the brigades or books printed on a press were trifles for the great unwashed. Widening their horizons to new and different worlds held no interest. The Emperor's delay in leading military action against the 'Persian infidel' agitating in the East provided the pretext they had been seeking. A nifty incitement was all that the 'riff-raff' had been waiting for. Everything was now in place to overturn the cauldron.

Historian Abdi Efendi narrated the events he personally witnessed and confessed in all sincerity that 'There were so many causes, yet there be little room for so long an account, and we had to content with this much,' in his report written in *taliq* calligraphy on coated paper, in a mere sixty-five

332

sheet volume, the gold-leaf rules and decorated headings notwithstanding. This short account, predictably, is highly subjective:

> These seditious wretches had been clustering for eight months in the City of Konstantiniyye: Patrona Halil of the 17th Company, of Albanian origin, and Muslı; and from the masters of the hounds, Master Ali, Blacksnake, Plane Tree Ahmed, Woodsman Ahmed, Emir Ali, Derviş Mehmed, Mehmed of Erzurum, and little Muslı; from the sword-bearers the Hajj Hüseyin of the Boxmen and İsmail the Greengrocer; and on the other hand some bird-brained thirty or so foot soldiers, seeking an opportunity – on that holiday there was none in the Doorstep of Felicity other than the district governor and Hasan Agha, the Commander-in-Chief of the Janissaries.[4]

Abdi Efendi was to ask himself later if any of the subsequent events could have been prevented had everyone been at this post and strict measures taken.

As for the army, they were all away on the business of pleasure, including the Grand Vizier and the divan council. Even the district governor himself was occupied with planting tulips in his garden. They thought this a once-in-a-lifetime opportunity; they gathered in three columns forthwith and unfurled their banners.

The rioters had started out as a few handfuls, but more and more joined the mob, and the chances of halting them diminished by the minute. Even the Commander-in-Chief of the Janissaries was unable to check his troops. The crowd grew into an irreversible avalanche of unmanageable dimensions, even the most timid nothing less than a brave rebel now, and bravely they poured into the streets.

The Grand Vizier İbrahim Pasha heard the news in his *yalı*, and complained, making inappropriate remarks in his fever'd state, 'Why has the district governor not overpowered these people, and punished them?' The district governor himself boarded a caïque immediately and left his own *yalı* for Konstantiniyye, seeking the answer to the question, 'What must one do to this brawl to dismiss it?'

It was too late to convene the ministers in search of solutions.

'Naught but what must be, must be...'

★   ★   ★

The Grand Vizier and his entourage fell victim to delayed intelligence on the movements of the rioters and their own overestimation of the rioters' numbers. By the time the numbers did rise, all exit routes had already been blocked. Guards entrusted with the security of the Seat of Felicity started looting their charge instead.

The First Division troops carried their cauldron to Etmeydanı. The 'cauldron overturners' had taken power, organised and established a chain of command.

★   ★   ★

The secret collaboration between Zülalîzade Arnavut Hasan Efendi and the leaders of the revolt was to surface later. Rumours of his wife's affair with the Grand Vizier had long humiliated Hasan Efendi. To add insult to injury, he had later – that is, two years before the revolt – been dismissed from his highly prestigious position as the Chief Judge of Konstantiniyye. It was payback time for Grand Vizier İbrahim Pasha as far as he could see, and he led the way. Drunk with the heady wine of revenge, he failed to see what lay beyond the immediate.

So His Majesty the Emperor had no option but to send his trusted chief steward to the bandits as an envoy. The chief steward arrived, and asked, 'Let us know what your demands are, and we shall comply,' and the rebels said, 'First İbrahim Pasha, then the steward Mehmed, and Şeyhülislam Abdullah Efendi, and some seven and thirty persons from the state, hand them over to us, we have no issues with our own emperor.'

These demands verily reflected Zülalîzade's secret desires; all he had to do was to feign despondency, the servant whose mouth is set in a grim line, circling around his master the Emperor as he rejoiced on the inside all the while.

His benefactor Sultan Ahmed had to make the heart-wrenching decision on the final day of September in the year 1730 to command the executioners to strangle the Grand Vizier. The least he could do would be to spare the man from certain torture; that, the Emperor could not bear.

* * *

No one would ever know quite what the Emperor thought or felt – the black torment of betrayal or the faint hope of a final lurch of salvation – as that other man who waited in the sword-bearer's room, resigned to his fate, removed the priceless emerald premiership seal from his inner pocket, handed it over to the *Kızlarağası*, was brought to the antechamber after everyone retired for the night and the executioner's noose was wrapped around his neck.

Sultan Ahmed never shared these thoughts even with Levnî.

Thus came the abrupt end of the grandest of all grand viziers, Nevşehirli Damat İbrahim Pasha, whose might had come close to that of the exalted sovereign, who directed the Ottoman Empire, who stamped his mark on a period in history, who renamed his home county, of unimaginable wealth and splendour, whose magnificence dazzled all, the favourite son-in-law and friend to the Emperor himself and his most trusted statesman. Such a legendary end, so blood-curdling and sensational!

> Grand Vizier İbrahim Pasha, his son-in-law the District Governor and steward Mehmed were massacred at two of the clock, and their corpses laden on ox carts were despatched to the mob in the square. The mob took down the corpses they fetched from the imperial palace and hung them high in the chamber in the square to inspect. They said, 'This is not Grand Vizier İbrahim Pasha; this man is uncircumcised, and he sports a tonsure, this man be an Armenian infidel,' and yet others said, 'This be a Greek infidel, Chief Furrier to the Grand Vizier, they are identical in height and girth and shape and beard, they could be brothers born of the same mother, and now the furrier has sacrificed himself for his master,' and so they flung the corpse onto the pack saddle of a donkey, taking him back to the palace, and when İbrahim Pasha's corpse fell to the ground, they lashed a rope to his neck and lashed that to the donkey's tail, screamed and yelled all the time as they carried him along the Imperial Way, left him at the Imperial Gate and asked the gatekeepers where the Emperor was and learnt that he was at the Procession Pavilion.

Abdi Efendi must have found the horror of those days hard to believe as he recorded the blood-curdling account of the midnight tale.

> They made for the place, offending His Majesty Sultan Ahmed with their grumblings. The Sovereign himself called out from the lattice of the pavilion, 'If that is not he, we shall personally hand him tomorrow,' sending an envoy to the mob as he moved to the Privy Chamber.

Gratitude for the generous accession tips Sultan Ahmed had distributed had long since dissipated in the hearts of the janissary commanders; there remained no trace of his initial determination to implement discipline, in particular in the officer and warrant officer ranks of the janissaries.

'The envoy has informed us that the mob is desirous of disposing of Sultan Ahmed and enthroning His Majesty Sultan Mahmud in his place.'

No number of heads he sacrificed could save Sultan Ahmed from this inexorable demand. He realised further resistance was futile; he no longer had a choice. Refusal to inhale the dust of the battleground instead of the floral breezes of the Seat of Felicity gardens had ultimately placed the Emperor of Tulips on this irreversible path.

He was prepared to abdicate in exchange for assurances of safety for himself and his children.

Mahmud and Ahmed
History repeats itself

'Never hand over the reins to your vizier; always monitor him, and never keep any one man in that post for five years or ten; and never take everything he tells you at face value! Never waste the treasury, and do your own work, do not trust others; here, my situation is an example to you. Strive always to appoint experienced people, and pray Good Lord on High for deliverance from the ill will of the servants! Never divulge your secrets to every man and jack of them, nay, even your own children, lest ye may later rue and regret a thousand times!'

Sultan Ahmed caught his breath. The final proclamations of his reign spoke of his human concerns:

'My children are entrusted to your care by God. Please treat them kindly!'

Sultan Ahmed had steeled himself earlier for the first of his hardest speeches with Levnî. The second concerned his brother's son, once he made the decision to abdicate without delay. He sent word for Crown Prince Mahmud to be brought over to the Imperial Gate, where he waited, in the middle of the night, not even waiting for daybreak.

Unable initially to understand whether to expect the executioner's silken cord or the bird of good fortune that was the throne, Mahmud stayed silent – but for the quietly praying lips – all the way, escorted by viziers and servants.

Every ruler experiences that awful fear at the devastating moment he hands over the throne, and Sultan Ahmed was no different. His memory reached twenty-seven years back, to the day when his elder brother Sultan Mustafa Han had been similarly deposed by rebels. Thus had ended Ahmed's sixteen-year-long seclusion in the cage; Sultan Ahmed had sat on the throne before standing to pray in gratitude. The first imperial decree he signed sentenced his own brother, the former Sultan Mustafa, and his five children including the then seven-year-old Mahmud, to the seclusion quarters known as the Boxwood Quarters... or simply the cage. And so history repeated itself as players merely swapped places.

Sultan Ahmed knew he would have this one single opportunity to advise his nephew Mahmud Han, his sincerity concealing the grief within, warning him against repeating his own mistakes was suddenly more important than anything else. This was his last speech as the twenty-third *Padişah* of the Ottoman Empire.

* * *

Sultan Ahmed's words hung in the air before the Imperial Gate; not reproachful as might be expected of a ruler deposed, but rather a father guiding his son, whose success is paramount to the senior man. Confessions of the errors of an entire period in history, its transgressions and bad luck too, these words spoke of experience, of maturity beyond any lust for power, not a desperate submission. Not entrusting all to his vizier, this was good counsel to the new Emperor, and the closest to a remorseful admission of guilt. Witnesses to this scene would have been moved by the former Sultan's exhausted disposition, barely disguised by his fortitude.

And finally, the former Emperor kissed his successor on the forehead. The young Mahmud Han kissed his uncle the former Emperor's hand, thereby courteously proving his undying respect. Sultan Ahmed's sons also took a cue from their father and kissed the hand of the new Emperor in indication of their allegiance.

Those present knew all too well they were witnessing the least hostile handover in all Ottoman history to date, and not a single vizier, battalion commander or Enderun official pretended to disguise streaming tears.

Sultan Mahmud Han donned the turban decorated with an aigrette in accordance with court custom and proceeded towards the throne in the Holy Mantle Chamber to 'be girt in sovereignty' whilst Ahmed, the former Sultan, and his sons turned their faces towards their new cage on earth in the imperial harem.

When the 'emperor-makers of the great unwashed of Konstantiniyye' determined the fate of the great Sultan Ahmed III in 1730, so came, also, the end of Sadabad. All that the new Emperor could prevent was its burning; instead, he had to offer to demolish it. Whilst those fabulous mansions, grandiose pools and even flowerbeds were reduced to ruins in a terrifying tornado, one endowment survived, one edifice that exemplified the spirit of an entire era: the Fountain of Sultan Ahmed stood, its floral reliefs and inscriptions intact, not a single one of those dotted green tiles dislodged, its gilding never faded, to immortalise the name and the glory of Sultan Ahmed for hundreds of years to come.

Levnî and Şebsefa
Reunion/farewell

As he grasped that his precious Emperor was poised at the beginning of the end, new horizons opened up before Levnî also, not that a single one piqued his interest: Sultan Ahmed's end also sounded the death knell for poetry and painting. History was to note that the famous artist and poet Levnî Abdülcelil Çelebi left behind nothing that could be dated to any time beyond the reign of Sultan Ahmed III. It was time to retire, but life still owed him one more thing. The time to postpone it was done.

He left the imperial palace quietly, this district he would never again visit, following a route only he knew; now in mufti, he went through Galata, walking calmly, indifferent to the panicking and aggressive crowds around. His indifference was an invisible coat of armour that protected his unchallenged progress. He finally arrived at a set of wrought-iron gates that once had symbolised power.

Only such a calamitous turn of recent events in Konstantiniyye could have caused the disorder at the *yalı* of Grand Vizier Nevşehirli Damat İbrahim Pasha, the statesman who no longer lived. Fatma Sultan had been disconsolate since she received word of her husband's fate, and her father's forced abdication and subsequent imprisonment in the cage had compounded her grief. Nevfidan Kalfa, her nanny since childhood, had taken control: having battened the gates, she was doing her best to pacify the terrified servants, eunuchs and the rest. Some had already run away, whilst others were scurrying hither and thither, not knowing what to do.

The companion succeeded in making himself known at the gate, which was opened in a hurry to admit him before clanging shut again.

The perfect servant, Nevfidan Kalfa always knew precisely what happened at home and in the city – which meant she knew about Levnî and Şebsefa. She invited Levnî into a suitable room, called Şebsefa, and disappeared from view.

They had such little time together. Who knew who would be flung where: when the mistress fell, so followed the slave down the precipice. Whether this was a reunion or a farewell, neither knew. There would be time yet for Şebsefa to lament her wasted youth.

*　*　*

So ended this era, not just for the Ottoman Empire, but also for Levnî. Now he had a much more modest objective: becoming an anonymous guest on that seasoned island, forsaking all desire, ambition and heartbreak, spending the rest of his days gazing at the veined trunk of an old cypress or the fragile petals of a young jasmine bloom, his eyes misting in the pine breeze that slipped into the sea like a tongue, unmindful of time, releasing the past from the burden of questioning. On the island...

İbrahim and Hüseyin
One-Eye and Manol
Time to settle debts

The site of the seraglio we now call Topkapı Palace has always commanded the finest scenery in all directions in the most prestigious location of the city, long before the arrival of the Ottomans. When Mehmed the Conqueror took the ancient city, the Byzantine Acropolis had been reigning supreme at this spot, that is, the heart of the city that was a palimpsest of ancient settlements and underground cisterns. These cisterns continued to service the new proprietors, the new palace of the Ottomans. The cistern before the imperial stables by Gülhane Gardens was one such, its entrance a low corridor, discreet enough for anyone to hide in, so long as he made it that far.

In the morning of that sleepless night when Crown Prince Mahmud ascended to the throne as the twenty-fourth Emperor of the Ottoman dynasty, as freshly baked loaves were carried out from the bakery in the First Courtyard to the palace proper, two fire-fighters emerged surreptitiously, unnoticed by the mob still reeling from the erroneous conviction that they had finally set things right, that the system to dispense the justice of their dreams had been achieved. The gatekeeper, recognising the Commander of the Fire Brigade Hüseyin One-Eye, who went in and out constantly and whose allegiance was never known, decided not to probe any further on this extraordinary day; the fire-fighter was accompanied by a middle-aged man of average height and no beard, and this man was unknown to the gatekeeper – he had to be one of the commander's constant loyal escorts. The only remarkable point was how astonishingly exhausted the man appeared.

* * *

No one commented upon the disappearance of Chief Furrier Manol Efendi, who had, for countless years, supplied his august patron the great Grand Vizier with the choicest sable, ermine and fox to line the silk kaftans with, and whose high prices had raised such envy; such things were not unexpected at times like these... No one would ever know whether he had been enticed with the promise, 'This is the last chance for your patron, the like of which cannot be found; and for you, one final secret service!'

* * *

Rumours that the beautiful wife of Zülalîzade Hasan Efendi had secretly run away were rife, but they went unproven.

Hasan Efendi's account of his dismissal of his wife ('I pronounced, "I divorce thee!" thrice, put her in a coach and sent her back to her mother in that small Rumeli town!') failed to convince his friends. Some, thinking they had recognised Mehtabe from her saffron silk cloak 'skirts flapping in the wind as she boarded a triple scull skiff going to Üsküdar' and the happy haste in the violet eyes peering out from the veil, never stopped gossiping.

Vanmour and Patrona Halil
His likeness captured on canvas

The painter recorded it all. A little contritely cursing the fate that placed him in the midst of this tempestuous time that ravaged through Konstantiniyye, his city, he still wanted to capture this insanity, this furore and terror, and preserve it all for posterity.

This man who called himself Patrona Halil, this man who was astonished by the slippery place his fate had suddenly picked for him, who mistook the shine of the slippery surface for splendour, who stumbled to disguise his own fright, who strove to put his limited intelligence to craftiness and who was destined, as a matter of course, to lose, this Bayezid bathhouse attendant: this man had piqued the painter's curiosity. An ignoramus with no understanding of history, of the rule as old as history itself: that the leader of a bloody revolt invariably was doomed to be consumed first. And even of those who understood how many had behaved differently? Those were the thoughts that went through Jean-Baptiste Vanmour's mind, as he worked before his canvas, isolating himself from the cataclysm that raged on and on outside: he was sketching the likeness of Patrona Halil, whom he had seen briefly from a distance, on one of those bloody days.

Standing upright before the confused mêlée in the background, seemingly confident, yet watching his back constantly, the figure bore an unsheathed sword. Below his narrow forehead a pair of eyes stared blankly, huge moustache barely able to cover an impudent mouth–suppressed insecurity feeding his belligerent defiance. He resembled an actor in a gigantic stage play. The painter had crammed a brace of figures to the edge; Patrona Halil's two henchmen with – again – huge moustaches only appeared as complementary elements. Vanmour worked unusually quickly on this occasion: here stood the finished painting already. This was more than a simple portrait: Master Vanmour had narrated the entire incident in the shape of one person, freezing time at his most victorious moment. Those who choked others prior to that moment would all too soon succumb to the same fate. Of this, the model portrayed had no inkling.

The painter wondered who would purchase this painting, where he would hang it and who would look upon it.

Afterwards
In the cage

Afterwards, Emetullah Sultan closed her sleepless eyes, imagining herself not in this plain room with the tiny windows, but back in her favourite place, in the bright and secure atmosphere of that Fruit Room where she had spent much delightful time. She reached out for the warmth of the wooden walls, seeking the texture of the oil paint depicting flowers and fruit, but in vain. The cold touch of the tiles beneath her hand brought her abruptly to the present: to the Boxwood Quarters, adjoining the Topkapı Palace harem, and totally cut off from its environment, that place darkened by tears silently swallowed for hundreds of years.

Wrenching herself from reality to seek sanctuary in the world of dreams had been her occupation of late, the only way to re-live the good times gone by and steel herself for their new life. The confiscation of her dazzling collection of jewellery had not upset her, gifts of the Emperor on this occasion or that over the years – even her favourite, the one item that symbolised her place in Sultan Ahmed's heart: that massive black diamond solitaire, which had attracted envious stares from every single woman. She cared not when she removed that ring and handed it back to the treasury, just as long as the gilded cage that isolated them from the rest of the palace did not fall between the two of them. The hardest to accept for his beloved wife Emetullah was the defeated look, the bowed head of the man still the most powerful in the world in her eyes, now under the watchful gaze of the harem eunuchs, like a declawed lion. She would defy their fate, standing by her man until the very end; she would offer him solace and joy for the rest of his days. As Sultan Ahmed had once instructed his Grand Vizier, 'The Chief Wife knows all there is to know about my circumstances; 'tis of her you must ask how I fare.'

Afterwards, the young prince Mustafa thought about how his admiration for his father grew in those life-changing days of the autumn of 1730, during all that time they spent imprisoned in the Crown Princes' Chambers. He was only thirteen years of age when he was placed in the Boxwood Quarters alongside his father. True, their lives had been spared, but this caged life was a fate worse than death, especially for his emperor father.

The only reason the former Emperor put up with these conditions was concern for the safety of his sons. Sultan Ahmed had no doubt that his bloodline would continue; it was this certainty that gave him strength. There was little he could actually do to protect his sons, but even his presence as the former sovereign sufficed to keep certain malicious intentions at bay. His nephew Sultan Mahmud Han was kindly and merciful, his respect for his uncle undimmed. Sadly, Sultan Mahmud had no sons of his own as yet, so his younger brother Osman took the senior-in-waiting position. The Crown Prince's rancour, possibly stemming from his hideous looks, in ironic contrast to the dynasty whose name he bore, intimidated everyone. The mere thought of what he would do once he came to power was terrifying enough.

Mustafa was convinced that his elder brother Süleyman – who had suddenly died of an unknown cause a few years earlier – had been poisoned by the abominable Crown Prince Osman, then second in line after his brother Mahmud. Osman's unimaginable gluttony, his bloated body, instability and sudden tantrums were no secret. So Mustafa started a course of a minute daily dose of poison to prepare his body against a poison attack. The bags under his eyes and the sickly yellow pallor of his young complexion did not escape his father's notice.

Crown Prince Mustafa's predilection for astrology discomfitted his father; yet since the time a stargazer had spoken of a long and great reign, it had been impossible to check the young man's interest. Mustafa sought to force the limitations of their environment set aside for them in the harem of the seraglio, in the Crown Princes' Chambers where he might end up spending who knew how long, perhaps the rest of their days, and sought to obtain books and all manners of instruments on divination.

Afterwards, life would go on in that section of the seraglio known as the Boxwood Quarters that was different from all others; life would go on in the hope that each new day might bring a change in fortune.

Afterwards
Elegy

Afterwards, the treasurer would record the jewellery confiscated from the body of the executed former Grand Vizier İbrahim Pasha; he began with 'a ring with twin diamonds'.

A huge ruckus blew up on Thursday
I who have built all these works
Did I deserve this calumny?
I cry having died of insults.

Go tell my son to don his black
Go tell my servants to look for me
Ruined is the palace in Üsküdar
I cry for it's left to the foe.

Help me, the forty-day mourners,
They said İbrahim Pasha is dead,
My corpse was fed to the dogs
I cry for my prayers untold.

I went to Üsküdar, lived there three month
I ran the council, concluded so much
I heard the rebels, lost my mind
I cry for having come into this evil world.

As calm returned slowly, and the rebels were arrested one by one, victims of their own insurgence, an unknown bard composed a mournful elegy that whispered around the city, sung softly in the squares, coffee houses, mansions and gardens, Grand Vizier İbrahim Pasha's lament echoed over and over again.

Afterwards
Nedim

Afterwards, a rumour spread concerning poet Nedim, renowned as Grand Vizier İbrahim Pasha's boon companion whose tulip-like eulogies had found much favour from the statesman: as he fled from the commotion, leaping from roof to roof, Nedim fell to his death at the palace. Very few people ever knew what really happened: an insane terror, worse than death itself, overwhelmed him and he vanished.

He worried himself to death in three months.

Ahmed and Levnî and Emetullah and Fatma and Mihrişah and Şermi and Hümaşah and Ümmügülsüm and Yirmisekiz Çelebi

After the end

Levnî joined his Maker in 1732, taking his fantastic secret with him. Others, very dear to Sultan Ahmed's heart, departed for eternity in the same year, only a brief interval between each death: Emetullah Sultan, his favourite wife, mother to his daughter Fatma Sultan; Mihrişah Sultan, mother to his crown princes, Süleyman and Mustafa; Fatma Hümaşah Sultan; Şermi Sultan, mother to his youngest crown prince Abdülhamid and finally, his precious daughter Fatma Sultan, as well as another daughter, Ümmügülsüm Sultan.

History has never adequately explained these strange coincidences.

Emetullah Sultan maintained her privileged position beyond her death, though she berated herself for dying with her job undone, abandoning her man; she was interred in Eyüp, at the feet of Mustafa Pasha, the conqueror of Cyprus. The princess and the three other wives were interred at the New Mosque cemetery.

When Mihrişah's son Mustafa ascended to the throne in due course as Mustafa III, he endowed a mosque in his mother's name in Üsküdar Ayazma, ensuring her name lived on beyond the centuries.

Levnî was interred in the flower garden of a religious lodge next to a small mosque, in a location that would either be swallowed up as the city expanded in time or be reborn one day, as an invisible part of these lands.

Yirmisekiz Çelebi Mehmed Efendi also died the same year, in exile in Cyprus where he had been since the Patrona Halil revolt; whether he had heard of the death of his friend, history has not recorded.

Sultan Ahmed survived in that gilded seraglio cage for another four years after the departure of his nearest and dearest. Sultan Mahmud, his successor, commissioned a magnificent dagger with emeralds on the hilt for Nadir Shah, but the Persian was assassinated well before he received this gift, which reverted to the Ottoman treasury.

Neither Sultan Mahmud nor his successor, his brother Sultan Osman, sired any children. It was Mustafa, Abdülhamid and later their sons who continued the bloodline. Sultan Ahmed III had bequeathed unto the Ottoman Empire an assured line of succession.

Unto the tulip gardens he left his shadow, never to vanish.

Glossary

Ağa, ~ Ağası, Agha	1. master/commander *(milit.)* 2. official 3. head servant of a household 4. eunuch in service
Baş Haseki, Birinci Kadın	Chief Wife
cirit	Ancient equestrian sport
çelebi	1. gentleman 2. intellectual, man of letters
damat	son-in-law
Darüssaade	'Abode of Felicity' i.e. seraglio, Topkapı Palace
Darüssaade Ağası	master at the Abode of Felicity; Kızlarağası; Chief Black Eunuch: top-ranking harem official
devşirme	levy of Christian children for imperial service, child tribute
divan	court literature, also an anthology or collection of poems
efendi	Sir, esquire
Enderun	1. Inner Palace 2. Inner Palace college
harem ağası, haremağası	black eunuch in harem service, chamberlain

kadın	1. woman 2. wife, consort
kethüda	1. steward 2. agent 3. official representative of an organisation 4. lieutenant or orderly *(milit.)*
Kızlarağası/Darüssaade Ağası	chief of the girls/chief black eunuch, top-ranking harem official
Konstantiniyye	'Constantine's City' i.e. Ottoman name for Istanbul
kul	1. servant of the Porte 2. palace official
Kul Kethüdası	A high-ranking officer in the janissary corps, third in rank after the commander-in-chief and the *sekbanbaşı*
medrese	seminary, a religious college, *madrasah*
mehter	the oldest military marching band in the world
Padişah	Ottoman Sultan regnant
Paşa, Pasha	1. general 2. high-ranking civil servant
Rumeli	'Roman Lands' i.e. western provinces of the Ottoman Empire
sipahi	cavalryman
Şeyhülislam	chief religious officer
tuğra	sultan's official seal
valide, Valide Sultan	mother, Queen Mother

Voyvoda	1. (Slav.) governor or duke 2. Christian vassal prince-governor of Moldova or Wallachia in the Ottoman Empire
Zağarcıbaşı	major, Master of the Hounds; commander of the 64th division of the janissaries

Dramatis personae

Ottoman Sultans

Sultan Mehmed IV 'The Hunter', r. 1648–1687
Sultan Ahmed III, r. 1703–1730
Sultan Mahmud I, r. 1730–1754

The Statesmen

Grand Vizier Nevşehirli Damat İbrahim Pasha, s.
1708–1730
Yirmisekiz Mehmet Çelebi, diplomat, ?–1732
Dimitrie Cantemir, Moldovan prince, Voyvoda,
    philosopher, historian, composer, linguist,
    ethnographer and geographer, 1673–1723

The Artists

Levnî Abdülcelil Çelebi, painter, ?–1732
Aşık Ömer, poet, ?–1707
Vehbî, poet, ?
Jean Baptiste Vanmour, Flemish-French painter,
1671–1737

The Women

Rabia Gülnuş Sultan, Chief Wife to Mehmed IV, and
    Valide Sultan to Mustafa II and Ahmed III
Emetullah Sultan, Chief Wife to Ahmed III and mother
    to Fatma Sultan
Mihrişah Sultan, d. 1732, wife to Ahmed III, mother to
    Mustafa III and Selim III

Rabia Şermi Sultan, ca. 1698–1732, wife to Ahmed III
and mother to Abdülhamid I

Lady Mary Wortley Montagu, 1689–1762, wife to British
Ambassador to the Ottoman Empire